Frank studied her with that implacable look of his. "I'll have to be closer to the problem to get the information you want."

He'll find out the truth.

Journey smothered the thought as soon as it skimmed through her mind. "Playing coy isn't like you. Stop hedging and spit it out."

He sat back. "The only way your family will let me through the door is if they think we're dating."

Dating Frank Evans? If Journey had a type—and she did—it was charming guys who didn't have a chance in hell of overwhelming her. Safe guys.

There was nothing safe about Frank. He was too big, too controlled, too dangerous. Being in any kind of intimate setting, even if it wasn't real, was the worst idea she'd ever heard.

"You want to fake date me to get close to the information you need to do the job." It didn't sound that unreasonable when he put it that way. "That's simple enough."

Frank raised a single eyebrow. "Duchess, let's be honest. There's nothing simple about this, whether you want to admit it or not."

Acclaim for Katee Robert's Novels

The Last King

"Intense, gripping, and full of unexpected steamy romance."
—*Fresh Fiction*

"Top Pick! The heart of this romance is the development of trust between Beckett and Samara, and Robert expertly unfolds it, revealing the emotional connection on both sides under the flash and fire of their irresistible chemistry. 4½ stars."
—*RT Book Reviews*

The Bastard's Bargain

"*The Bastard's Bargain* is deliciously gritty, darkly romantic, drop-dead sexy and thoroughly engrossing."
—*USA Today*, Happy Ever After

"*The Bastard's Bargain* might be the best book in this outstanding series."
—*Fresh Fiction*

Undercover Attraction

"Robert combines strong chemistry, snappy plotting, and imperfect yet appealing characters...This installment is easily readable as a standalone, and it's a worthy addition to a sexy series."

—Publishers Weekly

"*Undercover Attraction* is an amazing read...so addictive I want another fix."

—Fresh Fiction

Forbidden Promises

"A tension-filled plot full of deceit, betrayal, and sizzling love scenes will make it impossible for readers to set the book down. This installment stands alone, but new readers will certainly want to look up earlier books."

—Publishers Weekly

"4.5 Stars! My favorite book so far in this series! You will finish it in one sitting...This was one sexy ride!"

—Night Owl Reviews, Top Pick

An Indecent Proposal

"Robert proves she is one of the bright new stars of romance, and readers who love tortured heroes...will snap up the latest in her brilliantly imaginative and blisteringly hot O'Malley series."

—Booklist

"Top Pick! The chemistry between Cillian and Olivia is amazingly *hot* and the connection they have is wicked...Another amazing addition to a very addictive series. 5 stars."
—Harlequin Junkie

The Wedding Pact

"*The Wedding Pact* is original, and very cleverly plotted...And what can I say about the ending? Absolutely fantastic."
—Fresh Fiction

"I loved every second."
—All About Romance

The Marriage Contract

"Robert easily pulls off the modern marriage-of-convenience trope...This is a compulsively readable book! It's more than just sexy times, too, though they are plentiful and hot!...An excellent start to a new series."
—*RT Book Reviews*

"*Romeo and Juliet* meets *The Godfather*...Unpredictable, emotionally gripping, sensual and action-packed, *The Marriage Contract* has everything you could possibly need or want in a story to grab and hold your attention."
—Nose Stuck in a Book (ycervera.blogspot.com)

ALSO BY KATEE ROBERT

The Kings Series

The Last King

The O'Malleys Series

The Bastard's Bargain

Undercover Attraction

Forbidden Promises

An Indecent Proposal

The Wedding Pact

The Marriage Contract

THE
FEARLESS
KING

KATEE ROBERT

THE KINGS #2

FOREVER

NEW YORK   BOSTON

Copyright © 2019 by Katee Hird

Cover design by Elizabeth Turner Stokes. Cover copyright © 2019 by Hachette Book Group, Inc.

Forever
Hachette Book Group
1290 Avenue of the Americas, New York, NY 10104
forever-romance.com
twitter.com/foreverromance

First edition: February 2019

Forever is an imprint of Grand Central Publishing. The Forever name and logo are trademarks of Hachette Book Group, Inc.

The publisher is not responsible for websites (or their content) that are not owned by the publisher.

The Hachette Speakers Bureau provides a wide range of authors for speaking events. To find out more, go to www.hachettespeakersbureau.com or call (866) 376-6591.

ISBNs: 978-1-4555-9712-3 (mass market edition), 978-1-4555-9714-7 (ebook)

Printed in the United States of America

OPM

10 9 8 7 6 5 4 3 2 1

To Kesha—thanks for an amazing soundtrack for this book, and for never letting the bastards get you down

ACKNOWLEDGMENTS

It always feels a little strange to be thanking God for the inspiration and creativity that results in some seriously sexy books, but the ideas just keep coming and I am forever grateful for that.

Huge thanks to Leah Hultenschmidt for helping me make Frank and Journey's story the best version of itself. You always know what I'm trying to accomplish even if it doesn't show up on the page in the first draft, and it's been an amazing experience working with you!

Thank you to the art department at Forever for an amazing cover. You captured Frank in all his glory, and I couldn't imagine a better cover for this story.

Special thanks to Timitra, Diane, Jessica, Sheri, and Brooke for reading through and helping me get both Frank and Journey's experiences and history just right. Your thoughts and comments were exceedingly helpful. Thank you!

Writing a book is a strange process sometimes, filled with up and downs and the occasional spiral. Big thanks and hugs to Piper J. Drake, Åsa Maria Bradly, Kristen Nave, and Hilary Brady for always being there to give me the kick in the pants or the encouragement I needed to keep on keeping on. You're all rock stars and I don't deserve you!

Last but never least, all my love and thanks to Tim. Thank you for listening to my frustrations, celebrating my successes, never letting me get too down on myself—and always being willing to share the lime-flavored Otter Pops. Love you like a love song.

THE FEARLESS KING

CHAPTER ONE

Our father is back in Houston."

"That's hilarious. You should be a comedian." Journey King sat down in the chair across from her brother's massive desk and waited for him to laugh. But the devastating sympathy in Anderson's blue eyes told her that he wasn't joking. She cleared her throat, trying to speak past the sensation of it closing off her ability to take in air. "Oh God. No, he can't do this." She shivered, then cursed herself for showing even that much reaction.

"I'm sorry, Jo. I would've told you sooner, but I just found out thirty minutes ago he's on his way here."

Journey had always felt safe in the Kingdom Corp offices, totally in control, knowing she had her family at her back. But recent events had turned their world topsy-turvy and shaken some of that innate trust. With so many skeletons dancing in their closets, she should have expected her own personal one to come calling at the first available opportunity.

He's just a man.

The lie was as substantial as smoke. Elliott Bancroft

charmed everyone he met, masking the truth until up was down and down was up.

The silence threatened to suck her under. *No.* "No." She spoke aloud, trying to break the spell already weaving around her. "I will not let him win."

That battle was fought a long time ago. He won. You lost. You all lost.

Stop it.

Anderson rounded the desk as she shoved to her feet. "Jo…" He grabbed her hands, easily encompassing them in his own.

There wouldn't be time to run. Running and hiding had never worked with Elliott Bancroft anyway. She sank back into the chair, her body a marionette whose strings had been cut. "I'm okay." She wasn't, but if their father was on his way, Anderson needed to be focusing on the coming confrontation and not on her. She lifted her chin. "I'm okay. You should sit behind your desk. Start this off from the right position." The posturing wouldn't work, but it was *something*.

The door to Anderson's office swung open, and she tensed at the familiar footsteps even as she forced herself to twist and face him.

Elliott. Father. Monster.

Journey folded her hands in her lap. *Breathe. Just breathe. Do* not *react. If he knows you're afraid, it will make him happy.* "Elliott."

It had been…five years? Five years since she'd seen her father last, though she would have happily gone fifty more. He'd aged in that time, his skin darkened from too many hours in the sun, his dark hair shot through with silver. The blue eyes were the same, warm as a summer day...if one didn't know what lurked beneath. He'd turn more than a few heads in any room he walked into.

Except this one.

His smile widened when he caught sight of her. "Since you stopped taking my calls, sweetheart, I thought it was time to come to you." He spread his arms wide to encompass both Journey and Anderson. "Things are changing here at Kingdom Corp."

Journey forced her hands to relax. It didn't matter what he said or her reaction to it—the only thing that mattered was the truth, and the truth was that her mother would throw herself on a literal sword before she let her estranged husband anywhere near her company. He was bluffing. He had to be. "You don't have a say when it comes to Kingdom Corp. It's our mother's company." Or it had been. It belonged to Journey and Anderson and their other two siblings now. "She gave it to us when she left town." The paperwork still hadn't been completed because of all the red tape, but that didn't change anything.

It *shouldn't* change anything.

Elliott smiled. "Actually, the company isn't hers to give."

Her stomach twisted in knots, the knots growing thorns when Anderson didn't immediately jump in to contradict their father. The walls inched closer, the large room morphing into something too tight and close and cramped to fit three people. *Not enough air. I can't get enough air.* She lost the battle for calm and clenched the armrests of the chair.

Anderson shifted, drawing her attention to him like a drowning victim seeking a life preserver. His blue eyes, so similar and yet so different from their father's, held rage and regret. "Unfortunately, he's telling the truth. It appears the Bancroft family helped fund the initial seed money that got Kingdom Corp off the ground. Elliott stood as silent partner while our mother ran the company, but he's technically in possession of twenty percent of the company shares."

Quadruple what she and her three other siblings held individually. Journey gripped the chair tighter, digging her nails into the wood to keep herself from bolting. *Damn you, Anderson, you had to know this before today. Why didn't you tell me?* "Mother signed over her shares to you. That should put you firmly as the main share-holder with twenty-five percent."

If anything, Elliott's smile widened. "Her shares have to, by contract, be divided equally among our children. That puts each of you at ten percent—and leaves me as main shareholder. No, sweetheart, you won't get rid of me that easily. I'm here to stay." He shifted ever so slightly, and Journey flinched. Elliott chuckled and crossed over to sink gracefully into the unoccupied chair next to Journey. "Like I said, there are going to be some major changes happening here at Kingdom Corp now that I'm in charge."

I know what happens when he's in charge.

The pressure cooker inside her exploded, forcing her into motion.

She had to get out of there. Out of the office, out of the building. Getting out of Houston itself sounded even better, but that wasn't an option. Kingdom Corp needed her—and needed her more now than it ever had. The company was *theirs*, by right and by blood. She hadn't worked her ass off and bent over backward to meet her mother's every demand just to hand over the reins to Elliott fucking Bancroft.

"I'll talk to you later," she told her brother as she leapt from her chair and strode out of the room as quickly as she could in her heels.

Journey passed her office and took the elevator down to the ground floor. If she could just get to her apartment, everything would be okay. She'd cook some extravagant recipe that required intense concentration and blocked out all the jumbled thoughts kicking around in her head. She'd even work remotely so it wasn't a wasted evening. At some point, Anderson would come over and he'd anchor her until she was strong enough to face the world again.

If she went home and hid, *he* won.

Journey stopped on the sidewalk outside Kingdom Corp. Turn left, walk home, go through the same series of events she enacted every time her past showed up to slap her down.

Or turn right, and try something new. She didn't have to go home yet. She could walk for a while. Go get a drink. Dance a little. *Live.* Do something—anything—to prove to herself that she wasn't still that broken little girl.

Even if it was a lie.

* * *

Frank Evans kept one eye on the monitors as he went over the financial reports a third time. He'd purchased Cocoa's with the sole goal of getting access to Houston's elite who frequented the club, and several months in, it had already paid for itself several times over. Deals were made and broken within these walls. Now Frank didn't need an extensive network of people reporting information to him—he just needed the VIP section of Cocoa's.

It didn't hurt that the club made money hand over fist, either.

A stir on the cameras had him leaning closer with narrowed eyes. He knew who it was the second she strode into the VIP section simply by the way the men's body language shifted. They turned to Journey King like flowers seeking the sun. Even the women weren't immune, though most of their attention wasn't sexual in nature.

Frank could hardly blame them. He'd spent far too much time watching Journey since they met. She presented a puzzle box he couldn't unlock. The woman had more personas than he'd ever seen, and even with his substantial resources, he couldn't nail down which was the real woman and which was pretend. Party girl. COO of Kingdom Corp. Loyal daughter. Shunned almost royalty. Friend.

It didn't help that she was gorgeous and confident and showed every evidence of being a decent person despite having a harpy for a mother and working for company he disliked on principle. Her mother trying to have Frank's best friend murdered should have cooled his interest.

It hadn't.

He studied her as she cut around the dance floor and made a beeline for the velvet rope dividing the VIP section from the rest of the club. It created the effect of putting the rich and powerful on display for those drawn to that sort of thing, which should have been enough to dissuade said rich and powerful from showing up, but people with money were never logical when it came to soaking up attention from what they considered the rabble. Frank banked on it.

Even obviously distracted, Journey moved with the confidence of a woman who'd never once questioned her role in the world. And why should she? The King family was a staple in Houston since Journey's great-grandfather settled there and invested in the oil business. Though many of the families who'd done the same thing had fallen off in the intervening years, the King fortune and influence only grew.

Even splitting the family down the middle thirty years ago hadn't been enough to lessen that influence.

He expected Journey to take up residence on her favorite spot—the oversized throne that could have easily fit five people—but she strode to the small bar available only to the VIPs. She held up two fingers, and the bartender obediently lined up two shot glasses and filled them to the brim with top-shelf whiskey.

What the fuck?

Journey drank—all the Kings seemed to—but in the time he'd been watching her, moving just out of her sphere, Frank had never seen her drink destructively. She was now.

He should just leave her to it.

It wasn't his business.

He had a small empire to run and bigger fish to fry than Journey King. If she was in the middle of some kind of crisis, it sure as fuck wasn't Frank's problem.

Except...

He watched her down both shots in quick succession and hold up her fingers for two more. *She's running from something.* Why she'd chosen to run to *his* club and make it *his* business was beyond him, but he couldn't sit there and allow it to happen. Not on his watch. Three guys had moved to the bar just down from Journey's stool, and he didn't like the way they eyed her. Predators scenting weakness. "Goddamn it." It wasn't his business. He had people depending on him that actually needed and wanted his help. Journey King could take care of herself.

The trio of men had shifted closer, two on the left side of Journey and one on the right. She made all appearances of continuing to ignore them, but the tense line of her shoulders and the way she kept her gaze pinned on the bartender spoke volumes. He watched a few seconds more, gripping his pen tightly as the nearest man leaned over and spoke directly into her ear. *Here's where you tell him to fuck off.*

But she didn't.

Her shoulders bunched and she shifted slightly away from him—which put her up against the other two. Instead of coming back swinging like he'd seen in the past when someone stepped out of line, she shrank in on herself.

Something's seriously wrong.

Frank picked up his phone. "Dylan, I need you to send someone to collect Journey King and bring her to my office. Be subtle if you can, but get her the fuck out of there now." He hung up without waiting for a response. Dylan had been with his company, Evans, Inc, for years, and right now he served as the manager for Cocoa's while they cemented the changeover. He was a jack-of-all-trades, but over the last month, he'd done an excellent job of managing the club, so Frank intended to keep him in that position for the time being.

On the screen, a woman approached Journey, inserting herself between her and the pair of men at her elbow. *Smart of Dylan to send her instead of a man.*

Journey shifted and seemed to shrug off her fear for a few seconds. She pinned the camera with a smirk, a single eyebrow lifted, every line of her body conveying belligerence instead of the fear of expecting to be kicked at any moment. She flipped the camera the finger but didn't make a scene otherwise as she followed the woman out of the VIP section and toward the stairs that would lead up to his office.

To him.

Frank turned to face the door and braced himself. The few seconds of preparation didn't make a damn bit of difference when Journey marched in like she owned the place and flung herself into the chair across from his desk. The security cameras hadn't done her justice. They never did. Her little sister was the model, but Journey had the cutting kind of beauty that would have made a killing on the runway. Her long blond hair, big hazel eyes, and strong brows drew him in despite himself. After half a dozen business meetings, he should have been immune to her beauty. It was only a gift of genetics, after all.

"You summoned me?" She arched one dark eyebrow, though the earlier flash of attitude didn't quite hold. Something lurked in her eyes, in the tense way she held herself as if prepared to flee at a harsh word. Once again, he couldn't shake the feeling she was running from something.

But what?

Frank propped his elbows on his desk and studied

her. She'd always been lean, but she'd lost weight in the months since he saw her last, and dark smudges beneath her eyes hinted at sleepless nights or stress—probably both. *This will require careful handling.* "I'm calling a cab and sending your ass home before you embarrass yourself and your family." He gave his voice a bit of a lash, needing her to fight back, to regain her equilibrium. To get back to being the woman he'd come to expect.

Journey's mouth dropped open, which only prompted him to notice she'd painted her lips a bright pink. *Yeah, 'cause I definitely didn't notice before now.* She shoved her hair back. "You're out of your damn mind. You don't give a fuck about my family. Why should my embarrassing myself and them matter?"

"Because my best friend is your cousin and, like it or not, what you do reflects back on him." It wasn't, strictly speaking, the truth, but Frank wasn't all that interested in the truth. He was interested in getting Journey King the fuck out of his club before he did something unforgivable like involve himself in her problems. He knew better. Picking up strays might be a weakness he had, but he'd turned it into a strength and built an empire as a result.

Journey wasn't a stray. She was a fucking King.

She sat back, putting herself on display whether she meant to or not. Her dress was perfectly professional—hitting a reasonable two inches above her knees and with just enough give to the fit that it showed off her body without being actively provocative—but that didn't stop his gaze from catching on the slope of her small breasts, the curve of her waist, the long lines of her bare legs.

Trouble.

"I'll leave, Frank. No problem." She grinned, though it didn't reach her hazel eyes. "If you give me the building I've spent the last six months trying to buy from your contrary ass."

He stared. Of all the reactions he'd expected of her, tossing their thwarted business deal in his face wasn't one of them. He'd never had any intention of selling that damn building to Kingdom Corp, and Journey had to know it. "No."

She shrugged a single shoulder, her smile falling away. "Then I guess you're not getting me out of your club without causing a scene. The media loves to hate me, you know. I make excellent headlines. How much profit do you think you'll lose if it comes out that you blacklisted Lydia King's daughter?"

"Slow your roll, Duchess."

She straightened, eyes flashing. "For the last goddamn time—do *not* call me that."

Frank was supposed to be above petty bullshit. He'd worked damn hard to elevate himself over the mistakes his parents had made and the consequences those same mistakes generated. If he wanted to take someone down, then he took them down piece by piece. Methodically. Ensuring that, when he walked away, they wouldn't have the energy or the willpower to hold a knife to his back. All being petty did was create unnecessary enemies.

He didn't need help in that department. Frank made enemies simply by being what he was—a powerful black man moving among Houston's elite.

He couldn't seem to resist needling this woman,

though. He raked his gaze over her, forcing his expression to be impassive. "You can't bring up the media without mentioning the nickname they coined for you. They still use it. Might as well get used to it. You were the one who tried to marry into royalty."

Her pink lips thinned. "You are *such* a dick."

No point in denying it—it was the truth, after all. He reached for his phone. "I'm calling you a cab and you're going to get your ass into it, even if it takes me hauling you over my shoulder to make it happen."

She narrowed her eyes. "You'd like that, wouldn't you?" Journey pushed out of her chair and took two large steps to put herself right up against the desk. She planted her hands on the dark wood and leaned over, looking down her nose at him. "Get off your fucking power trip, Frank. You're nothing. You're less than nothing."

He sat back in his chair. Journey might be impulsive and speak before thinking when she was in social situations, but she was a damn professional the rest of the time. She wasn't like so many of the others of her kind. No matter what she thought of him, she wouldn't give it voice under normal circumstances. Trying to ice Frank out would only result in Kingdom Corp suffering the consequences when he blocked any future real estate deals they sought. She *knew* that, and if there was one god Journey King worshipped, it was Kingdom Corp. She'd never let something as mundane as personal opinion negatively affect her company.

He stood, using his size to push her back.

Except she didn't back up. She glared at him from the other side of the desk as if whatever had crawled up her ass was *his* fault. He braced his hands a bare inch from hers, leaning down to get right in her face. "Watch your tone, Duchess. The rest of the world might line up to blow smoke up your ass, but I don't play that game. Words and actions have consequences. You want to play in the big leagues? You better damn well act like it."

CHAPTER TWO

Journey could barely speak past the tangled mess of emotions inside her. Frank Evans was such a smug bastard, so damn sure he knew everything there was to know about everyone around him. It didn't help that he was absolutely gorgeous, a warrior in a three-piece suit. His dark brown skin gleamed in the low light of the office, his eyes seeming to swallow up the shadows. Everything about him was downright overwhelming, from his linebacker shoulders, to the well-defined chest that even his custom suits couldn't hide, to his sensual lips that never seemed to smile.

She straightened slowly. Not retreating. Restrategizing.

Journey held no illusions. Frank didn't give two fucks about her. He *did* care about her cousin, which was most likely the source of this little powwow. She lifted her chin. "You're not shuttling me out of here like some kind of dirty secret." If she left Cocoa's, there was nothing to do but go home. To *think*. To let the knowledge sink in regarding just how fucked her life was right now. *Frank thinks I can't roll in the big leagues.*

He had no idea just how big the leagues were that she played in right now. For Frank, it was all money and business and whatever real estate moguls did between buying up property after property.

For Journey, the stakes were so much higher.

"You're not a dirty secret, Duchess. You're a fucking mess." Each word cut through her, a knife to the chest, the stomach, the neck.

The fact that they were true only made it hurt worse.

She took a careful step back and then another. *This was a mistake. This whole thing was a mistake. I should have gone with my first instinct and run home. Trying to prove something is only going to result in my looking like a damn fool.* She couldn't say it aloud. There were only two people Journey trusted in this world, and Frank fucking Evans didn't make the list. She spun for the door. "Have a nice night, jackass."

Damn it. What was she doing? She'd just called Frank a jackass. Worse, she'd told him he was nothing—less than nothing. Journey closed her eyes and wrapped her arms around herself. If she needed an indicator of just how screwed up today had gotten, the poisonous words erupting from her mouth more than confirmed it.

Frank wasn't some stranger she'd never see again after acting like a jerk. He owned half of Houston, which meant Kingdom Corp—and Journey—came into contact with him professionally time and time again. He was also good friends with Journey's cousin, and he'd won over *her* best friend as well. Journey would have to deal with him outside of the professional sphere, too. *Oh, what a tangled web we weave.*

Damn it, I have to apologize.

"Frank." She spoke without opening her eyes. *Just get the words out and then you can leave. Just fix this.* "I was out of line. I'm sorry. You don't have to babysit me and I won't make a scene. I'll grab a cab right now and get out of your hair."

"Duchess." Instead of coming from behind her, his voice sounded in front of her. *Directly* in front of her.

She opened her eyes and bit down a yelp. Frank stood a few inches away. Even though she wore heels, Frank towered over her. He stared at her like he believed that if he focused hard enough, he could pull her thoughts from her head. *Trust me, Frank, neither of us wants that.* Finally, he frowned. "What's wrong? I thought it was just a bad day, but it's more than that, isn't it?"

The temptation rose to confess everything and throw herself on his mercy. He might not have a nurturing bone in his body, but he was all warrior. She'd bet her last dollar that he would have a problem with her father on sheer principle. Nothing personal, of course. Just taking care of business and cleaning up the trash. Everyone in Houston knew how *that* ended. People in Frank Evans's way didn't last long. She gave herself several seconds to picture her father's downfall, to luxuriate in the image of him broken and losing what little he cared about in the world. It would be glorious.

She couldn't do it.

To admit the truth was to open Pandora's box. Some things couldn't be unsaid, and while Frank might look at her like she was an idiot sometimes, he still saw her as a strong woman. Not a victim.

"Journey."

The shock of hearing her actual name from his lips

propelled her into motion. If he kept talking in that deep, steady voice, she'd compromise what little strength she had left. She'd spent too much of her life weak and depending on others to shield her. Doing it now, with a man who was barely more than a stranger? Out of the question. She had to leave and she had to leave now.

But when she moved, it was to sway toward him. Frank caught her hips, his big hands easily holding her in place. This was where he'd set her away from him and say something cutting to slam her back into reality.

Except he didn't say anything at all.

Frank's gaze went hot and his fingers pulsed on her hips, the slightest of movements that had her forgetting what little common sense she had left and tilting her face up to his. Their lips touched, and the world around them held its breath. *Another mistake in a long list of mistakes.* There was no backing down. No turning back time to pretend none of this ever happened. She shifted closer and pressed herself against his solid body. The man didn't seem to have a soft spot on him. *Good.* Journey ran her hands up his chest and nipped his bottom lip. Hard.

Just like that, the world sprang into motion again. Frank *moved*. One second Journey was wondering how far to take this, and the next he'd spun them around and pinned her against the door. He ran his rough hands down her sides, over her ass. Touching her everywhere. Anywhere. *Yes, yes, yes.*

He tore his mouth from hers and yanked her dress strap down to bite her shoulder. "You want a distraction, Duchess." He soothed the spot with his tongue and kissed her collarbone, the soft scrape of his teeth against her skin making her shiver. "I'll give it to you. On one condition."

She could barely think past his hands on her thighs, banding around them hard enough to bruise. Each touch. Each bite. Each rough kiss. It all towed her inch by inch back to earth, back to the person Journey King really was.

At least the person she was when her personal demons didn't show up to rub her face in the past.

No. No thinking. There's only Frank.

She arched against him, but he held her immobile. Journey cursed. "What condition?"

"After this, you tell me what's going on." He sucked hard on her neck, and her knees buckled. Frank spoke against her skin. "The truth, Duchess."

"Okay." She lied through her teeth. Anything to keep this going, to ground herself, to banish the fears nipping at her heels for a few minutes.

He lifted her and moved between her thighs, pinning her more effectively. It should have made her feel trapped, but she couldn't think about being held in place with Frank's tongue and teeth working her neck. He licked the pulse point in the hollow of her throat. "I'm not going to be gentle."

This *is what I need.*

She let her head drop back against the door, baring her throat to him completely. "I don't want you to be."

He leaned back enough to look at her—*really* look at her. "You just had two shots. If you're drunk—"

A laugh slipped free, a breath of fresh air clearing away some of the taint that had crept into her heart in the last hour. "Honey, it would take more than two to get me there. I'm no lightweight." Escaping her past would be so much easier if she could drown it out with only a few shots. Unfortunately, her entire family had too high of a tolerance for alcohol to make drinking her problems away an easy thing to accomplish.

He let go of one of her thighs and gripped her chin, his fingers little pinpricks of pain that had her hips moving restlessly against his. Frank met her gaze. "We all have demons, Duchess."

Not like me.

She couldn't handle kindness. It was too close to pity for the throbbing nerve she'd become in the months since the last phone call with her father. Having his barely veiled poison dripping in her ear was like standing on the tracks and feeling the first vibrations of an oncoming train. She'd instinctively known that call wouldn't be the end of it, that he'd play out one of his little games the way he had when his children were at his mercy—the kind of game that ended in blood and broken bones and psychological damage that a lifetime of therapy couldn't quite banish.

But instead of facing the ugly truth, she'd wrapped herself in comforting lies. *He's gone. He'll never come back. We'll never be at his mercy again.*

Look where that got her. Throwing herself at one of the few people in Houston who actually had the means to bring down Kingdom Corp—and would do it without a second thought if she gave him an in. *Awesome job, Jo. Way to make good life choices.*

Pressure clamped her throat, a curious burning rising with each ragged inhale. *Oh God, I'm going to cry.* Journey pushed on Frank's shoulders. "This was a mistake."

He hesitated but finally released her and stepped back, keeping one hand on her hip as if to ensure she didn't crumple at his feet. Since her knees *were* a little wonky, it was a good call. Her lips felt bruised and swollen, her neck tingling from his rough five-o'clock shadow, her thighs quivering from the feeling of him gripping her there.

She turned and grabbed the door handle. Frank was still too close, too big, too overwhelming. She could feel his gaze on her back. Waiting.

All she had to do was turn the doorknob and walk out of the room and he'd let her go. He'd given her a taste of what it would be like to take him to bed, and she didn't know if she'd survive it. Frank had all the markings of a control freak with a short leash, but there was no leash in evidence with his mouth against hers.

Which is the real Frank?

Does it matter?

She opened the door and looked into the hall. Half a dozen steps to the stairs leading down to the club where the pulsing beat of the music called.

Freedom. Or another kind of cage.

In the end, it didn't matter.

She shut the door and very deliberately locked it. *I choose this. If I choose nothing else, I choose this, right here, right now.* Journey unzipped the side of her dress as she turned to face Frank. He stood in the exact same place, watching her the way a hunting dog watched a wounded bird fall from the sky.

She slid her dress off her shoulders and down her body to step out of it, leaving her in only a black satin thong. She hooked her thumbs in the band, but Frank gave a sharp shake of his head. "Leave them on."

He crossed the distance between them in a single step, planting one hand against the door next to her ear. He didn't touch her, but his heat seemed to wrap around her, negating the chill of the air-conditioning. "Say no at any point, and this stops. No questions asked. I'll get you in that cab and make sure you get home safely. End of story."

She could have laughed. Who would have expected Frank Evans to have anything resembling an honorable streak, let alone with *her*? Journey reached up and very deliberately unbuttoned the front of his shirt. "Yes, Frank. I say yes."

* * *

Frank should have backed off the second he realized Journey was walking wounded. He should have done exactly what he'd originally planned and sent someone to escort her home to ensure she didn't do something she'd regret in the morning. He *should* have done a lot of things.

None of that mattered with Journey's French-tipped nails unbuttoning his shirt in a frenzy, as if she couldn't bear another second without their being skin to skin. She needed something, and he was in a position to give it to her.

What happens in the morning?

He kissed her to silence the voice of reason. There were a thousand better ways tonight should end, but Frank didn't give a fuck. She'd given him a taste and then had the audacity to look up at him with shadows in her eyes and say yes. He was a bastard and a half, but he intended to give her everything she asked for and more.

She shoved his shirt down his shoulders, bringing them chest to chest. If clothed Journey King was a source of temptation he'd never been able to combat, seeing her standing in his office wearing a little tease of a black thong…

No words.

Frank took two steps forward, bringing them solidly back against the door again. The rough contact seemed to center something in her, and her hesitance vanished. She arched against him, tilting her head back to offer her mouth. He bypassed her lips and dragged his mouth along her jaw to her ear. "I won't mark you anywhere that can't be covered."

"I don't care." She went for the front of his slacks, expertly undoing the hook and pulling down the zipper. "I don't want to think for a little while. Just keep touching me."

She's using me.

Another signal he should stop this. He was many things, but a sex toy didn't make the list. Neither did being a weapon a woman used in her quest for self-destruction, if that was tonight's goal. He gripped her hips, forcing her still. "Journey—"

She hooked her arms around his neck, dipping down so she met his gaze. "Just tonight, Frank. Shelve the questions for tonight." She bit her bottom lip and then seemed to force the rest of her words out. "I…need this. I need you."

The words hooked in his chest, threatening to override what little control he had left. Still, he held back. Fucking her tonight *would* be something she'd regret, no matter what she told herself now. But there were other options.

He could grant her a reprieve—just enough to take the edge off before he sent her on her way.

You're just looking for an excuse.

Damn straight.

He shifted his grip to run his thumbs under the thin band of her thong, tracing her hip bones. "Tell me what you need."

A hint of vulnerability glimmered in her hazel eyes. "Don't be gentle with me."

Deep down, a brutal part of him that he kept firmly leashed crowed in victory. He tried to drown it out with reason, but there was no place for reason with Journey slipping a hand into his pants and squeezing his cock in a grip that was just shy of vicious. He knocked her hand away and kissed her hard. Instead of melting against him, she met him thrust for thrust, tongue and teeth, with a frenzy that matched the beast rushing to the surface.

More. He needed more of this woman.

Frank lifted her and tumbled them to the floor, barely catching himself before his full weight hit her. Journey didn't miss a beat. She wrapped her legs around his waist and nipped his bottom lip again. Each move conveyed a desire no longer in check, an all-encompassing need only *he* could fulfill.

Do not *fuck Journey King on the floor of your office.*

He caught her hands and shifted to pin them beneath the small of her back. The only hope he had of keeping some measure of control was ensuring she didn't touch him. He shifted over her body, trailing kisses over each of her tight pink nipples and down her stomach to her silk panties. *Make her feel good. Make her forget whatever it is that's chasing her.* "Spread for me, Duchess." When she didn't move fast enough, he bit her thigh.

Instead of obeying, she clamped her thighs around his head. "More."

He did it again, working his way down one inner thigh and back up the other. Marking her. Frank dragged his mouth over her panties, and he couldn't contain a groan when he found her soaked. The scent of her need was more intoxicating than any whiskey he'd ever consumed. Consuming *her* sounded better and better. He licked down one side of the soft fabric and then closed his mouth over her completely.

Journey keened, her back bowing, her thighs shaking, her hips bucking against his mouth. Beneath the carefully cultivated exterior, she was a wild thing that had its wings clipped somewhere along the way. No one possessed that many restraints unless they were hiding something—or hiding *from* something. He sucked her clit through the silk, tonguing her even as he denied himself the removal of that last barrier. He could *taste* her, and it drove him mad. Frank released her wrists and gripped her thighs, forcing them wide so he had better access to her. *More. She's almost there.*

His cock was so fucking hard, he had to fight to keep from taking her right there on the floor. He fucked her with his tongue as well as he could without removing the panties. He growled, and her cry rose in perfect counterpoint. "Frank, please!"

No more playing around.

He sucked her clit hard, using his lips and tongue and teeth to work her until he had to pin her in place. Her legs started shaking and her cries rose, and still he didn't back off. Her entire body went tight as her orgasm rolled over her, the tension in her muscles turning her into a statue for one eternal second before she exhaled in a rush and went slack.

That's enough.

He rested his forehead against her lower stomach and closed his eyes. *Stop now. You gave her what she needed. If you keep going, you're taking advantage of a woman who wouldn't choose this otherwise.* He inhaled, but it only made things worse. He could smell her. It would be the easiest thing in the world to tug her panties to the side and lick her without any barriers in place. To tongue her pussy until she was back on the edge, begging him to make her come again and again.

Until they both lost control and he had her riding his cock.

Frank knelt between Journey's spread thighs and drank in the picture she made, her pale skin flushed with pleasure *he'd* given her, her eyes dazed and a small smile tugging at the edges of her lips. She lifted her head and looked down her body. "You didn't even take my thong off."

The fabric was wet from his mouth—from her desire. It felt as if another man had taken control of his body as Frank reached down and hooked two fingers around the soaked silk. He had to close his eyes as his knuckles brushed her clit, her wet pussy that was more than ready for his cock, and he pulled her panties off. He tucked them into his pocket as she watched. "I'll call you a cab."

Journey sat up, some of the pleasure leaving her face. "What?" Hurt lingered at the edge of her expression, and he could no more leave it unanswered than he could let her walk out of his office fifteen minutes ago.

He leaned forward and gripped the back of her neck, bringing her up to press her forehead against his. "If you fuck me tonight, you'll regret it, Duchess. You'd wake up in the morning and let shame override how good everything I'd do to you felt."

"I'm not saying you're right." She took a shuddering breath. "But I'm not saying you're wrong, either."

He didn't release her, couldn't force himself to let go quite yet. "Have dinner with me tomorrow."

"What?"

Even though he knew better, words spilled out. "You have a problem, Journey. Don't insult my intelligence by lying to me. We both know something drove you here tonight, and we both know that orgasm barely took the edge off of your fear." He released her neck and smoothed a hand over her hair before he could stop himself.

She reacted like he'd hooked her up to a live wire. Journey shot back until she hit the wall, her eyes too wide. "No."

He froze. *Why not?* Frank didn't let the question escape. He'd told her at the beginning of this that all she had to say was no to end things. She'd just called his fucking bluff. He let his hand drop and sat back on his heels. "I'll call you a cab," he repeated.

"That's for the best." She snatched her dress and pulled it on while he watched. Through it all, she didn't make direct eye contact again. Journey reached for the door and paused. "Frank..." She seemed to brace herself. "I appreciate the offer—I appreciate tonight, too—but..." She shook her head. "Good night, Frank."

He waited for the door to close to call down and ensure that Dylan had a cab waiting for her, and then he pulled his shirt back on. Frank stared at the door a long time, considering what Journey had—and hadn't—said. Given what he knew of Kingdom Corp and her family, the threat came either from her father's side or from within the company. Lydia King might be ruthlessly ambitious, but her one redeeming quality was that she seemed to love her children. She'd never do something to put that haunted look in her older daughter's eyes.

He should leave it alone.

He had enough bullshit to deal with without borrowing trouble.

If Journey couldn't handle whatever issues arose, then her older brother was more than capable. It was none of Frank's damn business, and they wouldn't welcome any assistance he offered.

Journey was not a fucking stray he could scoop up and incorporate into his business because she had nowhere else to go. She was a King. Bad for business and potentially bad for his friendship with one of the few people he cared about in this life—Beckett. If there was a woman in Houston completely off-limits to Frank, it was Journey goddamn King.

None of that stopped him from calling his second-in-command, Mateo. The man had barely picked up the phone when Frank said, "I need everything you can find out about changes that have happened at Kingdom Corp in the last twenty-four hours, and I need it by tomorrow."

"Sure thing, boss."

He hung up and sat back. It was just information. It didn't mean he had to do anything about it. Entirely possible that the issue was some internal conflict with employees of Kingdom Corp and that Journey had simply needed to blow off some steam. Simple. Nothing to concern himself with.

But every instinct he'd spent years honing shouted that Journey was in trouble—in *danger*—and he wouldn't be able to focus on anything else until he had an answer. Once he did...

Well, he'd decide his next move then.

CHAPTER THREE

Since avoiding Kingdom Corp wasn't an option, Journey put her sleepless night to work and went in before the sun had fully risen. Anything to keep herself occupied and not focus too hard on the thoughts chasing themselves round and round in her head.

I hooked up with Frank Evans.

She leaned back in her office chair and crossed her legs, her breath catching in her throat at the dull throbbing in her thighs from his bites. Journey closed her eyes. She shouldn't have kissed him. Or let him kiss her. Or whatever had happened that resulted in her mouth on his.

It didn't matter if he'd expressed interest a few months ago, or that she'd been drowning—was *still* drowning—and he'd represented a life preserver, if only for a little while. He obviously hadn't signed up for fucking her problems away. She shouldn't have even asked.

Shouldn't, wouldn't, *couldn't* ask.

Journey opened her eyes and pinched the bridge of her nose. Frank had allowed her a breath of fresh air last night, but it was over now. Time to slink back into the muck and figure out a way through their current mess. She grabbed her cell and dialed her older brother. Anderson would know what to do. He always did.

He answered on the first ring. "You're up early."

"I couldn't sleep. I tried, but..." The brief new memories Frank had given her weren't enough to stand against the cascade of poison hovering at the edge of her mind even on the best days. The last twenty-four hours hardly qualified as a *best day*.

"It's going to get worse before it gets better, Jo." He sighed, sounding just as tired and beat down as she felt. Here, on the phone, they didn't have to try to be strong or worry about the mask cracking and the wrong person seeing the truth. Journey and Anderson didn't play pretend for each other—they never had.

"I can handle it." It wasn't *quite* a lie. "It won't be forever, right? Elliott has never taken an interest in anything resembling work. Why should this time be any different?" She just had to hold on to what was left of her sanity until he left again. *Is this what my life is going to look like? Acting normal and well-adjusted in between tailspins every time he comes back to town?*

Her mother might have been a different kind of monster, but at least she kept the larger threats at bay with her presence. Journey gave herself a sharp shake. She couldn't afford to think like that. "He'll leave," she repeated.

"I'm not so sure, Jo. He's different this time. Focused. I don't like it."

"Me, either." She grabbed her favorite pen and tapped it against the desk. "When will you be in?"

He chuckled. "I'm here now." Footsteps sounded down

the hall, and then her office door opened to reveal her older brother. Anderson hung up and stepped into the room.

He looked so much like their father, it made her heart stop for several eternal seconds, but just like she had every time before, she focused on the differences. Anderson and Journey had their mother's mouth—generous but far quicker to frown than to smile in genuine warmth. Journey fought against the inclination, but Anderson had never bothered. He was taller than their father, too, and broader. Both her brothers leaned more King than Bancroft when it came to how deceptively large they were. Anderson hid it with expensive suits cut to minimize his sheer size. Bellamy didn't bother.

He shut the door carefully and took her in. She could actually *feel* him categorize the darker shadows beneath her eyes, the way her hand shook—just a little—and how lackluster her hair was after skipping her routine yet again. "You look like shit, Jo."

And he looked like he normally did—cool and in control. Anderson had always hidden his fear better than she had. Or maybe he truly didn't fear Elliott anymore. Maybe she was the only one who did. *Aren't you a little ray of sunshine this morning?* She cleared her throat. "Wow, thanks. I'll make sure to remember your supportive words when I shop for your Christmas gift."

He raised his eyebrows. "It's February."

"You don't say." She gave a mock gasp. "Only ten months to go. Anderson, I'd be really careful about playing your cards right or it's going to be 2007 all over again."

His lips quirked at the reference to the year she'd

bought him a pony and then badgered him until he took a picture riding it—which amounted to him standing over the tiny beast with a put-upon expression. It was one of her favorite pictures of her brother, one of the few times he wasn't perfectly put together.

He bypassed the chairs opposite her desk and rounded them to pull her into his arms. "I'll find us a way through this, Jo. I promise."

She closed her eyes and inhaled her brother's expensive cologne—the same stuff he'd used for damn near fifteen years. Here in the safety of his embrace she could almost believe that Anderson would take care of everything. Again. Journey allowed herself one last deep inhale, and then she took a step back. "Maybe we need to look at the possibility that there *isn't* a convenient way through this. What if he was just waiting for something to take out Mom so he could step in?" The thought raised the small hairs on the back of her neck.

She'd never put much consideration into her father's intelligence—he didn't need to be smart to destroy lives—and her mother didn't have much respect for him. When Journey was ten, Lydia had come home unexpectedly from a work trip and found her four children in the midst of one of Elliott's more creative punishments. He had them running around the house under the hot August sun for hours. By the time Lydia showed up, Eliza had fainted from heatstroke, and Anderson was carrying her as best he could.

Elliott never spent another night in that house.

Journey still didn't know what Lydia had done to run him out of Houston so effectively. Her mother didn't talk about it, and *they* were hardly going to bring it up. The

end result was the only thing that mattered—he was gone
and they were safe.

Until they weren't.

Her phone pinged, and then Anderson's did the same.
The sound snapped her back to the present. She couldn't
afford to let in the ghosts of their past. Her brother needed
her focused and standing at his side instead of cower-
ing behind him. Journey turned to grab hers, forcing a
laugh. "You still have that same notification for emails?
Anderson, we talked about this. It sounds like freaking
dial-up internet."

"It's nostalgic." He tapped out the pass code for
his phone.

"It's enough to give me anxiety just hearing it." She
opened her email and stopped short. "What the hell?"

"That fucking bastard."

She ignored her brother, scrolling through the extensive email as she read. She went back to the top and
read it again, part of her not quite believing this professional cutting down had been delivered by her father.
"He... What? He's vetting the board? *We* are the board."
When Lydia was still in Houston, the three of them had
effectively run the company, hauling the board in to vote
only when strictly necessary. The members of the board
were figureheads at best, which was the way everyone
preferred it. Why the hell did they need to be *vetted*?

Her phone rang, and she stared at it like it was a live
snake. "He's calling."

"Answer and put it on speaker." Anderson moved to
her back. He didn't touch her, but he silently offered his
support by sheer proximity.

She obeyed. Journey forced her spine straight. *It's just*

a phone call. He's not here…except he is here. We're not safe anymore. We never really were. "Early morning for you, considering your drinking problem, Elliott."

"That's a rich accusation considering what I know of your extracurricular activities." He sounded so satisfied, her stomach dropped and then rose at lightning speed, leaving her dizzy. Elliott continued, practically purring. "Rough night, sweetheart?"

Don't call me that. She bit down the response. He already knew far too many of her buttons—he *was* far too many of her buttons. Giving him more ammunition was out of the question. "I'm not sure what you're talking about. I'm in the office and you aren't, so…Who *really* had the rough night?"

He laughed, the sound so familiar, she sank into her chair and crossed her legs—*hard*—using the ache from Frank's bite marks to steady herself. *I'm not a child anymore. I'm a fucking adult and he can't hurt me.* She took a shallow breath. "Is there something you needed, or were you trying to ruin my morning coffee?"

Just like that, the charming daddy mask disappeared, replaced by the cold thing that dwelled beneath. "Going forward, anyone who serves on the board of directors will need to be approved. What happened with your mother was incredibly unfortunate and could have been avoided with a proper vetting process—one I fully intend to implement."

Dread weighted down her limbs. "Who's handling this vetting process—aside from you?"

"There are a handful of investors who haven't been pleased with the direction Kingdom Corp is going and who are eager to take a more hands-on role." She could practically hear his grin. "The vetting process begins this week. If anyone is found to be...unfit...they will be removed from their position within the board—and potentially removed from the company as well. We can't have *unfit* individuals in charge of any kind of operation. Wouldn't you agree, sweetheart?"

Me. He means me. I'm the weak link.

Anderson's hand closed around her shoulder, making her jump. He squeezed, his fingers digging in just enough that she managed to exhale the breath she'd been holding. "I'm not convinced a board you've helped bankroll is the most unbiased method of deciding if someone is unfit."

"You don't have to be convinced. This is happening. The board will make a decision based on the information given to them. I'm bringing in a psychologist to analyze every member and give the thumbs-up or thumbs-down."

"That's hardly legal."

His low laugh rolled down the line, making her stomach twist painfully. Elliott could be vicious, but he'd always been his scariest when he laughed. It was often the only warning they got before one of his creative games. The kind that ended in visits from the doctor the family had on retainer.

"Check your contract. You'll find it's perfectly legal." He paused meaningfully. "I'm sure you have nothing to worry about. It's not as if you're damaged goods and in danger of snapping under pressure. What could a shrink possibly find that would make them declare you unfit?"

Her mouth worked, but no words emerged.

Elliott didn't seem to need an answer. "I look forward to seeing your report on internal operations by Friday." He hung up.

She turned to Anderson. "He's going to try to oust us."

"It's looking like that." He took out his phone and started scrolling.

"What are you doing?"

He met her gaze. "We might not individually hold the majority of shares in the company, but if all of us stand against him, we might be able to at least slow this down until we think of a more permanent plan."

Journey pressed a hand to her chest. It took everything she had to force out the next words. "If we told...If we told the truth, they would declare *him* unfit."

"Jo, no." Anderson crouched in front of her and took her hands. He waited for her to look directly at him to keep speaking. "We have no evidence. No hospital records. No witnesses. Even if we could prove that he's a sadistic monster, the statute of limitations comes into play. It's been damn near twenty years. All telling the truth would do is reopen old wounds for the sake of his amusement. We'll find another way. I'll fucking kill him before I let him make victims of us again." His steady tone gave lie to any fiction she might spin about him bluffing.

Anderson never bluffed.

She gripped his hands tightly. "Don't you dare. You promised me you wouldn't."

"Fuck, Jo, I was nine. Of course I promised you then."

Anderson might cover up his scars better than she did, but times like these put them on full display. The wildness in his blue eyes was a look she hadn't seen in decades, the one that told her he didn't see a way out of this. She couldn't let him kill Elliott. Their father liked to use Journey to control Anderson, and time apparently hadn't changed that particular playbook of his.

As much as she hated dancing to her father's tune, she wouldn't let her brother throw away his life. Not now, when they'd worked so hard to do more than survive. She squeezed his hands harder. "You. Promised."

He hesitated for a long moment and finally exhaled, his shoulders dropping an inch in defeat. "Jo—"

"If you go after him, you're playing right into his hands. *Think*, Anderson. You know he has some kind of contingency plan ready in case you try to hurt him."

He released her and stood. "We'll fight this, Jo. We'll win."

She wished she believed that. Journey watched her brother walk out of her office and then sat there for a long time, thinking. Anderson would fight until his dying breath to ensure their father didn't win. If things started looking dire, he might do something he couldn't take back, promise or no. He'd throw away everything he'd worked so hard for. For her. For Bellamy. For Eliza.

She couldn't let him.

She stared at her phone. She'd been the victim, the helpless little sister, the one in need of being protected, for as long as she could remember. Journey had never been strong enough to fight her own battles. She wasn't sure she was strong enough *now*.

But she couldn't sit back and do nothing while Anderson went to war for them yet again, taking all the risks so no one else had to shoulder that burden. Elliott was focusing on her because she was the weak link, but the second he decided Anderson was more trouble than he was worth, he'd cut her brother's legs out from underneath him.

She couldn't let it happen.

Journey dialed before she could talk herself out of it. As soon as the line clicked over, she spoke in a rush. "I changed my mind, Frank. If your offer still stands, I...I need help."

* * *

Few things surprised Frank these days. People were nothing if not predictable, and he'd made his fortune being able to guess their moves before they made them. He hadn't expected Journey to call. He sure as fuck hadn't expected her to request his help less than twelve hours after he'd brought her to orgasm on his office floor.

He strode through the front doors of the Lotus, the restaurant he'd set as their meeting location. It was a little Greek place he'd scooped up right around the time he made his first million. The owners had been the same family since he was a child, and the recession hit them hard. They would have lost everything, so Frank had quietly bankrolled a face-lift and some key advertising for the place. He let them maintain independence for the most part, but they had meetings once a quarter to ensure the restaurant was following the trajectory he wanted for it.

Mira herself met him at the hostess stand. She looked like he imagined mothers were supposed to look—soft and curvy for excellent hugs, laugh lines from a life well lived, and a wardrobe of dresses in some of the strangest patterns he'd ever laid eyes on. Today, tiny cats danced across a minty background, setting off her brown skin and curly dark hair. "Mr. Evans! Let me look at you, let me look at you." She took his hands and held them out to the side, surveying his body critically. "Have you lost weight?"

"How could I, Mira? You send your son around once a week with your cooking." He pressed a quick kiss to her cheek and disengaged their hands. "The gyro on Monday was wonderful."

"Flatterer." She smiled. "You're here to meet the young lady?" She waggled her dark eyebrows. "Is it serious?"

He shook his head. "Sorry to disappoint, but it's business."

"This *is* disappointing. You won't be young forever." She shooed him. "Go to your meeting. I'll send the boys over with today's specials in a bit. Wine?"

He glanced at his watch. "It's ten in the morning."

"Iced tea, then." She didn't wait for an answer, which was just as well.

Frank gave himself a full ten seconds to enjoy the fond pestering. Before she died, his mother had been more occupied with escaping her pain in any way she could than she was with asking him about his life. It gave him a whole lot of freedom as a teenager, and he'd never felt the lack until he met Mira. She was what a good mother looked like.

No point in going over this yet again.

He made his way to the little table tucked into an alcove of sorts near a stained-glass window that over-looked the street. The morning sunlight shone through, turning Journey King into a piece of art, color washing over her blond hair and pale skin, painting her in reds and oranges and blues. She glanced up as he approached, but she didn't smile. She also didn't look like she'd gotten much sleep.

Frank thought over the information Mateo had provided this morning. Journey King wouldn't be the first person to have two shitty parents, and her lazy-ass father coming back to Houston couldn't be a pleasant thing. As best Frank could tell, Elliott Bancroft was a playboy who liked spending money more than he liked earning it, and between his wife and his family, he never went without despite showing no evidence of working a day in his life. If he was back in Houston and meddling with Kingdom Corp, he had some kind of ulterior motive.

Journey eyed him as if she expected him to come across the table at her. Skittish...edging straight into terrified. *What the fuck is going on?* He didn't have all the puzzle pieces, and the lack of information grated. Frank carefully leaned back, giving her the illusion of more space. "Considering how last night went, I didn't think I'd hear from you."

"You mean after the pity orgasm you gave me?" She lifted a single shoulder, as if she begged men to touch her—to fuck her—every damn day. "That's just sex, Frank. This is business."

Liar.

"I'm not petitioning for sainthood, Duchess. I don't dole out orgasms to brighten people's day."

Anger flared in her hazel eyes, pushing them closer to a true gold than a brown. Her tremors stilled, and she leaned back and draped an arm over her chair, giving him a lethal stare. *There she is.* Journey thinned her bright coral lips. "Could have fooled me." Another of those one-shouldered shrugs, as if last night hadn't meant shit to her. "It's irrelevant. The offer was a onetime thing. It's not my fault you didn't take me up on it."

Realization snaked through him. *I damaged her pride.* It was the only logical reason for her chilly attitude despite the fact that *she* sought *him* out today. He shook his head. "You were out of your mind with fear last night. I don't play the pity-fuck game, and I sure as hell don't get off on the knowledge that I'll be someone's regrettable decision when they wake up and realize what they've done."

"Frank Evans, so logical and cold." She laughed softly. "Who would have thought that the only time you warmed up was when you had your hands all over a woman?"

They could go round and round like this for hours and get nowhere. "You said you need my help."

Mira strode up with a tray of iced tea and water. She took one look at Frank's face, chose to silently place them on the table, and strode away. He'd have to apologize later, but he was too fucking frustrated in that moment to worry about it.

Journey picked up her tea and took a cautious sip. "You deal in information as well as real estate."

"That's hardly a secret." He hadn't gotten to where he was simply by being good with money and knowing which properties were worth investing in and which should be cut loose. In any business deal, the person with the most information had the power. It didn't matter who the players were outside of that deal, or how long their family had been in power in the city, or how large the number in their bank account. Information was the ultimate equalizer, and Frank used it ruthlessly. He'd paid too high a price not to learn that particular lesson.

The tension bled back into her body, starting at her shoulders and morphing her into a woman-shaped statue. Brittle. So fucking brittle. If he didn't know better, he'd think Journey King had a twin and *that* was who sat in front of him, rather than the gregarious woman he'd met months ago over a potential business deal. To see her fire doused so effectively... It made him want to bundle her off to anywhere but Houston until she brightened back into the woman he'd been so damn drawn to.

She wasn't his business—not if she wasn't prepared to offer something in exchange for his help. He had to remember that.

Journey reached for her drink and then seemed to think better of it. She folded her hands in her lap and met his gaze directly. "My father fully intends to remove me as COO of Kingdom Corp—and then I expect he'll go after my brothers' positions as well. If he succeeds, he'll run the company that my mother sacrificed everything for into the ground within five years. Sooner, more likely. I can't let that happen."

On the surface, it made sense, but it didn't line up with how hard she clearly fought to keep her expression placid. The company was something all Lydia's children loved to one degree or another. He understood wanting to fight for it—to do what it took to prevent an intruder from removing her and her brothers.

I could be misreading the situation.

He could be... but Frank didn't think so. "How does your father plan on removing you?"

"By declaring me incompetent." She gave a mirthless smile. "He's handpicking a board that will have the power to make that call, along with a pet psychologist to dance to his tune."

He studied her, considering the facts as he knew them. It sounded like the truth, but it still didn't shine a light on the greater picture. Journey King had plenty of resources if she chose to use them. More so, *Anderson* King was not an idiot, and he had to know that getting involved with Frank was a calculated risk that might not go in the King family's favor. Anderson didn't have the same racial and status hang-ups of most of the people who held power in this city, but he also wasn't stupid. Frank held no love for the Kings, even if his attraction to Journey defied logic. Pinning this deal on hope that his desire to get her into bed would outweigh his business plans was a fool's decision.

Which led him to exactly one conclusion. "Your brother doesn't know you're here, does he?"

"Bellamy isn't concerned with my movements." She said it so primly, he almost smiled.

Frank leaned forward, reclaiming the space he'd vacated earlier. "You know damn well I'm talking about Anderson."

She shifted, as if she couldn't decide whether to close the distance or put more between them. "Anderson can't know. That's part of the deal."

Interesting. "What, exactly, are you asking me for?"

"I need my father gone." She glanced around as if there were recording devices hidden in the room. "I mean, gone as in out of Houston like my mother is gone out of Houston." When he didn't respond, she sighed. "The usual scandal stuff won't work. He's been a scandal since he could walk—he's immune to it at this point. Old news. None of the cheating or alcohol or drugs will be enough. The Bancrofts are too established—and their pockets are too deep. They'll just pay someone off to sweep it under the rug. It has to be the right leverage, and I don't have the ability to find it on my own."

Why not? No one could get close the way family was able to, even family that was hated and untrustworthy. For better or worse, blood bonds bypassed all manner of things that should be deal-breakers—*especially* when someone was talking about a King or a Bancroft. Journey was both. He took a slow drink of his iced tea, letting her stew. "And in return?"

Another of those infuriatingly uncaring shrugs. "What do you want?"

You.

He stomped down on the completely irrational knee-jerk reaction. No matter what kind of bastard Frank was, he had a line he wouldn't cross, and that response jump roped right over the line. Repeatedly.

Elliott Bancroft's presence threatened to disrupt the power structure in Houston, as well as within the oil industry. While Frank didn't give two fucks about the oil industry, he *did* care about Journey's cousin, Beckett. Beckett's competing oil company would also be affected by any bold moves Kingdom Corp made with an unknown factor at the helm. All of it added up to bad news, and there was little Frank loathed more in this world than someone rocking the boat he'd spent years building and steadying. He would have moved against Bancroft the second he heard about this development, with or without Journey asking for his assistance.

But she was here, and she was willing to bargain.

He met her gaze steadily. "Two conditions. Kingdom Corp owes me a favor of my choosing down the road, no questions asked. It won't be anything that acts against the company's best interest, but it won't be comfortable, either. You also will reach out to your cousin and take him up on the offer he's repeatedly extended since things fell out with your mother." Beck wanted the King family reunited and the sins of the past put to rest permanently. So far, Lydia's children had resisted his overtures.

"You've got to be kidding. You're advocating for my cousin now?"

"My reasons are my own." He permitted himself a smile. "Never show how desperate you are when bargaining, Duchess. My conditions are perfectly reasonable. It's not as if I demanded you in my bed for the duration of our deal. We both know I could have and that you'd be more than happy to oblige."

Apparently he was twice the bastard everyone thought he was, after all.

CHAPTER FOUR

It took everything Journey had not to throw her iced tea in Frank's face. She'd expected him to demand a favor. Tit for tat and all that bullshit. She shouldn't have been surprised that he'd negotiated on Beckett's behalf. They were best friends, and Frank had risked a lot to ensure her cousin came out on top when he went toe-to-toe with Journey's mother. A couple of months wasn't long enough to combat nearly three decades of being told that the other side of the King family was the enemy, but Journey *could* envision a time when she took Beckett up on the olive branch he'd extended. He was dating Samara, after all, and if he was good enough for her best friend, then he probably wasn't a total piece of shit.

Reaching out to Beckett on *Frank's* terms?

No fucking way.

Easier to focus on that than on his non-threat about commanding her into his bed. She might not know him well, but their encounter in his office at Cocoa's was more than enough to get a read on him when it came to sex. He wouldn't make it part of the terms, and he damn well knew that *she* knew that.

Knowing the truth didn't make her want to wipe that smug look off his face any less, though.

She moved her hand away from her drink and linked her fingers in her lap. She would be calm. She would be controlled. She sure as hell would hold her temper because she needed his help. "What on God's green earth would make you think I'd put myself on the bargaining table for this?"

"Won't you?"

Two little words that sounded a whole lot more like a challenge than a question.

Her mouth dropped open. Frank gave her an arrogant smile that made her want to scream. "You forget, Duchess—you're not in a position to do anything but take my offer. *You* called *me*. I don't need this deal. Your father might be the scum of the earth, but he's nothing I can't deal with should I choose to. So far, I have no indication of how he'll conduct business, which means moving against him creates an enemy where I had none before." He propped his elbows on the table. There might still be a solid foot between them, but he seemed even bigger than he was up close. His cologne teased her, something subtle and yet startlingly male.

He smelled like the best kind of fucking.

Journey dropped her eyes, fearing what he'd see in them. "I understand that." She couldn't dredge up resentment, because he spoke nothing but the truth. He had the power. She had none.

As usual.

"In that case, I'll ask you again—take the terms, or stop wasting both our time."

She straightened her fork and moved her knife to the

exact distance from her plate on the other side. "How will this work? You can't just stroll into Kingdom Corp when it suits you. Even if Anderson is distracted with our father, he hasn't forgotten whose side you're really on." Beckett's. Not theirs. Never theirs.

For a long moment, she thought he wouldn't answer, but Frank growled and reached across the table to cover her hands with his own. Her heart leapt into her throat, its frantic beating stealing her ability to speak. Her flinch was as strong as it was involuntary, and Frank snatched his hand back before she'd completed the movement. "Duchess—"

"What's your plan?" she cut in. Journey took a shuddering breath and raised her gaze to meet his. There was no covering up her fearful reaction, but she'd be damned before she let him question it.

Frank studied her with that implacable look of his. "I can get a lot of information on your old man without too much trouble, but at the end of the day, your family holds the key. By your own admission, the normal methods won't work. I need to be closer to the problem."

He'll find out the truth.

She smothered the thought as soon as it skimmed through her mind. "Playing coy isn't like you. There's a solution you've already thought of. Stop hedging and spit it out."

He sat back. "The only way they'll let me through the door is if they think we're dating."

Dating Frank Evans? He was out of his goddamn mind. If Journey had a type—and she did—it was dashing metrosexual guys who didn't have a chance in hell of overwhelming her. Safe guys, even if it didn't look that way to the press or her brothers.

There was nothing safe about Frank.

He was too big, too controlled, too dangerous. She didn't think for a second that he'd hurt *her*—at least not physically—but he'd already proven time and time again that she wouldn't come out on top of their interactions. Putting them in any kind of intimate setting, even if it wasn't real, was the worst idea she'd ever heard.

It was pretty intimate when he had his mouth all over you.

She focused on the stained-glass window to avoid looking at him. She couldn't *think* with him so close, but that was Journey's problem—not Frank's. There had to be a way around this...but as the minutes ticked by, she couldn't come up with a single one that would fit the situation's needs as well as his solution. With a sigh, she nodded. "You want to fake date me to get close to the information you need to do the job." It didn't sound that unreasonable when he put it that way. "That's simple enough."

Frank raised a single eyebrow. "Duchess, you were coming on my mouth roughly twelve hours ago. It's complicated, whether you want to admit it or not."

She fought against the heat that threatened to spread up her chest. "Like I said before—that was just sex." It *hadn't* been sex, though. He'd tongued her through her damn panties, never giving her that much-needed contact. No matter how good the orgasm was—and it was beyond amazing—she'd wanted more. Admitting as much handed him even more power than he already had in this little exchange. She wouldn't do it.

"Just sex." No inflection in his words. He might as well have been talking about the weather.

She should get up and walk out. Journey had more than enough to deal with without letting Frank close enough to truly fuck up her life. It wouldn't be personal—she was sure of that—but it wouldn't take much for him to use this proximity to strike to the very heart of Kingdom Corp. Hell, she'd already all but paved the way for him.

She had no other options.

Elliott knew how she and Anderson operated—and how to use that to his advantage. No matter how strong she tried to be, he knew her buttons too well. She would break and bring Anderson down with her. Without Anderson, Bellamy and Eliza would topple like dominoes. Kingdom Corp would go down.

And it would be Journey's fault.

In the end, she didn't have a damn choice and they both knew it.

Journey held up a single finger. "I'll agree—on one condition."

"Duchess, this isn't a negotiation."

"It is now." She pointed at him. "I agree to your terms, as long as you promise not to use any information you gather against my siblings or my company."

The interest in his dark eyes sharpened, as if she'd just revealed more than she'd wanted to. Maybe she had. It didn't matter as long as he agreed. Frank considered her for a long moment. "This won't work if you're so busy protecting yourself that you're holding back information that will impede my ability to do this job."

She almost laughed out loud at the thought. "If I had the smoking gun linked to my father, I would have done it myself." No one cared about poor little rich kids whose daddy beat them. They didn't care about the years of terror he'd inflicted on his children. Even if they *did* and were willing to listen, there was no proof. It was his word against theirs, and she already knew which way the media would swing if it came to that. Beloved scoundrel of the Bancroft family versus the children of uppity bitch Lydia King? It was no contest in the public eye.

"Then we're agreed." Frank held out a hand.

She shook because she had no other choice. Certainly not because she wanted to feel his skin against hers again. His calluses scraped lightly against her palm, making her wonder what a man like Frank did to gain calluses. He wore a three-piece suit in the middle of a weekday as naturally as most men wore faded jeans, and as best she could tell, he worked something like eighty-hour weeks.

None of my business.

Journey realized she still held his hand, and snatched hers back. She reached for her purse. "If that's all—"

"It's not."

She froze. "I'm sorry?"

"Mira is about to bring us food, and then we're going to have a conversation." His lips twitched. If he were any other man, she'd assume she amused him. "Unless there's a reason you're leaving in such a hurry."

That wasn't a question. You don't have to answer it.

She ignored the not-so-helpful inner voice. "I can't be gone long, Frank. I realize being one of the richest men in Houston means you have an army of staff at your beck and call, but my company is in danger of going under— partly because of actions *you* took against my mother. Some of us don't have the luxury of being able to take a long lunch." Poking at him wouldn't do either of them a bit of good. She needed him, and he'd already agreed to help. Dicking around only threatened to ruin what little ability they had to fake a relationship long enough for him to do what was required.

His lips curved into a full smile, and she even caught a flash of white teeth. "Is that all? Funny, Duchess, but I was under the impression you were running because I make you nervous."

* * *

Temper sparked in Journey's eyes, a temper that Frank deliberately provoked as their conversation went on. He didn't know how to deal with her fear. *Just as well. It's not my business.* Journey *isn't my business.*

Mira strode up with a tray of their food and stopped short next to the table. "What did you do, Frank?"

He raised his eyebrows. "Why are you so sure I'm to blame?"

"Because I know you." She set the plates in front of them with the ease of long practice, and her gently chiding tone took some of the sting from her words. Mira smiled at Journey. "Don't let Frank scare you. He's all bark and no bite for someone like you."

The fact that she felt the need to put a qualifier on that statement meant she knew a lot more about him than he'd realized. *Of course she does. She's a mother.* Frank made an effort to keep himself toned down for Mira and her family. He liked them, and he was all too aware of what she'd think about the times when his only guiding light for his actions boiled down to one truth—power was everything. Sometimes that meant using information to push people into choices they wouldn't have made on their own.

Choices that benefited him and his company.

Journey's smile wasn't a fraction of its normal wattage, though not from lack of trying. "You sound like you know him well."

"I do. I've known Frank since he was, what, twenty?" She glanced at him for confirmation but charged on before he could grant it. "He helped my husband and me stay above water, and to prosper in the meantime. Don't let the growling and poor attitude warn you off—he's a good man." And then she was gone, marching back toward the hostess stand to meet a pair of women who'd just come through the front door.

"A good man," Journey repeated, almost to herself. She frowned. "How much did you have to pay her to get her to say that?"

He bit back a chuckle. "Mira isn't the type of woman who can be paid off for anything, let alone false compliments." He watched the woman lead the other two to a table, chatting all the while. "I've known her a long time. She's a nice lady."

"Yeah, I guess she is." Journey shook her head and picked up her fork. She set it down just as quickly, looking a little green. "Nothing personal, but I'm not hungry."

He considered that statement, weighing it. Granted, he and Journey had only shared a handful of meals that were all business related, but she seemed to go after food the same way she went after everything in life. Reveling in it. Frank took a bite of his chicken, still watching her. From Frank's information, her father had been back in town for only a few days, which didn't explain the evidence of prolonged lack of self-care that he saw written all over her. "You've lost weight."

"Why does that sound like an accusation instead of a compliment?"

He ignored that. "You're not sleeping, and your shaking hands are either a result of too much coffee to compensate or sheer stress. How long has this been going on?"

She gripped her fork like she wanted to stab him with it, and then very carefully set it down and lined it up perfectly with the knife next to it. "I won't let it negatively affect things going forward."

"It's already affecting things." He moderated his tone, smothering his frustration and leaving his words cold and clipped. "How long?"

Journey sighed. "Since before my mother left for New York. There was a... verbal confrontation with my father on the phone while things were going down with Beckett. It's not important, other than it dredged up some things I'm still dealing with. As a result, sleep is in short supply." She met his gaze steadily. "Like I said, I won't let it affect things."

Frank shook his head. "You can't keep going on like this, Duchess. You'll snap before I have a chance to do my job."

She thinned her lips. "Another condition?"

"Just speaking the truth. As soon as we came to an agreement, you became an asset. I take care of my assets." *That's all. It has nothing to do with hating to watch her unravel in front of me.*

She poked at her food. "I'm not an asset. I'm a person—a partner. If I'd wanted a babysitter, I would have hired one."

They could go back and forth on this until the sun went down, wasting both their time. She'd resist solely out of spite even though she had to know he was right in this instance. So be it. He'd find a way around her, just like he did with every problem that arose. If he had to play dirty to protect his investment, he would.

It was all about the bottom line.

Sure it is.

Frank changed tactics. "I need information." At her questioning look, he clarified. "The sex might be fantastic, but if I don't know a damn thing about you, no one in your family is going to believe we've been dating long enough to make your introducing me to them believable."

She opened her mouth, seemed to reconsider, and shut it. "That seems . . . reasonable."

"I think you'll find that I can be more than reasonable." He sank enough heat into the sentence to set fire to the room, enjoying the way she flushed in response.

Journey took a sip of her iced tea. "What do you want to know?"

He could pick up most trivial information through a background check, so he skipped over into the more intimate details. "How long have we been dating?"

"The first meeting." She answered without hesitation, no evidence of guile on her face. "We went out for drinks afterward and one thing led to another. Since my mother wouldn't be a fan and you didn't want to potentially damage your reputation while we worked on that real estate deal, we kept it a secret."

He remembered exactly how she'd looked at that first meeting. Journey wore a pair of gray tailored slacks, a white blouse, and fuck-me-red heels. The combination of buttoned up and risqué had intrigued him. It *still* intrigued him. As often as he thought he had a read on her, he realized he didn't know the first thing about her. Frank wouldn't have to fake his attraction, because if she was anyone else, the first time they met *would* have played out exactly as she described. "Good."

She leaned back and crossed her arms over her chest. "Let's see—I cook when I'm stressed. I run and lift weights in my home gym. I like catchy pop songs, but I'm a big fan of jazz, especially when I want to relax. I like audiobooks. My favorite color is turquoise, though I prefer it in my jewelry to my clothing." Journey narrowed her eyes. "I think that's enough to start with."

He wanted to know more, but he knew better than to push her now. Frank needed her centered and focused, and while stoking her temper might help with that, pushing too far would only create distance between them that they couldn't afford. "I'll leave it up to you if you want to tell Samara the truth or not."

"Not." She sat back and reached for her purse again. "If I tell her I'm fake dating you, then I have to explain why, and I'm not prepared to do that. I'd appreciate it if you gave me the same courtesy with Beckett."

What are you hiding that you don't want your friend and cousin to know about?

This wasn't just about Kingdom Corp. If it was, bringing in Samara Mallick was one of the better plays Journey could make. Up until a few months ago, her friend had worked side by side with her on a formidable team that even Frank would have reconsidered going against. Even though Samara had made the jump to Beckett's company, she still felt a degree of loyalty to Kingdom Corp—more importantly, to Journey.

I'm missing an important piece of information.

She stood. "I'll call you later and we'll get the next move set up. In the meantime, I wasn't joking about having work." Journey took one step away from the table and paused. "And, Frank...I do appreciate this. I know I'm not being as graceful about everything as I should be, and I'm sorry for that." She made a face. "I can't promise it will get better, though."

"If there's a way to get Elliott out of both the company and Houston, I'll find it."

She gave a jerky nod. "Thanks."

Mira barely waited for the front door to close behind Journey to approach the table. "Be careful with that one, Frank." He raised his eyebrows and waited. She huffed. "Don't give me that look. You know as well as I do that once you get past that sharp exterior, she's easily bruised. I've seen girls like her before. You be careful or you'll harm her."

"It's just business."

Mira snorted. "Whatever you have to tell yourself." She made a shooing motion. "If you leave through the kitchen, there's a plate of cookies my oldest dropped by this morning. Grab a few."

He obeyed because he knew it would make her happy. Frank paused for a few seconds in the kitchen and let himself enjoy the changes the years had brought this place. The front hadn't been altered beyond a much-needed face-lift, but as the investments had paid off, they'd upgraded every appliance back here. Mira always had liked her gadgets. He grabbed two cookies from the plate nestled next to the fridge and ducked out the back door.

Journey needed time to come to terms with their agreement. He understood that. He had his own brand of research to do before he saw her again.

Frank needed a plan of attack.

Elliott Bancroft would never see him coming.

CHAPTER FIVE

Eliza King stepped out from the private jet and glared at the sun beating down on her. "I hate Texas." The heat, the humidity, the people. In the seven years since her first modeling contract, she'd been back only a handful of times—and only under duress.

Everything had changed now, though.

She maneuvered herself down the metal stairs with ease despite her sky-high heels and wished she'd thought to bring a hat. She had a photo shoot in two weeks, and showing up with a sunburn would only piss off both the photographer and her agent.

A man climbed out of the waiting car, and she stopped short for a breathless moment before she recognized her older brother. "Bellamy!" Eliza dropped her bag and threw herself into his arms. The rest of this godforsaken state could melt into the Gulf for all she cared, but not her favorite brother. "I missed you so much!"

He lifted her off her feet easily and chuckled. "How the hell are you shorter than when I saw you last?"

"Shut up. I'm perfectly proportioned." She smacked

his shoulder. "You never came to visit like you promised." Her birthday had come and gone six months ago and she'd invited him to travel to Rio with her. When he'd passed, citing work, Bellamy told her he'd come to New York that holiday season for a week. She should have known better than to expect him to follow through.

Should have known better than to take it personally when he didn't.

Kingdom Corp came first. It had *always* come first for everyone in the family—except Eliza.

"You can put me down now, B."

"Sorry." He even sounded it, his regret poisoning her burst of good mood. Bellamy set her on her feet and held onto her long enough to ensure she didn't fall. Then he grabbed her bags and hauled them to the trunk. "I thought you said you were only coming back for the week."

"I *am* only back for the week." She'd answered Anderson's summons because she had no choice. Family was family, no matter how little she wanted to do with the associated business. Her modeling paid for pretty much anything she wanted, but Eliza was hyperaware of each passing year. She had an expiration date stamped on her forehead, and the money would dry up the day it hit. If she didn't find a replacement income before then, she'd be forced to rely on King money to live.

Which meant coming back into the Kingdom Corp fold like her mother had always wanted.

She slid into the backseat and scooted over so her brother could join her. As soon as he closed the door, she turned to face him. "All right, spill. Anderson wouldn't have summoned me back here for anything less than an all-out emergency, but he was sparse on the details." She tried not to resent him for that, but she didn't try very hard. As the oldest in the family, Anderson had always been destined for the CEO position within the company when their mother finally stepped down. No one had expected it to happen so soon, though.

Bellamy sat back with a sigh and loosened his tie. If Eliza wasn't aware of how dire the situation was, her brother showing up in a *suit* was enough to have alarms blaring. B preferred to dress casual, and as the head of security for Kingdom Corp, the only people he normally had to deal with on a regular basis were either family or his team. He wouldn't throw on a suit unless he'd just come from a meeting with an outside component.

His obvious reluctance to speak had her straightening. "You might as well tell me now. I'm going to find out soon anyway."

"Elliott is back."

Elliott. Never *Father*. Certainly not *Dad* or *Daddy*.

Bile rose in her throat, but many years of learning to control her expression kept the reaction off her face. "He's been back before."

"Not like this. He's not crawling around, asking for money. He's trying to step into the void Lydia created when she left town." Bellamy met her gaze, his hazel eyes showing a concern that left her cold. "I thought Anderson would run him out of town, but for some reason he hasn't—and he's forbidden me to do it."

Anderson had always stood between his siblings and the rest of the world, even with the eight years between him as oldest and Eliza as youngest. Maybe *especially* because of that age gap. When Elliott moved out, Anderson was twelve and Eliza was only four. He'd taken on

a more adult role, rather than the protective older brother
the way Bellamy was.

Of course, he hadn't interacted that way with Journey.

She shook her head. *No use thinking about that bullshit now.* She was here because he'd called. If things
went well, she'd be on a plane jetting off to a new photo
shoot inside of a week. Worst case, it might stretch into
two. Anderson couldn't expect her to stay longer than
that, and she would say no even if he tried to keep her
in Houston.

She *wasn't* back.

She refused to be.

* * *

Journey rolled over and picked up her phone. Seven
missed calls—Anderson four times, Samara once, Frank
twice. She dropped her phone and buried her face in her
pillow. Getting out of bed felt like too much energy right
now. She'd stayed late in the office last night, working to
mediate between two sales teams who had clashed over
a mismanaged project. Technically, that wasn't Journey's
job, but yesterday her father reassigned *their* boss to a
different department, so yet more requirements had been
loaded onto her until a replacement was found.

If she didn't know better, she'd think he was doing
it on purpose.

I do know better, and he is *doing it on purpose.*

She growled into her pillow. It was Saturday. She
might work more Saturdays than she didn't, but she
wasn't technically *required* to. There should not be so
many damn phone calls waiting for her. They also weren't

going away, and *she* wasn't going to get any rest until she dealt with them. Phone calls meant important, but not an emergency. If it was an emergency, Anderson would have sent someone to her apartment—or come himself. Ditto with Samara.

Frank...

Well, she wasn't ready to deal with Frank yet.

Coward.

So what?

She dialed Anderson before she could think too hard about the fact that she'd agreed to be in a fake relationship in order to bring down her father... *I'm living in a soap opera. All I need is an evil twin showing up and I'm good to go.*

The line barely rang when Anderson answered. "Are you okay?"

Journey sat up. "Yes, I'm okay. Why wouldn't I be okay?"

His pause spoke volumes. *Because you're a basket case combined with a tub of gasoline just waiting for someone to strike a match to watch you go down in flames.* He cleared his throat. "You didn't answer. I was worried."

"There's this thing called sleep. You should try it sometime." Even if she *hadn't* slept much last night. Every time she drifted off, that fucking recurring nightmare slammed into her. Running, always running, weights on her heels, footsteps sounding in pursuit, an enemy closing in behind her. And lining the trail, every single person she knew, none of them stepping forward to help. She always woke up just as hands closed around her upper arms, a scream trapped on the inside of her lips.

But she couldn't tell Anderson that.

Journey put everything she had into sounding calm and in control. "We can't focus on the enemy if you're so concerned about me that you're letting it distract you."

"Fuck, Jo, you're my sister. Of course I'm concerned about you." Footsteps sounded like he was pacing, probably in his office. "We've barely had two seconds to talk since he showed up, but I don't like this. It's more than the whole bullshit about declaring people unfit. That's just a distraction while he does whatever he's actually here to do."

Ice cascaded down her spine. She drew her legs up, even though she knew making herself a smaller target never actually worked. "What's his real goal?"

"That's the question, isn't it?" He cursed. "I'm sorry, Jo. I'm not trying to scare you. I'm just worried he's going to go after you."

Her mouth went dry and shivers worked their way through her body. Memories rolled over her, one after another. The edge of a razor blade against her hip, Elliott's casual voice in her ear warning her to stop shaking. The scream trapped in her throat as she hid with Eliza and Bellamy in the attic and listened to Anderson draw their father away. The hot curling iron.

Say something. You have to say something or he's going to ignore that childhood promise and then you're going to lose him.

Her breath hitched, but her voice came out halfway normal. "I can handle it."

"Jo—"

"I can handle it," she repeated, sounding like she actually meant it. "Anderson, you have to trust me on this."

He hesitated for so long, she found herself holding her

breath. Finally, he said, "I'm willing to let you play this out how you want, but the second I get proof that you—*any* of you—are in physical danger, it's over, Jo. I'm stepping in, and this time I *will* take care of the situation."

No way to misunderstand what *that* meant.

"I understand." She hesitated. "Anderson?"

"Yeah?"

"What if it really is that simple—that he just plans to take over and stay?"

Only the soft sound of her brother's breathing let her know he hadn't hung up. Finally, Anderson said, "I don't want to see you in the office today. You can work remotely if you're going to insist on working, but there's nothing here that requires your presence."

Journey closed her eyes. That wasn't an answer, which was an answer in itself. He didn't know what he'd do any more than she did. Despite everything they'd accomplished since those horrible years trapped in that house, they were still in danger of being outmaneuvered by their worst nightmare.

If she wouldn't let Anderson act as shield, she could at least remove her presence so he wouldn't be distracted worrying about her. "Okay. I'll see you bright and early Monday."

"Stay safe, Jo."

"You, too."

She hung up and stared at her bedroom door. She hadn't felt safe for months. She looked for the shadow in every light space, never truly letting her guard down.

Except here.

With a locked door between her and the rest of the world, she could settle in. At least in theory.

Journey sighed. Spending the day watching cheesy movies and wrapped in her fuzzy blankets sounded like a dream...but it was too close to truly hiding for her pride to handle. There were emails to answer, and she hadn't done a deep clean of her apartment in too long. Once those unsavory tasks had been conquered, she'd spend an hour or two cooking up a meal to reward herself.

Or maybe that's just a different kind of hiding.

Shut up.

She took a quick shower and called Samara after she got dressed. Since her friend didn't pick up, Journey sent a quick text: *Phone tag—you're it.* She couldn't deny the slightest bit of relief that she didn't have to deal with Samara yet, though. Her friend was one of the smartest women Journey knew, and it would take her all of two minutes to realize something was wrong and rush to her side. It made her smile to think about—she'd do the same for Samara—but Journey wasn't ready to throw open her closet door and let the skeletons out. Samara didn't see her as damaged goods now. Maybe she wouldn't even if she knew the truth.

But Journey couldn't guarantee it.

And because she couldn't, she wasn't willing to take a chance.

She stared at Frank's name on her phone. It had been two days since they spoke last. Maybe now was the time to call and figure out the first step in his plan.

Someone knocked on the door as she walked out of the bedroom. Journey froze, trapped between the desire to dive back under her covers and pretend not to be home and the need to *not* act like a goddamn victim another goddamn second.

She took the first step, and then another, making her way past the kitchen to the front door. *What the hell?* Journey paid through the nose for this place in large part because of its excellent security. No one should be able to get to her floor without being buzzed up first. Whoever was on the other side knocked again, more insistently this time.

It's a trap.

She edged closer to the door, as if whoever was on the other side could burst through at any moment despite the heavy-duty dead bolt. A quick check through the peephole had her heart slamming into her throat. *No.*

Her father braced a hand on the door and smiled. "I know you're in there, sweetheart."

There was no use pretending she wasn't. He wouldn't have shown up unless he was sure she'd be here. Journey rested her forehead on the door and closed her eyes. "Go away. I might have to deal with you in the office, but you're not welcome in my home." If she concentrated, she could almost pretend the thread of fear in her voice wasn't there.

"It's your choice." Elliott sounded perfectly reasonable. "It's come to my attention that Eliza is back in town. I'm due for a visit with my wayward youngest after all this time anyway."

Journey pressed her forehead harder against the door, the throbbing pain doing nothing to diminish her panic. She knew what happened next—what always happened next. No matter how calm or rational he seemed, Elliott would take his anger at Journey out on Eliza. Eliza, who had just arrived back in Houston and would be staying at a hotel. If he could get into Journey's building without raising any alarms, a hotel would be child's play.

Her sister would be hurt because Journey was too cowardly to stand her ground.

She took a shuddering breath and threw open the door. "What are you doing here?"

Her father walked into her apartment and shut the door behind him. "We haven't had a chance to reconnect. We're due for a talk."

A *talk*. She took several large steps back, edging toward the kitchen island. "You're here. Talk. Then leave."

"I'll leave—when I'm finished." He didn't move from his spot, his gaze sliding over her living room and kitchen, tainting everything in its wake. The fact that he was here at all contaminated her safe space.

She glanced over her shoulder, weighing the chance of making it to her bedroom and locking the door behind her. While the outer door to the main hallway was re-inforced, the interior doors weren't. *Easy enough to kick down if he's motivated.* No, she'd have to see this through one way or another. She tried to swallow past her fear. "What do you want, Elliott?"

"Elliott," he mimicked. His easy smile didn't reach his eyes as he tucked his hands into his pockets. "Is something wrong, sweetheart? You're acting rather combative considering all I've done is stand here."

He's baiting you.

She gritted her teeth. There might not be any witnesses, but any reaction would only encourage him.

Doesn't matter. React now or react later when he escalates. He always gets what he wants.

A sob caught in her chest, and she couldn't hold her ground any longer. Journey walked to the fridge, putting the kitchen island between them—and putting herself within reaching distance of the knife block on the counter. The knife wouldn't help. She'd watched enough true crime shows to know his superior reach and strength would only turn the weapon against her. It still made her feel safe. *A gun would be better.*

She took her time pouring herself a glass of orange juice. *Treat him like a hostile employee.* It wouldn't work for long, but it gave her the ability to clip out her words. "It's my day off and you're in my home, uninvited. Forgive me if my attitude is not up to par, but we don't have a relationship outside of work, and we will continue not having a relationship outside of work. If you have a concern within the confines of Kingdom Corp, you're welcome to email me and I'll take care of it as quickly as feasibly possible."

Elliott laughed, the sound oozing across the distance between them. "Fuck, you really are Lydia incarnate, aren't you?" He stalked closer and stopped just on the other side of the island as if gauging how quickly he could get around it. "You're just as much of a bitch as she ever was." His smile took on a sly edge. "But we already knew that, didn't we? If it was possible to cure you of that particular personality trait, my methods would have worked when you were a child."

All the air disappeared from the room. She grabbed the edge of the counter to stay on her feet, but it didn't stop her from swaying. "Fuck. You."

"Is that any way to talk to your beloved father?"

She couldn't move, couldn't breathe, couldn't do more than watch him round the corner of the island as he approached her. Journey tensed, a sound coming out of her mouth like a trapped animal. "Don't touch me."

He ran a single finger over her cheek, the soft touch taking what little strength was left in her legs. Elliott watched her sink to the ground, warmth bleeding into his blue eyes for the first time since he walked through her door. "You should know by now that you don't have a say." He crouched in front of her, too close, his sickly sweet breath choking her. "You're mine, sweetheart. You and your precious little sister and your brothers. You've always been mine, and you're always going to *be* mine. Don't think for a second that any of you can keep me from what I want." He smoothed his hand over her hair, a soft touch that heralded a closed fist or some kind of pain both more creative and horrifying.

Thud. Thud. Thud.

Someone was at the door.

Elliott jerked back, and she collapsed the rest of the way to the floor. He pushed smoothly to his feet and disappeared. She lay there, her cheek against the cool wood floor, and listened to him open the door. *He'll get rid of them and then...*

Then the nightmare would really begin.

A smooth voice saturated the dread pooling around her. "Everything good here? We had a complaint about someone trespassing."

Frank.

* * *

Frank stared at Elliott Bancroft for several long seconds and then looked over the man's shoulder and into Journey's apartment. *No sign of her.* It might not be enough to put him on high alert...if he hadn't seen footage of

Elliott bribing the guard at the security desk to get access to Journey's place. The man hadn't been inside her apartment for long, but Frank knew all too well how quickly things could get deadly. He'd gotten there in time. He refused to believe anything else.

But he might not have if he hadn't quietly purchased this building months ago when Beckett first started having issues with his wayward family.

If Frank hadn't tasked one of his men to keep an eye on the place a couple of days ago after he'd agreed to help Journey.

If, if, if.

He still couldn't see her. *Where the fuck are you, Duchess?*

He smoothed out his anger and banished his concern, leaving no trace of it in his face or voice. "Where is the owner of this apartment?"

The man gave him a charming smile. "She stepped into the shower. I'm not sure what this business about a trespasser is, but there's nothing wrong here."

Frank studied his face, finding no evidence of lying. Which just went to show exactly how dangerous Elliott Bancroft was. He glanced behind the man. The open floor plan didn't leave a lot of hiding places, and even if Journey was *that* willing to dodge Frank, she wouldn't be doing it while her old man stood there chatting him up. *Bedroom. Bathroom. That's it.* The shower wasn't on. Not surprising since Frank doubted Journey would just casually get into the shower while the enemy was in her apartment.

He met Elliott's gaze. The man hadn't recognized him, which was just as well. He was like all the other old rich assholes in Texas—he assumed Frank was the hired help based on the color of his skin. That used to irritate Frank to the point where he wanted to shove his identity—his power—in their faces.

These days, he used their racism against them. Frank let his shoulders drop half an inch. "Sir, I'm going to have to ask you to leave."

"This is my daughter's apartment." He smiled, as if that answered everything. To anyone who didn't know better, it might be enough. They would look at the charm and the familial connection and think nothing of a father dropping in on his daughter after a long absence.

Frank knew better.

Even if Journey hadn't asked for his help, he still knew better.

He dropped the apologetic tone and crossed his arms over his chest. Still polite, so very polite. "You see, sir, I know for a fact that she didn't buzz you up. As such, I'm going to have to ask you to leave. If she wants you here, she can always let you back in herself." *Over my dead body.* He had no right to the protective feeling that made him want to bash this man's face against the nearest wall to expel his rage. *I would feel that way if any other woman were in danger.* Journey being the injured party had nothing to do with the level of his anger.

Nothing at all.

Elliott seemed to weigh his odds of slamming the door in Frank's face and must have realized that Frank would haul his ass out of that apartment, Bancroft or no, father or no. "I can reschedule." He stepped around him and walked down the hallway as if going for a Sunday stroll.

Frank waited until the man entered the elevator to walk into the apartment and shut and lock the door behind him. "Journey?"

"Frank." Her voice was so soft, he wouldn't have heard it if the place wasn't dead silent.

He strode around the kitchen island and dropped to his knees next to her prone body. "Where are you hurt?" There wasn't any obvious damage, but her sweatshirt and leggings covered the majority of her body. A well-placed punch given by Elliott could do more than break bones. There could be internal bleeding or worse. He reached for her and hesitated. "Talk to me, Duchess."

"I'm okay." She pushed to a sitting position and leaned back against the cabinets, her eyes closed. "He didn't hurt me."

Her choppy breathing and the sheer lack of color in her face gave lie to her words. "You and I have a different definition of hurt." Even if Elliott didn't get a chance to do physical damage, there *had* been damage done. Her trying to downplay it only pissed Frank off.

Not about you.

Since she showed no signs of wanting to move, he slid back to brace against the cabinets opposite her, ready to jump forward if it looked like she'd tip. "You want to talk about it?"

"No." Journey pressed her lips together, eyes still closed. "Could you..." A shuddering breath. "Could you, like, just talk to me about nothing important? I just need a minute."

A minute to remember she was safe and that the danger had passed—at least for now. Frank stretched his legs out, careful not to touch her. Questions would only put her on the spot, and talking about any plans moving forward would add more tension, so he shifted to a relatively safe topic. "I've been friends with Beck since we were kids. I realize you're predisposed not to like him, but he's one of the best men I know. A little too willing to throw himself on his sword for the people he cares about, but no one is perfect. He's been acting a damn fool since he and Samara got together. It irritates the fuck out of him that she won't sell her condo and move into his, but I think he secretly enjoys the push and pull when they bicker about it." He paused, relieved to see some color working its way back into her face. "The asshole took me ring shopping with him last week."

That got a response.

Her eyes flew open. "He did *not*. It's only been a couple months since they got together. How the hell is he already thinking about proposing?"

He shrugged, enjoying her disbelief. She'd forgotten about whatever just went down with her old man, at least for a few seconds. "I asked him the same thing. He told me that when you know, you just know. Which is some bullshit, but they're happy, so who am I to judge?"

"A good friend, that's who." She pushed her hair back and crossed her legs, life bleeding back into her body. "If he proposes, she's going to say yes, and then we're going to have to talk them into a long engagement."

"I'll do my part." He studied her. She wasn't okay—not by a long shot—but she wasn't in danger of passing out on him anymore. Which wasn't to say she wasn't in *danger* anymore. He'd already fired the asshole at the security desk and replaced the man with someone Frank trusted, at least for the time being, but that didn't do anything to combat the fear he'd felt when he realized Elliott had infiltrated the building. If *he* felt that, he couldn't begin to imagine what Journey had experienced. "Do you want me to stay?"

Presumptuous? Fuck yeah. But he didn't want her to be alone, and she'd already proven that she wasn't willing to turn to her family for fear of dragging them down with her.

"No." She gave him a shaking smile. "I know this sounds dramatic, but I can't stay here. He...contaminated it." She pulled her legs to her chest and rested her chin on her knees. "It feels a little like running, but since Anderson banished me from the office this weekend, I might just get out of town for the night. Somewhere..."

Out of his reach.

That was the problem, though. Distance wasn't enough to put her fear to bed, and she'd spend yet another sleepless night listening for a footstep outside her door, sure that her father had tracked her down. Frank held out his hand, letting instinct drive him. "I have another option."

She blinked. "What option?"

Half a dozen possibilities arose, but none of them came out of his mouth when he spoke. "Come home with me."

CHAPTER SIX

Journey should have said no. She should have dredged up a smile and a confident tone and told Frank that she was just fine and could manage on her own.

She didn't say no.

Even if she left town, putting distance between herself and her father had never solved her problems. She'd spend the next thirty-six hours switching between berating herself for not being strong enough and staring at her hotel door, analyzing every sound in the hallway to determine if it was a threat.

It made her tired just thinking about it.

Going home with Frank wouldn't solve anything, but even though there was nothing *safe* about him, she knew that he'd never let Elliott through the door.

She sat there, trying to avoid being sick from the adrenaline letdown and fear turning her stomach toxic, and watched him move around her apartment. "What are you doing?"

"Put your head between your knees and take nice slow breaths."

She obeyed instinctively, and damn it, it helped.

Journey closed her eyes and inhaled deeply through her nose as she listened to Frank walk into her bedroom. *Oh well, let him snoop.* Several minutes later, he was back and urging her to her feet. "Time to go, Duchess." He gripped her elbow as if he wasn't sure she could make it on her own, and they headed down to the street.

"Just a minute." She fumbled for her phone and sent a quick text to Bellamy, asking him to keep a close eye on Eliza. Her father's threat might have been blustering, but she couldn't bank on it. She slipped her phone into her purse. "Okay, I'm ready."

Frank had parked his car a block down. The gray Audi R8 coupe was expensive and understated and probably had all sorts of extras under the hood. Kind of like the man himself.

He opened the door for her. "This is the right call."

"Whatever you say." Her voice came out dull and lifeless, but she didn't know how to fix that.

She didn't know how to fix *anything*.

Journey sat there, passive and silent, and watched the city scroll by. *Victim yet again. I had a chance to fight, and all I did was collapse in a ball and wait for him to hurt me. Pathetic. Worthless. Coward.*

"Whatever you're telling yourself, it's wrong."

Journey rolled her head to face him. Frank looked just as in control as he always seemed to—his big body effortlessly fitting into the driver's seat of his car. The only indication that his ease might be covering up something was the way he gripped the steering wheel as if propelling the vehicle through sheer will. She huddled deeper into her oversized sweater. "Have you added mind reading to your impressive set of skills?"

He shot her a look. "I don't have to be a mind reader. It's written all over your face. You're replaying what just happened and mentally whipping yourself for not doing more or reacting in a different way."

"I was within inches of the knife block." She hadn't meant to say it aloud, but once the words drifted into the air between them, she couldn't take them back. "I know half a dozen methods of self-defense, even if I don't keep up on practicing them like I should. I can shoot pretty decently. None of it mattered."

A muscle in his jaw jumped, but his voice was just as even as ever. "He showed up at your place—where you feel safe—unannounced and at an hour when you weren't expecting anyone." He flicked the blinker and changed lanes, taking them out of town and down toward the coast. "I'll bet he barely waited two minutes before he danced on every trigger you have."

Her stomach lurched, and she pulled her knees to her chest, trying to battle down the nausea. "How do you know that?"

"I've known men like him. He's a predator and a bully, and he wouldn't attempt to corner you when there was a chance someone else might step in."

If Frank hadn't shown up when he did...She reached over blindly, and he didn't hesitate to take her hand. He squeezed it hard, as if he knew she needed exactly that to ground her. *He already sees too much, and you just keep letting him see more.* It wasn't as if she had a choice.

No. Damn it, *no*.

She *had* a choice, and she'd chosen *him* to be the one to help her out of this mess. Journey stared at their linked fingers, his dark skin against her pale. "Why were you at my place today, Frank?"

"Because you're dodging my damn calls." He snorted. "For someone who said you needed my help, you have a funny way of showing it."

"I was busy."

"I don't doubt it. But we both know that was only part of it."

Since he was right, she ignored that. Journey told herself to take her hand back, but she couldn't quite translate the thought into action. "I don't know how my father got up to my floor." Her building was supposed to be one of the most secure in the city, and even that hadn't deterred Elliott.

Frank's hand twitched in hers. "He bribed one of the security guards."

That got her attention. She straightened her legs and twisted to face him. "How in the hell would you know that?" Journey took her hand back, something like anger flaring to life. It warmed her in a way nothing else seemed to these days.

Nothing but Frank.

She pushed that thought away and focused on him. "You hacked the security feed in my building." When he didn't respond, her jaw dropped. "Tell me you didn't."

"I didn't hack the security feed in your building."

Oh, *now* he found his words. She poked him in the shoulder. "That's not what I meant and you know it. Tell me you didn't buy my freaking building."

"It's not a recent acquisition, if that's what you're wondering."

Journey sat back. "You have some brass balls, don't you? How in the hell did you manage it? Bellamy tried when I moved in, but the owner wasn't interested in selling. *When* did you manage it?" She hadn't lived there all that long—a little over a year—and she would have known if Frank freaking Evans owned the building when she moved in.

His hands flexed on the steering wheel. "Several months ago. The owner just needed the right incentive to agree to the deal."

She just bet he did. She opened her mouth to tell him he was out of line but…Damn it, he *was* out of line. It shouldn't matter that he'd saved her before things got truly bad today, or that she understood his wanting to keep tabs on any King living in Houston. "It was no coincidence that you showed up when you did. You're having me watched."

"Protected," he snapped. "I'm hardly spying on you, and I only had one of my men keep track of your place *after* you asked for my help. You're welcome, by the way."

She crossed her arms over her chest. "You should have asked me."

"You weren't returning my calls."

Not much she could say to that. She glanced out the window and frowned. "Where are we going? I thought you lived in the city."

"I do. Most of the time." He took an exit. "I have a place close to the office where the commute passes for reasonable and where I can work after hours during the week or take meetings."

"You aren't going to take me out here to kill me and toss my body into the marshes, are you?"

He raised his eyebrows. "You have an overactive imagination."

"Oh, please. Give me a little credit. You might have done your research on me and Kingdom Corp, but I did the same for you." There wasn't as much information as she would have liked. She knew Frank grew up relatively well to do until his father was arrested for—and later convicted of—murder. The victim's family had sued and taken the Evanses for every penny they owned. There wasn't much record of Frank between the age of fifteen and nineteen, other than his mother dying, but he'd come into some money and apparently had an eye for investment. Within a year he'd turned a decent amount into something more. The rest, as they said, was history.

At least that was the official story.

The unofficial story was little more than rumors—and the reason she'd approached him in the first place. Frank Evans, who always seemed to know where to jump before the rest of the world saw the way the wind was blowing. Frank Evans, who was untouchable because key people owed him favors. Frank Evans, the dealer of information as well as property.

When he didn't immediately respond, she straightened. "Frank?"

"I'm taking you home, Duchess." He didn't look at her, but there was tension in his shoulders that hadn't been there before. "And then we're going to have a conversation."

Too much in that statement to fully unpack. "Why?"

He cursed. "Because you're scared shitless and you're not going to be thinking straight until you feel safe again. No one knows where I live—not even Beck. Sure as fuck not your old man. You can get your feet under you again, and we'll hit the ground running Monday."

"*Monday?*" She jerked her hand out of his grasp. "I can't stay there until Monday. That's two days from now." Two *nights*. Journey had every intention of keeping her hands off Frank, but even as shaken up as she was right now, she didn't like her odds of being under his roof for thirty-six hours without doing something unforgivably stupid. Especially if he really followed through on his promise to make her feel safe again. *Should have insisted on my original plan of leaving town alone.*

Frank took another turn, driving them deeper into the trees that seemed to have sprung up out of nowhere. "I'll get you back with plenty of time to make it to the office before anyone else. I have this fascinating technology called Wi-Fi, so if you need to work remotely, you're able to. Don't turn down a safe space just because I'm the one giving it to you."

He sounded so damn logical when he put it like that.

Likely because he *was* being logical and he *did* have a point.

Frank saved her, whether she wanted to admit it or not. He'd agreed to help her, even though he wasn't getting nearly as much out of the deal as she was, favor to Kingdom Corp or no. He wasn't the enemy, and treating him like one was a shitty thing to do.

She sat back. "I'm sorry."

"You don't have to apologize to me. You're shaken up and I'm here, so you're striking out." His lips twitched. "I can handle it, Duchess. Do your worst."

He couldn't handle her at her worst. She wasn't sure anyone could. That said, she appreciated the sentiment, the careful reassurance that he'd layered on over and over again. *You're safe.*

A shudder worked its way through her body, leaving her achy and cold and feeling like she'd just been dragged behind a car for half a dozen miles. "You have a shower in this place of yours?"

This time, Frank actually *did* smile. "I have five. You can take your pick."

He drove around a corner to reveal the house. No, *house* was too tame a word for the building they approached. Journey took in the overgrown-looking trees—the overgrown trees that were carefully trimmed back to prevent them from encroaching on the driveway or the house itself. The giant pillars in the front of it gave the building an almost plantation-like feel, right down to the faded paint, but the windows were clean, and she'd bet the place would pass any building inspection. "Dramatic."

"It keeps the door-to-door salesmen away."

And no one would ever look at this house and assume Frank Evans, real estate mogul, lived here.

Journey relaxed against the seat. "I like it." Better to focus on the house. Frank chose to bring her to it despite the fact that he apparently never brought anyone here. Easier by far than to deal with the shit show she'd just left.

It could have been so much worse.

Knowing that didn't make her utter failure to act any easier to bear. When it came down to the wire, she'd crumbled instead of fought.

Worst of all, she couldn't be sure she wouldn't react the exact same way if it happened again.

* * *

Frank ushered Journey into his house, keeping a close eye on her all the while. She seemed steadier on her feet since they'd started talking, but no one recovered from an attack that fast. And it had been an attack. Even without bruises to show for it, every bit of evidence pointed to Elliott having harmed her. Frank clenched his fists, doing his damnedest to smother the rage churning in his gut.

He hitched her overnight bag higher on his shoulder. "This way."

This place wasn't anywhere near as large as the King family home that Beck had inherited upon his old man's death, but it had five bedrooms on the second floor—two master suites—and half a dozen other rooms on the main floor. At the bottom of the stairs, Frank motioned for her to precede him.

Journey shook her head. "You never cease to surprise me." She pointed at the shining hardwood floors and then at the paintings hanging on the wall up the stairs. "The outside looks like some kind of Southern Gothic mansion that might fall down around your ears and is most definitely haunted." She turned that finger in his direction. "Inside, it's like a damn work of art."

"It's my home." The place he came to unwind. Where he didn't have to be on guard every second of every day. His sanctuary.

She turned in a slow circle, eyes narrowed. "Tell me the truth—you personally remodeled this place, didn't you?"

Guilt flared, and he cursed himself for the irrational response. "It was my first real estate purchase." At least he'd known enough at nineteen to realize he was too fucked in the head after his mother's death to be trusted to make good financial decisions. He'd thrown the majority of the money her life insurance had paid out into a year-long short-term investment fund, leaving just enough to buy this old house and a cushion to do what was required to make it livable.

It took him a year of nonstop work to get it where it was today, and he'd sloughed off the old Frank Evans in the process. Leaving that weak-ass kid behind was the best thing he'd ever done, and this house stood as a reminder that he'd never go back.

So many things encompassed in these four walls.

Journey shook her head. "Is there anything you can't do? Because you're giving me an inferiority complex."

"Sure." Frank shrugged. "I'm terrible at Monopoly."

She narrowed her eyes. "Did you just... You just made a joke."

Despite his humor, her hand still shook as she tucked a strand of hair behind her ear. Frank fought not to reach for her. She wouldn't accept any comfort he tried to offer, and he didn't know shit about offering it in the first place. "I'm setting you up in the room next to mine."

"Presumptuous."

He snorted. "It's a big house, Duchess. I don't want to have to stalk the halls hollering for you." He wanted to be close in case she needed him. *How many times do you have to think it for it to sink in? Journey King is not one of your strays. Her allegiance has never been and never will be to you.*

His suite was situated in the corner of the house farthest from the front door. It took everything he had not to offer to let her stay with him in the truest sense of the word. Her decision-making skills were no less compromised now than they'd been the other night while she was drinking. Frank was a bastard and a half, but he had to draw the line somewhere.

When Journey King came to his bed, it would be because she had no doubts about being there.

When, not if.

Fuck.

"Here you are." He walked into her room, dropped her bag on the floor by the bed, and turned so that he could see her reaction. The fact that he shouldn't care about her reaction held no weight. He did. Simple as that.

Her eyes went wide. "Damn, Frank. You should give your decorator a bonus." Journey froze and pinned him with a look. "There is no decorator, is there? You picked this—all of it. Every single thing in this house."

Even thrown off her stride, she was far too observant for his peace of mind. He looked around the room, trying to see it from her point of view. There was nothing overtly feminine about the large dark wood bed frame or the soothing gray tones he'd chosen for this space, and he'd purposefully kept it without any personal touches that would make a guest feel uncomfortable.

Not that he had had any guests until now.

He cleared his throat. "What makes you say that?"

"One, you're a control freak, and I just don't see you letting some designer into your place if you're as anal about guests as you seem to be. Two, you keep watching me for a reaction like you have a vested interest in what I think of the house. And three, I'm just magic like that." Her grin was much closer to normal. "The grays and white feel really soothing. It was a good call."

"Thanks…" He didn't know how to deal with the warmth in his chest that her words brought, so he moved to the bathroom door and nudged it open. "I'm assuming this shower will suffice."

She ducked past him, careful not to brush her body against his. "Holy shit, Frank." Journey stepped into the tiled-in shower and grinned. "You could have an orgy in here. Two orgies."

"Two orgies in the same room is a single orgy." He fought to keep his expression even. "Besides, I prefer my sex with a one-to-one ratio."

Journey ran her hand over the oversized clear tile blocks. "Don't we all? Seriously, though, this is amazing. You did this yourself?"

It was tempting to let her drive the conversation toward relatively safer topics, especially with her curiosity about his house waylaying her fear. But giving her that luxury was dangerous. Their arrangement was temporary and, goddamn it, he'd be an idiot to forget that. "We need to talk about what happened," he said bluntly.

Her smile fell away as if it'd never existed, leaving the drawn and exhausted woman in its wake. "Can I at least have that shower before you start your interrogation?"

He bristled at her hostility and welcomed it at the same time. It was better than the softer emotions that threatened at the sight of this woman in his home. He took a deep breath and squared his shoulders. "Cut the bullshit. *You* asked for *my* help. And I need information to be effective. Plus, we need to hammer out the last few details of the plan before Monday. We don't have time to pussyfoot around the issue."

"Fine." She crossed her arms over her chest and glared at a spot over his shoulder. "Give me ten minutes and I'll be downstairs."

"Take thirty. I have some calls to make." And she needed more than ten minutes to find her feet.

Sap.

Fuck off.

Frank stalked out of the room and downstairs, pointedly ignoring the sound of the shower being turned on. If he thought about it too hard, he'd picture Journey stripping out of her leggings and sweatshirt, picture the curve of her breasts and the way her hips drew his gaze to whatever tease of underwear she'd be wearing.

If he concentrated, he could still taste her on his tongue.

She'd welcome him if he walked back into that room, if only for the distraction he offered. Even after a single encounter, Frank knew what she liked. What she needed. He could give it to her now, could fuck her back to solid ground. All he had to do was walk back up the stairs, turn the knob, cross the bedroom floor.

"Shit." He scrubbed a hand over his head. He fought himself back from the edge, inch by inch. Touching Journey now was even more unforgivable than doing it when she was several shots in. If—when—she was in his bed, she'd be there because she wanted to be. Because she wanted him—not because she was running from something.

He stormed into his office and shut the door. It still wasn't enough distance between them, so Frank did the one thing guaranteed to get his goddamn head on straight.

He called Beckett King.

Thank fuck his friend answered almost immediately. "Hey, Frank."

"I need a favor."

Instantly, Beck's tone changed. "Sure. What can I do for you?"

He paced to his desk and then to the window, mulling over all the things he couldn't say without betraying some portion of Journey's dilemma. She hadn't sworn him to silence, but she very specifically hadn't gone to anyone else in her family with her problem—including her cousin. "Is Samara around?"

Beck didn't answer for a long moment. *Probably wondering why I didn't call Samara directly.* "She's in the office."

"You mind putting her on the line?"

Another pause, shorter this time. "Give me a few." Rustling came across the line as if Beck had stood and was walking out of his office and down the hall. Beck cleared his throat. "Are you in trouble?"

"Nothing I can't handle." It wasn't Elliott Bancroft that worried Frank. No matter how dangerous Elliott was, he was just a single man. The Bancroft family, on the other hand, added a multitude of complications. Frank didn't make a habit of disappearing people. It was messy business, and he knew all too well how the law would work against a black man, no matter how wealthy, if there was *any* hint of illegal acts. Often even if there *weren't* hints. What happened today had him reconsidering that policy.

Journey wasn't just a woman worried about losing her job because of her father.

No, she was in danger.

The problem was, Frank didn't know *what* kind of danger. He had no parameters for what to expect, and he could no longer trust himself to act rationally where

Journey King was concerned. He'd more than proven that today alone.

"What can I help you with, Frank?" Samara Mallick's voice on the phone was slightly tinny, indicating she was on speaker. Good. It meant he could convey his information to both of them at the same time.

"If I were to tell you Journey's father is back in town..."

All the warmth in Samara's voice disappeared. "Elliott Bancroft is scum, and nothing good can come of him being in Houston."

He already knew that, but her response confirmed what he'd suspected—whatever abuse Journey had suffered, Samara didn't know about it. It hamstrung him. Saying anything more put him at risk of alienating Journey, and if he pissed her off too much, she'd end their deal and try to muddle through things on her own. He had no doubt that she'd figure something out eventually, but she'd suffer harm in the process.

Harm he could prevent.

"She's with me this weekend, but you might want to give her a call on Monday." He hung up in the middle of Samara's sharp question and tossed his phone onto his desk. Maybe Samara could get something out of Journey now, but he wouldn't bet on it. Still, it would be good for her to have contact with her friend. He could see the walls going up around her as she tried to isolate herself to deal with this mess. Samara was busy enough with her own shit that she might not have noticed if someone didn't bring her attention to it—at least not right away. Frank merely corrected that.

And maybe pigs will fly.

CHAPTER SEVEN

Journey turned the shower as hot as it would go and stepped beneath the spray. She closed her eyes and let the scalding water beat against her back, pounding away the last of her shakes. *For now.* She was in over her head. No reason for that realization to be such a damn surprise, but Journey had fabricated a level of strength over the years that was just that—fabrication. Worse, she'd believed the fiction she'd spun around herself. Both the bad and the good.

Party girl. Spurned Duchess. Lydia King's protégé. Brazen bitch who didn't care what anyone thought of her. COO of Kingdom Corp. Independent woman.

Her father had been back in town for less than a week and it all crumbled around her in pieces. How strong was she when a single touch from him sent her to her knees instead of for a weapon to defend herself? How independent was she really if she needed someone to stand between her and her enemy?

First, Anderson had done what he could to protect her. And though their mother had never been loving or nurturing, Lydia hadn't hesitated the second she realized her children were in danger.

Journey didn't know how to fight her father when she couldn't be in the same room as him without curling into a ball and waiting for the inevitable attack. *I don't have to fight alone. Asking for help is not weak.*

She shoved the thought away and slicked back her hair. As tempting as it was to hide in the shower for the next hour or two, Frank wanted to talk about their plans, and the first step to kicking her father the hell out of Houston was getting dressed and having that conversation.

She had less than thirty-six hours to shore up her defenses so she was able to walk into Kingdom Corp on Monday as some semblance of the confident woman she'd shown herself to be over most of her adult life. It shouldn't seem like a Herculean task but...

She didn't know if she could pull it off.

One step at a time. Stop borrowing trouble.

Journey shut off the shower and used one of the big gray towels to dry off. It was fluffy and luxuriously soft, and she frowned at it as she hung it back up. Maybe it was nuts to expect Frank to have utilitarian towels and sheets and...

Warmth spread through her body at the thought of the sheets Frank had on his bed, warmth that chased away the tendrils of weakness still clinging to her beneath her skin. She already knew how good it felt to have his hands on her, his big body such a comfort. *God, would you listen to yourself? Frank doesn't* comfort. *He's a deceptively deep river that carves his way through any obstacle in his path. He* is *dangerous. You can't afford to forget that.*

Journey walked to the bag Frank had tossed at the end

of the bed and rifled through it. She wasn't sure what to expect since Frank was the one who'd packed for her, but there was a totally reasonable number of leggings, shirts, and underwear. Her fingers brushed her thick wool socks, and something inside her relaxed. Bundling up made her feel safe and comforted, which was part of the reason she kept her apartment temperature just above frigid. Frank's place wasn't anywhere near as cold, but she still pulled on the socks after she got dressed.

She stopped, her hand on the doorknob. Leggings and an oversized sweatshirt and giant wool socks did nothing to support the impression that she'd always fought to present to the world. To present to Frank. If she went out there now...

What's the alternative? Hiding in this room for the rest of your life?

Besides, that ship had already sailed when Frank found her in a huddled mess on her kitchen floor. There was no going back now.

She paused to pull her hair into a ponytail, squared her shoulders, and marched out of the bedroom. Journey considered snooping, but the last thing she needed was to piss off Frank, the one person capable of helping her out of her current predicament.

Besides, it's not like I'm going to sleep tonight. I'll wander after he's in bed.

And less likely to catch her.

She headed downstairs and followed the faint strains of some classical melody she couldn't quite place. It led her down a hallway with an arched ceiling and into what could only be Frank's office. She stopped inside the doorway and took in the space.

Large windows overlooked the trees surrounding the house, their branches allowing filtered sunlight through to paint the hardwood floor with intricate designs. The walls were a pale gray that, combined with the high ceilings, made the space seem even larger than it already was. Frank sat behind a pale wood desk that might have been feminine if not for the heavy lines of the piece. A matching cabinet housed a docking system his phone was currently hooked up to and a small potted plant.

He glanced up, his dark gaze as clinical as that of a doctor checking on a patient. "You look better."

It wasn't a question, and she had no way to address it without flat-out lying—she wasn't okay by a long shot—so she crossed to peer at his phone. *Violin Concerto in D Major.* "I didn't take you for a Tchaikovsky fan."

"It helps me focus." He closed his laptop and leaned back, giving her his full attention. The weight of Frank's gaze had her fighting not to fidget. She could feel it like a physical thing, tracing over her face and her shoulders, down her breasts and stomach, to her feet. And then back up again. It would have been easier to bear if it was sexual in nature, but he had the air of someone checking for wounds, rather than a man interested in ripping her clothes off and having her right there on the floor.

It didn't matter if her current state didn't drive Frank into a tizzy of lust. That wasn't why she was there. Journey resquared her shoulders. "It's time we talk about that plan of yours."

"What did your father do to you?"

It took everything she had not to flinch at his soft question. Journey stared at a spot over his right shoulder. "That's none of your damn business."

"I'm working blind here, Duchess. It would be helpful to know that history so I can anticipate his next moves."

What he said made sense, but she still wasn't prepared to trot out the stuff her nightmares were made of for strategic purposes. "He was abusive. Physical. Not sexual. That's all you need to know."

She didn't actually hear Frank sigh, but the slightest movement of his shoulders gave the indication of it. "Noted." He leaned back against his desk, the only warning she got before his tone lost its softness. They were down to business. "Your father has a long history of dancing right up to the edge of the law, but on the first pass of checking, it doesn't seem like he's ever broken it." He paused, obviously waiting for her to jump in, but Journey just lifted her chin.

Finally, Frank continued, "That said, I had my man look at why Elliott Bancroft suddenly decided to take an interest in Kingdom Corp." He held up a hand. "I know what he said. But he's spent his entire life dodging responsibility. Even if he planned on draining the company dry, that's still a hell of a lot more work than just taking the stipend Lydia had been paying him for the last twenty years."

Mother paid him off.

Journey had suspected, of course. Her mother was terrifying in many ways, but for Elliott to leave and never come back... for them never to have ended up divorced...

Lydia had done what it took to keep him out of their lives—and away from Kingdom Corp. The only thing Elliott loved as much as power over people weaker than him was money. It still made Journey twitch to think about. "You think he's got a larger plan."

"I think that's the only thing that makes sense." Frank stood and pointed to the overstuffed couch situated diagonally to the desk. "Sit down before you fall down."

"I'm fine." But she moved to the couch anyway. Her knees *were* still feeling a little wonky, and as aggravating as it was to take orders from Frank Evans, it would be worse to collapse in the middle of his office out of sheer stubbornness.

Frank joined her on the couch, but he kept the middle cushion between them. It was just as well. She wasn't sure what she'd do if he touched her now. Her demons rode her too hard, and Journey didn't trust herself one way or another. She was just as liable to jump him as she was to lash out.

She cleared her throat. "It's one of the Bancrofts pulling his strings if he's not here for a smash-and-grab. If he's got any loyalty, it's to his family."

"They're your family, too."

"No." She shook her head. "I mean, technically, yes, Elliott Bancroft is my father and he's a Bancroft and therefore my siblings and I are, too. But Mother drew her line in the sand when she gave us the King name." Journey gave a faint smile. "You can't be loyal to two masters. I'm a King."

Those dark eyes showed nothing. "It's possible the Bancroft family wants Kingdom Corp, and they're utilizing Elliott to do it since they obviously don't believe you and your siblings will fall in line. It's equally possible that Elliott has gotten tired of dancing to the tune his family has set and wants his own kingdom to rule, so to speak. Either way, we'll figure it out."

It sounded so simple when he put it like that. Hope

unfurled cautious wings in her chest. "You really think we can win." He was the one who helped Beckett prevail against her mother, so there was no reason to think Frank couldn't pull this off, too. It just seemed too good to be true.

"I wouldn't have agreed to do this if I didn't."

She had the insane desire to throw her arms around him and hug him for all she was worth, but Journey managed to resist the impulse. "Thank you."

"Don't thank me, Duchess. I'm not doing this for charity."

The reminder killed her good mood, though she fought to keep that truth off her face. "Right. Of course." She and Frank weren't friends—fake relationship, business deal, and one outstanding orgasm aside—and she couldn't afford to forget that. The only reason he'd agreed to help her was because he got something out of it. In all the chaos and emotional spiraling she'd done in the last few days, she'd lost sight of that along the way.

If you forget again, the damage your father can do to you will be nothing against the pain Frank Evans can cause.

* * *

Frank woke to the sound of footsteps in the hallway outside his room. In a single move, he was up with the shotgun he had stashed in the holster beneath the bed. No time to throw on clothes—not with the footsteps heading toward Journey's guest room—so he threw open the door and rushed into the hallway.

"Holy shit!"

He had the presence of mind to point the damn gun at the floor, but Frank's thoughts flowed sluggishly as he tried to reconcile the fact that there was no intruder. It was Journey. She stood in the middle of his hallway, her hands up in a defensive gesture, wearing only *his* T-shirt and nothing else. He blinked, but the image didn't morph itself into something more realistic. "What are you doing out here?"

"I…" She slowly dropped her hands to wrap around her body. The move pressed the white fabric against her breasts and, even in the low light, their curve was clearly defined. Journey's gaze dropped to the level of his hips and then shot back to his face. "I couldn't sleep."

"Then read a fucking book, Duchess. I could have shot you."

She edged closer, stepping into the moonlight spilling from the window at the end of the hallway. He took in the purple smudges beneath her eyes and the way her hands shook despite her relatively calm voice. *She's terrified.* Frank cursed himself for not realizing it before. He set the gun on a side table and held up his hands. "That came out wrong. I wasn't going to shoot you. You were never in any danger." She had enough shit to worry about without thinking he'd mistakenly put a round of buckshot into her chest.

Journey glanced at where he'd set the gun and then took another step closer. "You ran out of your bedroom door like you were about to face down an enemy." A small smile pulled at the edges of her lips, but it didn't reach her eyes. "If I wasn't ninety percent sure that it wasn't directed at me, the look on your face would have made me pee my pants in fear."

"I heard someone walking in the direction of your room and reacted." He didn't even stop to consider lying. Frank shook his head. *Shouldn't have handed her that piece of information.*

Journey, true to form, seemed to chew on his statement. "Would you have shot if it was an intruder?"

"You already know the answer to that question." In other circumstances, he would have hesitated. Frank was more than capable of handling himself in a fight, and it was easier to get the police on his side if he didn't murder someone in his house. Handing potential ammunition to enemies wasn't how he rolled—shooting an intruder would do exactly that.

But he'd also never had anyone under this roof but himself.

He could chalk up his over-the-top reaction to another person's presence, but the truth lay in a different direction. Journey had every single protective urge he possessed standing at attention and clamoring for him to step between her and whatever danger arose.

To do whatever it took to ensure she walked away from this situation as unscathed as possible.

"Frank."

He blinked, cursing himself for musing while they were in the middle of a conversation. "Yeah?"

"You're naked."

He bit back a response that could only be termed an invitation. Whatever Journey King needed, it wasn't him adding to her stress by throwing sex into the mix. His losing control at the club was a onetime thing—it had to be. Frank didn't like how easily she'd slid past his tried-and-true defenses and incited an inferno inside him.

One only she seemed to be able to quench.

"Give me two minutes." He grabbed the shotgun from the side table and stalked into his room. After safely stashing it beneath the bed, he pulled on a pair of lounge pants and headed back into the hallway.

Journey stood exactly where he'd left her, a strange expression on her face. She pressed her lips together and shook her head. "I don't know if I can do this."

The darkness lent a certain intimacy to their low conversation that he didn't know what to do with. Frank shifted closer. Mindful of her violent reaction last time he'd tried to comfort her, he kept his damn hands to himself. But that didn't stop him from wanting to trace the shadows beneath her eyes with his thumbs, to do something to ease the pain she obviously carried deep inside her. "You're stronger than you give yourself credit for."

"That's a quaint little saying." She huffed out a laugh. "It doesn't mean shit. I'm a mess and we both know it." She lifted a shaking hand and tucked her hair behind her ear. "No matter how good your plan is, I can't guarantee I won't fold at the most inopportune moment. It seems to be what I'm good at."

"Stop." He grabbed her wrist and tugged her hand away from her face. "Self-pity doesn't look good on you, Duchess."

"Is it self-pity if it's the truth?" She spoke so softly, he wouldn't have heard it anywhere else but in the silence of the space between them.

He tugged her wrist. "Come here." It had to be lack of sleep, but he just wanted to hug her until all her broken pieces fused together again. Frank knew better than to think he could heal another person. He'd learned the hard way that trying only brought sorrow and pain.

She shook her head. "No, I can't." Journey jerked her hand out of his grasp, but didn't retreat. She stared up at him, her hazel eyes too large on her face. "I want to. Fuck, Frank, even if it's a lie, I want you to hold me right now. I just... I can't."

Frank weighed the sentence against his interactions up to this point. There was something there, something he was missing, but he couldn't put his finger on it. If he had a brain in his head, he'd go back to bed and leave her to her midnight wanderings. So what if she'd be wasted and worthless tomorrow after a night spent among her demons? It wasn't his fucking problem.

I made it my problem when I set the terms of this bargain. Whatever you have to tell yourself to sleep at night.

"What do you need from me?"

For the first time since he reappeared in the hallway, she dropped her gaze. "Nothing you're willing to give."

Frustration raked at him. "I wouldn't have offered if I wasn't willing." He could have followed it up with so many things, but he kept his damn mouth shut. Journey didn't need him preaching at her about learning to accept help. She *had* accepted help, but he was the one shoehorning his way into other parts of her life. It wasn't his job to take care of her if she wouldn't take care of herself, but he couldn't bring himself to give a fuck.

"What happened in your office..." She cursed. "You know what? Forget I said anything. I'm already pathetic enough without throwing a pity fuck into the mix."

Frank rocked back on his heels. "We already established that I don't pity fuck, Duchess."

"Like I said—forget I lost my mind enough to say anything at all." She drew herself up until he was almost fooled that she'd actually shrugged off the entirety of the day and this conversation. "I'm going to go to bed."

"Journey." He waited for her to turn to face him before continuing. She looked so ... small ... standing there with her arms wrapped around herself wearing only his shirt. Breakable. He didn't like it. He didn't like it at all. "Would it help? Or is it just another form of harm?" He might want her, but he refused to be the cane she beat herself with.

She turned to look out the window, her words falling as softly as snow between them. "In the office was the first time I felt like *me* in months. You grounded me, Frank. With your hands on me, there was no past or future, and your mouth on my skin silenced every single skeleton rattling in my closet—at least for the moment. I don't regret what we did at all, and I know it doesn't make sense but—"

He couldn't have resisted Journey if he'd tried, and he didn't bother to try. Frank clasped the back of her neck and turned her to face him. "Let's make one thing clear."

"Just one?" Her faint smile actually reached her eyes this time.

"For now." He massaged the tense muscles in her neck, making sure to keep his grip firm. "There's no going back if you choose this. It's all or nothing."

She stared at his mouth but made no move to touch him. "I don't like being penned in, Frank." Journey dragged her gaze up to meet his. "Even if I did, you don't know me well enough to demand all or nothing."

He could lay it out there, could tell her that he'd had his

eye on her since the first time they met several years ago. It had never gone further than that solely because she was a King and Frank had enough enemies without borrowing hers as well. And there had been Beckett to consider. Hooking up with a member of Beck's estranged family would be a slap in the face to their friendship, and no sex was worth damaging that relationship. Not to Frank.

Things changed.

He wasn't willing to take a leap based on a couple of days' worth of up-close and personal interactions, but the deeper Frank delved into the maze that was Journey, the more he wanted to get to the heart of her. It wasn't smart.

In fact, it was downright dangerous.

He tightened his grip on her neck, enjoying the way she gasped and arched her back, instinctively offering her breasts to him. "I know enough, Duchess. Choose. All or nothing."

Still, she hesitated. "I need it like it was before. Rough and right there in the moment." Her hazel eyes begged him not to ask why.

He had questions, no matter that her issues weren't his business. The questions could wait—would probably wait forever. The tension in Journey's body spoke of a woman anticipating a blow, expecting him to tell her that what she wanted was fucked and to demand to know what had happened to her to make *this* her version of comfort.

Frank didn't say a damn thing. It wasn't his place to judge. Her needs matched his. What more was there to say?

A whole hell of a lot.

He took a slow breath, drawing oxygen deep into

his lungs and releasing his anger on the exhale. This wasn't about him. This was about her, about giving her a safe space in the only way she'd accept from him. For now. He wanted one thing he had no business wanting—her trust.

"I know, Duchess," he repeated. *Trust me.* Words he couldn't say because they would only ensure she would end this here and now, and that was something Frank refused to have happen. He might have rather started things between them when the world wasn't about to fall on their heads, but he'd learned to roll with the punches and make the best of any situation.

She swayed, leaning hard against his hand. "I'm in, Frank. Don't make me regret it."

Regret was the one thing he wouldn't allow between them. Which was why Frank kissed her hard. He took her mouth, reacquainting himself with the taste of her even as she went soft against his chest. She tasted like heaven, and he would have given his left arm in that moment to be able to take this where they both wanted it to go.

But not tonight.

Not like this.

Frank scooped her into his arms and strode for the guest bedroom. He kept a stranglehold on his control even as Journey kissed his shoulder, his neck, his jaw. Only the knowledge that he'd lose her for good if he let this happen tonight had him lowering her to her feet and kissing her again.

And then he stepped back. "Good night, Duchess."

Journey blinked. "But you just said..." Shock bled into something akin to hurt. "I see."

"I don't think that you do." Frank clasped her chin in

an unyielding grip. "What happened today fucked with you, Journey. You're on the ropes and you don't know which way is up, and I'm not such a bastard that I'll jump into your bed while you can't give consent."

"I *did* give consent, asshole."

"Yeah, you did." He leaned down and captured her bottom lip between his teeth, biting just hard enough to taste her gasp. "And I fully intend to take you up on it...but not this weekend." He forced himself to release her and step back.

He walked to the small bookshelf on the other side of the room. Every bedroom in the house had a selection of books he'd curated. Frank grabbed one at random and settled into the high-backed chair next to the shelf. He flicked on the light. "Sleep. Relax. No one is going to touch you this weekend—not even me. You're safe here."

Journey stared. "What are you doing?"

He held up the book. "I'm no professional audiobook narrator, but I'm more than capable of reading aloud." He read the title and sighed. "*Pride and Prejudice* makes for a good bedtime story, I guess."

She blinked a few times and then shook her head. "You might as well sit on the bed." She made a face. "I promise not to endanger your virtue."

It was a bad idea, but he recognized the stubborn look on her face. This wouldn't be a battle he'd win if he wanted to stay in the room. He waited for her to climb under the covers, and then walked over and gingerly sat on top of the comforter. He opened the book, but Journey laughed softly. "I have a better idea." She twisted to grab her phone off the nightstand and pulled up an audiobook app. She hesitated, her finger hovering over the screen.

"You said no one is going to touch me this weekend. What happens after this weekend?"

Frank settled back against the pillows and gave a tight smile. "After this weekend, all bets are off."

She lay down and pulled the covers up to her chin, leaving only her arm out. "I don't know if I thanked you for riding to my rescue but...thank you. You're going above and beyond the call of duty."

He didn't want her gratitude. "Start your book and close your eyes, Duchess. I'm here."

"Frank..."

He reached out, pushed the button to start the book, and laced his fingers through hers. She went tense at the contact, but the stiffness melted out of her body as the soothing tones of a woman who started talking about a trio of witches in a small town in Oregon. Frank kept a hold of Journey's hand as her breathing evened out and, within ten minutes, she was asleep.

He should have disengaged his hand and left the room then. Sex was one thing, but comfort was something completely different. It could lead to far deadlier emotions, and he knew better than to fall into that trap, even for a woman as engaging as Journey King.

He didn't release her hand.

He didn't leave the room.

He closed his eyes and let the story sweep him away. It was only for a little while, after all.

CHAPTER EIGHT

Frank dropped off Journey outside her place before the sun was fully above the horizon on Monday morning. "If you need anything between now and tomorrow, call me."

She didn't quite meet his gaze, just like she hadn't since Saturday night. "Thanks, Frank. I'll see you later." She made it two steps from the car and turned on her heel, her hair fanning out around her with the abruptness of the move. She ducked back into the car and pressed a quick kiss to his lips. "Seriously. Thank you." And then she was gone, disappearing into the doors in record time.

Frank shook his head and threw the car into gear, heading for his office. He'd put a lot of plans into motion over the years, but there was no way to anticipate Journey King. The mix of bristling hurt and sweetness never failed to surprise him, though she didn't seem to realize that there was a molten strength beneath it all. It wasn't his job to educate her—some people went their entire lives without allowing themselves to be forged into something new.

Remember that. Not my fucking job.

The building was quieter than he expected for a Monday morning, even as early as it was. He walked into his second-in-command's office and knocked on the doorjamb. Mateo turned away from his desk and nodded in greeting. He was a small Mexican man Frank had hired eight years ago. At the time, Mateo had debt collectors knocking down his door and a baby on the way. A mutual friend of theirs had pointed Frank in his direction, and neither of them had cause to regret that decision in the years since. Mateo's skills as a former Green Beret combined with a master's degree in business administration helped give Evans Inc a massive edge.

"Hey, you have a minute?"

"Pretty sure that's in my job description." Mateo grinned. "You're looking rumpled. Who is she?"

He shook his head. "Business first, then you can try to pry details about my private life out of me."

"Promises, promises." Mateo spun a pen around his finger. "I kept digging on Elliott Bancroft over the weekend. So far, nothing is popping. He racks up a truly outstanding amount of debt every couple of years, but someone always pays it off. Up until about five years ago, that someone was Lydia King."

What happened five years ago . . . ? Frank leaned against the doorjamb and crossed his arms over his chest. "She stopped paying him right around the time their youngest kid hit eighteen."

Mateo hummed under his breath and rotated his chair to face his computer. A few seconds later he nodded. "Yep. Right down to the month Eliza King turned eighteen. Interesting coincidence."

Frank had a feeling Lydia King could give him all

the dirt he could possibly want on Elliott, but calling her was out of the question. Not only would Journey be pissed, but if Lydia came back to Houston to protect her family, Beck would have to follow through on his threat to ruin her and her company. *A fucking mess* didn't begin to cover that situation. No, better to leave Lydia out of it completely.

"Find out who's paying his debts now." With a man like Elliott, following the money was their best bet at figuring out his agenda. He straightened. "Anything else I need to know?"

"There's a list in your office." Mateo's fingers flew over the keyboard, his tone distracted. "Nothing urgent, or I would have called you. I can handle anything you want to pass off."

"Noted." Frank was going to have to hand out significant bonuses this quarter to his key team. Between dealing with Beck's situation a few months ago, and now having to step out on operations to secure a favor from Kingdom Corp and Journey King, he was letting them take on more than he usually did. They were more than capable of handling it—Frank only chose the best to trust with running Evans Inc—but it felt strange to let the machine grind on without him at the helm 24-7.

He headed for his office, and he'd barely opened the door before his phone started ringing. Frank dug it out of his pocket. "Frank Evans."

"You know, I thought you looked familiar when we ran into each other, but I wasn't sure."

He stepped into his office and shut the door softly behind him. "Elliott Bancroft, I presume."

"The very same."

Elliott had no reason to recognize Frank—they'd never met before the incident at Journey's apartment—so he must have done some digging. It was the first step Frank would have taken if he was in that position. "I didn't expect to hear from you after our last conversation."

"Unfortunate business, that. You know how it is with family." A genial laugh that set Frank's teeth on edge. "What am I saying? Of course you don't. You're an orphan, I hear. Shame about your old man. Even bigger shame about your mama. Lucky you that she had that life insurance policy paid up, or we wouldn't be having this conversation right now."

Fury nearly stole his words. *Do* not *react.* If he told this asshole to keep Frank's parents out of his fucking mouth, it wouldn't do anything but tell Elliott exactly where to push to get a reaction. "You have a reason for calling, I assume."

"My girl didn't come home this weekend. You wouldn't know anything about that, would you?"

Frank stalked out of his office and back down the hall to Mateo's. He snapped his fingers at the man. Mateo barely got the pen and pad to him in time for him to write. *Get two men on Journey King. Subtly.* Mateo nodded and went for his phone.

It took everything he had to keep his voice calm. "Journey's an adult. She hasn't needed you for the last twenty years, best I can tell. No reason to think she's going to need you now."

"A girl never outgrows needing her daddy."

The smugness in the man's tone had Frank seeing red. This piece of shit had hurt Journey, even if he hadn't left a mark on her in the apartment. He didn't get to sit there and talk about her as if they had anything resembling a healthy father-daughter relationship.

Keep him talking.

Focus on the facts.

Before he could ask what the hell the man wanted again, Elliott continued as if they were having the nicest of chats. "You're a hard man to get a read on, Frank. I thought I recognized the Evans last name and, sure as shit, your daddy was the one who got too big for his britches all those years ago, and look where that got him. Shame he couldn't control his temper. That sort of thing run in the family?"

Frank gritted his teeth. He'd been dealing with attitudes like this since as long as he could remember. When he was a kid, that bullshit was leveled at his father—who had too much ambition for the color of his skin, according to those who held power. He had to be better than his political opponents, had to be damn near fucking perfect.

But no one was perfect.

Not even Henry Evans. *Especially* not Henry Evans.

He was a good father, and a better politician, but he was a shitty-ass husband. His selfishness led to the death of his mistress—his secretary—and he'd been convicted in the court of public opinion long before the judge and jury made it official.

"Get to your point."

"Now, now, Frank. We're having a nice little chat. Don't go and mess it up by being an asshole." The joking disappeared from Elliott's voice, revealing the truth of the man beneath it. "Your daddy killed a woman. It's my fatherly duty to ensure my daughter doesn't share the same fate as that poor girl. Journey's not thinking clearly or she wouldn't be with a man like you."

A man like you.

He could lie and pretend Elliott meant a murderer like his father, but he knew the truth. As a black man, he'd never be good enough for Journey in Elliott's opinion—in the opinion of far too many in Houston. No matter how noble his intentions, no matter how much power and money he accrued, the color of his skin would always outweigh anything else for some people.

Elliott numbered among them, which didn't surprise Frank in the least.

Frank couldn't change people's opinions, but he could damn well make sure he was too big of a fish to fuck with. If his father had the kind of power Frank wielded, he wouldn't have been charged with murder for what was obviously an accidental death, much less convicted.

He wouldn't have died in prison as a result.

Frank made an effort to unclench his hand. When he spoke, he kept his tone even and bored. "There's one key difference between me and my father, Elliott."

"Do tell."

"If I killed someone, it wouldn't be an accident—and the body would never be found." He hung up.

Mateo poked his head out of his office. "I have José and Ethan on their way to her place. If she's not there, they'll head to Kingdom Corp, but I told them to keep a low profile."

"Thanks." Frank walked back into his office and shut the door behind him. Journey wasn't going to thank him for the security detail, but he wasn't taking any chances with her safety.

She picked up almost immediately. "Hello?"

"Where are you?"

"Just about to walk out my front door. Why?" Nothing in her tone to suggest fear or that she was in danger.

"I have two men who are going to keep an eye on you for the time being. The situation has changed, and until I know how things fall out, you'll have a security detail on you whenever you aren't with me."

"What's changed?"

"Your father has made it clear he will try to get you alone, and my men will ensure that doesn't happen."

A long pause, as if she was weighing whether to fight him on this. "Are you sure it's necessary?"

"I wouldn't have assigned them if I didn't think it was."

Finally, Journey sighed. "Text me their names and photos. They can't come into Kingdom Corp for obvious reasons, but having a security detail makes sense."

That, more than anything, said she knew the stakes of this situation better than he did. Frank hesitated. "Something you need to tell me, Duchess?"

"You can't read my mind in addition to micromanaging every aspect of my life? Shocking." Her laugh sounded forced. "Just…don't underestimate my dad, Frank. He's smart and really good at pushing people's buttons to get what he wants. Be careful."

"I'm not the one who's going to be in the same building as him for most of this week." He hated reminding her of that, hated her sharp intake of breath in response.

"You're right. I'll be careful, too. Talk to you later." She cut off the call, leaving him fighting against the need to get back in his car and drive to her. To protect her.

Not part of the plan.

Nothing was going according to plan. He'd fully intended to keep his distance and operate like he always had. He hadn't expected Journey to get under his skin so effectively in such a short time.

And he sure as hell hadn't expected it to take more than a few hours' search to get the dirt he needed on Elliott Bancroft. *We're missing something there.*

He needed to find out *what* and to find out sooner, rather than later.

* * *

Journey had to give it to Frank—his men were *good*. After they introduced themselves and waited for her to verify their information, they melted into the foot traffic on the street as she walked to the office. She had no doubt they were close enough to deal with any potential threat that arose, but the one time she glanced over her shoulder, she hadn't seen either of them.

She barely made it to her office when she got the call that Samara Mallick was headed her way. Journey had expected her friend to show up at some point after she heard the news that Elliott was back in town—Houston's gossips would have the information by now—so she took a deep breath and tried to get her game face in place.

A few minutes later, the door flew open and Samara Mallick charged in. Her best friend shut and locked the door behind her, her black hair wild around her shoulders and a determined look in her dark eyes. "We're going to talk."

Journey held up her hands. "Whoa there, Turbo. You look like you're about to whip a gun out of your thigh holster and start shooting."

"If I see that piece of shit father of yours, I just might." Samara strode over and took her shoulders, peering into her face. "He's the reason you're not sleeping, isn't he? Damn it, Journey, you should have told me. I shouldn't have had to hear from Frank that Elliott's back in town."

Frank told Samara?

They were *so* going to have words about that the next time she saw him.

She opened her mouth to tell Samara she was fine, but the lie wouldn't come. She couldn't tell the full truth, but her friend at least knew part of it. "Him showing up is doing a number on me."

"I bet." Samara guided her to the couch situated against the wall opposite her desk. "I know I don't work here anymore, so you might not want to tell me, but—"

"He's the main shareholder now." It wasn't a secret, exactly. If Beckett didn't know already, he would soon enough.

"Shit," she breathed. "I bet Lydia is ready to chew through bricks at the idea of Elliott Bancroft at the head of Kingdom Corp."

"I don't think she knows." Her mother had taken losing Kingdom Corp hard, and leaving Houston even harder. They still spoke once a week, but Lydia flipped between asking five hundred questions about how the company was running and not asking at all. This most recent week had been one of the latter, which was just as well. She knew for a fact that Anderson hadn't told Lydia that their father was back, and Journey sure as hell wasn't going to be the one to mention it.

"That's for the best. If she comes back to Houston,

Beckett will do what he has to do and…no one wants that." Samara cursed. "What's Elliott up to?"

She couldn't tell Samara his plan, couldn't reveal just how flawed Journey was, right down to her core. If she was better adjusted, even a shrink who had been paid off by her father wouldn't be able to unsettle her enough to declare her unfit. She was the weak link, and if she confessed the truth, Samara would realize it. The only other time Journey had been perfectly honest with someone outside the family about the abuse she and her siblings had suffered at her father's hands was with her ex-fiancé.

It was the beginning of the end of their relationship.

Every time he looked at her after that, she'd catch a glimpse of a toxic combination of pity and disgust in his blue eyes. He might have really believed she was a victim instead of being damaged goods, but he wasn't prepared to deal with the level of baggage she brought to a relationship. So he'd bailed, leaving her to pick up the pieces and put on a brave face in the midst of a media storm that would have knocked her on her ass even on her best day.

If Samara reacted the same way upon hearing the truth…

Journey didn't know if she'd survive it.

Samara reached out and took her hand. "Is there anything I can do? Or, if not me, then Beckett? He'd be happy to help in any way he can." No censure in her friend's tone over the fact that Journey had been dodging her cousin's phone calls ever since he ran Lydia out of town. She might not hold that against Beckett, but she wasn't ready to take the first step in mending their broken family. Not yet. Not while she was so damn broken herself.

"This is one of those problems that needs to be handled internally." She squeezed Samara's hand. "I appreciate the offer, though."

"Uh-huh." She narrowed her dark eyes. "In that case, why don't we talk about the fact that you spent the weekend at Frank's place? Because I did not see *that* coming. How do you go from hating his guts to sleeping over?"

She didn't want to lie to her friend, but if Samara knew the truth, it would just spawn more questions Journey couldn't answer. Better a little lie now than the alternative. *The lies are adding up so freaking fast. Soon I'll be drowning in them.* "We're dating."

Samara blinked. "I'm going to need you to go back to the beginning and explain, starting with the fact that we talked last week and you didn't mention that you and Frank were seeing each other, let alone that it had progressed to the weekend sleepover stage."

Journey studied the photograph on the wall above their heads, the oak tree's leaves painted all the colors of fall. It usually calmed her, but she could feel the flush spreading up her chest to her cheeks. "We didn't want to tell anyone at first while we figured things out." She tucked a strand of hair behind her ear. "And this weekend wasn't like *that*. I had a fight with Elliott, and Frank just happened to show up right around the time things were getting ugly. He took my plans to hole up in a hotel personally and offered his house as an alternative."

Because it was Samara and because she and Journey were friends, her very real frustration crept into her voice. "He barely touched me the whole weekend. I slept in the guest bedroom for God's sake. And I didn't see him most of the time because he was holed up in his office working." She started to mention that he'd held her hand and listened to an audiobook the entire night, but it felt like revealing too much. Journey still wasn't even sure how she felt about it. She'd woken up Sunday morning with Frank's fingers still entwined with hers and his big body wrapped around hers.

Protecting her.

"Hmmm."

"Don't *hmmm* me. I can't help that I have terrible taste in men." She spent the entire time in Frank's house switching between obsessing over what waited for her back in Kingdom Corp on Monday and obsessing about the feel of Frank's mouth on hers. The end result was a shitty mood in which she wasn't inclined to give Frank the benefit of the doubt.

Samara shifted back and leaned against the side of the couch. "I mean, I can't say that I blame you. He's gorgeous and there's the whole helping me save Beckett's life thing, which puts me firmly on Team Frank. But normally when someone is still in the honeymoon phase, they tend to be less... cranky."

Journey gave her the expression that comment deserved. "You know me. Since when do I gracefully begin to date anyone ever?"

Instead of laughing, Samara sighed. "I know Adrian did a number on you, but—"

"Nope. Absolutely not. We are not invoking the name of my ex. It's been ten years, Samara. Does it still sting sometimes? Sure. But this isn't about him. This is about Frank being infuriating to the utmost degree and me dating him despite my better judgment."

Samara studied her nails for a long moment and finally

dropped her hand. "Shelving that topic for the time being—you've skipped the last two happy hours we've set up. What gives?"

Guilt flared. Journey started to go with the time-honored excuse of work keeping her too *busy* to spend time with her best friend, but it wasn't the truth any more than her dating Frank was the truth. Journey clasped her hands together in her lap. "I'm having a hard time with the transition since Mother left. Part of it is the longer hours, but we were already working that leading up to that whole mess. It's just..." She shrugged, going for nonchalant— as if she hadn't spent the last few months waking up in the middle of the night, covered in sweat and breathing hard, a scream trapped on the inside of her lips.

You didn't have nightmares Saturday night.

Yeah, not prepared to deal with that.

Journey ran a finger along the hem of her dress. "I turtled instead of being a good friend. I've been out a grand total of one time since you left Kingdom Corp, and it wasn't even a fun night out—it was me making bad life choices."

Samara's dark eyes seemed to read between the lines. "You know you can talk to me, right? We don't have to be the COOs of competing companies first and friends second. I'd do damn near anything for you if you needed me."

She knew that. Damn it, she *knew* that.

The temptation to spill everything nearly sent her to her knees. Her father's threats. Her weakness that she couldn't beat no matter how hard she fought. Maybe the burden would lessen if she could share it.

Sure. Dump your issues on Samara because you aren't

strong enough to handle them on your own. You already dragged Frank into this mess. Are you really going to pull your best friend in, too?

She managed a smile. "I know. I'm just at a point where I have to figure some stuff out, and unfortunately I have to do it alone."

Samara finally nodded. "Okay. I get that. You've had a hell of a lot of changes in a seriously short time, and needing to get your feet under you is totally understandable." She grimaced. "Though you don't have to justify that to me—really. I'm not trying to add to your stress level, but I miss you."

"Aw, honey, I miss you, too." She pulled Samara in for a quick hug, inhaling her lavender scent. "When all this bullshit has calmed down, I'm going to kidnap you for a weekend at the Hampton house or somewhere in the Caribbean. We both deserve a few days where the only things we have to worry about are turning over to sun our other sides and whether our drinks are getting too low."

Samara laughed. "Deal." She grinned. "Though if things go well, we can bring the guys along and have a couples' weekend."

Fat chance of that happening. "Ha ha. Very funny." Journey relaxed back against the couch. "Enough about me. Fill me in on all the giddy details of how things are going with my darling cousin."

CHAPTER NINE

After Samara left, Journey got through two meetings without the sky falling. Some days, her entire job seemed to be putting out fires, but she was good at it. There was nothing like two people walking into a room angry and frustrated—and walking out of it with a solution she'd helped provide. She smiled to herself and set down her pen. There was time for a short lunch before she met with Bellamy for their monthly check-in regarding all things security for Kingdom Corp.

She froze as someone knocked on her door, and then cursed herself for freezing. "Come in."

The woman who stepped into her office could only be termed *handsome*. She had a strong jaw and solid body, and her strawberry blond hair was pulled back into a no-nonsense low ponytail. Her gray suit was expensive but boring. All in all, it gave her a forgettable-type appearance...if they had met under any other circumstances.

She gave a cool, professional smile. "Journey King?"

"That's what it says on the plaque outside my office."

She set her pen down with care and forced herself to take a slow breath. Just because she didn't recognize this stranger didn't mean she was in danger. Her fight-or-flight responses were all jacked up, and she couldn't afford to start attacking anyone who crossed her path. "Can I help you?"

"I'm Dr. Alice Scott. I'm here for the first step of your evaluation."

Cold skittered down her spine, and she straightened. "I don't have an appointment on my calendar." No use in apologizing for her abrupt behavior. From the tight set of Dr. Scott's mouth the second she walked through the door, she already had a convenient diagnosis ready—at Elliott's bidding.

"I can reschedule if that's required." She reached for her pen, no doubt to write a note about how uncooperative Journey was.

"It's fine." She paused and made an effort to moderate her voice. "I only have thirty minutes before my next meeting, but we can speak now."

"Thirty minutes is more than adequate." Dr. Scott closed the door softly behind her and took in the office with a critical eye. "I like your art." Her tone said the exact opposite.

"Thank you." Journey gritted her teeth. "Please have a seat."

The shrink sank into her chair as gingerly as if it was covered in something disgusting. She flipped open her notebook and crossed one leg over the other. "We both know why I'm here, so I think it would be best to skip over the softball questions and get to the heart of things."

"No reason to waste both our time." Though that was

exactly what they were doing right now. Elliott wouldn't have brought in someone who was objective—he had a goal to accomplish, and this shrink would play a key part in that. He would have covered all his bases to ensure he ended up with the outcome he wanted.

"Your mother leaving under such sudden circumstances must have been difficult to deal with." Dr. Scott pinned her in place with hard blue eyes. "How are you holding up under the increased demands on your time?"

"To be honest, not much has changed." It was even the truth. "My mother appointed me as COO because she knew I could handle it, and she only micromanaged her pet projects when they came under my purview. The rest of the time, she was focused on the big picture, while I did my part to keep Kingdom Corp functioning like a well-oiled machine." She gave a tight smile. "If you'll excuse the pun."

The shrink made a note. "I have it here that Samara Mallick also left the company around the same time as your mother. Who's handling her duties now?"

"Anderson and I have split them."

"Hmmm." Another note. "You and Ms. Mallick were friends."

"We *are* friends—present tense."

She made that annoying *hmmm* noise again and sat back. "You don't think that friendship is in direct conflict with your current position within Kingdom Corp? She's now the COO of Morningstar Enterprise, is she not?"

This, at least, Journey had prepared for the second Samara left the company. Since they worked so closely for so many years, it stood to reason that people would wonder if that would affect their ability to work for competing companies going forward. "Samara and I are professionals. We're more than capable of being friends outside of work and competition within our respective positions."

"That's a rather optimistic outlook, don't you think?"

"Hardly." Journey gave her a hard look. "Samara was with Kingdom Corp for ten years. I know how she operates, both professionally and personally. As such, I can say with confidence that I'm correct. You're more than welcome to confirm that with Anderson." If her father thought he could use Samara to bring her down, he had another think coming. Their friendship brought up questions like this all the time, even when they had still worked for the same company. They'd managed to keep things separate when they needed to for the last decade— they'd do it for the next decade, too.

Dr. Scott recrossed her legs, apparently a signal of the subject changing. "You're dating Frank Evans."

That didn't take long for Elliott to figure out. "Yes."

"Another relationship that you can keep separate from Kingdom Corp."

It wasn't a question, so she should have kept her damn mouth shut, but Journey saw the writing on the wall. "If anything, my relationship with Frank is an asset to the company. While we also keep the professional and personal separate—shocking, I know—our being together may very well mean that he's more inclined to make favorable deals with Kingdom Corp."

"Those statements contradict each other. Either your relationship has nothing to do with your professional life or it's an asset professionally—which means you're also in danger of being influenced."

Journey caught herself white-knuckling the arms of her chair and released them. This wasn't going her way, but she'd be damned before she went down without a fight. Journey forced a smile. "Dr. Scott, I'm not sure how psychologists work, but within the oil industry, there's a significant amount of socializing and elbow rubbing between companies that are both allies and enemies. It's the nature of the beast. Personal bias, both positive and negative, comes into every single business meeting, whether anyone wants to admit it or not. Frank Evans made things very difficult for Kingdom Corp within Houston because he dislikes my mother intensely. I think it would be considered an asset that my relationship with him may open doors that have been previously closed to the company." *Chew on that, bitch.*

From the way the woman's mouth tightened, she wasn't a fan of Journey being so damn logical. Those cold blue eyes flicked up to her, crinkling a little at the corners, and that's all the warning she had before Dr. Scott said, "You seem rather confrontational, Ms. King."

"Excuse me?"

Dr. Scott's mouth quirked into something resembling a smile. "I believe you heard me. You knew a psychological evaluation was part of being the condition for holding a position on the board of directors. I haven't asked anything out of line, but you decided this was a fight the second I walked through the door. Why is that?"

Oh, so they were going to be honest. Great. Journey leaned back in her chair and stared at the woman. "You have one purpose here, and we both know it's not to provide an accurate report. My father has his plans in place, and you're on his payroll. So, yes, I'm confrontational.

You're wasting my time when you decided on the outcome before I said a single word."

"Interesting." Her pen scratched over the paper as she made yet more notes. "It's perfectly normal for girls raised without their father to have issues with authority, as well as feelings of abandonment. Neither of those things is your father's fault, you know. It's simply the natural reaction to the choice your mother made."

Her hands started to shake and her heart beat in double time. Rage blackened the edges of Journey's vision. "I'm sorry, could you run that by me again?"

"Which part?"

"You think that my mother is to blame for how much I loathe my father? That he *abandoned* us?" *That his leaving wasn't the best thing that ever happened to me and my siblings?* She could have laughed if she wasn't so close to screaming. "That's not even close to the truth. My father is a monster."

Dr. Scott's expression might have been sympathetic if it'd actually reached her eyes. "Ms. King, that statement alone, combined with your dating Frank Evans within twenty-four hours of your father coming back to town, speaks volumes. Your feelings for your father are getting in the way of your ability to function. Your decision-making skills are compromised—will continue to be compromised for as long as you avoid dealing with the issues your father's presence represents to you."

"Get out."

She ignored that and consulted her notes. "Your father isn't going anywhere, Journey. It would behoove you to mend the relationship between the two of you if you want to make a seamless transition."

The threat couldn't have been clearer if she'd spelled it out. "This session is over." Journey spoke through numb lips. "I have to get to my next meeting."

"We'll have another appointment later this week to continue this conversation." Dr. Scott rose as if completely unaware of the shit storm she'd stirred up. But, then, she'd done it on purpose. "Think about what I said, Journey. Kingdom Corp obviously matters a lot to you. I'd hate to see you self-sabotage and lose it."

Journey held it together as the woman left. She held it together as she crossed her office and threw the lock on her door. She even held it together as she sent Bellamy a quick text pushing back their meeting.

Then she sank onto her couch and pulled her legs up to make herself as small a target as she could. She couldn't close her eyes, couldn't risk being shoved back into the past and those nightmare years between four and ten. The way she learned to walk soundlessly to avoid alerting Elliott to her presence and provoking an attack. The look that would come into his blue eyes that made her stomach drop out. The teasing in his voice as he'd stroke a hand over her hair... right before the pain came.

No. I am not a child anymore. I am stronger than this.

She'd known Elliott would try to get her declared unfit. She should have anticipated that he wouldn't go about it in the most straightforward manner. If he wrote her off, he would incite Anderson to draw a line in the sand and, even with majority shares, that was one fight Elliott couldn't be sure he'd win. Not without heavy losses. Better to push and prod and provoke Journey to lose her shit so spectacularly that even Anderson couldn't argue that she should stay on in Kingdom Corp.

Her brother would make that call. She already knew he would. It didn't matter if it was to protect her—he would support Elliott's ousting her if he thought it would get her out of their father's crosshairs.

Journey rested her forehead on her knees, trying to *think*. She couldn't call Anderson. Now it was about more than protecting him. It was about keeping him from doing something unforgivable to protect *her*. He would remove her as COO until he could deal with Elliott, and that was something she couldn't allow.

There's a way out of this. There has to be.

If she played along and tried to "mend" the relationship with her father, he'd break her. They both knew he could do it, which had to be why the therapist took this route.

Breathe, damn it.

She bit her bottom lip hard, using the pain to steady the shaking ground she stood on. She hadn't been expecting the pointed questions about Frank. Something about him set her father on edge, which was why he'd had his pet shrink attack that relationship. *He's threatened by Frank.* But why? It wasn't just because of Frank's power within Houston. There were plenty of people that powerful, her cousin included, and Elliott hadn't singled them out. No, it was Frank specifically.

Surely it couldn't be as simple as the fact that Frank stood between him and Journey.

But what if it is? What if he's trying to cut away every single tether I have?

Journey crossed her office on shaking legs to grab her phone. She dialed almost from memory, letting out a relieved exhale when Frank answered. "Where are you?"

* * *

"Are you ready?"

Eliza smoothed down the long dress she'd chosen specifically for this meeting. It covered her from neck to ankle—too hot for Houston, even in February, but she'd suffer it gladly considering how like armor it felt. "Of course." She smiled at Anderson, which only earned her a severe look.

"Let's go. I have to be back in the office in an hour." He was always like that with her, as if the warmth he showed Journey used up what little bit of emotion he was capable of. All that remained for Eliza was disapproval so intense, she could feel it from three feet away.

It wasn't the outfit. It wasn't that she was in full makeup without a hair out of place. It wasn't even that she modeled for a living instead of dancing to the tune Lydia King set.

No, Anderson just flat-out didn't like *her*.

Eliza lifted her chin and fell into step beside him, refusing to let her brother outpace her with his longer legs. "I still don't understand why I was called home for this."

"We have to deal with him, which means you have to deal with him, too."

She wanted to slap that cold expression right off his face. "Yes, well, *I've* had to deal with Mother ever since she was exiled. She might be out of your hair, but she's essentially moved in with me while she supposedly scouts for other places to live." In the meantime, Lydia had begun meddling in every aspect of Eliza's life, and kept making worrisome comments about how shitty

Eliza's agent was at his job. If she didn't give the woman a project or a small country to conquer soon, Lydia would slip into her life permanently, and the small bit of breathing space Eliza had fought so hard for would disappear as if it'd never existed.

"It's nothing more than the three of us have been dealing with for the last twenty years, Eliza. It's about damn time you grew up."

Grow up, Eliza. Stop being such a spoiled brat, Eliza.

She swallowed a sharp response. It wouldn't make a difference, and they couldn't afford to be visibly divided when facing down their father, no matter their personal opinions of each other. Nothing she could say would change Anderson's mind, anyway. She wasn't brilliant, wasn't particularly business savvy, wasn't technically advanced beyond other people in her generation. The only thing Eliza excelled at was being pretty. She made it an art form, and was widely renowned for it.

But pretty only went skin-deep.

A fact her oldest brother never hesitated to remind her of.

He stopped just inside the door, his jaw tight. "If at any point you feel uncomfortable, we will leave. The only thing you owe him at this point is a meeting, seeing as how you're not officially an acting part of Kingdom Corp."

Even his help comes with thorns.

She lifted her chin. "I can handle it."

"All the same." He opened the door and allowed her to precede him.

The dim lighting gave her pause for half a heartbeat, but Eliza had walked runways where lights blinded her plenty of times before. This was nothing compared to that—even knowing what waited for her. The hostess caught her eye and led the way back to a private room situated in the far corner of the restaurant. It was called the Cellar, and the decor more than lived up to the name, the exposed brick and flickering candlelight raising the small hairs on the back of her neck.

Or maybe that was the man who pushed slowly to his feet at their approach.

Elliott held out his hands, and there was nothing she could do but take them and let him tow her closer. He brushed a perfectly polite kiss against her cheek, but bile still rose in response. *Show no fear.* "Elliott."

"Eliza. Thank you for making the time." As charming as ever, all warm voice and easy smiles. If she hadn't seen the moment when the peace turned to nightmare, she might not have believed it possible of this man. Even so, Eliza knew all too well that she'd been spared the worst he had to offer—something her siblings held against her, even if they weren't aware they were doing it.

"Let's keep this short." Anderson held out a chair for her—as far away from their father as the table allowed. The move warmed some of the cold from her body, even though she knew he did it more to spite Elliott than to protect her.

Stop feeling sorry for yourself.

Easier said than done.

She sank into the chair and arranged her long skirt around her. "I'm surprised you're back in Houston, Elliott. I thought you hated this place."

"Oh, that." He waved it away. "Home is home, regardless of the baggage that comes with it. Isn't that right, Andy?"

"It's relative." The words were so clipped, it was a wonder he didn't chip his tooth.

Eliza shifted, drawing both men's attention to her—and away from each other. "You said you had a specific reason you wanted to see me?"

The smile fell away from Elliott's face, leaving a serious mask in its place. The earnest father, who wasn't willing to spare the rod for fear of spoiling the child, but who would do it out of love rather than anger. It was as much a lie as anything else about him. "You've done good, my girl, but it's time to stop playing around and come home."

She sat up straighter. "What are you talking about?"

"Your siblings have all done their duty to the family." He twisted his mouth as if sharing an inside joke just between the two of them. "Now it's your turn." He reached across the table and covered her hand with his own, and it took everything she had not to drive her fork into the fleshy part of his forearm.

The room fell away around them, the rushing sound loud in her ears overwhelming everything else. But not loud enough to drown out his next words. "It's not so much to give, really, my girl. Asher Bishop is attractive enough, and he's got the kind of money that can ensure you keep up the lifestyle you should be accustomed to."

"Explain what the fuck you mean, old man," Anderson snarled.

Elliott never took his gaze from her. "It's already set in stone, Eliza. You're a vital part of securing a merger that will move Kingdom Corp into the big leagues, where it's always belonged." His smile widened, as if he thought she'd be pleased with this turn of events. As if he dared her *not* to be happy. "No point in theatrics or threats. What's done is done."

It took two tries to get her words into the air between them. "What are you talking about?" she repeated.

"You're going to marry Asher Bishop, linking our future with Cardinal Energy, both in family and in business."

CHAPTER TEN

Frank walked into the hotel lobby approximately thirty minutes after Journey called. Regal Legacy Hotel and Spa was one of the fancier properties that had gone up a couple of decades ago, parked right in central downtown Houston. It boasted some of the biggest events in the city throughout the year, in addition to the spa being a draw for the rich and bored when their lives got to be too stressful.

He found Journey in the bar off the main lobby, staring into a glass of whiskey. There was no one around this time of day, so Frank strode through the empty tables and slid onto the next bar stool over. He ran a critical eye over her. In the few hours since he'd seen her, she'd lost the slightly rested look she'd acquired over the weekend, but she wasn't close to her breaking point, as best he could tell. "Strange place for a meeting."

"Is it?" She shrugged a single shoulder. "We're supposed to be newly dating. It's not out of the realm of possibilities that we'd meet up to bump uglies."

"Bump uglies. Is that the technical term?"

Journey twisted to face him. She'd changed clothes since he saw her last, and now she wore a knee-length body-skimming deep blue dress with a square neckline. Again, she wore fuck-me shoes, this time strappy black ones that crisscrossed at her ankles. The dress shone slightly in the low light, an invitation to touch that he had no business taking her up on. Her breath hitched and he watched her nipples press against her dress. She let loose a soft curse. "How can you look at me like that and kiss me like you mean it and then just...walk away? Am I really that disposable to you?"

Surprise had him speaking ill-advised words. "Not disposable. Never that." He motioned for the bored-looking bartender to give him the same drink Journey had. "I meant what I said over the weekend—I want you in my bed because you want to be there, not because you're hurt and looking for a parachute while in a free fall."

"Frank." Her smile made something uncomfortable twang in his chest. "I'm never *not* in a free fall. Most days I just hide it better. Maybe I had a chance at being healthy once, or maybe that option was taken from me a long time ago, but the end result is that I'm stuck in a cycle of maintaining and clusterfuck. The clusterfuck times have been decreasing over the years, and getting further and further apart, but all it took was a few specific dominoes lined up, and down I go." She mimed tipping the first domino. "So if you're waiting for the stars to align and me to be in perfect emotional health before you fuck me...I hope you're not holding your breath."

Layers upon layers in those words. Frank didn't do well with broken things. Discarded, things, yes. He excelled at seeing the strength in people despite their circumstances and offering them the opportunity to stand on their own—and he obtained their undying loyalty in the process. Loyalty was just another kind of power. He didn't *fix* people. He didn't even know where to start. The one time he'd tried—with his mother—her spiral had taken her to a place so dark, there was nothing he could do. She died, and he learned his lesson. *Never again.* "Duchess, you need a white knight. I'm not that. I'm never going to be that."

She picked up her glass and drained half of it. "I don't need a knight, Frank. I need a goddamn sword and the skills to save myself. I've played the part of damsel in distress. It's not a comfortable fit for me." She met his gaze steadily, a tangled mess of emotions lurking in those hazel eyes. Anger. Fear. Despair. Desire. "Know anyone who makes a mean suit of armor?"

She's not asking me to fix her.

He nodded in thanks at the bartender when the woman deposited a second glass of whiskey in front of him. "I know what you think of me, but I'm not in the business of dealing harm to those who don't deserve it."

"Who said I don't deserve it?" She huffed out a soft laugh. "God, Frank, you should see your face. So serious. I'm not asking you to fuck away all my broken edges. I'm telling you that I'm an adult and can make my own decisions and accept the consequences. I want you. You want me. There isn't a single reason we shouldn't be upstairs in a room right now having outstanding sex."

Why was he fighting this so hard?

You know why.

He downed his whiskey. "We need to have a

conversation about why you called me today. I'll get us a room so we can have some privacy for it."

"Conversation, sure." She set her empty glass next to his.

Damn it, the woman drove him out of his fucking mind. Frank captured her wrist, forcing her to look at him. "You've said your piece, and so have I. Ultimately that changes nothing. This is a business deal, Duchess."

The desire died in her eyes, leaving only the toxic mix of fear and despair. "I hear you, Frank. Loud and clear." She turned and strode away, leaving him staring after her.

Goddamn it, he was making the right call. It didn't matter how her ass filled out that tease of a dress or how good she smelled or how badly he wanted to do whatever it took to chase the darkness from her eyes and make her forget for a little while. It wasn't his job. His job was to find Elliott Bancroft's weak spot and exploit it enough to banish the man from her life.

Distraction meant danger for her.

But she's in fucking danger right now, and I'm only making it worse.

And round and round he went.

There was no black and white in this situation—only gray. Frank couldn't shake the feeling that one wrong step would send Journey tumbling past the point of no return and leave her truly broken.

He couldn't be responsible for that.

He paid the bartender and followed her at a more moderate pace. By the time he reached the lobby, Journey had a hotel key in her hand. She didn't look at him as he fell into step beside her and they walked to the elevator. Silence reigned on the ride up to their floor and the short walk to the room. She closed the door, twisted the lock, and then slumped against it. "I just can't help but keep throwing myself at you, no matter how many times you tell me no. Isn't that the definition of insanity?" She laughed, the sound filled to the brim with despair. "I'm drowning, Frank. No matter how many moves I make, he's always two steps ahead, and he knew exactly what buttons to push to make the ground fall out from beneath my feet."

Frank stopped thinking so damn much and reacted on instinct. He pulled Journey into his arms and held her tightly. She felt so slight like this, as if a sharp word would send her breaking into a million pieces. Finally, slowly, she lifted her arms and hugged him back. "Is this a pity hug?"

"What happened this morning in the office, Duchess?"

She tensed and then buried her face in his shoulder and let out a shuddering breath. "My father hired a shrink to come in and evaluate those holding executive positions in the company to see if they were fit to serve on the board—and maintain their jobs. She ambushed me today, and even though I knew it wouldn't go my way, she basically had a bullet-pointed list designed to hit every single weak spot I have." Another of those heartbreaking laughs. "I have more than a few."

From a tactical standpoint, it made sense, but that didn't stop Frank from wanting to bash that bastard's face in for subjecting her to this. *War. This is war. You can't afford to forget that.* "I'm sorry."

"Don't be. The timing caught me off guard but the line of questioning didn't." She rubbed her nose against his shirt. "You smell criminally good."

"Thanks."

"Right. Focus." Some of the tension bled out of her body and she melted against him. "There was one part of the so-called session that surprised me—she was hyper-focused on my relationship with you." Journey raised her head to look up at him. "Something about you, specifically, has him pissed. I thought it might just be because you're a force to be reckoned with inside of Houston, but the same applies to my cousin, and he hasn't made any effort to contact Beckett." She sighed. "I guess it could be old-fashioned racism, too. I just don't know."

"I think a good portion of it actually is old-fashioned racism." He considered keeping his cards close to his chest, but ultimately Frank had no more answers than Journey did when it came to the question of Elliott's fascination with him. "But you're right—there's more. He's a bully and I challenged him when I showed up at your apartment. If he views you as his, that territorial feeling might be enough to drive him to attempt to run me off."

"That sounds like him. He can't stand losing, and my mother made sure he lost all four of us. He obviously never got over having his toys taken away."

"Duchess—"

"You're right. I'm sure you're right. It's the only thing that makes sense." Her gaze fell to his lips and then jerked back to his eyes. "Sorry. I'm focusing. I promise."

All his reasons for staying the hell away from Journey King disappeared in the face of her disarming smile. She fought so fucking hard to be strong, to not need anyone around her. She stood there in his arms and did her damnedest to respect the lines he kept drawing in the sand.

Fuck it.

What was one more sin to weigh his soul down?

Frank kissed her.

CHAPTER ELEVEN

Journey should have told Frank to fuck right off with his mixed signals. She should have gathered up what remained of her tattered pride, walked out of the hotel room, and shut the door firmly behind her. She *should* have done anything but slide her arms around his neck in silent demand for him to give her more. To make her forget.

Touch me. Purge the poison, if only for a little while.

It would come back. It always came back. Within hours, she'd be choking on the past and fighting herself as hard as she fought the new threats her father had leveled at her.

But she wouldn't be doing it while Frank had his hands on her.

He kept one arm around her waist, clenching her to him, and lifted the other to grip the back of her neck. It grounded her, a physical reminder of where she was, of who touched her. *Frank.* He lifted his head slowly and studied her mouth as if memorizing the curve of her lips. "You're sure."

It wasn't quite a question, but she nodded as much as she was able. "Yes."

Still, he didn't move. "You know the rules—you change your mind, we stop. No questions asked, no explanations required."

Journey closed her eyes and inhaled his scent. This might very well be a pity fuck, but she couldn't bring herself to care. She needed what he offered, no matter the motivation behind it. *I chose this. That* was the only thing that mattered. "Kiss me again, Frank."

This time, he didn't hesitate. He took her mouth, shifting his grip to bracket the front of her throat, guiding her to the angle he desired. His body caged her without crushing her, taking what he wanted even as he created space for her to kiss him back. Somehow holding her down and lifting her up at the exact same time.

She'd never felt more free.

Yes. This. She pushed up on her toes and surrendered everything. Right then, in that moment, she was safe. Frank would fuck every thought from her head. He would leave marks on her body to remember him by, but he wouldn't harm her. She wanted everything he'd give her.

Everything and more.

He let go of her waist to yank her dress up so he could cup her from behind, his hand sliding roughly down the center of her ass to push two fingers into her pussy. She jumped and then moaned, pushing back against the intrusion, trying to take him deeper. He turned them without missing a beat and half walked, half carried her backward to the bed. Frank lifted his head enough to say, "I make a wrong move, you let me know."

It was more command than question, but she was already nodding. "Don't stop."

He withdrew his fingers, but before she could mourn

the loss, he pulled her dress off and tossed it over his shoulder. Her bra and panties followed, leaving her naked and him fully clothed. She froze, but he was already moving, using a hand on the center of her chest to guide her back onto the bed. "Leave the shoes on."

She propped herself onto her elbows and watched him strip, each move as efficient as everything he seemed to do. The suit jacket was draped over the desk chair, followed by the tie. "I want to see."

He turned to face her as he unbuttoned the dove gray shirt, revealing an intoxicating slice of dark brown skin and a muscled chest that spoke of serious control and countless hours in the gym. "God, Frank, you're sexy as fuck."

"The fact you can say that while looking like you do right now…" A muscle twitched in his jaw, and his dark eyes went scorching hot. "Spread your legs for me, Duchess. Let me see how much you need what I'm going to give you."

She obeyed immediately, scooting back onto the mattress enough that she could prop her heels on the edge of it, giving him exactly what he'd commanded. Journey watched him through half-closed eyes as she ran her hands over her breasts, pausing to pinch her nipples, and then down to stroke her thighs.

His movements lost their fluidity and he yanked off his pants quickly enough that she was worried he'd popped a button somewhere, but then nothing mattered because he stood before her, gloriously naked. He produced a condom from somewhere and rolled it on quickly. Anticipation coursed through her, molten and wicked and needy. "I don't want to wait any more."

"Tough shit." He hit his knees in front of her and grasped her thighs in the exact same place he had in his office. His fingers dug into the muscle, the instant ache drawing a gasp from her lips. Then his mouth was on her pussy, kissing her thoroughly. He *claimed* her, alternating between fucking her with his tongue and giving her little nips that made her nerve endings spark in response. Through it all, he kept a viselike grip on her thighs, anchoring her in this moment, in this hotel room, with *him*.

She reached down and clasped his wrists as he sucked on her clit, working her with his tongue and just the slightest edge of his teeth. Somehow he knew exactly what she needed, exactly where to draw the line to keep it from being too much. Pleasure and pain coiled inside her, intrinsically linked until she didn't know which was which. "Frank, oh fuck, *Frank*."

He didn't stop, didn't slow down, didn't do anything but continue the delicious assault with his mouth. There was no teasing, just the full-throttle rush toward the orgasm looming through her entire body. It hit her between one breath and the next, bowing her back and curling her toes in her shoes, drawing his name from her lips, though whether it was benediction or curse was beyond her.

She barely had a chance to release his wrists when he flipped her onto her stomach. The mattress dipped beneath his weight, and his thighs roughly pushed hers wider. He covered her with his body, his chest solid against her back. It felt so good, she moaned. He drew her hair aside and kissed the back of her neck as he reached between them and positioned his cock at her entrance. "We good?"

"Don't you dare stop," she gasped.

He set his teeth against the back of her neck as he shoved into her to the hilt. She whimpered even as she tried to take him deeper, to have him fill her even more, until he chased away the empty spots lurking in her soul. Frank caught her wrists and pinned them to the bed as he leveraged himself back to withdraw and slam into her again. His rough breathing was direct counterpoint to hers, the only other sound in the room the rough contact of flesh against flesh.

She loved every second of it.

"We're not done yet, Duchess." He released one hand and then he was against her back again, bearing her down even as he slid a hand between her thighs to pinch her clit. "I've been imaging how good it would feel to have you coming on my cock since that night at Cocoa's. You know the one."

She knew. It was the first indication she'd gotten that Frank had fire barely banked beneath that cold and perfect exterior—and that it might be aimed right at her. "I know."

"Thought you might." His strokes became rougher, less controlled. "I've had the taste of you on my tongue ever since I licked you through those fucking panties on my office floor. Every time I've jacked myself since then, I picture ripping those fucking things off and sinking between your thighs just like I am now." He bit the spot where her neck met her shoulder, and it was too much on top of everything else.

Journey buried her face in the comforter and sobbed as she came. Her orgasm swept away every single thought in her head, leaving only blessed silence, and still it wasn't enough. She arched back against Frank, tilting her hips until he hit that delicious spot inside her with every thrust, needing him to take the dive off this particular cliff with her. "Come inside me, Frank, I want to feel you."

He cursed against her skin, and his entire body went taut. As if she'd drawn his orgasm out of him against his will simply by commanding it. He shifted to collapse half on top of her but where he wouldn't crush her. "How the hell can I have just come and already want you again?"

"I don't know." She turned in his arms and took one of his hands to press it between her thighs. "But keep touching me." She caught her breath as he slid two fingers into her. "Yes, like that."

He stroked her lazily, his gaze never leaving her face. "I have an hour, Duchess."

She toppled him onto his back and straddled him, riding his fingers even as she leaned down to kiss him. For the first time in months, Journey felt something close to the woman she'd fought so hard to become. It was an illusion, but a welcome one all the same. She shifted to nibble on his square jaw. "How many of those condoms do you have stashed?"

His lips quirked. "Three."

"Then let's put them to good use."

CHAPTER TWELVE

Frank checked himself in the mirror to ensure he hadn't missed a button. The image reflected was almost enough to have him canceling his meeting with Mateo and climbing back into bed with Journey. She lay propped against the headboard, her legs tangled with the sheet and her breasts unabashedly bare. She glanced up from her phone and met his gaze, a small smile tugging at the edges of her lips. "That was some afternoon delight."

Afternoon delight.

Such a quaint description for something that wasn't the least bit quaint. He and Journey had come together like a hurricane meeting a tsunami, a clash so intense, it was a surprise the hotel still stood around them. His gaze traced the faint marks on her chest from his mouth, the slightest bruise from his hands on the one thigh he could see...*Fuck*.

He never lost control.

He couldn't afford to, not when he knew all too well what lay down that path. His mother's face flashed through his mind, her lively smile dimmed and her body ravaged by the sickness she was too broken to even *try* fighting, her eyes harsh with the truth that life never hesitated to kick someone like them when they were down. All because she'd loved his father so fucking much, losing him had meant losing a part of herself that she could never reclaim. *That* was the result of letting lust slip its leash.

The result of love.

Heartbreak that made it impossible for her to keep putting one foot in front of the other.

Heartbreak his father had caused when he became just another Icarus who thought he could have it all without paying the price that power cost.

Journey already teetered on the edge. If Frank wasn't careful, he'd be the reason she tipped past the point of no return—and took him down with her.

She must have seen something on his face because her expression fell and she went back to her phone. "Call me when you figure out the next step?"

Shit. He didn't know how to do this. He wasn't used to walking on eggshells for fear of damaging the people around him. Frank's team might have come to him while they were down and out, but they could all haul their own weight—together and individually—and he never had to fear that a sharp word would do more than give them pause. He cleared his throat. "Have dinner with me tonight."

"No." She didn't look up from her phone. "Samara and I are meeting for drinks—not at Cocoa's, so you don't have to worry about running into me and having to play the part. I'm not going to get in the way of your investigation. Well, I'm not going to get in the way any more than I already have." She typed out something, a small line appearing between her strong brows. "I realize that playing my therapist wasn't part of the plan, so you'll be fairly compensated."

He was across the room before he registered his intent to move. Frank propped his hands on either side of her body and leaned down. When she still didn't look up, he growled. "Stop doing that."

"Stop what?" Something horrifying like a quiver shivered through her voice. "I'm trying to retreat behind the already-established lines. Thank you for grounding me, but since you made your opinion of me more than clear, I will do my best to ensure it doesn't happen again."

He simultaneously wanted to kiss her and throw something. "Journey, look at me."

Slowly, oh so slowly, she raised her gaze. Her hazel eyes shone too brightly, but none of her obvious distress showed elsewhere on her face. He didn't touch her, but he didn't back off, either. "I don't make a habit of mixing business with pleasure, but you're hardly a burden. If you didn't notice, I was in this bed with you as an active participant." He clasped her chin, tilting her face up to meet his. "I said I don't pity fuck, Duchess, and it's the truth. So you can get that thought right out of that busy brain of yours. I wouldn't have declared my intent to get you into my bed if I didn't mean it. Did I intend for it to happen like this? No. Am I going to let you retreat behind that wall you're building as fast as you can? Fuck no." He pressed a quick kiss to her lips.

"I don't understand you."

"Plenty of time to give it a shot." He backed off and pulled on his shoes. "Do you have plans tomorrow night?"

Her frown stayed in place, but she slowly shook her head. "No."

"Now you do. I'll pick you up at six." He swiped his wallet off the dresser and paused. "Want me to call you a car?"

Journey tossed her phone onto the bed beside her. "I'm more than capable of calling one myself." She hesitated. "Thank you, though."

There was nothing else to do but leave. "I'll see you tomorrow."

"Happy hunting."

He walked out of the hotel room, pausing to ensure that the door shut fully behind him, and then headed for the elevator. In the lobby, a pair of men caught his eye and motioned him over. Recognizing Ethan and José, he veered toward them. Ethan hung back, seeming to watch everything and nothing, but José stepped forward to meet him. "Hey, boss."

"Any trouble?"

"Nothing like that." José was a tall, thin man who usually drew second looks from every woman in the room from ages fifteen to eighty-five. He had a smile he used as a weapon to charm information out of resistant people, and he was damn good at it. Add in the fact that he had a decent head on his shoulders, and he was one of the best assets Frank had.

He waited, and José finally said, "It's not my place to question the setup you have going."

"You wouldn't be on this if I didn't value your opinion. You have a problem—stop the bullshit runaround and spit it out."

José focused on a spot roughly three inches over

Frank's left shoulder. "Your girl needs to communicate her movements for us to be effective. We wouldn't have known she left the building if not for the fact Ethan here was taking a smoke break around the corner and saw her go. Do we know the level of danger?"

"Not yet. Could be nothing more than threats. Could be more serious." He wasn't willing to take a chance either way. No matter what happened with him and Journey, he sure as fuck wasn't going to sit idly by while her old man ran rampant over her. Or worse. "I'll talk to her."

"Appreciate it, boss. Having to cover what exits we can in case she pulls a rabbit makes us both less effective."

"Noted. Thanks for bringing it to my attention." He waited a beat. "Is there anything else?"

"Nope."

"Report to Mateo tonight after she gets back to her place, and we'll have an update for you." He turned and headed for the main doors. Journey didn't seem to have a problem with his keeping men on her, but doing that in theory versus having to report her movements...She would see it as a confinement and chafe at the restrictions. He didn't want to think her old man would actually put her life in danger, but he couldn't afford to assume otherwise.

Frank normally lived by the rule that no risks brought no gains, but in the time since his mother died, he'd never had something he wasn't willing to risk.

He did now.

* * *

Journey made it back to the office in time for her rescheduled meeting with Bellamy. They kept it brief and to the point—the only current threat to their company was Elliott fucking Bancroft. At least they were in agreement about that. She managed to focus as they went over the reports—a couple of cyberattacks that Bellamy's team had no problem repelling, and one asshole reporter who wouldn't take *no comment* for an answer—and then there was nothing left to stall with.

She stood and smoothed her dress down. "Eliza's back in town?"

"Yeah, she's been back since Friday." He glanced at his watch. "She had a meeting with Elliott an hour ago. Honestly, I expected a text letting me know she's on her way to the airport by now." He said it with fondness, but Bellamy had always held a soft spot for their baby sister's antics.

Journey couldn't afford to. "That didn't last long." She was self-aware enough to know part of her issue with Eliza was simple jealousy—her little sister had never had a problem drawing a line in the sand and sticking to it, even if it meant abandoning everything they'd been taught from the cradle to want. She left Houston at sixteen and hadn't looked back. Every time Journey had seen her since, Eliza had a glow about her that only came from true freedom.

"What do you expect, Jo?" He frowned at her. "She might have shares in Kingdom Corp, but she's not really interested in the company. It's not like we're bankrolling her lifestyle, either—her modeling gig more than pays for it."

She bit back a sharp retort and deflated. "I know. I'm sorry. I'm not exactly the best sister lately, am I?"

He shook his head. "You and Eliza have your

differences, just like she and Anderson have their differences. Just...don't take your issues out on her. That's all I'm saying."

"You're right. I know you're right." She managed a smile. "I'll call her and invite her to happy hour tonight with me and Samara."

Bellamy raised his eyebrows. "Is that your idea of a good time or a punishment?"

"Hey! Don't be a jerk. You know damn well that Samara and I know how to have a good time." Or they had up until their respective responsibilities caught up with them—just like they always did. She sighed. "On second thought, if she hasn't already skipped town, I'll take her out to lunch tomorrow."

"That's a better idea." His smile died. "We won't let him win, Jo. I know it feels like Anderson and I aren't doing anything while he zeroes in on you, but we are."

That's what she was afraid of. When they were children, she and Anderson had intentionally drawn their father's wrath to keep him away from their younger siblings, to shield them from having to grow up making the choices—the sacrifices—required to keep each other safe. At eight, Bellamy already knew his role in their fucked-up little family. Protect Eliza. She was too young to handle anything Elliott could level at her, and too young to have the control necessary to escape the worst of his wrath.

One look at his face was all she needed to recognize that Bellamy wouldn't be standing in the background this time. "You let me and Anderson handle it, okay?" Her phone buzzed and she cursed. "Damn it, it's Mother."

"Are you going to answer?"

"No." She sent the call the voice mail. Journey didn't

have anything to tell her that wouldn't send her mother into a murderous rage. After they had taken care of their father, she would let their mother in on just what the bastard had planned, and how they'd managed to circumvent him.

To do anything else was to invite ruin.

She walked toward the elevator and cursed when her phone buzzed again. *I swear to God, Mother...* Journey froze at the unknown number. Better to let it go to voice mail, but... "Hello?"

Her father's voice slithered through the line. "Quite a long lunch you took today."

Her heart skipped a beat. "I had a meeting."

"Lies don't become you, sweetheart. I had hoped your mother would raise you better than to shirk work for a man, but then you've always had a habit of letting me down, haven't you?"

She flinched. If she concentrated, she could hear the sound of the belt slapping his palm as he crossed the room toward where she cowered, his expression remorseful. *You've let me down again, sweetheart.*

Then the rest of his words penetrated. He knew where she'd been—who she'd been with—and intentionally used the familiar threat... "You leave Frank the hell alone, Elliott. He has nothing to do with this."

"He made his choice when he stepped into a situation that was none of his business." He laughed softly. "Almost quitting time. I wonder if that low-rent boyfriend of yours managed to make it back to the office without a problem. He doesn't exactly work in the safest part of town."

Even after all these years, she could read between the lines. He wouldn't bring up Frank without a very specific reason. *Frank's smart and capable and he would never let my father get the drop on him. Except he's focusing on protecting* me, *not on watching his own back.*

No, you're being paranoid. He's just grandstanding to throw you off. Frank isn't in any danger.

Is he?

She cleared her throat and put as much cool confidence into her tone as she could. "Is there a point to this conversation, Elliott? Or did you just call to make vague threats?"

"I would never threaten, sweetheart. Words only work when there's action to back them up."

How many times had she heard him say that exact thing? Too many. As much as Elliott liked to threaten and manipulate, he loved using his fists even more. Or a belt. Or whatever lay close at hand, the more creative the better.

Journey's stomach clenched, and she forced herself to punch the button to call the elevator, to step inside the open doors, to take it down to the lobby. Every instinct screamed at her to run to her office, to throw the lock, to curl up on her couch with the lights off until the shaking passed and she felt moderately in control again.

She didn't have the luxury of breaking down now. Not if her father was threatening what she thought he was threatening. "If you do anything to him, I will—"

"You'll do what you've always done, sweetheart," he cut in. "You'll curl up and take it, because you are weak and that's what the weak do."

"I am *not* fucking weak." The words felt like a lie on her tongue, but her fear for Frank kept her moving. Journey hurried out of the elevator and into the lobby, half expecting that this was all some elaborate game and that *she* was the intended victim. But no, there was no one around except the two men Frank had assigned to watch over her.

Does Frank have a security detail for himself?

Damn it, you know he didn't assign one.

"I'd appreciate you not taking that tone with your father." He sounded as pleasant as if sitting down for afternoon tea. "A man like Frank is beneath you, sweetheart. He can dress himself up in all the three-piece suits he wants, but it doesn't change who he is. Trash. He might have convinced the rest of Houston into thinking he's something to be feared, but trash always gets taken out eventually. He will, too."

"You're bluffing." He *had* to be bluffing.

"You know better." He hummed a little under his breath.

Her throat spasmed. "If you did something to him—"

"I have no idea what you're going on about, sweetheart. *I* was merely calling to point out that if you're going to be predictable and insist on meeting your...boyfriend...at a hotel in the middle of the day, someone will take notice. And that someone might not be as kind and loving as I am. They may very well snatch one or both of you off the street. If that were to happen...I can't stand the thought of what would happen then."

"Sure sounds like you've given it at least some thought," she gritted out. Frank's men jumped to their feet as she strode toward them, and she jerked her chin toward the street. "You won't get away with this, Elliott. I won't let you." *Frank has to be okay. He* has *to be. I don't know what I'll do if Frank's not okay.*

"I would never hurt someone you care about,

sweetheart. That's something only a monster would do."
He laughed a little. "Enjoy the rest of your night." Elliott
hung up.

One of the men stepped forward. José, she thought his
name was. "Problem?"

"Take me to Frank. There's trouble." Frank might be
okay right now, but it didn't mean he'd stay that way.
Elliott didn't bluff. Something about Frank had gotten
under his skin, and he would scratch at that itch until
he demolished it.

Until he demolished Frank.

Frank wouldn't bend like Journey. It wasn't in his
nature, and Elliott had to know that. No, her father would
go straight for breaking him. She could pretend Frank
would see him coming a mile away, but Journey had
thrown Frank off his game today. He would be distracted,
and Elliott was smart enough to use that against him.
To hurt him.

To kill him?

She wouldn't put anything past her father, not once
he'd fixated on an enemy.

I have to get to him. I have to get to him now.

She headed for the doors, José on her heels. He caught
her arm as they hit the sidewalk. "Ethan is bringing the
car around."

She started to say they didn't have time for that but
forced herself to stop and think. Flagging down a taxi might
mean action right now, but it would take time they couldn't
afford to waste. Ethan was one of Frank's men. He had just
as much interest in keeping Frank safe as she did.

On that note . . .

Her hands shook as she dialed Frank's number. *Please*

pick up, please be okay, please don't have let him hurt you. She almost cried out with relief when he answered in a low tone. "Duchess? Is everything okay?"

"Where are you?"

Instantly, the hint of softness disappeared from his voice. "At the office."

"Stay there." His office had to be safe. Frank was too smart to work in anything other than what qualified as a fortified building. "I'm on my way. Just…stay there."

"What happened?"

She couldn't answer that without getting into Elliott's call, and if Frank thought Journey was in danger, he would ignore her warning and come for her. *Which will play right into Elliott's hands.* Maybe. The problem was that she didn't know *what* her father's plans were.

Her heart beat in time with her panicked thoughts. "Promise me you'll stay at the office. Ethan is driving us there. We're on our way."

Silence for a beat. Two. "Okay, Duchess. I'll be here waiting."

It was as good as she was going to get. "Thank you." She ended the call as a black SUV pulled up to the curb in front of her, Ethan at the wheel. José opened the back door for her, and Journey slid in. She stared at her phone the entire trip to Frank's office. A live snake in her hand would have been less dangerous.

At any moment, her father could call to gloat that he'd done exactly what he threatened, that he'd drawn Frank out of his office and removed him from the equation. *That he took out the trash.* Frank was trash? The very idea would have been laughable if she didn't have panic beating frantic wings inside her. Frank was the best of men. Ruthless, yes. Ambitious, without a doubt. But with a core of goodness that anyone who dealt with him for any length of time could see.

It had just taken Journey a little longer than most.

She slipped her phone into her purse and stared out the window, silently counting down the blocks to Evans Inc's building. Journey had never been there before, but she knew where it was located—*everyone* knew where it was located. Including Elliott, no doubt.

As they pulled up to the sidewalk, Frank stepped out of the doors and strode to the car. Journey muttered a curse under her breath even as she drank in the sight of him. No injuries. He was there and he was safe and Elliott hadn't gotten to him.

Yet.

Frank yanked open the door and stuck his head in. The relief on his face would have been comical under any other circumstances. "You're okay."

"Get in here." She grabbed a fistful of his shirt and towed him into the backseat with her. Journey didn't take a full breath until he shut the door behind him, and even then, she was too aware of how exposed they were sitting here on the street. They could go back to her apartment or to his...but ultimately they would be vulnerable. *Frank* would be vulnerable. "I need to get out of town," she blurted.

He sat back and looked at her. Those dark eyes missed nothing. "He threatened you."

No, he threatened you. If she told him the truth, he would brush her off. Frank had power in spades and he wasn't stupid or complacent...but he wouldn't expect Elliott. No one expected Elliott.

She couldn't tell Frank the truth. Not yet.

But if he wouldn't go to great lengths to protect himself... maybe he would to protect *her*.

She took an unsteady breath. "Yes."

Frank leaned forward. "Ethan, take a roundabout route to Journey's apartment. We'll be inside long enough to pack and then we're heading to the airport."

Thank God. She grabbed his hand. "My family has a place in the Hamptons. It's safe, and it'll get us—me—out of town for a few days." Long enough to figure out the next step without having a target painted on Frank's chest.

An insufficient Band-Aid to a very large problem, but she wouldn't be able to breathe until she knew he was safe—*really* safe.

He gave her another of those long looks. "That will work." Frank typed out a quick text on his phone and then pulled Journey closer to tuck her beneath his arm. The warmth of his big body reassured her better than anything else could. "I have new security being installed in your building, and it will be ready in a few days. He won't get to you again—not like he did before. I'll make sure of it. I'll keep you safe, Duchess."

"Okay," she murmured. Journey laid her head on his shoulder, making plans of her own. *I won't let him hurt you, Frank. No matter what it takes, I'll keep you safe, too.*

CHAPTER THIRTEEN

Frank didn't realize that Journey had made alternative plans with Ethan until the man drove them to a private hangar at the airport. The plane sitting outside it wasn't overly flashy as such things went, but there was no mistaking the King family jet. He pinned Journey with a look. "This isn't necessary." One thing Frank had never bothered to put money into was private transportation like this. It was easy enough to book an independent company for any traveling he needed to do, and he made a habit of resisting the urge to prove that he had the biggest dick in the room by making new-money purchases on things like jets and stupidly expensive cars and the like.

"On the contrary, it's entirely necessary. As he's more than proven by this point, Elliott isn't above bribing people to do his dirty work. This plane is owned by my mother, and the staff is hers."

He hated to burst her bubble, but Frank still didn't know what had caused her reaction today. He'd left her in the hotel, looking a little lost and a little confused, and now she was sitting next to him, practically vibrating with nervous energy and shooting him looks like she wasn't quite sure he was real. "Duchess, everyone has a price."

Journey rolled her eyes. "Yes, I'm aware of that. Just trust me on this—the staff of the plane isn't bribable. Not by Elliott, anyway." She opened the door and climbed out. "I'm sure you have calls to make, so you might as well do it now while you have some privacy. I have to talk to the pilot." She strode to the stairway leading to the plane's door and disappeared inside, leaving him staring after her.

He'd seen Journey King weak and flailing. He'd seen her drunk and laughing her ass off. He'd seen her coolly professional as she gave a presentation.

He'd never seen her take charge so efficiently before.

There was no doubt from the moment she picked him up outside his office. It wasn't like the last time her father cornered her, where she'd needed Frank to step in and bolster her strength. Everything from her tone to the way she held herself was different this time.

He didn't know why.

The entire drive to her apartment, he'd braced himself for her to come apart at the seams, to need him to hold her together. It never happened. When they arrived, she'd turned into a whirlwind, throwing together a small bag, and then muscling Frank into the elevator and down to a waiting car. All the while, acting like there were snipers on the roofs and boogeymen lurking just out of sight.

There was definitely something going on that she hadn't told him about.

With a muffled curse, he called Mateo. The man answered instantly. "You okay, Frank? You went outside and never came back."

"There was an incident."

Silence for a beat. Two. "Do you need backup?"

"No, I have it handled." There was no reason to think Elliott would follow them to the Hamptons—not when his plan was based so heavily in Houston. It gave them the window of time they needed to get security in place without Frank worrying about Journey. "I have the security being reconstructed in Journey King's building, so I need you to put someone on it until it's completed."

"I'll oversee it personally."

"Thanks, Mateo." He glanced out the window, but Journey hadn't reappeared yet. "Ethan."

The man nodded and got out of the car to head into the plane. Frank trusted his men with his life—with Journey's life—but he'd found out the hard way that it was better not to let the left hand know what the right hand was up to. "You didn't get a chance to update me before I was called away. Anything useful?"

"Not quite. A string of mistresses longer than my left leg. Two look like they were paid to abort his love child, and one disappeared off the face of the earth after he was done with her. I'm looking into the circumstances around that—if she disappeared or if she *disappeared*."

Knowing what he did of Elliott, none of that surprised him. "Who paid them off?"

"Wasn't his wife. She doesn't seem to give a damn who *he* fucks as long as he stays the hell out of Houston. Nearly impossible to track the funds because they came from an offshore account, but my money is on Elliott's mother, Esther Bancroft. She's one mean lady, and fiercely protective of her little monster."

It might be a pressure point to examine. If they could

convince Esther Bancroft that Elliott was up to no good in Houston, she might pull funding until he fell in line. It was a long shot, but they couldn't afford to ignore a potential solution. One never knew how things would shake out. "Keep digging. A man with his habits and history hasn't kept his nose clean all these years. There's something we can use. We just have to find it."

"Sure thing, boss." Mateo hesitated. "You coming back to the office today?"

"I'm taking an unscheduled trip. I'll be back in a few days, but I'll be in contact the entire time."

Mateo very carefully didn't ask *why* he was taking an unscheduled trip. Or point out that Frank didn't do unscheduled—not when he had as many balls in the air as he currently did. "You want me to move your meeting with Jacob about Cocoa's to early next week?"

"Yeah." He looked up as Journey strode back down the stairs and headed toward the SUV. "I've got to go. Keep me updated."

"Will do."

He hung up and joined her outside. Frank ran a critical eye over her. She'd changed in her apartment and now wore black leggings and a long shirt that hit her around midthigh. She was flushed, but aside from the looks she kept shooting at the other hangars, she didn't seem much the worse for wear. "Now's a good time to tell me what the fuck is going on."

"I'll tell you when we're in the air. Come on. Ethan got the suitcases, so the only thing missing is you." She took his arm and tugged him behind her.

Frank allowed it, his mind whirling to click the pieces together with each step he took. It wasn't until the plane door closed behind him and the tension bled out of Journey's shoulders that he understood. "He didn't threaten you."

She dropped into a seat and waited for him to take the one opposite. Journey leaned forward and shook her head. "No, he didn't threaten me."

The plane jerked into motion. Frank shot a look at the window and gritted his teeth at the sight of the pavement running past. "What did your father say, Duchess?"

"He knew about this afternoon." She wouldn't quite meet his gaze. "And he's furious. He isn't the type to issue explicit threats, but he came closer than I've ever heard him today." She finally looked at him, her hazel eyes filled with too many things. "He'll kill you, Frank. Or make you disappear."

"I'm not going to be brought down by the likes of Elliott King." Better men than him had tried and failed, but telling her as much now wouldn't accomplish a damn thing.

She shook her head. "You're not listening to me. He won't come at you in a fair fight. He'll play on your weaknesses—he'll use someone you care about to get your guard down—and that's when he'll strike. You can't defend against an attack you don't see coming."

Frank sat back, shock temporarily stealing his ability to respond. This wasn't about a threat leveled at Journey like he'd thought. She was reacting differently because, this time, the perceived danger was for *Frank*.

She frowned. "Are you okay? You've got a weird look on your face."

"Your father didn't threaten you again. He threatened me."

Guilt flared across her features, but she set her jaw in a way he was coming to recognize. She wasn't sorry that she'd let him believe she was the intended victim in the most recent threat—and she'd probably do it again if given half a chance. Journey lowered her voice, but she didn't look away. "I won't let him hurt you. Not because of me. Not at all."

"You don't have to protect me, Duchess."

She didn't blink. "If I don't, who will?"

Frank didn't have an answer for that. He didn't know if there *was* an answer for that. People didn't protect him. He protected his people. He was the one who'd fought tooth and nail for power to be able to do so. Because he'd looked around after his father was arrested and realized that if he waited for a savior, he'd be waiting his entire life.

Their world looked at people like him a certain way, and he'd never be able to change anyone's prejudices by being a good person. No, the only way people changed was because they were forced to, and the only thing capable of *that* was power.

If Frank's father had the kind of power he now wielded, maybe things would have fallen out differently. Then again, maybe not. He'd been a black man on trial for killing his white mistress—in Texas. If there was ever a deck stacked against someone, it had been stacked against Henry Evans.

But if he'd been powerful enough, maybe those charges wouldn't have landed in the first place. Those assholes wouldn't have dared put him on trial with nothing but circumstantial evidence.

Henry Evans was determined to be a real-life superhero. Larger than life and putting the wealth and influence he'd worked his ass off to acquire to good use to help those who couldn't help themselves. In his ideal world, that was the only logical course for rich men to take—to give a hand up to those who needed it, who could spend their entire lives fighting and never make it to the next tier. People had loved him for it. *Frank* had loved him for it.

And it was all a lie. His saintly father was fucking his secretary, and then, when she threatened to go public with it, their fight ended with the woman dead at the bottom of a staircase. It didn't matter that Henry hadn't pushed her—that she'd lost her footing and fell. The jury didn't give a fuck. Neither did the media. They saw their chance to take him down—a black man who'd gotten uppity and threatened the status quo that Houston's elite fought so hard to maintain—and they gleefully took it. All while Frank and his mother were forced to watch as their life was dismantled, piece by piece.

His father had single-handedly ruined their family, and Frank learned an invaluable lesson. The world wanted to see men like him burn for simply being born with a darker tone of skin. One mistake was enough to knock his father off the tightrope he walked, and a lifetime of good deeds didn't hold water in comparison. The only way to keep himself and the people he cared for safe was to accrue power. To shove his presence in the faces of those who wanted to crush him beneath their boots. To make his existence impossible to ignore. To make him fucking untouchable.

If his father had learned that lesson, he wouldn't have died in a prison shower.

His mother wouldn't have spent years fleeing the heartbreak she never got over—right up until it killed her.

"I don't need anyone to protect me."

Journey gave him that sad little smile that made his chest ache. "Everyone needs protection sometimes."

* * *

Journey's phone rang as they turned onto the long drive that would lead to the Hamptons house. She'd been expecting the call, and there was no point in trying to put it off. "Anderson."

"Funny story. I get out of a hellish meeting with Elliott only to be informed by Bellamy that you took *Frank Evans* to the Hamptons house. Jo, it's Monday. What are you doing?" He lowered his voice. "We can't afford to make a misstep right now. Elliott is playing a deeper game than I expected, and I don't know if I can block his moves as well as I'd hoped. He just informed Eliza that she's going to marry Asher fucking Bishop to help secure a merger with Cardinal Energy."

What are you up to, Elliott? "He can't coordinate a merger without board approval."

"He *has* board approval." Anderson cursed. "We only hold two spots—Bellamy isn't even on the board of directors. While we were focusing on Elliott showing up, he's already managed to turn the majority of the board to support him. They voted on it this morning."

"Fuck."

"That about sums it up."

The rest of what her brother said caught up with her. "Wait, back up. Why the hell would Eliza have to *marry* him? This isn't medieval Europe. We don't have to barter our sister to secure a business deal. He just signs on the dotted line and that's that." She was oversimplifying, but the fact still stood that there wasn't a damn reason to turn her sister into an unwilling bride. Because Eliza *was* unwilling—there was no way she'd agree to that unless she was under duress.

"It might be as simple as getting her out of the way. I don't know. I just don't fucking know." Anderson cursed. "I'm in over my head, Jo. I can't be everywhere at once, and every time I turn around, another thing I've fought to protect is being thrown to the wolves."

She pulled up in front of the house and held up a finger to keep Frank in his seat. Journey climbed out and shut the door, walking several steps away from the car. "He threatened Frank."

"Why the hell would he decide it was a good idea to fuck with Frank Evans? He's risking alienating a potential ally. Frank's allegiance is to Beckett—always has been."

Oh right, I didn't tell him. Guilt flared, and she did her best to ignore it. "I'm dating Frank. I didn't exactly make it public knowledge for obvious reasons, but Elliott made a surprise visit to my apartment last Friday, and Frank happened to show up around the same time."

Silence reigned. She paced away from the car and back again. Every instinct demanded she start talking—babbling—and try to explain herself to avoid her brother's anger. Or, worse, his disappointment. She didn't. Anderson might get pissed sometimes, but it was only on her behalf. *He* would never hurt her, and even if fighting with him was the last thing she wanted to do, she would do it if it meant keeping him safe.

He couldn't go after their father directly. She'd originally concocted this plan for fear that Anderson would
kill their father and pay the consequences. Now, Journey
couldn't shake the belief that if Anderson challenged
Elliott, their father would kill *him*.

She had to keep him out of it.

"Andy, talk to me."

The use of her childhood nickname for him had him
cursing all over again. "He was at your place."

At first she thought he meant Frank, but realization
stopped her in her tracks. "Nothing happened. Frank
arrived before... Well, I don't know what he planned, but
Frank ran him off." *Because I couldn't. Because I wasn't
strong enough.*

"Stay in the Hamptons, Jo. I'll cover for you."

Oh, she didn't like this turn. She didn't like it one
bit. Journey clutched the phone to her ear. "Don't do
something you can't take back. Promise me."

"No." He paused. "I'm not going to take him out into the
Gulf and toss him off that fucking boat of his. Yet. But I
want you out of this. Stay there until I deal with him."

Fat chance of that. She hadn't been thinking back
in Houston—just reacting. Her first instinct was to get
Frank somewhere safe and out of her father's reach.
That didn't mean they were going to stay safely tucked
away while someone else fought her battles—again. "I'm
coming home in a couple days," she said gently. "I'm not
sitting this one out."

Anderson sighed. "I don't suppose there's anything I
can say to get you to stay out there."

"There's not. I'm sorry I left so unexpectedly, but..."
She glanced at the car, not the least bit surprised to

find Frank's gaze on her. "They could have killed him. Because of his connection to *me*. That makes him my responsibility." It didn't matter that Frank wouldn't agree. It was the damn truth.

"Some other time, we're going to talk about the fact that you're dating Frank fucking Evans and didn't bother to tell me." The sound of a door opening and closing in the background. "I have to go put out some fires."

"I'm still taking my meetings for the week via conference call."

"I thought you were taking vacation days." His voice warmed, and she could perfectly picture his smile. "Make sure you get out to the beach while you're up there. Might as well take what enjoyment you can before you come back to this shit show."

She laughed softly. "It's February."

"Still."

"I will. I promise."

"Call if you need anything."

"Same goes for you." She waited for him to hang up and then turned back to look at the eyesore that was their Hamptons house. Oh, it was a study in perfect lines and expensive taste, from the grounds unfurling on either side of the looping driveway to the perfectly manicured landscaping on the back side of the house that led down to the perfect private beach. Inside was even more luxurious, every piece handpicked by her mother. It was just…too much. She had so many good memories here, but it was hard to forget that she was King first and everything else dead last when faced with the physical representation of her family's absurd wealth and history.

Journey checked her watch. She had an hour before her last meeting of the day, and she fully expected some kind of contact from her father once he discovered that she'd used the company jet without asking permission.

Frank climbed out of the car and moved around to the trunk to grab their luggage. One look from him told her not to bother offering to help. Why would she? He wasn't just a man. He was Frank Evans the Untouchable. A man who didn't need help from someone like Journey.

And, damn it, that stung.

She pressed her lips together and focused on following Frank up the front steps of the house. Her adrenaline high had worn off sometime in the last hour or so, and she needed a few minutes to center herself and figure out what happened next. As soon as Frank had time to do the same, there would be yet another battle over the fact that she'd had the audacity to mislead him in order to protect him.

At least she could look forward to *that* argument. The man might infuriate her more often than not, but going round after round with Frank gave her equal parts enjoyment and frustration—at least before the events that brought Elliott Bancroft to Houston. She wanted that back, wanted to meet him on equal ground instead of being this quivering, weak thing that she'd become.

I don't know how to do this.

Stop overthinking. It never did a damn bit of good anyway.

Frank opened the door and raised an eyebrow. "Secure."

"Give me a little credit. I called the service we use to keep this property maintained and asked them to freshen up the place before we landed." She jerked a thumb over her shoulder. "Did you think I just keep a car at the airport indefinitely?"

"I wouldn't put anything past the Kings." The comment held no heat, though. He stepped into the house, leaving Journey to follow him.

She pointed to the bottom of the stairs. "Leave the suitcase there." Journey didn't wait to see if he'd follow her command. She just strode past him and down the wide hallway leading deeper into the house. She'd left detailed instructions with the staff—she didn't want anyone here for the duration of their stay. The company that maintained the house and property were known for their utmost discretion, but it would be all too easy for Elliott to slide into the spot left by Lydia and take over their loyalty.

The kitchen was her favorite part of the house. It was stupidly oversized—just like everything else— but the white-on-white color scheme, combined with massive windows that overlooked the ocean, created a calming effect. One of the windows could be opened garage door–style so food could be served directly from the kitchen to the outdoor lounge and let in the ocean breeze. Journey bypassed it and pulled open the fridge and freezer. "Good."

She felt more than heard Frank come to stand at her back. He didn't touch her, but with the cold blast of air from the fridge, she fancied she could feel the heat rising from his body. "I'm going to get food started. Why don't you go upstairs to the office and start working through the couple dozen phone calls we both know you're dying to make?"

Silence for a beat. Two. Finally he said, "You have a security system in this place?"

"Yes."

"Set it." His footsteps sounded, leading back the way they'd come in.

Journey closed her eyes and allowed herself a single inhale and exhale before she moved to obey. There were far too many windows in the house to withstand anything resembling an attack, but with the system armed, at least they would get warning.

You sound like you're going to war.

Isn't that exactly what's happening?

CHAPTER FOURTEEN

Journey lost herself in the methodical motions of measuring and cooking. She got chicken marinating in the fridge and chopped the veggies to roast. Since Frank still wasn't downstairs by the time she finished prepping for dinner, she whipped up a batch of her brownies and slid them into the oven just in time to take the scheduled conference call. She got the laptop going and keyed in her information to start the call and then threw the bowl and utensils in the sink while she waited for the other two participants to connect.

Ronnie arrived first. She blinked into the camera, her close-cropped black hair making her dark eyes seem even larger on her face than they actually were. "Where are you? Anderson said you had to take an emergency trip, but he didn't deign to drop any other details."

"That's because it's none of your business, snoop." She laughed, sliding into her workplace persona with ease. It helped that she liked Ronnie. The woman ran the tech department for the company, and she had earned the position at a younger age than anyone else in Kingdom Corp history.

Ronnie didn't get a chance to reply before George appeared in a third video, his expression as dour as ever. "Ladies."

"George," Journey answered for both of them, which was just as well. If Ronnie and George could manage to spend more than two seconds in the same space without sniping at each other, this call wouldn't be necessary in the first place. "Why don't we get right into the thick of it? What's the problem this time?"

"Ronnie's department is over budget this quarter—again." A pleased glint appeared in his blue eyes, which didn't bode well. "Seeing as how that's the third quarter in a row, Mr. Bancroft has given me permission to lay off ten people within the department."

"You can fuck right off with that noise, George!"

"Ronnie, enough." Journey inflected steel into her tone, and the other woman went silent, though she obviously wasn't happy about it. Fine. She could be pissed. Journey was pretty fucking pissed right now, too. She stared hard at George. "You know as well as I do that all layoff orders come from *me*. Not from Elliott. He's not the CEO, no matter what he's acting like at the moment, so you might want to wipe that smug look off your face, George."

"If that bastard lays off one of my people, we all walk. See how he likes *that*," Ronnie snarled.

She could actually see the framework that held Kingdom Corp together shaking. This would be the first casualty when the wave broke, but it wouldn't be the last. Elliott might have the power, but he obviously didn't know shit about running this company or he wouldn't have played things like this.

Unless he wants *it to explode so he can blame me for it.*

She had held her anger at a slow boil since getting the call about Frank, but it ratcheted up several degrees in response to her suspicion. She'd worked too damn hard to let him take Kingdom Corp from her. Oh, she was sure Beckett's offer to hire her and her siblings still stood—he was the kind of guy who wouldn't go back on his word— but *that* company wasn't hers. It wasn't the place she'd fought on behalf of for her entire life. It was as much her family as her actual family was.

She had to do something, and she had to do it now.

"George, we both know for a fact that engineering is under budget this quarter. Take the excess from them and spread it around as necessary to cover the tech department. Assure them that it's a temporary situation and they'll be compensated accordingly. I'll set up a meeting with Jenna to discuss it next week." She held up a hand when he went to speak. "I want you to think very carefully about the words you're about to say. If they're going to further inflame this situation without offering a useful solution, I highly suggest you keep them to yourself."

He clamped his mouth shut and glared at her. *Thank God.* She nodded. "Good. In that case, we'll go over financials once I'm back in the office. Under no circumstances are you to enact any orders from my father without running them past either Anderson or myself first." She swallowed hard. "Until he does or does not take an official role within the company, he has no authority and will be treated as such." She'd pay for that order. She had no illusions about *that*. It didn't matter. Journey could take whatever damage her father dealt.

Kingdom Corp couldn't.

"Ronnie, I want a full financial workup explaining

how this happened." She ignored the betrayal on the other woman's face. "You have a budget, and part of your job is working within it. If it's not an appropriate budget, we can revisit it, but going over is out of the question. If you do it another quarter, then something has to give. Do you understand?"

Ronnie reluctantly nodded. "I'll put together the report for you."

"Thank you." She looked at both of them. "Is there anything else requiring my immediate attention?" After they both gave a negative, she closed out the call and stood back with a slow exhale. That hadn't gone as well as she would have liked, but it was far from the worst situation she'd had to muscle her way through. The next step was smoothing Ronnie's ruffled feathers, and getting George's head in the game instead of on the layoffs he'd been deprived off, but both of those things could wait. They needed to stew a little bit in the meantime, otherwise she risked undermining her authority.

The oven dinged, drawing her back to the present. She frowned at the clock above the microwave. Frank had been upstairs a seriously long time at this point.

She pulled the brownies out of the oven, set them aside to cool, and then rushed upstairs. The room she'd set Frank up in was empty, but faint light shone beneath the bathroom door. Journey hesitated for all of a second before she turned the door handle and strode into the bathroom.

And stopped short.

Frank was in the shower.

She stared at the outline of his big body, only slightly distorted through the clear curtain. He had his hands braced on the tiled wall and his head bowed beneath the spray. She couldn't actually see the lines of water lovingly tracing the muscles of his back, but Journey had no problem mentally tracing those same lines.

The absolutely insane desire to strip off her clothes and join him in the water rose, and she had to clench her hands to keep from doing exactly that. She'd all but kidnapped the man and brought him to another state. Her father wanted him dead in the most literal way. There were a thousand things she should be doing right this second to ensure that the world didn't fall out from beneath them, and jumping into the shower with Frank didn't number among them.

No matter how much she wanted to.

I need to get dinner in the oven. Yes. That's what I need to do. And maybe if she took a couple of minutes, she could regain the equilibrium she'd been missing since all this began.

Too bad she didn't like her odds all that much.

* * *

In the hours since they'd arrived at the house, Frank had managed to get through two rescheduled meetings about property he'd recently acquired, answer two dozen emails, and shower. Every once in a while, he'd hear Journey downstairs puttering around, a check-in that relaxed him in a way that he wasn't prepared to deal with. Later, when the fate of their little corner of the world wasn't hanging in the balance, he'd examine his complicated feelings for Journey King at length.

Now wasn't the time or the place for it. He'd just pulled

his shirt over his head when his phone rang. He glanced at the screen. This conversation had been coming from the second he agreed to help Journey. "Hey, Beck."

"It's time you're straight with me, Frank. I'm willing to give you the benefit of the doubt because of our history and our friendship, but only if you stop dicking me around now."

He bit back a sigh. "I'm not intentionally keeping things from you."

"Bullshit. You drop me a cryptic phone call about Journey King, and then, next thing I know, Samara tells me that you're dating her. The timelines don't match up, because you sure as fuck would have told me if you were dating my cousin while my aunt was trying to have me killed."

No use arguing with that. He never really intended to. It had taken Beck a little longer than Frank expected to put it all together, but he was understandably distracted with his new woman and running Morningstar Enterprise. "I have things under control."

"Of that, I have no doubt." Beck hesitated. "Shit, Frank. When I was in trouble, you didn't hesitate to drop everything and help me. Obviously something's going on with Kingdom Corp and you're neck deep in the mess. My cousins won't ask me for help, but I damn well expect you to."

Despite everything, he smiled. He enjoyed the fuck out of his friendship with Beckett King. Even when the rest of his life had gone to shit in the worst way possible, Beck remained the one true thing that he could set his compass by. They didn't talk about their teen years much, about when Beck was still reeling from his mother's death and clashing weekly with his father, or when Frank had watched *his* old man taken away in cuffs and had to weather the media shit storm that rose in the aftermath. Or the fact that Frank's mother had chosen to let death take her, rather than fight to stay in the world with her son.

But they'd been there for each other through it, constants in each other's lives in the way they couldn't be in their own.

He pinched the bridge of his nose. "You know Elliott Bancroft is back."

"Yeah." The anger changed in Beck's voice, becoming colder. "He paid me a visit today, all smiles and charm, wanting to put the sins of the past to rest and all that bullshit."

"What did he want with you and Morningstar?"

Beck laughed, but not like anything was funny. "To partner up to usher in a new age where Kingdom Corp and Morningstar Enterprise are the behemoth that crushes anything in its path. He didn't say merger, but it was there between the lines."

"He didn't think you would agree to that."

It wasn't a question, but Beck answered all the same. "I didn't get the impression that he was particularly torn up when I told him to kick rocks, but I'm still keeping an eye on my key employees in case he decides to pull a page from Lydia's playbook and poach someone." The slightest of pauses. "We aren't talking about me, though—we're talking about you and my cousin."

Frank hadn't really thought he'd get away with that subject change, but it didn't hurt to try. "She's in trouble, Beck. Big trouble. I agreed to help when I thought it was merely business, but best I can tell, Elliott is setting up to actually hurt her—not just remove her as COO." He walked to the vanity that was set up opposite the bed. "Apparently the bastard took exception to me personally, because he's decided to focus his threats on me and Journey for the time being, rather than on the rest of his children."

"He's threatening *you*?"

"Yeah. It's nothing I can't handle, though." He cleared his throat. "Be careful, Beck. Whatever hard-on Elliott has for the Kings might not extend to you, but you can't know that."

"Save some of that worry for yourself. Elliott is a concern, but if you break Journey's heart, Samara will go on a warpath. Take it from me—you don't want that."

No, he didn't. He liked Samara, and he didn't want to cause her unnecessary grief. He couldn't even defend himself without exposing that things were more complicated than he wanted to admit. This might have started out as a fake relationship, but he and Journey had muddied the waters beyond repair. "I'll keep that in mind."

He ended the call and went in search of the woman in question. Sounds in the kitchen drew him in, and Frank stopped just outside the doorway and watched the one-woman whirlwind. She dashed some unidentified spice onto the dish on the counter and then swung around to slide it into the oven. Then she was off, snagging two wineglasses in one hand and a bottle in the other.

She turned and startled. "Jeez, Frank, you're as quiet as a cat." Journey made a face. "Well, as a traditional cat. Every single cat I've ever owned has been clinically insane and vocal about it."

Her frenetic energy drew him in despite himself,

dousing his questions for the time being, and he walked through the kitchen to the bar stools set up opposite the peninsula from where she worked. "How many cats are we talking about?"

She held up the wine bottle and set a glass in front of him when he inclined his head. "Four cats, all owned individually. The first was Cletus, which was our family cat when I was six." The light died in her eyes, but she shook her head and poured him a healthy glass of wine. "He liked to wander the halls at night and sing the song of his people until he woke up the entire household. My father killed him, though we told Eliza that he was going on grand adventures to keep her from feeling too bad about it. She didn't take his abandonment well, and Anderson caught her at the edge of the yard one night going out to search for him." She poured herself a glass of wine. "Then maybe we would have lost her, too."

Elliott killed their cat. *Fuck.* He tapped his finger on the marble countertop. "Lot of responsibility on you two, taking care of your younger siblings."

She laughed. "Really, Frank? I'm pretty sure you sprang from the womb as a fully grown human being, complete with impressive walls and that exact look on your face."

He didn't make a habit of thinking about his childhood up until age fifteen because the betrayal lay too damn thick over everything. If his old man had been content with what they had instead of trying to expand his influence—legit motivations or not—then maybe power wouldn't have gone to his head. Maybe he would have stayed faithful.

Or maybe it wouldn't have mattered in the end,

because the hounds of Houston would have come hunting at some point to set the balance right and remove Henry Evans from the picture, one way or another.

Frank wasn't sure what he believed, but it was a moot point all these years later.

There was such a hopeful aura about Journey, he couldn't shoot her down like he might have under other circumstances. "We had a dog when I was a kid. A mutt with the auspicious name of Gomez." The dog had preceded Frank's existence by a few years, and Gomez had become a partner in crime through all of his earliest memories. He'd buried Gomez himself when the old fellow died a peaceful death right before Frank turned twelve.

Journey's smile went wistful. "Did you two have a lot of grand adventures?"

"They seemed like it at the time."

"They always do." She walked over to check on a pan of what looked like brownies and then covered them with a plastic lid.

"You know, when I told Ethan to take us to the airport, I had a specific destination in mind." A property in Florida that he rarely visited, but kept up to date with the best security money could buy. A place he'd had every intention of convincing Journey to stay until he could deal with the growing threat back in Houston. When she finished her glass of wine in several large gulps and poured a second one, Frank considered how best to bring her around to the subject. He sighed. "Duchess...we're in the Hamptons."

She studied her wineglass. "Hmmm, yes."

That wasn't encouraging, but he couldn't seem to leave

this alone. "You went behind my back and conspired with my men to change the plans. You brought me to the Hamptons."

"You said that already." She sighed and set the glass down, meeting his gaze directly. "You were threatened, Frank. Because of me. He wants to *kill* you." She lifted her chin, her hazel eyes blazing. "He already took too much. He's not going to take you, too. I won't allow it."

Journey looked like some kind of avenging angel with that expression on her face, and he sat back. "You were worried about me." Not worried. Terrified and furious. She'd wanted to *protect* him. *Him.* Frank fucking Evans. The one who took care of the others around him. The one who'd worked so damn hard never to need protection again. "Duchess, I have it handled."

"You can lie to yourself, Frank, but you damn well better not lie to me. You *don't* have this handled any more than I do." She reached for her glass of wine. "And *that* is why we're in the Hamptons."

CHAPTER FIFTEEN

Journey had suffered through some awkward dinners in her life, but this one took the cake. Frank barely looked at her, as if her stating the obvious was some unforgivable sin he didn't know what to do with. That was fine. She didn't know what to do with their current situation, either. They were outgunned and outmanned and just flat-out outmaneuvered.

Again.

She picked at her food, but her chicken didn't offer up a neat solution. Instead, she kept going back to the shock on his face when he realized she'd brought him here to protect him. Shock, and something like anger. Because her protection didn't mean shit, and everyone knew it. She couldn't even protect herself. How would someone as strong and composed as Frank ever believe that she could protect *him*?

I'm damaged goods.

No matter how hard I fight, I'm never going to escape that label. Even with Frank.

She drained her second glass of wine and poured

another. Thank God for small favors—her stomach didn't rebel at the alcohol. She glanced up to find Frank studying his plate as if it held the answers to the universe. *I can't do this right now.*

"I'm going for a walk." Journey shoved to her feet, considered her glass, and then grabbed the wine bottle. She held up a hand despite the fact that Frank had made no move to follow. "I just need some space."

Still nothing.

Well, then, that was that. Journey remembered to de-activate the alarm at the last second, and then she pushed through the glass doors and out onto the patio. It wasn't enough distance—not when she could feel Frank's gaze on her back—so she charged forward to the path leading down to the beach. It was colder than Texas, and she welcomed the chill and the icy-feeling steps against her bare feet.

He didn't trust her.

She let loose a helpless laugh and took a long pull of the wine. Of course he didn't trust her. Even if she hadn't been an enemy before this whole thing started, she'd proven time and time again that when her father pushed just the right pressure point, she'd crumble. She *wasn't* trustworthy. Not to stand strong—sure as hell not strong enough to watch Frank's back.

I want to be.

She was trying. She'd gone to therapy—real therapy, not that shit show her father required—and had done all the exercises, read all the books. The kicker was that Journey *had* been healing. Her black spirals were further and further apart, her needing to call on Anderson dwindling until they had something resembling a more normal sibling relationship.

Until Elliott came back and shoved his presence into her safe space at every available opportunity, causing the memories to erode her strength and threaten to suck her under—for good this time.

She used her free hand to rub her bare arm against the chill that was rapidly progressing to downright cold. The empty beach dulled the sharpest of edges as she started walking. It was only a couple hundred yards long—plenty for a single private property—but it gave her space to move.

Frank knows what Elliott did to us.

She could still picture her ex's face when he realized the depth of what she'd suffered. Revulsion, anger, and pity all mixed up in what was a death knell for their relationship. The engagement hadn't lasted another month. His words rolled through her, the memory of how he wouldn't meet her gaze making her eyes burn even after all this time. *I can't fix you, Journey. I wouldn't even know where to start. The thing I liked about us was how uncomplicated we were and this…This is complicated.*

Complicated.

She snorted and took another, longer pull of wine. Complicated didn't begin to cover it. At least Frank never looked at her with pity. Anger, yes. Boatloads of anger, though it was rarely directed at *her*. Frustration aplenty. A healthy dose of lust.

Too much to ask for him to look at me with respect, I suppose.

"Duchess."

She startled and spun, sending sand flying. Frank stood a few feet away, his hands in his pockets. He eyed her as if trying to gauge her mood. *Well, that makes two of us.*

Finally he shook his head and shrugged out of his jacket. Before she realized his intent, he wrapped it around her shoulders and zipped it up, cutting her bare arms off from the cold wind coming from the ocean. It also trapped her wine bottle within the jacket, but she managed to extract it and get her arms into the sleeves without making an ass of herself.

And still Frank didn't say anything else.

Journey started to lift the bottle again but aborted the move halfway through. "I'm not going to walk into the ocean or anything stupid like that. You don't have to babysit me."

It was hard to see in the light of the crescent moon, but he might have raised his eyebrows. "I don't think you're suicidal, Duchess. I came out here to apologize."

She stared. "What do you have to apologize for?"

"I obviously gave you the wrong impression."

"No, I think you were pretty damn clear about what you thought of my ability to protect you." And, damn it, it stung. No matter how justified his belief was, she selfishly wanted *one* person in her life to believe she was capable of standing on her own—of standing between them and the monsters.

Frank turned to look out over the water. The moonlight played along the planes of his face, as if it couldn't resist touching him any more than she could. He sighed. "It's not personal."

That surprised a laugh from Journey. "Bullshit."

"What?"

"Bull. Shit," she bit out. "If I was Beckett—"

"If you were Beck, I'd react the same damn way." He crossed his arms over his chest and glared at her. "We each have a role to play in this life, Duchess. *I* protect. Beck wouldn't let me step in with your mother, and I value his friendship too much to shit on his wishes. He handled it, yeah, but he didn't ignore my offer of help out of sheer pride, either."

She waited for him to realize the irony of what he was saying, but he just kept watching her with that implacable look on his face. Journey dug her toes into the sand and huddled deeper into his jacket, letting the faint scent of him wrap around her like some kind of security blanket. There was something there, something in his voice...

The truth all but landed at her feet.

He thinks he *failed. It's not that I tried to protect him—he would be handling it as gracefully if* anyone *protected him.*

Relief swarmed her, leaving exhaustion in its wake. At the end of the day, it didn't matter if Frank didn't believe Journey could stand as an equal or if he legitimately didn't believe that *anyone* could stand as his equal. He'd reacted poorly, and she turned it around and made things all about her. As if her pain was the only thing that mattered.

Frank was more an enigma than anyone she'd ever met. Something happened to make him cling this tightly to the role of protector. *Not his father, though that was a fucked-up situation. It has to be his mother.* "Frank...what happened to her?"

He didn't pretend to misunderstand. What little openness he had left in his expression disappeared, transforming him back into the cold real estate mogul she'd first met. "Leave it alone, Duchess. That has nothing to do with anything." He shook his head and softened his tone. "Just...let it go."

Without another word, he turned and headed back toward the house, leaving her alone on the beach.

* * *

Frank knew Journey trailed him back to the house, but he didn't look back. Past and present clashed in a toxic mix inside him, Journey's sad determination melded with his mother's despair and eventual resignation. They weren't the same. His mother stopped fighting after his father went to prison. Between one day and the next, she gave up and became a shadow of the woman she'd been. Not even her teenage son could convince her that life was worth living once she took that first step—though Frank hadn't realized that truth until many years later. He couldn't have stopped her from making the choice she had, couldn't have *saved* her.

Different situation. Different circumstances.

Journey is a different woman.

For all her jagged edges, he couldn't imagine Journey slipping softly into death's dark embrace. She would fight until the bitter end, even if it was a losing battle. She wouldn't give up facing a sickness any more than she was giving up facing her own personal boogeyman. Elliott scared the shit out of her, knocked her down again and again, but she still climbed back to her feet and kept going forward, step by stumbling step.

Frank opened the sliding door and moved back to let Journey precede him. She shot him a look but walked into the house and set the bottle on the counter. He waited for her to rekey the alarm. Now was the time to head up to his room and reestablish the boundaries they'd trampled all over today. They couldn't be what each other needed, and muddying the waters further was a mistake. But when he opened his mouth, that wasn't what came out. "Come here."

"You sure?" Her mouth quirked, as if she'd tried to fake a smile and her face hadn't cooperated. "Because a hug might be too much like leaning on another person for you to stomach. I might crumble and then where would you be?"

Frank held out a hand and motioned her forward imperiously. "You aren't the only person with scars in this room, Duchess. Makes us prickly bastards, but we're stronger because of the pain we've gone through."

Still, she didn't move. She just stared at him with those big hazel eyes as if trying to read his mind. "I don't know what you're smoking, but I'm not stronger because of what I went through. Or did you miss that time I was curled in a ball on my floor because of a single fucking touch?"

Frank wished he could go back in time and deal with Elliott Bancroft at her apartment differently. The man hadn't shed nearly enough blood in payment for the damage he'd inflicted. "You survived, Journey. You kept living and didn't give up because of the hurt writhing around inside you. You're a successful professional, and you've managed to hold down at least a handful of healthy relationships with your siblings and with Samara. That's winning from where I'm sitting."

She looked at him like she'd never seen him before. "I don't understand you."

He didn't understand himself in that moment. It wasn't his job to fix Journey, but he'd gone from thinking she needed to be fixed to appreciating her jagged edges and wicked charm. She might be more complicated than most people he'd met, but she wasn't truly broken. No matter what she believed about herself.

Something I'd do well to remember. "Let me hold you."

Another hesitation, shorter this time. She took the two large steps between them cautiously, as if expecting him to rescind his command, and then slipped into his arms. She pressed her face against his chest, her soft words almost felt more than heard. "What happened to your mother, Frank?"

He tensed. He'd only meant to offer her comfort, to apologize again for being short with her. He didn't want to do *this*, didn't want to drag his old pain kicking and screaming from the box in the back of his mind where he'd kept it locked away for so many years.

Would she even understand if he tried to explain? Frank rested his chin on the top of her head. Journey had displayed her demons for him again and again. Maybe it was time he shared a few of his own, no matter how the words felt like shattered glass in his throat. "My old man didn't last a year in prison after his conviction. He was shivved in the shower about eight months into his sentence. He never got a chance to file the appeal that might have set him free." And while Henry Evans was a cheating asshole, he wasn't guilty of murder. An appeal might have meant freedom if he'd lived long enough to file it.

"Shit, Frank."

"Yeah." He hugged her tighter, inhaling the citrusy scent of her shampoo. "My mother just...gave up. She managed to hold down a job to pay the bills, but she checked out and nothing could check her back in." The first year or two, he'd done everything he could to snap her out of it. Part of him believed that if he was just good enough, she would come back to him. Solid grades, half a dozen scholarships and even more grants so she wouldn't have to worry about killing herself to pay for his college, not even a *hint* of trouble or girls or normal teenage bullshit. None of it mattered. "She was diagnosed with breast cancer the month after I left for college."

Getting the next part out was more difficult, the end of the story one that he didn't want to give voice to, as if he could change the way things happened by not talking about it. *Talk about it or not, the past is the past.* "She refused treatment. She just...resigned herself to dying. Within six months, she was gone." He hadn't found out until a week later that she'd kept current with her old life insurance policy—one that paid out to the tune of two million dollars. She might not have loved Frank enough to fight to live, but she'd loved him enough to ensure he was taken care of after she was gone.

Cold comfort, that.

"Jesus." Journey clenched him to her, as if she could squeeze away his past.

"It was a long time ago." Fifteen years, to be exact. It struck him that, in another couple of years, he'd have spent more of his life an orphan than he'd spent with parents. He smoothed a hand down her back. "Come to bed with me, Duchess."

She hesitated but finally nodded against his chest. "The only thing to do at this point is call the day to avoid it from getting worse." Journey stepped back and looked around the kitchen. "It doesn't *seem* like the ten plagues of Egypt are going to descend on us, but better safe than sorry."

"I don't know—the day isn't complete without a bunch of locusts making an appearance."

She jerked to a stop. "Did you just... You *did*."

"What?"

"You just made an honest-to-God joke. Again." She smiled. "Dang, Frank, I'm going to have to be careful. At this point, I actually *like* you, and you fuck like a dream. You aren't a secret duke or something, are you? Because the only way you could be more perfect was if there was a title involved." She strode away before he could answer, which was just as well. He didn't know how to respond to that.

He might look like the full package on paper, but the truth was that Frank was shallow. Barring Beck, his friendships were surface level and wouldn't withstand any amount of stress. He dated, but the specter of his parents' relationship hung over his head, a cloud he couldn't escape. Letting someone close like that, loving them with everything he had... All it did was open a person up for devastation. He chose relationships based on a genuine understanding of what he could and couldn't give emotionally, and he and his partners usually parted amicably enough as a result.

There was nothing amicable about the wild feeling in his chest whenever he was in the same room as Journey.

If today had proven anything, it was that he couldn't guarantee her safety. Elliott had outmaneuvered Frank once, which meant it was possible he'd manage it again. If he hurt Journey...

Frank's chest went tight and his gut churned at the damage Journey might suffer if he didn't protect her. It made him want to wrap her in a bulletproof suit and ship her off to New York to stay with her mother until he figured out a way through this. To stay *safe*.

Because he didn't know what he'd do if she was harmed.

He couldn't afford to let his feelings about her screw with his control, but that ship had sailed. He was self-aware enough to realize that. The only thing he could do was deal with the fallout.

Frank followed Journey upstairs and found her in the room she'd sent him to earlier. She caught his expression and shrugged. "The family suites are on the other side of the house, and all your stuff is already here. No reason to move."

It felt like they'd stepped into a parallel universe as Frank brushed his teeth next to her and they both stripped before climbing into bed. Frank pulled her to him and tucked her against his chest. A heartbeat passed, and then another, and she still stayed rigid in his arms. He smoothed a hand down her spine. "Relax. We both need this after today."

"Right, the locusts." She draped her arm over his chest, and the worst of the tension slowly bled out of her body. "This is weird, right?"

"This is comfort."

"I thought fucking was comfort."

He rolled his eyes at her cheeky tone. "Close your eyes and go to sleep."

Her eyes drifted shut, but it was a long time before she fully relaxed and her breathing evened out. Frank lay there and watched her sleep—watched *over* her while she slept. If he let himself, he could imagine countless nights stretching out before them, all beginning just like this—with Journey asleep and trusting in his arms and with him letting the steady sound of her heartbeat lull his eyes closed. Nights that morphed into mornings and days and back into nights.

Yeah, if he let himself, he could imagine an entire fucking future with Journey King.

* * *

Eliza glanced over her shoulder and shoved her suitcase into the trunk of the car she'd borrowed from Bellamy. She swore she could feel eyes grinding into the space between her shoulder blades, but the street was mostly deserted outside her hotel. *Doesn't matter if my father* does *have someone watching me. It's too late to stop me now.*

She slammed the trunk shut and hurried to the driver's door. She'd booked the last flight out of Houston immediately after that disastrous meeting with Elliott and Anderson. By tomorrow, she'd be safely back in New York and beyond her father's reach. *Marry a stranger for the sake of Kingdom Corp? He's out of his goddamn mind.*

Her phone rang as she threw the car into gear, and she almost didn't answer it. But it was Bellamy, and if Eliza owed anyone in the family an explanation, it was her brother. "Hey, B."

"Why do you sound like you're in a car?"

"Because I am." She stopped at a red light and checked the time. *Not too long now. It'll be okay.* "I'm going back to New York."

A pause, like she'd shocked him. "Where are you, Eliza? Just stay there and I'll come get you."

Hurt grew jagged tendrils in her chest. She'd thought that, of all of them, Bellamy would understand that she needed to go. Apparently she was wrong. "I can't stay. I won't allow him to turn me into some trophy wife for the sake of a fucking merger."

"Goddamn it, you're not listening to me. I'll drive you to the airport myself, but it's not safe. Just pull over. I'm on my way."

The light turned green and she pressed the accelerator. "What are you talking about?"

"Elliott—"

Movement out of the corner of her eye made her look just as a truck smashed into the side of her sedan. The impact shattered the windshield into a thousand pieces and crumpled the car around her even as the airbag deployed, punching her in the face.

The last thing Eliza heard was Bellamy yelling her name.

CHAPTER SIXTEEN

At the end of the best night's sleep Journey had in six months, she woke up on Frank's chest. Drooling. *Oh my God.* It couldn't get any more awkward—in addition to pushing him to tell her things he obviously didn't want to last night, now she was doing *this*.

She slid back carefully and headed for the bathroom. He still wasn't awake when she got back, which indicated a level of trust that he'd never admit to aloud. She watched him sleep for a few seconds, but the only thing worse than drooling on a sexy man was getting caught watching him sleep like the ultimate creeper.

She pulled on a pair of leggings and a tank top and headed down to the kitchen. Journey considered the mess they'd left in the kitchen the night before and grabbed an apron. *Might as well make myself useful since I'm up.* She tied it around her waist and got to work.

It took less time than she expected, so she started on a breakfast potpie. A little too complicated to feed two people, but after last night, Journey needed the busy work to keep her from overthinking things.

Frank knew her ugly truths.

He knew and he hadn't turned away from her.

It really wasn't *that* high of a bar to set, but she could count on one hand how many people had cleared it—and still have fingers left over. A lot of fingers. She sighed and finished chopping the potatoes. Next up was grating the sharp cheddar that would seal everything together in the pie in the most delicious way possible. Then some bacon and eggs, and it would be ready for the oven.

She transferred the cheese to a bowl and stared at it for a long moment. Frank had a lot of secrets in his past, too. She'd known some of them—everyone knew what Henry Evans had been convicted of—but his mother's fate had never made the news. It should have.

Now she understood more about why Frank operated the way he did. He'd had a taste of what happiness might be, and then life had orchestrated to kick him in the teeth over and over again with the loss of both his parents. No wonder he fought so hard for power—it represented a wall of protection for him and everyone under his care. It ensured he'd never share his parents' fates. That the people who condemned his father would never get the chance to condemn Frank, that he'd never have to sit idly by while someone he cared about wasted away.

If she let him, he'd play prince to her damsel in distress, shutting her away while he rode off to fight the dragon.

She couldn't let him do it. She *wouldn't* let him endanger himself while she sat safe and secure somewhere else.

Not going to solve any problems staring at this half-made potpie.

She threw together some homemade crust and had just

popped the whole thing into the oven when a floorboard creaked behind her. Journey rose and turned around to find Frank standing in the doorway of the kitchen. He looked just like he had the night before, a little tired, and almost...*Hesitant* wasn't the right word. *Worried* definitely wasn't, either.

Cautious.

As if by stepping into the kitchen—into her space— he might be doing something he couldn't take back. He crossed his arms over his chest and surveyed her. "If you could see yourself right now, Duchess."

She glanced down and winced. Flour streaked the black leggings, and the frilly apron looked absolutely ridiculous. "As difficult as it is to believe, this wasn't yet another sad attempt at seducing you, Frank. Promise." Her joke fell flat into the new awareness in the room. She smoothed a hand along the embroidered picture on the apron—bright multicolor flowers. "I'm just going to...go change into something clean."

She made it to the doorway, but unless he moved, she'd have to drag her body against his to leave the room, and that just didn't seem like the best of ideas if she wanted to keep from throwing herself at him yet again. Journey waited...and waited some more. She managed to dredge her gaze up and froze when she caught him staring at her mouth. "Frank?"

"I promised myself I wouldn't do this. That I wouldn't go down this path." He reached out and tugged her apron, loosening the ties around her waist and causing the fabric to sag. He hooked his big hands into the fabric of her tank top. "Tell me to stop."

There was only one of them capable of putting the

brakes on this situation—and it wasn't her. She licked her lips, and he cursed when he noticed the movement. Journey lifted her arms and held her breath as he tugged her shirt off. She shimmied out of her leggings and kicked them in the opposite direction of the oven. The move left her naked but for the apron tied around her waist. *So much for playing hard to get.*

All the while, he watched her. *Waiting for permission.* God, didn't he know by now that she was a sure thing where he was concerned? Journey caught his wrist and pulled him toward her as she backed into the counter. "I don't want you to stop."

He was on her instantly, claiming her mouth as he lifted her so she could wrap her legs around his waist. Frank took three steps and set her on the counter, sending up a cloud of flour. He shoved her apron up, twisting it around her body so it covered absolutely nothing, but he didn't take it off. "You look like a wet dream, Duchess. I never figured I'd go for the Betty Crocker bullshit, but waking up and coming downstairs to see you bending over, that tight little ass framed by the apron's bow?" He pushed two fingers into her and grasped the back of her neck with his free hand, bending her over the counter. His kissed the curve of first one breast and then the other. "How's a man supposed to keep his head with you looking like this? *Feeling* like this." He pushed a third finger into her as if demonstrating his point.

It took two tries to get her voice under control. "Is that a trick question?"

He circled her clit with his thumb, his dark eyes stormy. "Does it sound like a fucking trick question?"

Got you riled, didn't I? His earlier words came back

to her. *I promised myself I wouldn't do this.* If Journey had a little more pride, she'd shove him away and tell him to come back around when he actually chose this. Chose *her*.

It would never happen. She knew Frank well enough now to know that.

She should tell him that she didn't want scraps at his table. That she deserved better than that.

Instead, she gripped his shoulders and gave herself over to everything he did to her. The rough rasp of his stubble against her breasts, his fingers working her, his muttered curses against her skin...It washed away everything except the here and now. Nothing else mattered but the pressure already building inside her, a pleasure Frank seemed to draw out without even trying. If she let him, he'd bring her to orgasm several times and *then* he'd take his pleasure.

No.

No fucking way.

If she was going over this edge, they were going over it together. She reached blindly into the drawer to her left, scrambling until her fingers grazed a familiar foil packet. Journey yanked it out and tore it open.

Frank narrowed his eyes. "Did you just pull a condom out of your kitchen drawer?"

"Yes." She shoved his pants down and gave his cock a single stroke before she rolled it on.

"I'm going to need you to explain that magic trick."

"No magic." She kissed his shoulder, his neck, his jaw. "My family hasn't come out here for a 'family' vacation in about a decade, and Mother prefers Europe to something so pedestrian as the Hamptons. So in the past, we've partied here, and it pays to have protection within easy reach because alcohol is killer on self-control."

He might as well have been a statue for all he moved, his fingers still speared deep within her. "Did you fuck a lot of boys here, Duchess? Let them lift you onto the kitchen counter like I am now?" The growl in his voice made her nipples pebble almost painfully.

Frank Evans was *jealous*.

She hid her grin, enjoying the fluttering feeling in her chest entirely too much. "I prefer to fuck behind closed doors under normal circumstances." She let go of him and leaned back to prop her hands on the counter behind her, well aware of the wanton picture she painted. Her apron strings tangled between her breasts, and the rest of it was in a ball against her side, leaving her pussy exposed as well, his fingers still inside her. "Though I'm considering changing my policy. This is sexy as hell."

"Fuck. That." He pulled his fingers out of her, but she barely had a chance to mourn the loss when his cock was there, shoving into her roughly.

She laughed. She couldn't help it. He looked so damn furious, the temptation to keep screwing with him was too much to ignore. He deserved it after that bullshit comment about not wanting this. Journey pressed hard against the hand he still had clasped around the back of her neck. "Do you think the boys would like this, Frank? Because I sure as hell do."

He looped an arm around her waist and yanked her almost off the counter. "No one else, Duchess." He fisted the front of her apron, using it as leverage to fuck her harder.

"Or what?" He slammed into her, grinding them

together, and she bit back a moan. It would be easy to just give in, to let him steamroll her. He'd made it so good for her... and then she'd fling herself right back into uncertainty afterward. If Frank felt enough to be *jealous*, then he was in just as deep as she was.

And, damn it, she wanted him to admit it.

Journey reached up and hooked the back of his neck, mirroring the way he held her. She arched up so she could whisper in his ear. "Or what, Frank? From where I'm sitting, all you've done is tell me how much you don't want this—don't want *me*. You don't do complicated and you don't do broken, and we both know I'm both." She hitched a breath, her breasts rubbing against his chest. "I might forget my pride when I'm around you, but there's only so long I'm going to beat my head against this particular wall. This might be the last time, it might not be, but eventually I *will* move on to someone who actually wants me." She nipped his earlobe. "And when I do, I'm going to ride his cock until he sees stars and worships the ground I walk on."

He leaned back. On anyone else, his expression would be called a grin, but Journey knew better. It was a warning, the same way a wild animal flashed its teeth before it attacked. "You'll be bored within a week, and you'll break the poor fuck's heart in the process."

She went to smack him, but he caught her wrist easily—and then captured her other one to pin them both against the small of her back. This hadn't been what she intended when she baited him, but she was in too deep to go back now. "Yeah, well, that's my choice."

"Wrong, Duchess. *I'm* your choice and you damn well know it." He rolled his hips, rubbing against the spot on her inner wall that drew a whimper from her lips. "It makes you crazy that you want me." Frank lifted her, keeping her wrists pinned, and walked Journey to the dining room table they'd eaten at the night before. He shoved the centerpiece out of the way and laid her onto the cool wood. "About as crazy as it makes me wanting you." He withdrew from her, and the sound of a chair scraping over the hardwood floor was the only warning she got before he sat at the head of the table—right between her spread thighs.

* * *

Frank took out all of his frustration on Journey's pussy. He fucked her with his tongue the way he needed to fuck her with his cock. He wasn't stupid. He knew exactly what she was trying to pull with that little stunt with the condom and throwing the idea of other men in his face. It didn't matter if the idea of her with someone else drove him out of his fucking mind. It *couldn't* matter. He liked her entirely too much, a sensation that undermined his control simply by breathing the same air as her.

To feel more?

That way lay ruin.

He gave himself over to punishing her with his mouth, letting her know in no uncertain terms that for the time they were together, her pleasure was *his* to deliver. But when she came with a cry loud enough to rattle the windows, it only made the turmoil inside him worse. Because it wasn't enough.

He wasn't sure it would ever be enough.

Frank shoved to his feet and kicked the chair out of the

way. He guided his cock into her and reached up to bracket her throat. "No one else, Duchess," he repeated.

Those hazel eyes saw right through all his bullshit to the wild thing beneath his skin. She called to part of him on a fundamental level that he didn't know how to deal with. Journey licked her lips and pressed her throat more firmly against his palm. "I'll consider it."

His control snapped. Frank gripped her hip with his free hand, pinning her in place as he fucked her slowly, letting her feel every inch of him in torturous detail. "I know what you're trying to do."

"Do you?" She swallowed hard enough that he felt it. "Prove it."

"You want me to fuck you hard enough to break this table. To drive you out of your damn mind and leave marks all over your body that will have you walking funny for a week."

She grinned. "Come on, you know that sounds like a dream."

"Not this time." He kept up the slow strokes. "You aren't in control, Duchess. It's time you remembered that." He narrowed his eyes at her hands gripping the edge of the table. "Over your head."

She hesitated, but ultimately obeyed, stretching her arms over her head and lacing her fingers together. He released her long enough to untangle the apron and toss it aside. Frank ran his hand up the center of her body to take her neck again. "You're with me."

She met his gaze directly, fully present in what they were doing. No hesitation. No fear. "I'm with you."

He started moving again, picking up the motion that made her eyes go heavy-lidded and her body writhe as much as he'd allow. It felt good, so fucking good, to be inside her, to know that he was the one putting that hazy look on her face and chasing away her shadows.

Like maybe his armor wasn't as tarnished as he'd let himself believe.

Frank guided her legs up to rest on his shoulders. The new position allowed him deeper, and she made that sexy-as-fuck whimpering sound with every stroke. He kept going, driving her slowly, inexorably back to the edge again. This time, when she came, he couldn't restrain himself. He pounded into her, pursuing his own pleasure even as she went wild beneath him. Frank came with a curse and braced a hand on the table on either side of Journey's limp body.

She wiped her forehead, leaving a trail of flour across her skin. "We're fucked, Frank."

Fucked about summed it up. "I know." No matter what he told himself—told her—his response just now spoke louder than his words had. If he was actually able to leave Journey King the hell alone, the thought of her moving on to someone else wouldn't make him damn near homicidal. He dipped down and pressed a kiss over her heart. "Come on." He helped her to her feet as the oven timer dinged. "What's that?"

"Breakfast." She grinned. "Or maybe what we just did was breakfast and this is brunch? It doesn't matter. It's desperately needed calories." She went to grab her apron off the floor, but Frank got there first.

He held it just out of reach and pointed at her discarded clothing. "Go put on some clean clothes before you burn off something vital. I'll get the damn breakfast out of the oven."

She raised her eyebrows suggestively. "Come now—
I've been cooking naked since I moved out on my
own. I have more than enough experience protecting my
important bits."

He blinked. Picturing her in *his* kitchen, wearing
nothing but that ridiculous pink apron... *Fuck.* "Get
dressed."

"Bossy." She put a little swing into her walk as if she
knew he couldn't keep his eyes off her ass. Flour marked
her skin, and there was a nearly perfect white handprint
on her hip that had him wanting to follow her upstairs
to ensure that whenever she thought of this house, it was
attached to memories of coming on his cock.

Get the fucking breakfast, asshole.

He managed to find the pot holders and get the thing
out of the oven, and then he cleaned up the mess they'd
made. A couple of minutes later, he heard Journey rushing downstairs and turned to meet her in the doorway.
The look on her face stopped him cold.

She held up her phone, her skin bleached of color
and her eyes too wide. "Eliza's been in an accident. We
have to go. Now."

CHAPTER SEVENTEEN

The trip back to Houston simultaneously took too much and too little time. Journey couldn't seem to sit still, and Frank was smart enough to leave her alone as she paced back and forth in the plane. After they landed, he drove her to the hospital in silence, seeming to sense that she wasn't capable of holding a conversation.

No reason at all to blame herself for what happened to Eliza. People got in car accidents all the time, and it was never part of some sinister plan.

But no matter how many times she told herself that, she didn't quite believe it.

Frank pulled to a stop outside the hospital and grabbed her hand before she could rush from the car. "Duchess, look at me."

Each second she sat still instead of rushing to her baby sister's side was sheer agony. "I have to go."

"Journey." He tightened his grip until she lifted her gaze to his face. His expression might be the familiar cold lines, but there was sympathy in his dark eyes. "Sure you don't want me to go in with you?"

No. "Yes." She swallowed hard. "Anderson is closing

ranks, which means family only." She refused to think about who else was considered *family*. It didn't matter if Elliott showed up—Eliza needed her, and so Journey would deal with their father. Full stop. She managed to squeeze Frank's hand. "I appreciate it, though."

"If you change your mind, or need anything, call me. Doesn't matter the time."

Warmth flared, eating away at the coldness that had wrapped around her as soon as she got off the phone with Bellamy. "Thank you." She hesitated. "Would you do me a favor?"

"Of course."

So easily, he answered her, as if favors were something Frank Evans handed out for free. *Something changed between us, something big.* She didn't have the time or energy to pick apart *what* it was right then, but she appreciated it all the same. "This sounds crazy paranoid, but is it possible to pull the traffic cameras where she had the accident? I guess the cops will probably do that, too, but I'd feel better hearing the news from you." It wasn't that she didn't trust the police, exactly—more that Journey didn't trust *anyone* beyond a short list that included Samara, her siblings... and Frank.

"Consider it done." He leaned forward and pressed a quick kiss to her lips. "I'll text you when I have it. Good luck, Duchess."

"Thanks." She'd need all the luck she could get at this point. She grabbed her purse and opened the door. "Seriously, Frank—thanks. For everything."

He leaned over so that he could see her better. "I'll see you tonight, Duchess. Text when you're leaving here and I'll meet you at your place."

By all rights, she should tell him to get the fuck out of there with that kind of talk, but the truth was that the thought of going back to her empty apartment with the events of the last week hanging over her head wasn't a good one. If he was going to offer to stay over, she wasn't going to tell him no. "I'd like that." Journey shut the door before she could expose any more weaknesses than she already had.

She followed Bellamy's directions to the waiting room outside the ICU. Journey loathed hospitals, from their dull color schemes to the faint smell of antiseptic cleaner that seemed to permeate every inch. And, underneath it all, suffering. She wasn't sure if she believed in the supernatural, but if ghosts existed in any form, they haunted the walls of places like this, their energy affecting every single person who walked through the doors.

Both her brothers sat in the waiting room, and they looked up as she walked through the door. She tensed. "Elliott?"

Anderson grimaced. "Hasn't seen fit to make an appearance."

Thank fuck. Journey slung her purse onto the floor and took the seat between her brothers. "What happened?" Bellamy hadn't conveyed more than the basics over the phone—Eliza was in a car crash and in serious condition, followed up by directions for when she arrived.

"Hit-and-run." This from Bellamy. He dropped his head into his hands. "She was leaving Houston—going back to New York—and I tried to get her to stop." He cursed. "I was on the phone with her when the accident happened."

"Oh, Bellamy." She started to reach for him but

hesitated. They weren't exactly a touchy-feely kind of family, and it might make it worse. *Stop making excuses.* Journey held her breath and gingerly rubbed her brother's back. He shuddered, which was almost enough to make her snatch her hand back, but then he reached out and clasped her knee with a shaking hand.

She looked at Anderson. "How is she?"

"She got out of surgery right before you arrived." He looked at his watch. "It took twice as long as it should have, and no one will tell us anything but that we need to wait for the surgeon. She's alive. That's all I know."

"God," she breathed, even as her mind raced. She'd known it was serious from Bellamy's reaction, but if Eliza had been in surgery for *hours*...It was so much worse than she'd imagined.

Tension laced through her body as footsteps sounded in the hallway, approaching the waiting room. She reached out and touched Anderson's shoulder. "Someone's coming."

No one relaxed as two uniformed officers stepped into the room. The men were cast from the same mold—fit and straight-backed, expressions wiped from their faces. The older one had silver coloring his temples, but otherwise they might have been related. The younger one took them in at a glance. "You're Eliza King's family?"

Journey glanced at her brothers in turn, but they just stared at the cops, as if their baby sister being in danger had broken something in them. She squeezed Anderson's shoulder and kept her other hand on Bellamy's back. "Yes, we're her siblings."

The cops exchanged a look, and the younger one took up a position just inside the door while the older one strode over and sank into the chair across from them. He leaned forward and braced his forearms on his thighs. "As I'm sure you're aware by now, your sister was involved in a car accident late last night."

Why are they telling us something we already know? Journey shook her head and tried to focus. "Did you find the other driver?"

A muscle jumped in his jaw, though his expression remained frustratingly bland. "It was a hit-and-run. The other car left the scene."

Bellamy lifted his head at that. "You'll have pulled the traffic cameras."

Again, that twitch in his jaw. "There was nothing identifiable about the vehicle. It was a dark truck without plates, and the windows were tinted dark enough that the driver isn't identifiable. We're checking local repair shops, but I'm telling you right now that it's not looking promising."

Something isn't right.

Bellamy practically growled. "Tinted windows and a missing plate don't sound like an accident."

"We have no evidence suggesting otherwise."

She stared hard at the cop and then looked at his partner, taking in the way he kept his gaze pinned to the window in the waiting room—and the thin bead of sweat along his hairline.

"Last time I checked, a hit-and-run is a crime in the state of Texas," she said. "There's got to be something more you can do to catch whoever did this."

The cop pulled a card out of his pocket. "If you have further questions, feel free to call my supervisor."

This wasn't how the police conducted investigations.

Journey might not spend a lot of time up close and personal with the law, but even she knew that. A crime had been committed, and, as such, they should be investigating to the fullest extent of their abilities.

She barely waited for their footsteps to fade before she pushed to her feet. "What the hell was that about?"

"That's what I'd like to know. I saw her car, Jo—it looks like a crumpled Coke can. There's no way another vehicle should have been able to do that damage and drive off before the police arrived. It doesn't make any fucking sense."

She ran her hands through her hair. "They have to know this was intentional—that she was targeted. That changes this from a simple hit-and-run into attempted murder. Why aren't they doing anything about it?"

"You know why." Bellamy leaned his head against the wall behind his chair and closed his eyes. "The cops we talked to right after we got here were different ones, and they seemed much more willing to help find answers. Strange coincidence, them being reassigned and those two assholes ending up with a case they're all too eager to close."

"You don't know they were reassigned." He opened one eye and pinned her with a look, and she sighed. "Okay, I'm reaching. You can't honestly think Elliott got to them."

"Don't be naive, Jo." This from Bellamy. He stretched out his legs. "The Bancrofts are just as powerful as the Kings."

Damn it. *Damn it*. She paced from one side of the room to the other. "There's got to be something we can do, someone we can go to."

"It won't work."

She spun on Anderson. "How can you know? You haven't even tried."

She stared at her brothers, the two steady beacons in her life. They were crumpling around her. Anderson might cover it up better, but it was there in the tightness around his mouth and the way his eyes seemed to see something a thousand miles away. He was fighting for control, to be the calm leader that he knew they needed... and he was failing. Bellamy wasn't even trying to keep a steady face, his frustration and anger riding close to the surface, but then he'd always been closer to Eliza than the other two.

Her brothers needed her.

They needed someone to step up and relieve the burden, at least for a little while.

She never would have considered it would be her. *She* was the weak link, the one who spent the majority of this mess trying not to fall to pieces while everyone else stood strong.

She gave her brothers what she hoped was a reassuring smile. "I'm going to go see if I can track down some information and some coffee. Just... hang in there. She got through surgery. Eliza is tougher than anyone gives her credit for. She'll be okay." The words felt like a lie, but neither of them called her on it.

None of the nurses had any information for her, so she collected the coffee and headed back to the waiting room. She barely made it into the room when the surgeon appeared in the doorway. He was an older black man, his short hair gone silver and laugh lines bracketing his mouth. He wasn't laughing now. "You're Eliza King's family?"

"Yes." Journey stepped forward, aware of Anderson and Bellamy standing and moving to either side of her. "Is our sister okay?"

"She came through surgery just fine, and she's awake." He hesitated. "She doesn't want to see you—any of you."

* * *

Frank swung by the apartment he kept in the city long enough to shower and change, and then he headed to the office. He'd already asked Mateo to pull the traffic cameras before they'd taken off, so there should be answers by now. It was a struggle to focus on the facts and not think about the lost and determined look on Journey's face when he'd left her in front of the hospital. She wanted to go in alone and he respected her choice—but that didn't mean he liked it. Ethan and José were already on their way to the hospital to ensure nothing went sideways, though he doubted Elliott would be so blunt.

Then again, he'd never expected the man to go after his youngest daughter, either.

Make no assumptions. We don't know what happened yet.

Maybe not in facts, but he knew what his gut said— Elliott was somehow responsible for Eliza's accident. Whether it was to bring Journey back to Houston or for some other reason remained to be seen, but the timing was too neat to be coincidental. Journey took Frank and bolted out of Elliott's reach and, within twenty-four hours, a terrible accident befell one of her siblings, forcing her to return. Not only that, but she wouldn't be thinking clearly because she was worried about her sister.

What better time to strike?

It's what Frank would do, though he never had to stoop to harming people to get what he wanted. Not physically, at least. There were so many more effective ways to hamstring a person without lifting a hand. Obviously, Elliott had never learned that particular lesson.

He took the steps two at a time, heading for Mateo's office. Something about this situation had bothered him from the beginning. Elliott was crafty—there was no denying that—but why not make his move years ago if he was really after the power?

Because Lydia King was still in Houston. Even with the power of the Bancrofts behind him, only a fool would underestimate that woman.

Mateo looked up as Frank walked in, his expression severe. "Your girl has gotten herself into a vipers' nest by accident of birth, and it's going to get worse before it gets better." He turned his monitor so Frank could watch the grainy black-and-white video he'd already queued up. It showed a dark sedan sitting at a stoplight. The light turned and the car started forward, right into the path of an SUV. The impact crumpled the car in on itself as the SUV pushed it through the intersection and out of view of the camera.

Shit.

Frank walked over and leaned down. "Play it again. Slower." The second the SUV came onscreen, he said, "Pause." Frank pointed at the grille. "You see that?"

"Reinforced bumper." Mateo leaned forward and frowned. "Hard to tell, but it looks like a rack you'd find on a cop car or armored vehicle."

"Not something you see around here a lot." Frank dropped into the seat across from the desk. Those kind of aftermarket bumpers weren't exactly rare, but they were usually on trucks or SUVs that spent a lot of time on roads where wildlife was an issue—hit something with it, and the bumper would save the front end of the car in most cases. There were pavement princesses who had their shit all geared up like they thought they were some kind of badass, but…Coincidences upon coincidences. Too many to write off.

"They planned this to do the most damage they could." He stared at the screen. "If they wanted her dead, better to hit from the driver's side, but there is the chance someone might jump the green light and get in the way, lessening the impact. He didn't try to stop, didn't try to slow down. How did he know she was going to be at that intersection at that time?"

Mateo tapped a few keys, bringing up a different window on the screen. "She was staying a few blocks away while she was in town. Had a meeting with her father and oldest brother midafternoon, and came back all flustered looking." When Frank shot him a look, he shrugged. "Come on, boss. You didn't order the other siblings watched, but you would have eventually. I just anticipated your order."

Since he *would* have ordered it if he wasn't so damn preoccupied with Journey, he just nodded. "Something upset her enough at that meeting to bolt. Ten to one she was headed for the airport." She wouldn't have gotten far without the private jet, but easy enough to buy a commercial ticket this time of year. It wasn't as if Eliza King was hurting for funds.

"She called to have help bringing her luggage down to the car."

Which was how they knew exactly when she'd be at the intersection. She took the most direct route to the airport, and it was late enough that traffic wasn't a huge issue. Child's play to plan an ambush.

He tapped the arm of his chair. "Her old man didn't like that she wasn't going to play ball." The was the only explanation. Unless... *Wonder if Journey knows what that meeting was about?* It was entirely possible that Elliott had put out the order to stop his youngest daughter from leaving Houston by whatever means necessary. But if that was the case, why not just arrange to have her nabbed off the street? She wasn't an active part of Kingdom Corp. She held no value as far as the company was concerned, inherited shares aside.

So why was she in a meeting with Elliott and Anderson?

Frank ran a hand over his face and made a mental note to ask Journey about it when he saw her. "Let's treat this as a separate incident for the time being and assume it's not part of Elliott's overarching plan." All of Elliott's actions up to this point had been directed at removing his children through bullying and intimidation. While he was more than capable of violence, murder was still a big step to take—and it *was* attempted murder. There were a thousand different ways he could have stopped Eliza from getting to the airport without endangering her the way the hit-and-run had. Elliott was too smart to escalate on this scale.

Unless he was desperate.

It still doesn't make sense. I need more information.

Frank's phone buzzed, and he frowned when he saw Beck's name. "Hey."

"You got time for a drink?"

He checked his watch. "It's not even noon, Beck."

"I have something I want to talk to you about."

That much was obvious. His friend wasn't the type to grab a drink in the middle of a workday, no matter how stressful life got. And he sure as fuck wouldn't call Frank to do the same without cause. It was just as obvious that Beck didn't want to talk about it over the phone. "Yeah. Normal place?"

"See you there."

He hung up and found Mateo watching him. "What?"

"That's some cloak-and-dagger shit right there, boss."

Frank rolled his eyes. "No more so than what we were already doing." He sat back. There were a couple of options available moving forward, and he didn't like any of them. Elliott's determination to take control of Kingdom Corp stemmed from either one of two places—him owing money to someone scary, or the Bancroft family finally utilizing him in their quest to devour any and all lucrative businesses in Texas.

He could have Mateo keep pulling the financial string, but at this point it was unlikely anything new would pop. Frank could arrange a meeting with Esther Bancroft and try to get a feel for the woman, but without more information and an ace or two in his pocket, that would tip their hand without any real benefit. All while keeping a close watch on Journey and hoping like hell he could counter Elliott's next move before someone else got hurt.

Fuck. No good options.

The look on Mateo's face said he'd realized the same thing. "What's next?"

That was the question. "We need to know what went

on in that meeting with Eliza and Anderson. I'll talk to Journey King, but I want secondary confirmation."

"Consider it done. I have a friend whose cousin works at the Cellar. I'll see what I can find out."

"Thanks." He pushed to his feet. "I'll be back in a few hours."

It was time to get some answers. What the *fuck* was Elliott up to?

CHAPTER EIGHTEEN

Eliza still wouldn't see them. It didn't matter how much Journey argued with the nurses and doctors, she was turned away every time.

In the end, there was nothing they could do about it.

She almost called Frank, but she was feeling too damn raw to handle the intensity that arose from being around him. *Not from being around him, Jo—from being* with *him.* It wasn't the sex that changed things for them. It was the fact that she'd ripped herself open in front of him time and time again and it didn't seem to faze him or make him think less of her. Journey didn't know how to handle that. Frank was so damn overwhelming, and it would be so incredibly easy to just roll with it and let him guide them to wherever he wanted to go.

She couldn't.

She refused to.

The one thing she needed most was control, and it was the one thing neither of them had around each other.

She called Samara instead. Her friend arrived in record time, and Journey barely waited for the car to slow for her to jump into the passenger seat. She frowned at the buttery-soft leather. "Wait a minute—you don't have a car."

"Correction—I didn't have a car. But since I'm driving out to Thistledown Villa a couple times a week and Beckett and I have such insane schedules, I bit the bullet and bought one." She checked her blind spot and pulled into traffic. "How's Eliza?"

"She won't see us. Not even Bellamy." She crossed her arms over her chest and slouched deeper into the seat. "He's crushed that she won't let him in the room."

"Hmm." Samara took a turn, heading in the direction of Journey's apartment.

"Don't *hmmm* me. She's my sister. She's hurt and she's vulnerable and she shouldn't be alone right now."

"I'm not arguing with you." Samara's tone was as dry as the desert. "Though you're obviously pissed about something. Is it a belated freak-out over Eliza or is it something else?"

Too many things to list without a couple of bottles of wine and a conversation she wasn't sure she wanted to have. Frank knowing the truth about her history was different from telling Samara.

"Journey, you know you can talk to me, right?" Samara huffed out a breath. "Something is bothering you and has been bothering you for a long time. You've lost weight and you have this look in your eyes..." She pulled into the parking garage of Journey's building. "If you don't want to talk to me about it, I understand, but you have to talk to *someone* about it. I'm not going to sit here and let you waste away."

Samara was the best of friends and Journey didn't deserve her.

"I love you." The words just burst out.

Samara parked. "I love you, too."

Did she really think that Samara would look at her differently if she knew the truth? Journey closed her eyes and inhaled deeply. Maybe it was time to stop treating her abusive childhood like her dirty little secret and thrust things out into the sunlight. "Can we talk? Really talk?"

"As if you have to ask." Samara held up her phone. "Takeout?"

"Yes, please and thank you. I just need a shower and to change and then I'll tell you everything." They headed upstairs, and it wasn't until Journey unlocked the door that she remembered Frank's concern about her security. *It's fine even if whatever new upgrades he ordered haven't been finalized yet. Frank fired the guy who let Elliott up and replaced him with someone trustworthy.* The knowledge didn't stop the small hairs from raising along the nape of her neck, but she still opened the door and stepped into her apartment.

It was untouched.

She blew out a breath. "Wait here for a second, okay?" Journey walked into the room and waited until Samara closed and locked the door behind her. Then she did a full sweep of the apartment. It didn't take long to ensure no one was lying in wait. As best she could tell, no one had been in there since she left. She hesitated in her bedroom, and then unlocked her gun case and took out her .22. Journey had a license to carry concealed, but she rarely hauled her gun around with her.

That changed now.

She popped out the clip, checked to make sure there wasn't a round in the chamber, each move as automatic as breathing. When she was fifteen and her grades and mental health were suffering because of nightmares, her mother dragged Journey to a private shooting range every day for a month straight. It was a nontraditional method of dealing with her fear, but learning to control her breathing and narrow her focus as she sighted down the barrel at the target *had* helped.

Time with her mother had helped more. That month cemented Journey's determination to make herself a valuable asset for Kingdom Corp—for Lydia.

Satisfied everything was in working order, Journey replaced the clip and walked back into the main room to set the gun next to her purse on the kitchen island. She had a holster around here somewhere, but she'd find it later. "Okay, we're good."

Samara watched her closely. "Beckett said it was serious, but he doesn't know as much as he wants to about what's going on."

No, he wouldn't. Her siblings and their cousin had been kept apart from birth by virtue of their parents' vendetta against each other. Beckett had hardly grown up with an idyllic childhood, but he didn't know the dirty details about what went down in Journey's household those first ten years.

No one did.

Journey smoothed her hair back. "Just give me fifteen minutes to jump in the shower."

"Take your time." Samara started typing on her phone.

Journey knew herself well enough to know that if she waited too long, she'd chicken out and she might never gather up the courage to take this flying leap again. So she washed up as quickly as she could, pulled on a pair of faded jeans and her favorite tank top, threw her hair into a ponytail, and walked back out into the main living area of the apartment.

Samara sat at the kitchen island, her dark brows drawn as she read something on her phone, an array of takeout food in front of her. She looked good. Her black hair fell in thick waves around her shoulders—a style she'd rarely worn when she worked for Kingdom Corp—and her brown skin had a healthy glow that only seemed to come alongside true happiness. Being in love obviously agreed with her.

She looked up when Journey approached, and gave a soft smile. "Feel better?"

"As good as can be expected." She took the seat next to Samara and pressed her hands flat to the marble countertop. "My father abused me as a kid—he abused all of us, though Eliza was young enough to be spared the worst of it." The words felt like stones dropped into the still silence of the room. She took a slow breath, but the sky didn't come falling down around her, and Samara didn't jump to her feet and flee the room. That made it easier to keep going. "I don't really know when it started. I was that young. It was just the way things were. He stayed home with us while Lydia traveled and spent most of her time in the office, and so he had free rein. He was ruler in our fucked-up little kingdom, and he got off on the power he held over us. There was..." She shook her head. "I don't know what was worse—the mind games where he had us convinced that we were the ones forcing him to take these measures, and then playing one of us against the others to get us to do what he wanted. Or the punishments that we invariably earned by not being good enough."

Next to her, Samara had gone so still, Journey wasn't sure she drew breath. "I'm so sorry, Jo."

"My mother caught him in the midst of one of the punishments when I was ten. I..." She stared hard at her hands. "I know Lydia is a monster. I'm not an idiot. What she did to Beckett and Nathaniel was fucked up beyond all reason. But she *saved* us, Samara. She ran him out of the house, out of the damn city, and she ensured that he didn't come back. I don't know what would have happened if he'd stayed. Maybe he would have killed one of us eventually. I just don't know.

"I went to therapy. Lots of therapy. I was...I was muddling along just fine, but he's back and he's setting me up to get fired on account of being unfit to hold the COO position." It was as if the past had been a festering wound inside her and last night with Frank had lanced it. The words weren't easy—never that—but she could actually give them voice. "I went to Frank for help." She let loose a hoarse laugh. "Which, in hindsight, seems like a weird choice."

That should have been the end of it, the worst of the dark secrets she'd been carrying inside her for far too long. But Journey found herself continuing. "He's more than helping me. It was supposed to be a pretend relationship, a way to get him near the family without anyone suspecting anything. But it's turned into something that might be real if we could get out of each other's way long enough to see if it's possible." She shook her head. "That might be the craziest part of this."

"Journey." Samara reached over and covered her hand. "Thank you for telling me."

She knew that tone, the gentleness covering a fury that

rode far too close to the surface. She'd felt it on Samara's behalf more than once over the years, and she knew what would happen if she didn't defuse it right at that moment. She turned her hand over and laced her fingers with Samara's. Sure enough, her friend's hand vibrated with little shakes, betraying how deeply affected she was. "I can't let anyone else stand between me and this mess. Not Anderson. Not Frank. Not even you, Samara."

Finally, her friend sighed, and it was as if the tension left her body. "You're sure?"

She wasn't. All evidence pointed to this blowing up in her face, but between her suspicions about Eliza and what Elliott threatened to do to Frank, Journey wasn't willing to risk anyone else getting hurt. "I'm sure. I'm done letting other people fight my battles. It never felt like I had the courage or strength to stand on my own, but I'm going to jump and figure my way out on the way down."

* * *

Frank walked out of the bright Houston sun and into the dimness that was the Salty Chihuahua. The little bar had been a favorite of his and Beck's since they were old enough to drink, and it always felt a little like coming home. The vintage pinup posters on the walls and the stylized table legs that looked like women's legs were just the icing on the cake to the strangeness here. Nothing had changed in the last thirteen years, and he imagined he could walk through those doors thirty years from now and it would be like entering a time warp.

He made his way back to their normal table, but stopped short when he realized Beck wasn't alone.

Anderson King sat next to him, and the man looked up as Frank approached, his blue eyes not showing any emotion. "Evans."

"Anderson." He nodded. "Beck."

"Sorry, Frank. Anderson called me when I was on my way over here, and I figured it would be better to cut through all the bullshit and lay our cards on the table." Beck waited for him to take a seat in the booth before he continued. "We all want the same thing—Elliott Bancroft out of Houston and away from Kingdom Corp."

Frank didn't give a fuck about Kingdom Corp. If Elliott wanted to drive that goddamn company into the ground, he was more than welcome to it. But Frank knew Journey well enough by now to know that she'd go down with that ship, and *that* he couldn't allow. Elliott had already hurt her enough; she wasn't going to lose the company she loved because of him, too. "I'm listening."

Beck shot him a look, but it was Anderson who spoke. "I couldn't figure out what the hell was going on with you and Jo, but she asked you to help, didn't she? That's the only goddamn reason I can think that you'd even be part of this conversation." He leaned, every move telegraphing arrogance. "We've got it covered, Evans. You're no longer needed."

For fuck's sake. He forced himself still, smothering any physical reaction that showed just how close to the mark Anderson had hit. "From where I'm sitting, you need all the help you can get." He pulled his phone out of his pocket, brought up the video, and spun it around to face the other two men.

Anderson watched it all the way through twice and cursed. "I knew it wasn't an accident, but they set it up to do as much damage as possible with that single hit." His composure dropped for the breadth of a moment, but he regained control quickly. "I should have known she'd try to run. Eliza wasn't going to let anything threaten her freedom—not even Elliott." He shook his head. "I'd be proud of her under other circumstances."

Beck leaned forward. "Why did Elliott bring her back to Houston?"

Frank owed his friend a bottle of his best scotch for asking the question. Anderson would bristle and bitch if Frank had broached it, but Beck was different. They might never be friends, but King blood ran thicker than most—at least when everyone got out of their own damn way. Without their parents in the picture, Frank suspected the King cousins would mend the bridges burned thirty years ago and move forward as a unit, even if they retained their competing businesses.

Anderson hesitated, but if he had figured his way out of this situation, he would have done it when Elliott first showed up. He was obviously outmaneuvered by his father, and not in a position to turn away assistance, even from Frank and Beck. He picked up the beer in front of him and took a long pull. "He's organizing a merger with Cardinal Energy, though it only goes forward once Eliza and Asher Bishop are married."

"A marriage to cement a merger?" Frank raised his eyebrows. "Outdated, don't you think?"

"It doesn't matter what *I* think. Elliott pulled that shit off all on his own. I tried to go around him to finesse the deal, but the Bishops won't talk to me, and the board of directors seems to be permanently unavailable." He cursed. "I only had a couple hours before I heard about

Eliza's accident, but I *will* get her out of this. I just need time. She didn't give me any fucking *time*."

"It doesn't make sense. If the marriage is the determining factor for the merger, then keeping Eliza safe and in good health should be Elliott's priority. What the hell does he gain from nearly killing her?" Frank picked up his beer and set it down again without drinking it.

"He doesn't deal well with people defying him." Anderson moved his beer bottle a precise inch to the left and glared at it. "He's capable of anything."

The whole thing reeked of a personal vendetta, which made sense if they took it as Elliott reclaiming what he felt Lydia had stolen from him.

Or punishing the children who escaped him.

Frank shook his head. This meeting wasn't going to get them anywhere. They could spend hours going back and forth. It wouldn't change anything, and Journey wouldn't be in any less danger.

He slid out of the booth and stood. "I suggest you get a secondary security detail on both Eliza and Bellamy for the time being—as well as on yourself. Better to be paranoid than to be dead."

Beck propped his elbows on the table. "Where are you going?"

"To do what I'm good at—fixing the fucking problem."

CHAPTER NINETEEN

After Samara left, Journey strode into her bedroom and grabbed her phone. She had two missed calls from her mother. She hesitated. Telling Lydia anything at this point was a risk, but there was a chance her mother might have valuable information about Elliott—information that she could leverage into forcing him to leave. She took a slow breath and dialed her mother.

Lydia didn't make her wait. "You've been avoiding my calls."

"I know. I'm sorry. Things have been complicated." She walked to the window in her living room overlooking the street. Nothing seemed amiss out there, but Journey still moved to her door and double-checked the locks. "Elliott is back in town."

Silence for a beat. Two. "Has he hurt you? Any of you?"

Warmth flooded her chest, tangling with the betrayal she still hadn't quite dealt with. Her mother was just as capable of evil as her father, but Lydia had never hurt a child—would never hurt a child. *It's just the adults who have to watch out for her.* "He's made a play for

Kingdom Corp. Why didn't you tell us that he helped get the company off the ground?"

"Because he didn't," Lydia scoffed. "Elliott likes power, but he'd never part with the kind of capital I needed at the time."

She stopped short, her mind racing. *If not Elliott, then...* "Esther." Elliott's mother. Journey's grandmother.

"Yes. Whatever he's doing there, she's the one behind it." Lydia lowered her voice. "If you need me—"

"No, absolutely not." She put as much calm assertion into her voice as she could. "You know what will happen if you come back. We have things covered."

Despite her lying through her teeth, Lydia accepted that. "I expect you and your siblings in Monaco for Christmas this year."

That broke the tension better than anything else could have. Journey rolled her eyes. "Mother, it's February. Christmas is ten months away."

"All the same." Lydia hesitated, but when she spoke, steel laced her tone. "You can deal with Elliott, Journey. He's going to try to convince you that you aren't capable, and your brothers will try to step in, but you *can* deal with him. Break him. Don't let him break you."

She found herself smiling despite everything. "I'll deal with him. And we'll be there for Christmas."

"See that you are. Good luck, though you don't need it." She hung up, leaving Journey staring at her locked door.

Her mother seemed to have every confidence that Journey could handle the situation and that they'd all be vacationing in Europe over the holidays to celebrate.

She blew out a breath. "Okay. I can do this...Okay."

She scrolled through her contacts and dialed, holding her breath and praying she wasn't making a terrible mistake.

The line clicked over. "Yes?"

She swallowed hard. "Hello, Grandmother."

"Journey. So wonderful to hear from you. It's been quite some time." If Esther Bancroft was surprised to get Journey's call, she gave no sign. But, then, if Lydia's suspicions were correct and she was the one behind Elliott's determination to take over Kingdom Corp, Esther had to know one of the King children would be calling eventually.

"I know. I'm sorry." She wasn't. The Bancroft family had rallied around their discarded son after Lydia threw him out. Though her mother kept her from the worst of it, Journey vividly remembered eavesdropping on a meeting with Lydia and her lawyer where they discussed how ugly the battle had become. She had never filed for divorce, and Journey firmly believed that it was because the Bancrofts threatened to take the children and ruin her business in the process. Elliott had generations of family prestige and money to fall back on and ensure he got his way. Lydia had no one, not after her split with the rest of the Kings.

After the lawyer laid out how awful their chances were and left, Lydia had called her brother Nathaniel— the only time in Journey's living memory that she'd done so voluntarily. She'd...she'd *begged* him for help.

And he refused.

Lydia had no choice but to bend to the Bancroft family's wishes and stay married to Elliott, and one of those wishes entailed mandatory visits to the family home in Dallas during the summers. Journey had fought hard against going, but her mother finally sat her down and stressed the necessity of using every weapon available.

The second Eliza turned eighteen, they were free. The visits stopped, and she hadn't had to endure more than a quarterly phone call since.

Esther's definitely going to hold that against me.

"Grandmother, I think it's long past time we had a talk. Are you in town?"

"I just arrived from Dallas this morning," Esther said.

If she hadn't suspected Esther was aware of what Elliott was up to, her grandmother's presence in Houston would have announced it in blinking neon. The only time she came into town was to deal with something that couldn't be delegated, preferring to stick to the Bancroft estate just outside of Dallas, running a good portion of Texas from her drawing room. "Are you available?" She checked her watch. Frank said he'd come over tonight, which still gave her plenty of time to meet with her grandmother and get back to the apartment before he did. Journey wasn't stupid enough to go somewhere without telling anyone, but she didn't want company for this particular meeting.

"For my beloved granddaughter? Be at the apartment I keep in town within the hour."

Journey gritted her teeth and then forced a smile, hoping it would translate into her tone. Her grandmother held a place of power in any negotiation they had going forward, and they both knew it. No reason to hand her yet another weapon. "I'll see you then."

"I'm looking forward to it."   •

I'll just bet you are. The only thing the Bancrofts loved was power. Esther, in particular, had scared the shit out of Journey as a child. She had a way of looking at a person as if she could see down to their very soul—and she always found them wanting.

Journey changed into a fitted black dress that managed to be her version of demure, and pinned her hair up in a simple style. She would have to hurry to make it inside of the hour timeline, but the only thing guaranteed to distract her grandmother from her purpose was showing up inappropriately attired. *God forbid.*

My family's priorities are so fucked up.

After letting José and Ethan know where she was headed—and waiting for them to grab their car so they could drive her over there personally—she arrived at her grandmother's Houston residence.

The high-rise building was on the newer side and so expensive that the suites were mostly owned by out-of-town billionaires. Journey waited for the doorman to check her info and then left the men in the lobby and headed up to her grandmother's floor. Stepping off the elevator was like stepping into the past. Esther had apparently decided to bring a little piece of home with her when she visited, because the suite was decorated identically to her rooms back in Dallas, right down to the little Pomeranian statues arranged carefully on the vanity. *Creepy, as always.*

Esther rose as Journey walked in, as regal as a queen. Her cloud of white hair was pinned perfectly in place, and she wore a designer dress that managed to convey wealth and power without beating the viewer over the head with it. She extended a gloved hand. "Granddaughter."

So we're going to play it like this.

Journey stalked to Esther and placed her hands over

the old woman's. Despite having left seventy in the rearview several years ago, age hadn't conquered Esther yet. She stood straight, her face smoother than it had any right to be. *Probably bathing in the blood of virgins.* "Grandmother."

"It's been some time since I've seen you." She held Journey's arms out and cast a critical look over her. "Stressed and brittle isn't a good look for you, my dear."

She extracted her hands and took a small step back. "As usual, your warmth astounds me."

"Attitude." Esther shook her head. "You get that from your mother. My Elliott never talked back the way you children do."

No, he always kept a calm and cheerful voice when he was giving his children a lifetime's worth of scars.

Over the years, they'd gone through this song and dance more times than Journey could count. "As delightful as this is, I'm not here so you can tell me all the ways I've disappointed you over the years. This isn't about family. This is business." The Kings might not differentiate between the two, but the Bancrofts sure as hell did.

Esther stilled, shifting from grandmother to a cold stranger in the space of a heartbeat. This was the woman who had taken a prestigious family name and old money and turned it into an empire that spanned a good portion of the country. "You should have led with that." She motioned to the dark wood table situated in the corner opposite the door. "Tea?"

"No, thank you." She didn't necessarily think her grandmother would poison her, but she'd also never thought that her father would orchestrate a car accident that put Eliza's life in danger, either. The rules on what was and wasn't possible seemed to change daily, and she wasn't going to get caught flat-footed.

Esther took a seat opposite her and waited for Journey to do the same. She folded her hands. "Now, what is it that brought you to my door?"

The phrasing made her sound like some kind of Mafia boss, which should have been absurd, but only a fool underestimated Esther Bancroft, blood relation or no. Journey lifted her chin. "I want you to call off your dog. You've made your point—Kingdom Corp owes its existence to you. Tell me what you want and I'll see it done—on the condition that Elliott leaves Houston and never comes back."

Esther considered her, the steely blue eyes that ran through the Bancroft family showing nothing. "Never come to the negotiation table from a point of anger, my dear. It makes you look weak."

Damn it. She held her grandmother's gaze, refusing to look away or show how overwhelmed she felt. "If you want to nuke the company, there are more effective ways to do it than letting your youngest son meddle with everything because he thinks he's untouchable." She paused, smothering any show of emotion. Esther wouldn't respect it, and it would only undermine Journey's argument. "Which leads me to the conclusion that you want Kingdom Corp mostly intact for whatever you have planned. With Elliott at the helm and the rest of us driven out, all the key employees will be gone within a month—two at the most. He's been here a week and he pissed off the tech department so thoroughly, they would have walked if not for me. That would be impressive if it wasn't so damn dangerous."

A slight tightening around Esther's mouth betrayed her irritation, though it didn't show on the rest of her face. "I have no idea what you're talking about, but my Elliott is more than capable of running the business if that's what he's decided to do. I'm not his keeper."

Journey snorted. "You don't believe that any more than I do. He *requires* a keeper. He's a mess. He's always been a mess."

"And you've historically had issues with your father." Esther narrowed her blue eyes. "You're too old for such petty vendettas, my dear."

There was nothing petty about her issues with Elliott, but she wasn't stupid enough to trot them out now. It would make more sense to hand a loaded gun to her enemy and paint a target on her chest. Esther and the rest of the family considered Journey and her siblings as Kings, rather than Bancrofts. What they would do for each other, they wouldn't do for *them*.

The image of her mother after that meeting with the family lawyer skated through her mind. The only time she'd ever seen Lydia look something close to defeated. *If my mother couldn't best them, how in the hell do I think I can?*

She shoved the dark thoughts away. She had to power through this as if Esther were just another business competitor. *That*, Journey could handle. "Even if you— excuse me, I mean Elliott—had planned on replacing key employees, replacing an entire department is costly and ineffective. We have the best Houston has to offer on staff, and you won't convince them to stay with him helming the ship."

Esther sipped her tea from its porcelain cup. It had

frolicking kittens painted on the side, which just added to the surrealism of the moment. "You assume that your father isn't making choices to best benefit the company. You're taking this whole thing rather personally, aren't you?"

"Choices to best benefit the company. Funny you should say that." She folded her hands in her lap. "Explain to me how orchestrating a hit-and-run that almost killed Eliza is benefiting the company?"

That got Esther's attention. She straightened, something resembling worry flickering across her face. "Is she well?"

"As well as can be expected considering the circumstances. Quite a coincidence that she was on her way to the airport to jet out of Houston and never return when it happened."

Understanding dawned, quickly replaced by cold calculation. "You can't honestly think that your father had anything to do with this. Eliza is instrumental in moving Kingdom Corp into the future. Elliott wouldn't endanger that over something as petty as her leaving town." Esther sighed and leaned back. "You always were a dramatic child. Elliott would never hurt one of his children. Never."

Frustration bloomed, and she had to press her lips together to stop from screaming at her grandmother. Hurt was the only thing Elliott was capable of doling out to his children, and Esther wasn't stupid. Even if she didn't believe Lydia's claims on behalf of the children, she was more than capable of looking into things and coming to her own conclusions. Whether she had done that or not was irrelevant. She knew what he was accused of, and she had the gall to make that statement to Journey's face.

There would be no winning this argument today. Esther was too smart to concede anything now, but she was also too smart to let her son continue fucking things up. She would rein him in. She had to if she didn't want a full-on rebellion on her hands. The only reason she would have sent in Elliott was to ensure what passed for a bloodless coup.

She knew that wouldn't happen now.

Journey would go down fighting, which meant things would get very, very ugly.

Very ugly wasn't good for business, and if there was one thing Esther prized above all others, it was business.

Journey set her jaw and stood. "Thank you for seeing me." She turned and strode toward the door.

She barely made it three steps before her grandmother's voice stopped her.

"I hear that you're seeing that boy, Frank Evans." She tsked. "Honestly, Journey. Even if you're set on infuriating your family, dating one of *his* kind is going too far."

She spun on her heel and glared. There was no mistaking what Esther meant. "Racism isn't a good look for you, Grandmother." There was so much more to say, but Journey reined in her rage. It didn't matter what Esther thought of Frank. He was better than her—better than all the Bancrofts piled together. She lifted her chin. "I highly suggest you bring your mad dog to heel before he does something irreparable. Time is of the essence."

She walked out and this time her grandmother didn't call her back. It was just as well. Journey had nothing else to say.

She had to believe there was still time to save the company. To save what was left of their family.

She pushed the button to call the elevator, and a prickle crept down her spine. Journey turned, her hand going to her purse where she'd stashed her gun, but the hallway was empty. A flash of a reflective surface caught her eye, dragging her attention up to the camera situated in the ceiling. Many residences had security cameras—her own included—but she couldn't shake the feeling that someone was on the other side of those cameras.

Someone who wanted to hurt her.

She deliberately turned back to the elevator doors, tracking the ascending numbers. Journey pulled out her phone and called José. She barely waited for him to answer before she cut in. "I'm getting in the elevator in approximately thirty seconds and coming down to the lobby."

"Trouble?"

Thank God that Frank's men were just as astute as he was. "I don't know, but I'd rather be paranoid given the current circumstances." She'd forgotten about her security detail too many times already—an unforgivably stupid sin. They were there for her protection. Using a tool at her disposal didn't make her weak. It made her smart.

The doors opened and she stepped into the elevator. Journey kept her phone handy during the descent, but no one joined her. It was just as well. With her nerves strung tightly enough to snap, she couldn't be sure of her response to a perceived threat. Or if she'd even be able to register a perceived threat from a real one.

Stop thinking like that. Get to the lobby, get the men, get the fuck out.

She walked into the lobby and breathed a small sigh of relief as José flanked her. He moved close in enough to say, "Ethan has secured the car. He's out front. I've got your back covered."

"Thank you." She kept moving, scanning the faces of the people scattered through the lobby. No one seemed particularly interested in what she was doing, but that didn't change the crawling sensation just beneath her skin. *Something's coming.*

Her phone buzzed in her hand. She stopped short at the sight of her grandmother's name. Journey glanced at José and followed his silent direction to the black SUV waiting at the curb. Once she was inside, she answered. "Twice in a single day, Grandmother. I'm honored."

"I've considered the information you brought to me, and I'll investigate the attack on Eliza." No hint of frailness or age in Esther's tone. Just pure command. "In the meantime, I will remove Elliott from his current position—on one condition."

"I'm listening."

"You and Anderson will vote with the board every time, without fail."

Journey glared at the back of the seat in front of her. "You mean we'll play the part of puppet for you and jump when you say jump."

"Call it what you wish. That is my condition." Esther's voice softened. "I wouldn't be opposed to seeing you children more often."

Trap.

Nothing good came from her grandmother playing the gentle relationship card. There was nothing gentle *or* grandmotherly about Esther, and the fact that she thought Journey was stupid enough—or emotionally wrecked enough—to fall for it irked her. "I'll discuss your terms with Anderson and Bellamy." She took a careful breath. "In the meantime, as a show of good faith, you will call off Elliott."

Esther laughed. "There's some Bancroft in you, after all, isn't there?"

"No, Esther. I'm all King." She hung up and slouched back against the seat, every muscle in her body going slack and weak.

That's when the shakes started.

She nearly dropped her phone as she dialed her older brother. *Keep it together. You're safe. She can't hurt you. Elliott can't hurt you. You're winning.*

This doesn't feel like winning.

It felt a whole lot like defeat.

"Jo?"

She ran her free hand over her arm, debating asking Ethan or José to turn on the heat. "I just talked to our grandmother."

"Grandmother... You talked to *Esther*?"

"Yeah. In a strange turn of events, she's in Houston right now." Her sarcastic comment fell flat. "She agreed to call off Elliott."

"For a price."

"Yeah, for a price. She wants control of Kingdom Corp, one way or another. In exchange for removing Elliott, she wants us to vote with the board majority every time." The fact that their grandmother had control of the board was something Journey would have to think about in greater depth. She'd known many of those men and women for years—decades in some cases. Flipping their loyalty hadn't happened in the last couple of weeks—the last couple of months, even.

Esther had been planning this coup for a long time, a spider constructing a web around an unsuspecting fly, waiting for the moment when it moved into just the right place to trap it and strike.

I am no fly.

We *are not flies.*

"If we agree to that, we might as well let Elliott take over, and walk away. It accomplishes the same damn thing."

She bit back a curse. She didn't disagree with her brother, but he was missing one very important point. "We can't fight if we lose our positions within Kingdom Corp. We sure as hell can't win. If Esther can take over the board, then we can damn well take it back. Agreeing is just a quick patch until we come up with a better plan." When Anderson didn't immediately speak, she leaned her head back against the car seat and sighed. "Yielding a single time doesn't mean we're weak. It doesn't mean she wins."

Silence for a beat. Two. "I don't see a way out of this, Jo. I thought I had things under control, but after Eliza..."

"I know." Anderson wouldn't be coming in with a last-minute solution to save all their asses. Not this time. "Give me twenty-four hours to figure out a game plan and then we'll give our answer to Esther."

He exhaled harshly. "I can do that."

"Thank you." She hesitated. "It will be okay, Anderson. We'll find a way through this. I promise." Journey hung up and leaned forward to catch Ethan's eye. "Take me to Frank."

CHAPTER TWENTY

Frank glanced up as Mateo walked into his office. No mistaking the look on his second's face. "You found something."

"I found something," he confirmed. He drank from a giant mug of coffee, and his dark face was drawn and exhausted. Frank made a mental note to double Mateo's hazard pay for pulling this shit together in such a short time. The man set the mug on his desk and passed over a manila folder. "I compiled this last night..." He looked at his watch. "Well, technically this morning."

Frank flipped through the information, dread curling through him with each word he read. "That dumb fuck."

"That about sums it up."

He kept reading. They'd thought they found all of Elliott's debts—and that they all had been paid by his mother. They were wrong. Frank looked at the numbers, at the zeros behind them. "Four *million*? How the fuck did he dig himself that deeply?"

"He was paying it off at first, probably from money supplied by Lydia King, though it's damn near impossible to track." Mateo lifted his mug in the direction of the file. "The fact I managed to pull that much together is a testament to how good I am at my job."

"Trust me, you'll be compensated. More than compensated." Frank finished reading and sat back. The picture painted by the file wasn't a pretty one. A decade of loans from the Russians, of all people. Elliott had paid them back repeatedly...until six years ago, when the repayments stopped, but the spending didn't. He shook his head. "Ivan Romanov gave him enough rope to hang himself with."

Mateo nodded. "If he hasn't already called the debt due, he will before too long."

There were other ways to pay. Frank knew better than most the value information held. The Bancroft family had its fingers in more pies than anyone knew, from overseas trade to arms manufacturing. Elliott could be doing anything from insider trading to allowing Romanov to smuggle things in or out of the country.

"What I don't get is why he didn't go running to Mommy with this." Mateo leaned his head against the back of his chair and closed his eyes. "She's paid off every other debt he's acquired."

That, at least, he had an answer to. "Bancrofts aren't stupid enough to get caught with ties to the Russian mob. Admitting he owes them money is putting the entire family name in danger if it comes out—and it will." The only reason it hadn't until now was that the information was leverage Ivan Romanov no doubt held over Elliott's head.

I could buy the debt and be the one holding that bastard's leash.

His people depended on him to keep them safe, but Journey was relying on him as well. A soft snore made Frank sigh. Mateo had fallen asleep in his chair. If he left him there, the man would wake up with a crick in his neck. He set the file on the desk and clasped his shoulder. "Mateo, use my couch." Frank quietly closed the door of his office behind him and made his way to Mateo's desk, where he could continue to consider this new information.

The facts didn't change on his second read-through of the brief—or his third.

Mateo had anticipated his needs, and there was a Post-it note with Romanov's number on the last page. Frank studied it for a long moment. Getting into bed with organized crime wasn't part of the plan.

But if he didn't do something, Elliott would keep going after Journey—after her siblings.

He could kill someone if they didn't act fast.

He took a slow breath and dialed the number Mateo had provided.

"Ivan Romanov."

That didn't take long. "My name is Frank Evans of Evans Inc in Houston. I have a business prospect for you."

A pause, and the man's Russian accent thickened. "I'm listening."

"A mutual friend of ours, one Elliott Bancroft, owes you a significant amount of money. I'm willing to negotiate terms so you stop putting pressure on him. I have information I think you might find valuable in your business dealings."

Another pause, longer this time. Finally, Ivan chuckled,

the sound rumbling down the line. "I like you, Frank Evans. You have balls, and a man like myself can appreciate that. But the debts have already been paid for the man of who you speak."

What? "By who?" He spoke without thinking.

"I'm not in the habit of giving information for free."

A bargain, then, but one with different parameters. Frank leaned back in his chair, tension working its way through his shoulders and cascading down his back. "Information for information, then."

"There is word of a merger with Kingdom Corp," Romanov hinted.

Easy enough to answer that question that isn't a question. "I have it on good authority that Kingdom Corp is acquiring Cardinal Energy in a merger, though I can't speak to the terms of the deal."

"Good. Good. This is good news." Ivan laughed, the sound booming down the line. "The man's debts were purchased by a close relative of his. Nice older woman, though she is strong enough to scare weaker men out of her path."

Esther. It has to be.

"A pleasure exchanging information with you, Ivan."

The amusement fled from the Russian's tone. "Do not call this number again." He hung up.

As soon as Frank set his phone on the desk, it buzzed with a text from Ethan. *Incoming.*

Frank pushed to his feet and strode down the hallway. It hadn't been all that long since he'd seen Journey last, but the sheer relief he felt down to his very bones as she made her way toward him rocked him back on his heels. *Safe. She's safe.* Her dress and understated pumps made it look like she'd just come from the office, but the last he'd heard, she was with Samara.

Journey walked herself right into his embrace as he raised his arms and folded her into him. Frank stroked a hand down her back, the touch soothing something inside him. He turned his head and pressed a kiss to her temple. "Things with Samara went well."

"Yes, though I didn't come from there just now." She hugged him tighter. "I may have handled the Elliott issue, but we have bigger problems."

No misunderstanding that. "Esther."

"Yeah." Journey leaned back enough to meet his gaze. "How'd you know?"

It was on the tip of his tongue to say *lucky guess* the way he would to Beck or anyone else who asked. Frank smoothed the hair back from her face, letting his touch linger on her cheekbones. "Mateo dug deep enough to get the name of the person Elliott owed money to. We had a short but enlightening conversation."

A line appeared between her strong brows. "That sounds very vague and sinister."

"I told him about the merger." More honesty, pouring from his mouth as easily as his next exhale. He wouldn't apologize for monetizing that information, but he also wouldn't lie to her about it. "If he's as smart as his reputation says he is, he'll use it to his advantage, and the only thing either of us is guilty of is insider trading."

Her lips quirked the slightest bit. "Plenty of people have gone to jail for insider trading, Frank. It wasn't worth the risk. I got the information we needed without having to do anything illegal." She sighed. "Did you even think to ask what I knew before you made that call?"

He hadn't. He'd only thought of protecting her, not of asking her insight. Frank opened his mouth, but he didn't know what he was supposed to say. "I take care of people, Duchess. It's what I do."

She didn't move back, but he could almost see the distance between them growing vaster, a sinking hole deep enough to swallow the unwary. Journey gave him a sad smile. "There's no shame in leaning on other people occasionally." She shook her head and stepped out of his arms. "Is there somewhere we can talk privately?"

There was no one in the hallway but them, but he nodded to Mateo's office. Once they were closed inside it, Frank leaned against the door and watched Journey pace. "I'm sorry I upset you."

"Is that what you think the problem is?" She gave a mirthless laugh. "Even if it was, that's a half-assed apology if I've ever heard one. 'I'm sorry I upset you' means that you're sorry I'm upset but you'd do it again in a heartbeat." She held up a hand before he could speak. "It's a moot point. I just came from meeting with my grandmother."

It took him precious seconds to make the jump with her. Frank was still focused on her dismissal of his apology and then... "Your grandmother. Esther Bancroft is in Houston?"

"Yes." She perched on the edge of the desk and met his gaze. "She has control of Kingdom Corp's board. We knew that—Elliott wouldn't have been able to come in like he did without board support—but she explicitly stated it. She'll call off my father if Anderson and I do her bidding when it comes to the company." She wrapped her arms around herself. "I don't see a way out of this.

I know there has to be one, but I don't see it. This is
exactly what that crafty bitch wanted. She sends in Elliott
to terrorize us, and then we trip all over ourselves to give
her control just to get him out of our lives." Journey's
hazel eyes shone a little and she shook her head. "I hate
that it's working. I hate that she played us like this."

"Esther Bancroft has been doing this sort of thing a
long time." Really, it was a brilliant play. With the shares
Elliott owned in the company, Esther could have made
her move at any time, but she must have put these pieces
into place and just waited for the timing to be right.
Frank couldn't have handled it better if he'd tried. "Elliott
crossed a line with what happened to your sister. For a
man who's usually so subtle about his torment, he seems
to be losing control."

"Yeah. Maybe." Journey seemed to realize she was
clutching herself and dropped her arms. "As long as my
brothers and I can keep our current positions within the
company, we have a chance to oust the Bancrofts."

She was so focused on the company, she wasn't
looking at the other potential outcome if Elliott was once
again banished from Houston. "He'll come after you.
After all of you, but after you specifically."

"It's entirely possible." She lifted her chin. "But I'll
burn that bridge when I come to it."

He released her hand and shoved to his feet, agitation
driving his movements. "He's got you over a barrel,
Duchess. This isn't a fight you can win on your own."
Regret hit him the instant he gave the words voice.
The one constant Journey held was that she wanted—
needed—to fight her own battles.

And he'd just told her that she couldn't.

Frank turned to face her. "I'm sorry."

"There are those words again." She leveraged herself off the desk and straightened her shoulders. "I know I'm a mess, Frank. I've been pretty honest about that from the start. It's nothing new, and throwing it in my face because you're scared is a really shitty move. I might be broken, but I'm not a glass figurine you can bundle up and stick on a high shelf to protect. I'm a person, and I'm muddling through things as best I can. I won't be stupid, and I definitely won't put myself within striking distance of him, but I will not cower and hide with so much at stake."

He could lose her.

It wouldn't happen because things fell apart in a mundane way, because she realized that Frank's damage and hers were a recipe for disaster when thrown together. Losing her like that would tear out his fucking heart, but at least give him the comfort of knowing Journey was going on with her life. Living. Breathing. Pulling her tattered strength around her and moving through her days with purpose.

He could lose her in the same way he'd lost his mother and his old man.

At the very core of his being, Elliott was a bully. Since he couldn't lash out at his mother, he would lash out at his children.

At Journey.

This position within Kingdom Corp was the first real power Elliott had in his life. Running Kingdom Corp, especially in the wake of his hated wife's departure, *was* personal. He'd see Journey and his mother's collusion as an attack against him, and he'd come gunning in the only way he knew how.

This time, he wouldn't hold back.

Frank was sure of it.

Even with two of his best men watching over her, that bastard could still find a way to get to her. It could be as simple as lying in wait in her parking garage and shoving her into the trunk of a car. Or accosting her in a stairwell. *I know how that ends.* With her bent and broken at the bottom of the stairs. Too many scenarios kept playing in his head of Journey dead and gone, the life bleeding out of her hazel eyes.

And I can't stop it.

Frank dropped to the sofa against the far wall. "He *will* hurt you," Frank said. The only reason Elliott hadn't done something irreparable up to that point was that pushing her out of the company she lived and breathed would hurt her more. Without that option, Elliott was a wild card. He would destroy his children if he could. Frank nodded to himself. "I've been working on increasing the security in your building. The goal was to have it done before we came back from the Hamptons, but obviously that time-line changed. It will be finished in a few days. You'll stay with me in the meantime."

She raised one eyebrow, a deep understanding shifting through her hazel eyes. "I see." Journey laughed softly. "God, you really are a big spiky marshmallow, aren't you? Did you try to pull this shit with Beckett when he went toe-to-toe with my mother?"

"Beck's just as stubborn as you are, and that time I backed down. But I won't make the same mistake twice. It kills me that so much was stolen from him."

"Frank..." She reached up and cupped his jaw. "You can't save everyone."

"You don't think I know that? If I could have, I would have saved my parents."

There it was. Out in the open. He'd been so fucking powerless when the cops came and took away his father, and during his mother's rapid decline when he watched her slip through his fingers more and more with each day that passed. If she'd agreed to surgery and chemo, there was a chance she could have beaten the cancer, but she decided to forgo treatment. She died a little more each day and *there was nothing Frank could do to stop it.*

Just like he hadn't been able to save Beck from a soul wound.

Just like all his precautions hadn't saved Journey from being hurt.

He ran his hands over his head. He never lost control. *Never.* But these days he was a runaway train and there was no stopping it until he eliminated the threat. Taking Journey somewhere he could ensure her safety was the only thing that would calm him.

But she'd been hauled around enough in her life.

"Come home with me." He stopped and tried to moderate his tone. "Please, Duchess. I refuse to lose another person I love over something I can prevent."

Journey moved to stand in front of him and stared up into his eyes for a long moment. He was too fucked up to maintain his normal calm mask, and whatever she saw there was enough to have her nodding. "I just need to run by my place to pack an overnight bag." She held up a hand when he would have protested. "This is just for tonight, Frank. You can't hide me away in your secret house outside Houston and go to battle on my behalf. Anderson and I have a decision to make—Bellamy, too—

and that can't wait." She shook her head. "Plus, I've already dropped the ball enough when it comes to my job. If I'm gone longer, the whole place will be falling apart."

"Duchess—"

"That was not a request—that was me stating my plans."

If he didn't accept them, she wouldn't leave with him. That much was clear. "My men stay in the room with you while you're in the Kingdom Corp building."

She opened her mouth, seemed to reconsider, and closed it. "They can stand by my office door and glower at anyone who walks past." When he hesitated, Journey sighed. "Frank, no matter what you think is going to happen, I do have meetings that require confidentiality. I'm not calling the trustworthiness of your people into question, but the fact remains that they will stand outside a closed door while I conduct my business. Understood?"

How had he mistaken this woman for a broken thing? She might be bruised and a little battered in both body and soul, but that just made her strength shine brighter. If circumstances hadn't taken her down her before now, they wouldn't.

Elliott has to have realized that by now. He's got to know he can't undermine her and discredit her because she's found her legs and she's not going to bend to his will. He never expected her to go over his head to Esther, and he's going to be furious when he finds out.

He's going to want revenge.

He didn't say it aloud. Journey had to know, even if she wasn't willing to admit it. Either way, the bastard wouldn't get to her tonight. "I understand."

"Good." She turned and headed for the door. "Let's go."

* * *

Eliza woke to both her brothers in her room. She stared dully at Anderson talking softly with the nurse and Bellamy slumped in the chair next to her bed as if he'd been there for a long time. Maybe he had. The drugs they pumped through her IV were strong enough that she slept more often than she didn't, which was just as well.

At least in her dreams, nothing had changed.

She touched the bandages covering her face. She'd seen the damage this morning when they switched the dressings. Brutal cuts crisscrossed her face and a good portion of her shoulders, chest, and arms. Her lower half hadn't been spared, either. When the car crumpled around her, the metal had shattered her hip and left leg. The doctors assured her that the surgery had been successful, and though it may take one or two more, she would walk again.

Eliza didn't fucking care.

She closed her eyes, listening to the nurse murmur that she'd give them some privacy, and then the door shut. It was only then that she said, "I told them I didn't want to see any of you." She didn't even *sound* like herself, her voice raspy and hollow. Fitting, in a way. The rest of her was ruined—why not that, too?

"Eliza." This from Bellamy at her side.

She didn't open her eyes, couldn't see the pity on his face, couldn't handle knowing that her brother thought less of her. Even without looking at him, she knew what he was thinking. "It's not your fault, Bel. Even if you'd been driving, it still would have happened." The cops had already been in to talk to her that first day, though they couldn't be clearer in their disinterest in following up on whoever did this to her. *Fine by me.* She'd have the reminder every time she looked in the mirror. The people of Houston hated the King family as much as they loved them. Going from fashion model to scarred freak would create a media sensation all on its own. She didn't want to be dragged through a trial—both in the courtroom and by the press.

No, better to let it all fall away.

"The doctor says you'll make a full recovery," Anderson said. He sounded closer, his big personality taking up too much room. He'd always been like that, the type to take charge of every situation he came across.

Well, too damn bad. She wasn't a situation. She wasn't even a problem he could solve.

Eliza pulled her blankets higher up her chest. Her hip and leg were encased in metal and plaster, so that the left side of her body lay exposed for anyone to see how truly fucked up she was. *A full recovery.* The very idea was laughable. She might walk again, but there was no recovering from this.

Her face would scar. Not the kind that could be covered up with the right makeup and careful lighting. Hideous red jagged marks that rent her features like a mirror someone had thrown a chair through.

Her career, her *life*, was over.

When she didn't respond, Anderson continued, "I know Elliott has this bullshit merger in place, but I'll find a way around it. If they want a merger, we can make that work, but I'm not *selling* you to secure it."

Who would want to buy such a broken thing, after all?

"Eliza," Bellamy said again.

She couldn't turn from the pain in his voice despite her best efforts. She reluctantly opened her eyes to find her brother staring at her. The only other time she'd seen that look from Bellamy was when she'd come home after her first school dance, her mascara running rivers down her face because her idiot date had thought her being a pretty blonde meant she was down to fuck him in the locker room. Bellamy had taken care of her, calmed her down, and disappeared for several hours.

She still didn't know what he'd done to her date, but when she saw the guy the next Monday in school, he looked like he was about to pass out as he stammered an apology.

No one had asked her out for the rest of her high school career, expedited as it was.

"B . . ." She couldn't tell him she was fine. He wouldn't believe it, probably because it was a bald-faced lie. Eliza hadn't been further from *fine* than she was in that moment. "I'll survive." A much weaker reassurance, but closer to the truth. Survival required the bare minimum, after all. One foot in front of the other, an inhale followed by an exhale. Life dragged on for everyone, including her.

She cleared her throat. "I really would like to be alone."

Bellamy didn't look away. "You'll be here for a couple more days and then you're coming home." He probably meant that to be comforting, but it sounded like a special kind of hell. She'd die before she let her brother—or anyone in her family—become her caretaker.

A battle to fight when we get there.

The nurse ushered them out shortly after, for which Eliza was grateful. She didn't trust herself not to strike out like the wounded animal she was. It wasn't her brothers' fault that Elliott had effectively sold her to secure his merger, and it sure as hell wasn't their fault that someone had hurt her. Whether they targeted her because of the merger itself or because she was trying to flee it was anyone's guess.

She. Didn't. Care.

Her phone buzzed and she sighed when she saw her agent's name—again. There was no avoiding this, no matter how much she wanted to. Eliza sucked in a breath and answered. "Diego, hey."

"Are you okay?" He cursed. "You're alive, which is something at least. I told you not to go back there, Eliza. This shit..." More cursing. "It's bad."

It struck her that he wasn't talking about the accident. Eliza clutched her phone tighter. "What's going on?"

"Word got out before I could control the story. I don't know how they found out, but every single account you have dropped you. This morning. You're unemployed, honey."

She closed her eyes against the burning that started there. She would *not* cry, would not break down. Diego might not know how they found out, but Eliza had no illusions. As if her fucked-up face wasn't enough of a message, whoever did this to her had ensured she had nowhere to run once she recovered.

As if anyone would have wanted her after they saw how she looked now.

It took her two tries to get her words in order. "This is it for me, Diego. Once all the payments clear for the work I've already done, I'm out."

"Honey, we can find a way. Those assholes aren't the only names in the business, and you're Eliza fucking King. You're too good to go out like this."

He wouldn't say that if he could see her now, broken and disfigured. "It's over. I'm done." She hung up before he could say anything more. It was nothing more than the truth, but Diego was persistent and brilliant. If she let him, he'd spin a hopeful future around her that would light the way through her recovery and keep her going.

It would be a lie.

It was over. Her modeling career. Her independence.

She looked down at her mangled body and bit back a whimper. Even the stupid marriage merger wouldn't survive *this*.

Who will want me now?

She knew the answer before the question finished.

No one.

No one would want her, not now. Not ever again.

CHAPTER TWENTY-ONE

It wasn't until they arrived at Frank's place that it hit Journey—*Frank Evans told me he loves me*. She sat in his surprisingly cozy living room and stared at the steaming mug of tea in her hands. *Frank loves me*. And she, asshole that she was, hadn't said anything back.

He walked into the room, having disappeared briefly to change into a pair of lounge pants and a T-shirt. It should have made him look rumpled and at home, but there was nothing rumpled about Frank. She'd bet that he ironed that white shirt recently.

"I love you, too," she blurted.

"I know." He didn't even miss a step as he prowled around the living room, checking the windows as if expecting someone to burst through them at any moment. He shot her a look. "I knew the second you whisked me away to the Hamptons to keep me safe."

She set the tea on the table and glared. "Way to take the wind out of my sails, jerk."

"What we have is hardly a traditional relationship." He gave a half smile. "Life would be simpler if it was."

"You mean if my abuser father wasn't probably going to try to kill both of us before the month is out? Or the part where you helped my cousin banish my mother from Houston?"

His brows drew together. "Do you blame me for this?"

"No, of course not." She sighed. "It's entirely possible that Esther would have removed Lydia herself once she got tired of waiting for someone else to do it." The Bancrofts wouldn't have been satisfied with exile, either—not when they knew exactly what Lydia King was capable of. Journey reached for the tea again but aborted the move when she saw how badly her hands shook. "I don't want to give in, Frank. I know it's the smart thing to do, but I want that bitch out of my company and I want my father out of Houston."

Frank crossed the room to stand in front of her. He picked her up before she had a chance to protest, and strode out of the living room and toward the stairs. "Enough."

"Enough?" She shifted, but he just clenched her more tightly to his chest.

"We can talk this thing to death, but there isn't a damn thing we're going to accomplish tonight. Tomorrow you will sit down with your brother and figure out your next steps, and I will get my team together to start digging into the Bancrofts. Your father is the most immediate threat, and Esther will lighten up on the pressure if she thinks you're bowing to her will. My team is the best. If there's something to find—and there is—then we'll find it." He toed open the door to his bedroom and walked in without turning on the light. "If I thought for a second it wouldn't backfire, her paying off a Russian mobster would be leverage enough. But it's too dangerous. The Russians don't play by the same rules we do."

He sounded so damn grumpy that, despite everything, she smiled. "That offends you deeply, doesn't it?"

"We're not talking about any of them. Not for the rest of the night."

She eyed him. "What *are* we talking about?"

"Us." Frank set her on her feet and just as carefully pulled her dress over her head. He smoothed his hands over her body as if assuring himself that she was there and whole and okay. *Just like I did to him a couple days ago.* The thought might have made her laugh if it wasn't so damn sad.

"Is there an 'us,' Frank?" She grasped his wrists, stopping him from stroking her sides. "Because I think we're both fucked up enough to realize that love isn't the stuff of fairy tales. It doesn't earn you a happily ever after." Journey huffed out a sad little laugh. "If it even *is* love. We're probably getting infatuation mixed up with real feelings, and isn't *that* sad?"

"Duchess, look at me." He waited for her obedience before continuing. "Neither one of us came into this thing blushing virgins. Do you have a habit of getting starry eyed for every single man you've ever fucked?"

"Don't be absurd." She glared, but the effect of it bounced off his serious expression, so she gave up. "I see what you're saying, but the question still stands—is there really an us?"

He lifted one hand, hers still attached to his wrist, and sifted his fingers through her hair. Journey pushed off his chest and half turned away from him. "You don't do broken things, remember? I'm not going to just be magically fixed because I've fallen for you. You're going to keep trying to protect me, and I'm going to keep trying to fight to be a full partner. We'll be in a perpetual standoff."

"Broken things scare the shit out of me because there's no easy fix." His voice roughened and seemed to reach across the distance to slide down her spine. "Even if I could keep you safe from the enemies circling, I can't keep you safe from *me* fucking up."

Her throat burned and she blinked rapidly, still not looking at him. "Then I guess that's that."

"Is that how you want it to be?" He sounded closer, but he didn't touch her again.

"No! How the hell could you say that?" She spun, nearly slamming into him, and skittered back a step. "I want you, you arrogant, stubborn asshole. I don't know how to do this. I don't know how to be someone who isn't carrying around a lifetime of baggage, but I..." Realization dawned, sowing strength into her muscles and straightening her spine even as her words evened out. "I want this. I want you—us."

"That's all that matters, Duchess. We just have to jump together. We'll figure out the rest on our way down." He said it so calmly, as if he had no doubts that they'd figure out how to fly together, instead of crashing themselves to pieces on the rocks below. Frank held out his hand. "Will you jump with me?"

She wanted to take that hand so badly, she shook in an entirely different way. "If we do this, it will never be equal. I'll always be the broken one, and you'll always be the protector trying to step between me and the rest of the world. I'll resent you. You'll smother me."

He *laughed*, the ass. "If you really think that, you

haven't been paying attention. I'm not keeping score, but I'd say we're pretty damn equal." He sobered. "You were right before. I should have got a hold of you first instead of doing even the smallest deal with the Russian. I made the wrong call."

This thing didn't look like she'd always imagined her perfect relationship. They fought. A lot. He was pushy and just as arrogant and stubborn as she'd accused him of being. Frank would never, ever just roll over because she demanded it. And sometimes he might refuse to do so just to prove he could.

But...

This was also the man who had listened to her pour her darkest poison out without looking away. He'd listened to her boundaries—her triggers—and done his best to work around them so she always felt safe. Not comfortable. Not by a long shot. But Frank would never harm her on purpose.

She pressed her lips together. "There's a decent chance that my father is going to find a way to shove me in front of a moving SUV or maybe ensure I suffer some unfortunately lethal accident." She'd fight to survive. The little girl who had closed her eyes and waited for the pain to end didn't exist anymore. She had people she cared about—people she loved—and Elliott had already proven that he would hurt them if given half a chance.

If Journey couldn't dredge up the strength to fight him on her own behalf, she'd do it on theirs.

"We'll take him down, Duchess—just like we'll take down any enemy that comes at us in the future. Together."

She took a half step toward him. "How can you be so sure about all this?"

"Because I know *you*." He tapped the spot over her heart with a single finger. "This shit with your old man knocked you for a loop, but every other obstacle you've come across in your life, you've faced down without blinking. You protect the things you love with a ferocity that I am intimately acquainted with." He took her hand and mirrored the motion, touching his chest. "Because it's the same thing I have coiled and snapping inside me. Like recognizes like. Even if it took me a little too long to figure it out."

She could keep arguing, but he had an answer to every issue she threw at him and . . . truth be told, Journey didn't *want* to prove him wrong. She wanted to be the ferocious woman he saw in her. The one who would go to battle at his side as a full partner, who he'd trust to watch his back against any threat that arose. "Okay."

Frank smiled, a full, happy smile that lit up his eyes. He pulled her against him and took her mouth, growling when she immediately opened for him. Journey went for the buttons of his shirt, but he stopped her. "Slow tonight, Duchess. Let me make love to you."

In the end, there was only one thing to say to that. "Yes."

Frank released her and stripped quickly, until he stood before her gloriously naked. The faint light from the setting sun stole across his dark skin and lovingly traced every curve of carved muscle. He walked to his dresser, and she had to clench her jaw to keep from moaning at the sight of his ass. Journey had never considered herself an ass woman before, but she had the insane urge to sink her teeth into his.

Frank turned and raised his eyebrows. "Checking out my ass?"

"I'm not even sorry." She registered what he had in his hands, and fear battled desire, the twin flames threatening to scorch her from the inside out. "I know you said to trust you, but bondage is going to throw me right off the deep end." She'd never let someone tie her down before, had never been able to stand the thought of being that helpless again...

She took a step back. "No."

"Journey." The snap in his voice made her stop retreating long enough to look at him. Frank held up the pair of ties. "They're not for you. They're for me."

She blinked. "You want *me* to tie *you* up?" In every single sexual encounter they'd had, Frank was the dominant one, the one who took charge and kept them both in the moment even as he drove her out of her mind with pleasure. It came as naturally to him as breathing, and for him to hand that control to her floored her.

"I trust you."

The simple words left her weaving on her feet. *He trusts me.*

Frank hadn't moved. "It's your decision, Duchess."

"Yes."

I want to show him how much I love him.

She walked over on unsteady legs and took the ties from Frank's hands. "Lie down." She watched as he obeyed, a heady feeling coursing through her body, chasing away the last remnants of fear. He reclined on his back in the middle of the blue bedspread, and Journey crawled onto the bed to join him. She decided straddling him was the best way to go about this. "Arms over your head." She tied his wrists to the metal close enough that he wouldn't wrench a shoulder, but far enough away that he shouldn't be able to get too much leverage—theoretically, at least.

Journey sat back and took in the picture he presented. She frowned. "Something's missing." She looked around and her attention caught on a trio of candles situated on the dresser. *Perfect.*

It wasn't until she had retrieved a lighter from her purse and set flame to their wicks that she realized Frank wasn't exactly a candle type of guy. "Ex-girlfriend?" Jealousy snapped vicious thorns through her at the thought of another woman sharing this space with him, putting her mark on his home effectively enough that he hadn't bothered to erase evidence of her even after the relationship was over.

"I like candles." A thread of amusement in his voice told her that he knew exactly where her thoughts had gone.

She transferred the candles to each side of the bed and paused to make sure they weren't going to set fire to anything. The flickering light teased Frank's skin much the same way the sunset had, giving the room an intimate, sensual feeling. Journey returned to the bed and ran her hand down the center of his chest. "Spend a lot of time in the gym?"

"Most days." His muscles clenched beneath her wandering hand. "Helps me focus to burn off energy."

"I'll bet." She leaned down and dragged an open-mouthed kiss along the same path her hand had taken, stopping short of where his cock strained, as if reaching for her. "How's that been working out for you lately?"

"It hasn't."

She laughed against his skin, letting herself sink into this moment. Nothing existed outside of Frank's bedroom. It was just the two of them, and the riot of emotions they'd coaxed from each other. Emotions she could show him without fear of a flashback or panic robbing her of control.

It was only her and Frank.

Journey moved to straddle his stomach, keeping well away from his cock, and smoothed her hands over his chest. "You look good, Frank." Strong. Steady. Sexy as fuck. She dipped down and flicked first one nipple and then the other with her tongue. He tensed beneath her, watching her with eyes that seemed to swallow up the faint light from the candles.

"Let me see you, Duchess."

She straightened with a slow smile and ran her hands over her lace-covered breasts. He twisted his hands around to clench the metal headboard, and his obvious fighting for control only heightened her desire. She shrugged off the straps of her bra and let them fall so only the cups over her breasts kept her shielded from his gaze. "Like this?" Emboldened, she leaned back and spread her knees a little, waiting for his gaze to fall to her thong before she tugged the fabric to the side. "Or did you mean like this?"

Frank hissed out a breath. "You know what I want."

Yeah, she did. That didn't mean she was going to give it to him. Yet. She stroked her clit with her middle finger, watching him watch her. "It's not as good as what you do to me, but I think I could get used to this power exchange."

He glared at her finger. "Stop taking what's mine, Duchess."

"What's yours is whatever I decide to give you." She

pushed the finger into her, whimpering a little at the expression on his face. If she wasn't careful, she could get herself off like this, finger fucking herself on top of Frank with his eyes on her. *Not yet.* Journey bit her bottom lip and held up her finger. "Open."

He parted his lips, holding perfectly still as she slipped the finger that had been inside her between them. The passiveness barely lasted a heartbeat. He sucked her finger and raked his teeth gently down the sensitive skin as she withdrew it. "More."

"Demanding for someone who's tied on his back."

He gave her another devastating grin. "I know what you want, Duchess." Frank licked his lips. "Climb up here and pull those panties to the side. Hang on to the headboard while you ride my mouth. It's been too long since I've had a taste of you."

She pretended to consider, as if he couldn't feel her clenching her thighs around his torso at the scene he'd described. "Yes . . . with one caveat."

Frank raised a single brow and waited. Journey leaned down to kiss him, needing to be closer, to have him going as wild beneath her as she felt. She didn't stop until they were both breathing hard and she was doing her damnedest to remember why she wasn't going to ride his cock right then and there. *Having him tied down is probably the only chance I'm going to have to do this.* Journey nipped his bottom lip and shifted to whisper in his ear. "I've wanted to suck your cock since that first night in your office." This time *he* clenched beneath her. She writhed against him, desire almost getting the best of her. "So, yes, I'm going to ride your mouth, while you're in *my* mouth." She grinned. "Want to race to orgasm?"

His curse came out strained. "Hard to declare a winner in that scenario."

"That's because we both win." She sat up. "I was going to take my panties off, but I like the idea of revisiting our first time, don't you?" She looked around the room. "Do you have those ones stashed around here somewhere?" Journey leaned back and wrapped her hand around his cock. "Did you jack yourself to the memory of me like you promised?"

"You know I did."

"Then I think you deserve a reward, don't you?"

* * *

Frank instinctively pulled at the ties keeping him from touching Journey as she lowered herself onto his face. His first taste was pure heaven, but that was nothing compared to the sound she made when she sucked his cock deep into her mouth.

The moment seemed to freeze in time. It was too good, too fucking perfect to have her mouth on him as she squirmed against *his* mouth. Trying to guide him to her sweet little clit as if he had intentions of going anywhere else.

He dragged his tongue up her center and then circled her clit, wishing he had his hands to hold her hips in place. If he wasn't careful, he'd blow before she got there, the hot wet clasp of her mouth a temptation he wouldn't have been able to resist even if he wasn't desperate for her. He clamped his lips around her clit and sucked hard, and she let go of his cock to cry out. "Oh, God, *Frank*." He did it again and again, edging her toward that sweet oblivion, needing to feel her come apart all over him.

She jerked away, too fast for him to catch one last taste, and scrambled down his body. "You would be the only man who managed to top while he's tied down and I'm riding his face."

"You love it."

"No. Well, yes." She shook her head, her blond hair sliding over her face even as she seemed to struggle for breath. "I can't concentrate when you're doing that with your mouth."

He didn't want her to concentrate. He wanted her wild with abandon—with trust. He needed her as crazy for him as he was for her. "Make love to me, Duchess."

She bit her bottom lip and gave his cock a stroke. "It's hard to resist you when you put it like that."

"Then don't resist me." He gritted his teeth as she gave him another stroke. "Ride my cock. I want to watch you use me for your pleasure. We have all night. You want to suck my cock after that? You won't have to tie me down to do it."

She smiled almost shyly. "Promise you'll let me have my filthy way with you and won't pull that caveman shit where you toss me to the mattress and fuck me like you can't get enough."

"No." The affronted look on her face drew a laugh out of him despite the situation. Or maybe because of it. "I love fucking you like I can't get enough. It happens to be my favorite thing—because it's the goddamn truth. I'll never get enough of you, Journey."

And hell if that didn't scare the shit out of him. He'd gotten this far in life because he compartmentalized. Strong emotions—love—had the potential to become a glaring weakness, an Achilles' heel that anyone with a brain could exploit.

If anyone threatens her, I'll burn the world to the ground to keep her from harm.

It wasn't a comfortable thought. It sure as fuck wasn't a *safe* thought. But then, Frank had left safe in the rear-view mirror the second he'd brought Journey to orgasm on his office floor. That had been his point of no return, even if he didn't recognize it at the time. His first taste of her had incited a need he would happily spend a lifetime assuaging.

She grabbed a string of condoms from the nightstand. "You've got that look on your face." She moved to straddle him and kissed his chest. A crinkle of foil and then her hands were on his cock again, rolling on the condom even as she watched him with those witchy hazel eyes.

"What look?"

"The dangerous sexy one that's possessive as all get-out." She positioned his cock at her entrance and sank onto him in a smooth move. "The one that should scare the shit out of me and send me fleeing into the night."

"You're too brave to run scared, Duchess. Not from me, and not from anyone else." He thrust up as she sank onto him again, but his position only offered him so much leverage.

It was worth it to see that look on her face. Her cocky smile that had been missing for far too long, her movements sure as she rode his cock, seeking her own pleasure. *Fuck, she's perfect.*

Beautiful and strong and fucking perfect.

She circled her hips in a move that had him digging his heels into the mattress in an effort to drive into her. "*Journey.*"

"I like it when you say my name." She planted a

hand on his chest and leaned up to untie first one hand and then the other.

Frank kept gripping the headboard. "You sure?" This moment was too perfect to ruin because either of them wanted to push her too far, too fast.

Journey took his hands and placed them on her hips. "I want all of you, Frank. Your trust, your dominance, your strength. Give it all to me."

His heart damn near grew ten sizes at her words. "Ride me, Duchess."

She gripped his biceps and started moving, every sinuous roll of her hips driving them both closer to the edge. It took everything Frank had to keep still, to let her stay in the driver's seat. He kept his grip on her hips, urging her to maintain the relentless pace that would take her exactly where she needed to go.

"God, that feels good." Her eyes slid shut and she whimpered, her strokes becoming more irregular. Frank stroked her clit with this thumb, watching her face all the while. He wanted to see the moment she came undone, that she gave everything to him.

Journey dug her nails into his arms and cried out, her back bowing as her pussy clamped tight around his cock. It was too much and not enough, and he thrust up into her again and again, needing to follow her over the edge, to share this fucking perfect moment with her. He came with a curse and her name on his lips.

She rewarded him with a sweet smile and slumped onto his chest. Journey pulled his arms up to wrap around her back like he was her favorite blanket. "It shouldn't be possible that the sex keeps getting better and better, but it does."

"I know." He kissed her temple and held her close. There was no telling what the future would bring, but they had right now and it was enough.

"Hey, Frank?"

"Yeah."

"I really do love you. It's not a situational thing. It's an all-too-real thing."

He held her tighter, never wanting to let her go. "I know, Duchess. Mine is an all-too-real thing, too."

"Well...good."

He grinned against her skin. "Are you hungry? I have some food stashed in the kitchen."

"Starving." She sat up and shook her out hair, looking like some kind of sex goddess. "Food and fucking. Frank Evans, you really do know the way to a girl's heart."

CHAPTER TWENTY-TWO

After a night spent in Frank's arms, Journey woke up in his bed alone. She stretched and smiled without opening her eyes. The invisible sword might be hanging over their heads, but it was hard to be truly afraid with her body still aching from what Frank had done to it. What they'd done together.

I love Frank Evans.

He loves me.

We're going to try to do this for real.

If they could get through their current situation, they'd actually have the time and distance to figure out if they *could* be together. She sat up and pushed her hair out of her face. Esther was scarier than Elliott in a number of ways, but Journey didn't freeze up at being in the same room as her grandmother. *That* was a battle she could fight.

It might even be one she could win.

She smiled. *God, is this what hope looks like?*

She tried to call Anderson, but he didn't answer. Journey checked the clock—six in the morning—and decided against leaving a message. Instead she sent him a text. *We need to give Esther an answer today. I'll be in the office later this morning, but if you're free earlier, let's meet.*

Satisfied she'd gotten that ball rolling, Journey called Bellamy. Despite the early hour, he sounded wide-awake when he answered. "Hey, Jo."

"How's Eliza doing?" It still bothered her that her sister wouldn't let them into the room after her accident, but Journey could understand to a certain extent. That didn't mean she was going to let the directive stop her. She'd already been a shitty enough sister without abandoning Eliza when she needed Journey the most.

He sighed. "Not good. I mean, she's going to make close to a full recovery. The doctor is confident she'll walk and run again, though the limits of that will be something Eliza has to figure out for herself when the time comes." He hesitated. "Her face is bandaged up. She had close to eighty stitches on her face and shoulders alone. She's…she's going to scar."

The implications settled across Journey. A scarred model was an unemployed model, even with today's slowly advancing ideas of what beauty was. Even if she could still work, people would always compare Eliza now with Eliza before the crash. It would be hell. "Shit." She threw the covers back and stood. Moving made it easier to think. "We'll find a place for her. If she doesn't want to be part of the company, then we'll find something else."

"I've never seen her like this, Jo."

She spun on her heel and started for the bathroom. "You saw her?"

"Yeah, Anderson talked his way into the room and we were there when she woke up yesterday. That spark, that defiance, is gone. It's not just the pain meds and the accident. It's like she's given up."

"We won't let her give up." He was closer to Eliza than anyone, but maybe this was a job for a sister, not a brother. Journey dug through the overnight bag Frank had stashed in his bathroom, looking for clean clothes. "I'll check on her before I go into the office to meet with Anderson. And I'll talk to her doctor and see if we can get her moved to in-home care. Hospitals suck the life out of even the strongest people, and she's not in a good place for that shit. If we can get her home, then we can figure out the rest." She stopped short. *Which home?*

Bellamy must have sensed the direction of her thoughts. "With Mother gone, her place is empty. I can get people in there to set up the spare suite for anything Eliza needs."

She took a steadying breath. *Focus. One step at a time.* "First we need it cleaned out. A total spiff-up job that includes moving Lydia's stuff into her suite. She didn't have a lot of knickknacks, but her stamp is all over that town house." A few years ago, Lydia had edged out the competition in a series of three town houses in downtown Houston, a reasonable commute from the Kingdom Corp offices. She'd combined them into a home with four bedrooms, a library, an office, and half a dozen other smaller rooms for entertaining. A huge space for a single woman—both then and now—but it would more than do for Eliza. "After I talk to the doctor, I should have a list of things we need to bring Eliza home."

A sound brought her head up, and she paused when she found Frank leaning against the doorframe. "I'll call you when I know more." Journey hung up and straightened. "My sister needs me."

"I gathered. You going into the office afterward?"

"Yes. There's really only one option at this point, and it's to agree to Esther's terms." She pressed her lips together. "Does that offer to dig up information still stand? I think we're going to need all the leverage we can find to get her boot off our collective necks."

"The offer stands. I'll get Mateo started on it this morning." He crossed to her and pulled her into his arms. "Promise me you won't do anything dangerous today, Duchess."

She smiled up at him. "Only if you promise me the same."

"Consider it done." He kissed her, but before she could sink into the sensation of his mouth against hers, Frank gentled it and stepped back. "As tempting as it is to join you in the shower, I have a meeting later this morning that I can't miss."

Disappointment was tart on her tongue, but she couldn't argue with his reasoning. If they got distracted, they could get lost in each other for hours, and there were too many important things going on to hide out in Frank's house and wait for it all to blow over.

Because it wouldn't blow over. It would explode in their faces.

Journey ducked into the shower to get the water going. The glass separating the shower from the rest of the room had an abstract pattern etched on it that made her think of snowflakes, but she could see Frank's indistinct form on the other side. "What's the plan?"

"I could ask you the same thing."

She made a face at the blur of his image. "I'm going to get Eliza out of the hospital." She soaped herself down and resigned herself to using dude shampoo. "All she can do in that room is think about what she's lost. It's not good for her."

"Duchess."

"Oh, okay, fine. There's also the fact that it's not secure and she's weak and drugged up and it wouldn't take much to make sure she goes to sleep and never wakes up." Saying that to Bellamy would send her brother into protective mode, which would lock *everyone* down. Journey couldn't afford to have her movements restricted right now, and Bellamy wouldn't think too hard about her having an ulterior motive for bringing Eliza home because the reasoning she'd given him was sound.

She rinsed off and just let the water run down the tense muscles between her shoulder blades. Epic sex and too many orgasms to count had gone a long way to smoothing her frazzled edges, but it still wasn't enough to mute the reality of their current situation. She didn't think even a freaking horse tranquilizer would be enough to actually check her out at this point. Journey shut off the water and stepped out to find Frank waiting with a towel. "I would really appreciate it if you'd spare a team to keep Eliza safe until the end of this." She should have gotten over her pride and asked him for it from the start. They knew what Elliott was capable of when provoked, and she'd still tried to stick her head in the sand.

She dried off, conscious of Frank's gaze on her. It wasn't hot this time, more like he didn't really believe she was okay. "I'm fine."

"You're not."

They squared off. She had a feeling that any hint of weakness would see Frank wrapping her up and locking her in this house while he went off to battle the dragon. Well, fuck that. Journey had finally found her spine, and she wasn't about to lose it just because the thought of her in danger made *him* uncomfortable.

But she wasn't stupid, either.

"After I handle the Eliza situation, I'll be going into the office to meet with Anderson and hash this mess out. I'll take whoever you want to send with me." She held up a hand. "Two men. I don't need a small army surrounding me, no matter what you think." It would be comforting to be in the center of men Frank trusted to keep her safe, but that wasn't what standing on her own looked like.

He seemed to consider arguing but finally gave a short nod. "Two men, and they go with you everywhere."

"Fine." Her stipulations from the night before still stood, but there was no reason to fight about it again. They'd compromised, which was more than she could have hoped for considering how deep Frank's protective instincts ran. He loved her, and if he thought he failed her…Journey didn't like to think about what it would do to him.

I can't live my life in a glass box because I'm afraid of him getting hurt.

She'd tried that. She'd failed, and when her father shattered the box around her, it had almost sliced her to pieces in the process. Never again. Journey walked to him and went on her tiptoes to press a soft kiss to his lips. "I promised I'll be careful, and I meant it. Trust me to keep my word."

"It's not your word that I'm worried about, Duchess."

He settled his hands on her hips and tugged her against him. "How are you feeling today? Truthfully."

"Truthfully?" She considered lying, but he'd see right through it. "I'm stressed that this is going to blow up in my face and that someone I care about will get hurt because I'm not smart enough or fast enough to fix things before they spiral further out of control. I'm worried about a dozen different things, all of which are jockeying for position in the front of my mind." In addition to all the life-and-death family shit, she still had to sit down with Ronnie and figure out how to get the tech department back within their budget, and then deal with George and his shitty-ass attitude.

Just thinking about it made her want to take a nap.

She braided her hair and pinned it up in a look that was a little boho for her tastes, but since Frank didn't own a hair dryer, it was the best she had to work with. Journey pulled a dress out of her bag, considered it, and traded it out for a pair of slim black slacks and a red blouse. *If I have to run, pants are a better option.* Paranoid thoughts, but it wasn't actually paranoia if people were truly out to get her.

One thing at a time.

First she had to ensure Eliza was safe. That had to be her top priority right now. A close second was getting their company out of the fire, at least for the near future.

Journey straightened her shirt and tucked a stray strand of hair back into her braid. "I'm ready."

It almost felt like the truth.

* * *

Leaving Journey on the curb in front of the hospital—again—was the hardest fucking thing Frank had ever done. He kept thinking about what could go wrong the second she left his line of sight. It took everything he had to drive away and leave her there with Ethan and José flanking her. They would keep her safe. There was no other acceptable outcome.

Not to mention she'd never forgive him if he tried to keep her away from this mess.

He checked the time and headed for Morningstar Enterprise. Beck met him as he stepped off the elevator. His friend cast a critical eye over Frank. "You look pretty damn happy."

"I…am." The words tasted strange on his tongue. Strange, but not unpleasant.

Beck stared for a long moment and then burst out laughing. "Holy shit, you're in love. That's the only thing capable of making this shit show of a situation with my family look even remotely positive." His dark eyes took on a crafty gleam. "How is my cousin, by the way?"

"Journey is fine." And she'd damn well stay that way with Ethan and José watching her back. He followed Beck into his office and took the chair across from the desk. "We need to fast-forward on your reconciliation with your cousins."

Instead of sitting behind the desk, Beck took the chair next to Frank. He frowned. "What the hell is going on, Frank?"

Frank hesitated. He trusted Beck with his life. No question. But did he trust Beck with Journey's? By telling Beck exactly how bad things were over there, he'd be opening the door to more corporate warfare. Beck knew *something* big was happening because of the meeting with Frank and Anderson the other day.

Stop second-guessing yourself. You know Beck. You trust Beck. The man is not going to turn mercenary just because you suddenly have more at stake in this situation.

"Esther Bancroft has orchestrated a hostile takeover of Kingdom Corp. She turned the board at some point, and she sent in Elliott as soon as Lydia was gone to soften your cousins up to seeing things her way." It really was a brilliant plan as such things went. "She offered them a deal—she'll send Elliott back into whatever hole he was hiding in as long as Journey and Anderson fall in line."

"Hmmm." Beck sat back and drummed his fingers on the armrest. "She doesn't have to play nice with them. If she has the board, she has the company. Even as COO and CEO, Journey and Anderson can only do so much without board approval. She's hamstrung them."

"Yes." Frank had already put some thought into this. "But if she wants a healthy company—and all evidence says that she does for bargaining purposes, if nothing else—then she needs to keep the status quo. I don't expect she plans to keep them on indefinitely. Once she's accomplished what she's set out to do, she'll kick them to the curb. I'd wager she already has that exit strategy in place." It was what he would have done in her place.

"What do you need from me?"

Just like that. No hesitation. No trying to figure out how to turn things to benefit himself.

I'm an asshole for doubting him, even for a second.

"Journey and Anderson are meeting this morning to figure out their next step. Getting Elliott out of Houston is worth temporarily agreeing to Esther's demands. If you'd be willing to work together to oust the Bancrofts, it would be useful."

"Of course." Beck nodded. "They're in this mess in part because of the ultimatum I offered Lydia. I owe it to them to help."

"That's bullshit." Even if he wanted his friend's help, he couldn't let that guilty nonsense stand. "Lydia made her bed when she went after you. She wouldn't have stopped until you were dead, and you damn well know it. I didn't see any of her kids jumping up to stop her when she was plotting murder. You don't owe them shit."

Beck gave a half smile. "They're family, Frank. I meant it when I said I wanted to mend bridges, and so I'd offer to help solely for that reason. Plus, Samara and Journey are friends—and apparently Journey matters a lot to *you*." He shrugged. "The whys are less important than the hows. I'll reach out to Anderson this afternoon."

"Thank you."

"You don't have to thank me." Beck shook his head. "And you also didn't have to come in here with your reasoning all laid out as if I was going to tell you no. Fuck, Frank, you don't ask me for shit. You never have. Short of murder, I'm going to do whatever I can to help you."

Part of him had known that, but hearing it spoken aloud still startled him. "I've asked you for shit before."

"No, you haven't. Not since we've been adults. We're friends, but you are always there when I need you, and you haven't asked me for a single damn thing." Beck met his gaze directly. "You didn't even want me around after your mom passed, Frank."

"Beck—"

"I get it. I do." He pushed to his feet and ran a hand through his dark hair. "And I didn't need you to reach out just to make *me* feel better, but it set the tone for our friendship after that." He smiled. "My point is that it's nice to finally be the one helping out."

Frank opened his mouth, reconsidered, and shut it. He pushed slowly to his feet, feeling as ungainly as he had as a stupid teenager. Before his world went up in flames. Before everything had changed. He hesitated, but Beck was his family. The only family he had left.

"Losing her broke me, Beck," he said quietly. "I begged her to take treatment. I guilted her and pleaded and yelled and cried, and she never wavered. She chose death, and kept choosing death every single fucking day from her diagnosis until she took her last breath." Even after all these years, it hurt to say it. "I couldn't face anyone after that. Not even you. The ground was gone beneath my feet and up was down and down was up and all I wanted to do was destroy the last few things in my life that mattered to me. If I'd reached out then, it would have been to burn our friendship to the ground."

Beck didn't seem to breathe. "I wouldn't have let you."

"Maybe. Or maybe I would have done something unforgivable." Frank shrugged. "I don't know. But even in the midst of all that shit, I knew I didn't want to lose you. So I left first, at least until the world stopped spinning on its head."

Beck crossed the space between them and pulled him into a rough hug. "You stubborn asshole." He released him and stepped back. "We'll get through this." His grin turned wicked. "Samara mentioned something about a double-date vacation."

Frank snorted. "Yeah, yeah. Let's survive this shit before you start planning out the rest of my life." Though he kind of liked the picture that presented. Spending time with the two people who he cared most about in the world when things weren't burning down around them. Some relaxation and a break from Houston—and Journey in a string bikini.

Focus on dealing with the enemy and then worry about the aftermath.

He clasped Beck on the shoulder. "Thanks. We'll talk more soon."

"Hey, Frank."

"Yeah?"

The amusement drained from Beck's face, leaving concern in its wake. "Be careful. Esther Bancroft isn't someone to fuck with. We'll get her out of Houston, but in the meantime...just be careful."

"I will."

He took the elevator down to the parking garage. Frank headed for the SUV he'd chosen to drive today, rather than his Audi. Eliza King's hit-and-run was at the forefront of his mind when he and Journey left his house this morning, and as much as he enjoyed the Audi, it wouldn't take a hit the same way the SUV could. He checked his phone, but other than a text from José saying that Journey was still at the hospital and safe, there was no news.

The vehicle chirped as he unlocked it, but the sound was immediately drowned out by the wail of an alarm several cars down. Frank hesitated. There was no reason to think that alarm had anything to do with him, but he recognized Beck's silver BMW as the source of the sound. Strange coincidence, if someone believed in that sort of thing.

He didn't.

Frank edged to his SUV and grabbed his gun from the holster near the emergency brake. He stopped at the rear of the vehicle and looked around, but there was no one in sight. There had to be *something* going on, because car alarms didn't just go off for shits and giggles. He kept the gun at his side and stalked toward Beck's car.

Nothing.

He keyed in the code—Beck had been using the same goddamn PIN since he was sixteen—and the lights and sound obediently died. Frank hissed out a breath and shook his head at himself. Car alarms were the biggest waste of fucking money in existence, and he needed to be careful going forward because he was obviously jumping at shadows.

"Put the gun down."

Frank froze. The voice came from behind him and to the left—near the front of the car next to Beck's BMW. *Elliott's* voice. *Fuck.* "That was a cheap trick."

"You'd be surprised how often cheap tricks work. Put the gun down or I'll put two in your back. Imagine how prettily my daughter will cry over your casket."

Frank weighed his options. He could try to turn and shoot, but Elliott had the drop on him. He'd get at least one shot off before Frank could turn fully, and one shot was all Elliott really needed.

Too risky.

He set the gun carefully on the ground. "There."

"Kick it away—under the car...Good boy." Elliott chuckled. "Now, let's go for a drive."

CHAPTER TWENTY-THREE

It took longer than Journey would have liked to get the doctor to see things her way, but when she badgered him about how he was going to guarantee Eliza's safety, he'd finally agreed to sign the transfer papers. All that was left to do was bring Eliza around.

She stopped inside the door to Eliza's room, shock derailing her drive. Her sister looked just as terrible as Bellamy had said. Bandages wrapped half her face, and a cast encompassed the left side of her lower body. *Oh, honey.* Her sister stirred, and Journey wiped all sympathy off her face. Eliza wouldn't see it as sympathy. She'd see pity.

And she'd hate Journey for it.

She took a shallow breath and straightened her shoulders. "Hey, Eliza."

"Hey." The word came out duller than she expected. As if her sister could barely put forth the effort to communicate. *I was right about getting her out of here.*

Journey strode to the bed and peered at the IV machine. "We're taking you home."

"Home..." Interest threaded through her voice, though the word slurred a little. "You don't mean New York."

"No, honey, I don't mean New York." Bellamy would coddle Eliza. Anderson would swing between wanting to handle her with kid gloves and bungling it because he didn't do handling well. Someone needed to lay things out straight. Eliza might be the favorite baby sister, but she was still a King. She'd survived, the same way they all had, and she'd been living on her own for years. She was made of tougher stuff than their brothers gave her credit for.

Tougher than Journey gave her credit for, too.

She met her little sister's blue gaze. "Bellamy is getting Mother's old place ready for you. We'll have an in-home nursing staff until you're recovered, and then I expect there will be some kind of physical therapy, though it's up to you to decide if you want to do that in-home or go to them." The interest faded from Eliza's face, so Journey pulled out the big guns. "The accident wasn't an accident."

Eliza tensed. "You seem so sure."

"And you don't seem surprised." She grabbed a chair and pulled it over to sit next to the bed. Maybe looming over her sister wasn't the best choice for this conversation. Frank's men outside the door would ensure they weren't interrupted. "What do you remember about the crash?"

"Nothing. One second I was driving, the next I was flying." Eliza glanced at her phone sitting on the table next to the bed. "But I'm not stupid. Either Elliott didn't want me leaving—and wanted to send a message to you—or someone doesn't like the fact that I'm part of the bargain for this fucking merger."

Her sister knew it wasn't an accident. She'd sat here, alone and helpless, maybe waiting for someone to come finish the job. Anger pulsed through Journey and she clenched the arms of her chair. "I'm going to take care of it."

Eliza's eyes flew open. "Jo, no. Let Anderson handle it. Or call Mother. She's always been so damn good at fighting our battles. I don't want any of you hurt because of me." She reached up and touched her own lips. "Damn it."

Journey had thought she was sparing Eliza by withdrawing, by them *all* withdrawing over the years. They never talked about what happened in that house. Oh, Anderson was always there if Journey needed an anchor, and she knew he dealt with his demons by sweating them out. Even Bellamy showed the strain occasionally by appearing at work after what was obviously a sleepless night, face drawn and shadows lurking in his eyes.

But not Eliza.

Never Eliza.

If one of them got out unscathed, it was supposed to be her. She was only four when Lydia saved them. Surely all she had were patchy memories? *How would I know if we never talked about it?* Journey cleared her throat. "He's not going to win, Eliza. And he's sure as fuck not going to hurt you. I won't allow it."

"Jo—"

Something clanged outside the door. Journey shot to her feet, her heart racing. *We're in a hospital. There are sounds in a hospital.* Every instinct she had shouted that she was lying to herself. Bad things were happening.

She shot a look at her sister in the hospital bed. Bad

things had been happening for a long time. She wasn't going to let Elliott take anything more from Eliza—from any of them. "If I'm not back in a few minutes, hit that buzzer and call Anderson."

"Jo!"

But she was already moving, striding to the door and slipping into the hallway. Ethan stepped in front of her, his hand up as he spoke into his phone. He hung up and slipped it into his pocket. "There's no reason to panic."

"People say that directly before they give you a reason to panic." She looked up and down the hallway, but there didn't seem to be anything amiss. Certainly nothing to explain the alarm bells pealing through her head. "What's going on?"

"Mateo just called to ask if Frank came here instead of the office."

She stared. "Why would he come here?" She charged back into Eliza's room and dug her phone out of her purse. Journey dialed Frank, even though she knew Mateo would have tried to call Frank already. It wasn't as if he was screening his calls. She was so focused on waiting for the voice mail to click over so she could move onto the next step that she didn't realize someone had answered until breathing skated across the line. Journey froze. "Hello?"

"Hello, sweetheart."

Every single nerve in her body froze solid and encased her in ice. "Where is Frank?" She spoke through numb lips, her mind struggling to reconcile her father's voice coming through the line when she was sure she'd been calling Frank's number.

Elliott spoke as if she hadn't asked a question. "You

never were particularly good at doing what you're told. Ever the disobedient daughter."

"Where. Is. Frank?"

"You took something I valued greatly." He trailed off, as if musing to himself. In the distance, a familiar sound shushed through the line. "You had to know that would require punishment."

That got her moving. She snapped her fingers at Ethan, who fumbled to hand her a pen and paper. Journey scrawled out *He's near water* and held it up for Ethan and José to see. As they rushed for their respective phones, she took what passed for a steadying breath. "If you hurt him, *you'll* be the one who's punished."

He laughed. "Please. We both know better."

"Elliott—"

"I'll be sure to tell him you said good-bye." He hung up before she could say anything else.

Journey cursed. "This is bad." She glanced at Ethan and José but they were on their phones, in the middle of two different conversations. As much as she wanted to rush out of the hospital, she couldn't do it until they had a plan in place. *Hold on, Frank.*

Ethan hung up first. "Elliott's got his yacht docked at the marina. If he's somewhere near water, that's got to be it."

"Mateo's tracing Frank's phone." José paced from one side of the room to the other. He opened the door enough to check the hallway and shut it again. "Thanks, Mateo." After slipping his phone into his pocket, he turned to face them. "He's at the marina."

"Okay." Journey ran her hands through her hair. She turned to find Eliza watching her. "I have to go."

"I know." Eliza might have smiled, but it was hard to tell with all the bandages. "Good luck."

"Thank you." She was going to need it. Journey motioned to the men and they headed out. It wasn't until they hit the parking garage that she spoke. "We need cops and we need your men there." One look at their faces said what they thought of that, but she didn't give a fuck. "We need cops," she repeated. "They can't ignore the possibility of a shootout or murder in such a public place. They can't afford to."

Ethan jumped into the driver's seat, and José held the door open for her in the front. Neither of them said a word about her accompanying them, which was just as well.

If they tried to stop her, she'd go through them to get to Frank.

She listened to José start making calls, waiting long enough to ensure he had, in fact, called the cops, and then Journey called Anderson. Voice mail. She cursed. "I don't know where the hell you are, but I *need* you. Elliott has Frank. They're at the marina. I'm going after him." She hung up. It was only then that the reality of the situation sank in.

Elliott had Frank.

He wanted to kill him.

To punish *her*.

She gripped her slacks with shaking hands and stared straight ahead as Ethan navigated through Houston's streets. Not fast enough. Not nearly fast enough. If Elliott got to open water, it would significantly delay their ability to stop him. He'd have all the time in the world to hurt Frank. To dump his body into the ocean once he was finished with him. To sail away to some un-extraditable country.

If he hurts Frank, there's nowhere on earth he can go where I won't find him.

She clenched her jaw until black spots danced along the edges of her vision and red washed over everything. There was no room for fear.

In the backseat, José cleared his throat. "Backup is roughly fifteen minutes behind us, maybe more. I can't speak to the police timeline."

Journey closed her eyes, counted to ten, and opened them again. "We can't afford to wait for them—any of them."

"Agreed."

Thank God. She took a steadying breath. "I don't suppose you two have experience with hostage extraction?" It came out as a lame joke, but neither Ethan nor José jumped in to tell her no. She turned to look at Ethan. "You do, don't you?"

"We have experience in a lot of things." He held the steering wheel in a white-knuckled grip, which belied his calm tone. "It's part of the reason Frank has us on your security detail."

She filed that piece of information away to ask Frank about later. Because, damn it, there *would* be a later. Journey nodded at the road. "Drive faster."

Minutes later, Ethan pulled into the parking lot and turned to her without shutting off the engine. "We do this by the book, Journey. Our men are on the way, and we're not rushing in there like idiots and getting anyone killed."

Frustration sank jagged claws into her. "You don't honestly expect me to sit here and wait for backup." Even now, Elliott could be leaving the marina. He could have already *left*. She pulled her purse closer to her. Drawing a gun on men whose only job was to protect her put Journey in a really shitty category of people, but she didn't give a fuck. Frank needed her, and she wasn't going to let these men stand in her way. No matter if they were allies or not.

José leaned forward to shoot her a look from between the front seats. "No need to pull that gun. We're going in. But you will follow orders and you will stay between us the entire time."

"Done." In that moment, she would have said anything to get them to turn off the damn car and go save Frank, and they must have known it.

Ethan shook his head and climbed out. "Frank's going to kill us for this, you know."

"Nah." José gave a tight grin that didn't come anywhere near his eyes. "He'll just give us a dressing-down for the ages and then suspend us with pay until he's cooled off."

She didn't know if this was some kind of ritual of theirs or if they were trying to make her feel more at ease, but Journey slipped her purse over her shoulder and followed them down to the massive docks where the boats were kept. She let their words wash over her, let the ease of their conversation about what Frank would do to punish them wrap around her like an air bubble. There was no *if* they got Frank back. It was *when*.

Journey appreciated their confidence, even if she wanted them to hurry the fuck up.

"Company," José murmured.

"I see them."

Journey followed their gazes to the pair of men headed

toward them. The two guys couldn't have screamed *paid muscle* more if they had the words painted across their foreheads. Black fatigues, too-tight black shirts, intense expressions on their faces.

Not to mention the guns they had nestled into shoulder holsters.

"We'll take care of this, Journey."

She nodded and then cleared her throat. "Yeah. Sure." She looked beyond the approaching men and missed a step. There it was—the *Queen Bitch*. Elliott's yacht.

It was starting to pull away from the dock.

"Ethan!" She pointed.

He stepped forward, but the man closest to him swung. Ethan cursed and ducked beneath the punch. "Don't you dare, Journey!"

If she didn't move now, it would be too late. Finding and commandeering a boat would take too long, if they could even do it at all. Once Elliott hit the Gulf, he could go anywhere—do anything.

Fuck no, he won't.

She bolted, slipping between the two fights that began as the second man engaged José, having obviously decided that Journey was the lesser threat. He wasn't wrong, and she used it to her advantage. Journey sprinted down the dock, her low heels drawing dull thuds from the slatted wood beneath her feet. The gap between the yacht and the dock grew, but this was her only chance. She wouldn't miss it.

She leaped from the edge of the dock.

Journey hit the side of the yacht with a bone-crushing force that drove the air from her lungs, but she managed to get her arm around one of the railing posts. She hung there for several long seconds, waiting for someone to come investigate or for her strength to give out and dump her into the water.

Nothing happened.

She risked a glance over her shoulder to where the fight was still going on in earnest. It was obvious Elliott's two men were outmatched, but it was equally obvious that by some unspoken agreement, Ethan and José were dragging it out.

To give me time.

She took a deep breath and, on the exhale, hauled herself up and through the gap in the railing to the deck. No time to rest. The space was too open. All it would take was someone up above to look down and they'd see her sprawled there.

Journey kicked off her shoes and grabbed them in one hand. She stood and hurried to the door leading inside. A quick pause to pull her gun out of her purse and shove her shoes in and she was ready.

Liar. You aren't ready. You don't have special training. You're not a fucking marine who knows how to handle extractions without someone getting killed.

Shut up. I'm here. I will *save Frank.*

She slid soundlessly through the door, forcing her breathing to slow and even out no matter how thin the air seemed or how strong the urge was to gasp her inhales. No sounds but the faint hum of the motor as Elliott guided the yacht farther from the marina.

Farther from safety and watching eyes.

Journey ducked into the first door she found—a bedroom—and typed out a quick text to both Anderson and Ethan. *I'm on the yacht. Send backup.*

Anderson responded immediately. *Get off that fucking boat right now, Jo. RIGHT NOW.*

Too late.

She made sure her phone was on silent and vibrate was off and slipped it back into her purse. No telling how long she'd have cell reception on the water. Journey didn't make a habit of taking boats out of the sight of land, and so she had absolutely no frame of reference.

She had to believe that the men would continue with the rescue plan.

That they'd be able to track the *Queen Bitch*.

Don't think too hard about everything that could go wrong. It's outside your control right now. Frank is the priority.

With that in mind, she stowed her purse in the closet. Her phone would be useless before too long, and hauling around the bag would just slow her down. She loaded her gun, ensuring there was a bullet in the chamber, and paused. *Am I really going to shoot someone?*

The first thing her mother taught her upon putting a gun in her hands was not to even bother carrying it if she wasn't prepared to use it. It was part of the reason Journey usually kept it locked in her closet instead of on her person, despite having a current permit to carry concealed. With the biggest threat supposedly out of her life, she had never thought she'd actually be in a position where she might have to shoot to kill.

She tightened her grip. This wasn't about her. This was about Frank.

I'll do what I have to do.

Journey padded back into the passageway. She took a second to orient herself and then headed for where the ladder should be. Most yachts were arranged in a vaguely similar pattern, so she should be able to make her way to the upper decks—and the navigation system—through the center of it. She strained to listen with every step, sure that someone would jump out and attack, but the thing was deserted.

In some ways, that was worse.

Elliott didn't want any potential witnesses for what he planned for Frank.

She found the ladder with little difficulty and started her ascent, her gun held carefully in front of her and her gaze trying to take everything in at once. The faint sound of voices reached her as she hit the second level, and Journey plastered herself to the bulkhead. Several seconds passed and the conversation didn't get any louder. A few steps further and she recognized Frank's deep voice and her father's amused tone.

That bastard won't be amused for long.

She edged up the last few steps in a crouch. The men were both to the left of the ladder opening, but a half wall blocked her view. It was possible they weren't alone, and that the third person was some highly trained professional who would shoot her the second she came into view...but it was a chance she'd have to take.

She straightened, her gun held steady in two hands. The tiny flicker of relief at the realization that there was no one else died as she took in the scene. Elliott stood at the navigation system, a gun a few inches from his hand. Frank knelt on the floor at his feet, blood seeping from where it appeared he'd been pistol-whipped in the face, his hands fastened behind his back with a zip tie.

Her father shifted to face her fully, and she focused on him. "Do. Not. Move."

Elliott lifted his hands slowly, a grin pulling at the edges of his mouth. "Or what, sweetheart? We both know you're not going to pull that trigger. You don't have it in you."

She adjusted her grip on the gun. Even knowing it was only a few pounds, her arms shook with the effort of keeping it steady. It wasn't a position she could hold indefinitely, and Elliott was probably betting on that. "Move away from the gun. Slowly."

Instead of obeying, he slouched a little, looking for all the world like he was settling in for some good gossip over an expensive drink. "I'm surprised you made it past my men. I'll have to have a chat with them."

She tensed, and then cursed herself for showing even that much reaction. Journey knew all too well what his *chats* entailed. She shifted a step to the side so that she wasn't at risk of tumbling back down the stairs if the yacht made an unexpected movement. "Get away from the gun. I won't tell you again."

"You know what I don't understand?" He crossed his arms over his chest. "Why him?" Elliott nodded at Frank, who watched the whole thing with cold, dark eyes.

Waiting for his moment.

Journey gave her head a small shake when Frank looked at her. If he tried to jump her father, Elliott would grab the gun and shoot him. At that range, there was no way he'd miss, and a couple of rounds to the chest might not be fatal, but she wouldn't risk it. She refused to let him risk it.

Elliott snorted. "He's not going to listen to you, sweetheart. The fool loves you. He'll jump in front of an entire clip's worth of bullets if he thinks it'll save you. Honestly, it's sickening. Love makes you weak."

"No, it doesn't." Without love, she wouldn't be here. Even if it ended in disaster, Journey was *here*. She wasn't waiting for someone else to save her. She was facing her own goddamn monsters. "On your knees, Elliott."

"If you insist, I—" He moved. Her father lunged for the gun, just like she'd known he was waiting to do. His hand closed around the weapon.

Journey pulled the trigger.

Her gun bucked in her hands, but she was expecting it. She pulled the trigger twice more in quick succession, her mother's voice in her head. *If you have to pull the trigger, you make damn sure they're not going to get back up again.*

Red bloomed on her father's white shirt in a cluster in the center of his chest. His gun fell from nerveless fingers and he hit his knees. He blinked at her as if he'd never seen her before. "You shot me."

"Yes, I did." She kept the gun trained on him as she slid a step closer to Frank. Her shoulders ached from the effort, but she wasn't about to let her guard down now.

"You..." He touched his chest and looked at his red-stained fingers. "I didn't think you would."

"You don't know me anymore." She cast a quick look around, but there was nothing sharp sitting conveniently close. She stalked to Elliott as he collapsed onto his back. Journey kicked the gun farther from him. *I shot him. I shot my father.* She took a shaking breath and went to her knees next to him. A quick pat down found a knife in his pocket. A fancy switchblade that probably cost a small fortune.

Elliott's hand closed around her wrist, but there was no strength in his grip. Blood flecked his lips, and his blue eyes were glassy. "You'll never be rid of me."

"I'm already rid of you." She hurried to Frank.

He shook his head as if waking from a dream. "You came for me."

"Of course I came for you, you ass. I wasn't going to let him kill you." Journey touched his head gingerly. The wound was still bleeding, though not freely. No telling if he had a concussion until they got him into the hospital. She sawed through his zip ties and sat back on her heels. "I don't suppose you know how to drive a yacht?"

"Journey." He rubbed his wrists and then took her by her shoulders. "You came for me."

She cupped his face gently. "I'll always come for you, Frank. I love you."

* * *

Frank pulled her into his arms and hugged her tightly, not sure if she was shaking or if he was. "Don't ever do that again, Duchess. I swear to fucking God, if you scare me like that again, I'll put you over my knee and paddle your ass."

She laughed against his chest. "I hate to be the one to tell you, Frank, but that's not exactly a deterrent from where I'm sitting."

"You *won't* be sitting for a fucking week when I'm through with you."

Another of those intoxicating laughs, though it faded far too fast. She twisted to look at her old man. "He's dead."

"Yeah, he is." Frank would have spared her pulling the trigger if he could have. He'd held his fucking breath until he went light-headed while she faced off with her father, waiting for his opportunity to leap at the man.

It never came.

Journey didn't need him to save her. She saved herself, and him in the bargain.

It wasn't over yet, though.

He forced himself to let go of Journey. "We need to get the hell back to Houston."

"Yeah." She wiped the back of her hand across her forehead. "Anderson and your men are coming—and probably the cops or Coast Guard or whoever handles crimes on the water."

He looked back at the spot where Houston had disappeared on the horizon. She'd had backup, which was more than he could say. She'd covered all the bases. "I love you."

"I know." Journey's breath hitched. "Let's get off this fucking boat."

"Took the words right out of my mouth." Frank started for the navigation system when the yacht lurched hard enough to throw both him and Journey to their knees. "What the fuck?"

She scrambled to her feet and ran to the railing to look over. "Uh, Frank?"

"Yeah?" He climbed to his feet again.

"I think we have bigger problems." She pointed to a plume of smoke curling from the rapidly tilting yacht.

Frank grabbed the railing to steady himself and cursed at the sight. The yacht gave another lurch, and his palms went clammy when he realized they were much, much closer to the surface of the bay than they had been a few seconds ago. "Who the hell blew a hole in the yacht?"

"Uh, now might be a good time to mention that my brother was *really* insistent I get off this boat. I don't think he meant like *this*, though." She gulped. "I'm not exactly a great swimmer, Frank."

Fuck.

They did not survive this long to drown before help could get to them. Frank grabbed her hand. "I need you to jump, Duchess."

"Jump?"

"If we don't get off this fucking ship, it will suck us down when it goes under. We have to get clear." He started searching the area, yanking the cushions from the bench seat and testing them. They weren't life jackets, but they would float. *It'll have to do.* He thrust one at Journey. "Come on." He hauled her down the stairs to the main deck. Their best chance lay in jumping from the bow and swimming like hell. He climbed over the railing and waited for her to do the same. After the slightest hesitation, Journey followed him to the edge.

"Jump, Duchess." Frank didn't give her the chance to change her mind.

He pushed her.

Frank kicked off his shoes and followed her into the water. He hit and went under for several precious seconds before he swam to the surface. Journey sputtered a few feet away and shoved her wet hair from her face. "You pushed me!"

"Yep." He snagged the pair of cushions and shoved one at her. "We have to swim. Now."

Journey nodded and fought her way through the water
in the opposite direction from the yacht sinking beneath
the surface. *Too slow.* Frank followed her, muttering
encouraging words when she flagged, all of his focus
on getting them as far away from that fucking boat as
possible. He wasn't sure of the radius of the drag—
only that it existed—and he was taking no chances with
Journey's safety.

She came for me.

He'd never seen anything so beautiful or terrifying as
his woman stepping out with a gun in her hand and fury
and determination written across her features as she faced
down the man who had spent far too many years terroriz-
ing her. She did it for *him.* For herself, too, but the only
reason she was there today was because of *Frank.*

"Frank," Journey gasped. "I'm so tired."

"Keep going, Duchess. We're almost far enough." He
paced her. "Then you can rest."

"Can't believe you pushed me," she muttered, picking
up her pace again.

He glanced back to see the last few feet of the
yacht disappear. The slightest of tugs pulled at him, but
that was it. *Far enough. Thank fuck.* "We made it." He
stopped her with a hand on her shoulder. "Float on your
back. Keep the cushion at chest level and cross your arms
through the strap."

She obeyed and gave a short laugh. "You experience
much in the way of shipwrecks, Frank?"

"My first one." He waited to make sure she was secure
and then mirrored her position. "Help is coming."

"If they were tracking my phone—if that's even something you can do over open water with no cell towers

around—then we're in trouble. It's at the bottom of Trinity Bay."

"They'll find us." Pieces of wreckage floated around them, and if the Coast Guard got involved, there would be helicopters. Even in a boat, it would be possible to spot them.

They just had to survive long enough for help to get to them.

"Hang on, Duchess. Help is coming."

CHAPTER TWENTY-FOUR

The cushions weren't really meant to act as flotation devices. Journey held hers in a death grip and did her best to lie on her back in a dead man's float...and not think about the dead man currently occupying the waters of the bay somewhere near them. Frank floated next to her, the soft splashes of his kicks somehow making their isolation worse. They weren't *that* far from the coast—less than ten miles, for sure—but it might as well have been on the moon for her ability to swim there.

She looked to where the yacht had been up until a few short minutes ago. After they'd jumped, it disappeared beneath the waves terrifyingly fast, taking her father with it.

Hopefully.

Journey jerked her gaze to the sky, still a perfect blue. "I was going to jump," she said again.

"I know. I just sped up the process."

The vast space beneath her made her skin crawl. She'd swum in Trinity Bay more times than she could count, even out this far and farther on party boats when she was younger. It had never bothered her before. If she thought too hard, she could almost picture Elliott's lifeless body rising through the water below them and... "Talk to me, Frank." When he didn't immediately start, she bit her bottom lip hard. "I'm starting to freak out and I'm pretty sure if I freak out, we're both going to drown, so I need you to talk to me."

His shoulder bumped hers as they floated closer together. "We're getting out of this, Duchess. Help is coming." A variation of the same thing he'd been saying since they hit the water.

She wasn't sure if he believed that any more than she did. Time ceased to have meaning once she jumped onto the yacht, but she was relatively sure that they'd barely been in the water an hour. If someone hadn't shown up yet, maybe they weren't showing up at all. She closed her eyes against the burning there that had nothing to do with the sun. "I killed him." She waited for guilt to cripple her, to seep through every part of her until nothing remained untainted.

It didn't come.

"Do you regret it?"

"Not in the way you mean." She pressed her lips together, tasting salt that she could almost convince herself came from the sea around her instead of the tears trickling from her closed eyes. "I should regret it. Murder is a big deal—the biggest deal, even—but the only thing I regret is that he didn't live long enough to be prosecuted and spend time in prison. To experience even the smallest slice of suffering that he dealt out over his lifetime."

Easy enough to speak this awful truth. It was only the two of them here in this moment, the endless sky overhead and unknowing deep beneath. "I'm not sorry. I would do it again."

Frank's hand found hers in the water. "You have nothing to be sorry for." His fingers clasped hers long enough to give a comforting squeeze before he released her. "I would have spared you that if I could have."

"I know. Just like I know if you'd tried, he would have killed you." Journey shook her head, her hair a strange weight in the water. "No, this was the only way. I *know* this was the only way."

"I'm here, Journey." He spoke quietly, his words blending with the soft sounds of water around them. "Not just right now. For always."

Journey kicked lightly until she bumped Frank again. "I want to go on a real date. Not a fake one because we're keeping up appearances. Not a weekend away because we're in danger and we need to wait it out. A real date with two people who are into each other."

"Who love each other."

She smiled, tasting salt. "Who love each other."

"Saturday."

She blinked. "What?"

"I'll pick you up at seven on Saturday. Pack a bag."

"Frank, real dates don't include needing a bag packed." Her arms started to slip from the cushion, and she spent several painful seconds trying to readjust. Desperate to ignore the fact that she most certainly wouldn't be able to hold on to it indefinitely, she focused on their conversation. "Real dates are the traditional dinner and maybe something afterward, then you drive me home and we make out on my front porch while I try to pretend like I'm not sure if I want you to come up. Eventually, I get over my bullshit and drag you to my apartment and we spend the rest of the night banging like it's going out of style."

His dry laugh lingered in the air above them. "We've already established that nothing about this is traditional or expected. Why would a real date be?"

A valid point. She shivered. Her skin felt clammy. *Losing heat.* It wasn't *that* cold in the water, but it was colder than her body, which was enough to fuck her up over time. "So what happens on this nontraditional, unexpected real date?"

"That, Duchess, you'll have to wait and see." He went still. "Do you hear that?"

"Don't toy with my emotions, Frank." But then she heard it, too.

A boat's motor.

Journey twisted and kicked, trying to get her head high enough out of the water to see. A rapidly growing black dot appeared, heading their way. "Friend or foe?" Her gun was long gone. They were both tired and waterlogged, and if the boat was filled with Elliott's men coming to finish the job, they would just have to drive right over Journey and Frank a few times to make it work.

You are just a little ray of sunshine, aren't you?

"Frank?"

He lifted a hand to shield his eyes as he trod water. He didn't seem to have the same difficulty that she did, which meant he probably could have started swimming the second the yacht went down and been halfway back to the coast by now. He hadn't. He'd floated next to her and talked her down even though there was no way he was any surer of rescue than she was. His expression cleared. "They're mine."

"Thank fuck." She couldn't make herself let go of the cushion as the boat approached and coasted to a spot next to them. She recognized Ethan and José among the half dozen men leaning over the side to help them.

Frank jerked his chin at her. "Journey first."

She went under as she let go of the cushion, but strong hands grabbed her shoulders and hauled her up. Her legs went out the second she hit the deck, and she slumped into a boneless heap in the middle of the boat. One of the men—a rough-looking guy with a sunny smile—wrapped a solar blanket around her while two more helped Frank into the boat. He knelt next to her and cupped her cheek. "You good?"

"Yeah." She would be.

He apparently didn't have the same weak legs thing going on that she did, because Frank stood and addressed the man at the wheel. "Dylan, get the Coast Guard on the line. We have to get ahead of this." He turned back and crouched in front of Journey. "We play this my way, Duchess. Your father kidnapped me and I shot him in self-defense."

She shivered and pulled her blanket more firmly around her. "That's not what happened."

"I know that. You know that. But I'm not letting you take the rap for this if things go badly."

It was on the tip of her tongue to ask why they didn't just turn around and drive away and leave Elliott to his watery grave. She knew the answer. There would be questions. A Bancroft son, even a shitty one like her father, didn't just disappear without Esther whipping the entire city into a frenzy in her efforts to find him. With her reach, she might even be able to manage to get both the state and feds involved. Eventually, they'd find the yacht, and they'd find what was left of Elliott.

Maybe they'd realize Journey and Frank were involved. Maybe they wouldn't.

But it wasn't a risk either of them was willing to take.

That made sense. Letting Frank potentially take the fall *didn't*. She knew what would happen if he confessed to shooting her father. Esther would jump at the chance to bury him. The self-defense plea would be overturned and he'd be prosecuted for murder. He'd be convicted.

Just like his father was.

She wouldn't allow it. This was her mess, and she'd dragged him into it from the start. Journey wouldn't let him suffer the consequences that were hers to bear. She reached up and grabbed his hand, forcing as much strength into her grip as she could. "The gun was mine and if they recover the body and do a ballistics test, they'll figure that out. We play this straight, Frank. Promise me."

He hesitated, and finally nodded. "If that's what you want."

"It is." Journey pulled him down until he was even with her. "Besides, I have Frank Evans in my corner. How could I not come out on top of this shit show?"

"I'm in your corner and you're in mine." He pressed a quick kiss to her lips. "Call your brother and update him. I'm going to take care of this, Duchess. I promise."

* * *

"Tell me what happened."

Frank pinched the bridge of his nose and bit back a sigh. He hadn't *really* expected the cops to believe his and Journey's story, for all that it was true, but he'd overestimated his patience—and how long it would take his attorney to show up. All he could think about was how shaken and exhausted Journey looked when they'd led her to a separate room for her own version of this particular hell. She needed him, and he was stuck talking to this fucking detective. "I'm not saying a damn thing without my lawyer—which I've mentioned several times at this point."

The detective ignored that, musing aloud, "Seems you and Elliott Bancroft had some bad blood. A man like you dating his girl. Father's not going to be too keen on that."

Patience.

It didn't work. All he could see was the shadows beneath Journey's eyes, hear the hopelessness in her voice when they'd been clinging to those fucking cushions and praying like hell his men would show up in time. She'd been so afraid, and he hadn't been able to assuage those fears a single damn time since they'd been together.

She's alive. That's all that matters.

"Did you give Journey King medical attention?"

The detectives exchanged a look. "The girl's fine."

The door opened and a small Chinese woman strode through it. "You two—out. You—stop talking."

Thank fuck.

The detectives grumbled, but Frank had never seen anyone contradict Naomi Jiang when she got that look on her face. His gratitude dried up when she leaned a hip against the table he was handcuffed to and scowled. "You really stepped in it this time, Frank. Since when are you dating Journey King?"

"That's relevant...how?"

"It's relevant because the King family generates its own media circus just by breathing. Being accused of murder—or being a victim of kidnapping—only adds to the flames. Tell me exactly what happened so I can get you out of this mess."

"So you can get us *both* out of this mess." He held her gaze. "She's with me. That's not up for negotiation."

"For fuck's sake," she muttered. "Look, you're not even in hot water at this point despite how it looks." She motioned at the cuffs. "You kept your mouth shut, and I could deal with a few racist cops in my sleep." She glared. "Your girl is not my problem. Keeping you out of jail— and out of a potentially harmful media storm—is."

"Fix it, Naomi."

"Fine." She pushed off the table and smoothed her hands over her impeccable deep blue dress. "You're both lucky that fixing these things is what I do. Hang tight and don't say another word, or I swear to God, I will shove you onto a plane to a country without extradition today."

The threat didn't mean a damn thing. Between his injuries, several witness accounts about Elliott's behavior toward Journey, and other testimonies about what happened today, the detectives would reach the truth. Eventually. He was just fucking tired of waiting. Journey needed food that didn't come from a vending machine and the space to settle her nerves after everything that had happened.

He fully intended to provide her that safe space.

First, he had to get them the fuck out of this police station.

An hour later, Naomi had managed exactly that. She walked Frank and Journey to the entrance to the station and pointed an imperious finger at them. "Stay in town. Keep your noses clean. This isn't over, but once they compile the evidence and follow up on all the information you shared, you should be in the clear." She narrowed her eyes. "Unless you're lying to me, in which case we have bigger problems."

Frank wrapped his arm around Journey's waist and tucked her against the side of his body. They both wore the ugly gray sweat suits the cops had provided to replace their soaked clothes, and the material scratched at his skin. "I know better, Naomi. We both do." Journey nodded in confirmation.

That seemed to satisfy Naomi—marginally. "I don't expect them to haul you back in before Monday, so we'll set up a meeting to go over any developments. If something changes, you call me first, and don't you dare talk to anyone without me. Got it?"

"Got it."

She nodded. "Then get your asses out of here. You both look like shit." She turned on her expensive designer heels and marched away to terrorize someone else.

Journey huffed out a laugh. "I like her."

"Of course you do. She's fucking terrifying." He kept his arm around her as they descended the steps and waited at the curb for the car service he'd called. "Let's get you home and showered and fed."

A car pulled to the curb, but it wasn't a stranger behind the wheel. Bellamy King leaned over and rolled down the window. "Get in. We have a situation."

Journey tensed against him. "What's going on?"

"Grandmother is on her way to Kingdom Corp. She wants all of us there."

Frank tightened his grip on her. "Fuck that. The company shares move to Anderson with Elliott's death—not Esther. Your sister almost died. She's not doing anything but going home right now."

"No." Journey pressed her hand to his chest. "We're going. She still has board control, and that makes her dangerous even without majority shares. I won't be the weak link." She twisted to look at him. "If you need to leave—"

"Get that thought right out of your head, Duchess. Where you go, I go." He opened the passenger door for her, and then climbed into the backseat once she was settled.

Bellamy didn't move. "You okay, Jo?"

Frank kept his snarl under wraps. It was obvious that her little brother loved her, and just as obvious that he didn't know how to handle the fact that he hadn't been there for her. The question was both testing the waters and a peace offering of sorts.

She settled back into her seat with a sigh. "Getting there, Bel. Getting there."

They didn't speak another word until Bellamy pulled into a parking spot in the garage of Kingdom Corp. He hesitated and then said, "I'll give you two a minute. Esther will be up in Anderson's office when you're ready."

Frank watched him walk away from the car. "He's about as subtle as a brick to the head."

"Bellamy's better when he sees things from a distance." She didn't move to open her door or turn to look at him. "He also doesn't like feeling helpless."

You don't have to do this. He knew better than to speak the words. Today had more than proved Journey was strong enough to stand as a full partner, to protect him as much as he protected her. He trusted her to draw the line when she needed to. If she said she could handle it, then she could.

But that didn't mean she had to stand alone.

"What do you need from me?"

She sighed. "I should tell you that I need you to leave so I can do this myself, but the thought of going up there and facing her down after everything that's happened... I can't do it."

"There's no shame in asking for help, Duchess. It doesn't make you weak. It makes you smart."

She twisted to look at him around the headrest. "I know that." Her hazel eyes seemed almost brown against the chalkiness of her skin and with her blond hair tangled around her face. She looked like she'd been to war and back, which was nothing less than the truth.

He waited. This was the defining moment for them, more than anything that had come before. The immediate danger had passed—whatever Esther's game was, her goals that day wouldn't involve threats.

Journey *didn't* need him.

Not anymore.

She gave a half smile. "It would make me feel better if you were there with me when I faced her."

Not to fight her battles—to support her while she fought her own.

He reached up and smoothed back her hair. "Anything for you, Duchess."

* * *

Journey probably should have asked Bellamy to swing by her place on the way over so she could change, but she perversely wanted her grandmother to see exactly what Elliott had brought about.

They took the elevator up to the executive floor. Frank stayed half a step behind her, offering her his silent support, and she loved him so fucking much for realizing she needed to do this—and not trying to stop her in an effort to protect her. He'd never chain her to him. He would, however, stand by ready to catch her while she learned to fly with her newfound wings.

They found both of Journey's brothers and her grandmother in Anderson's office. Esther stood at the window looking out over the view, probably placing herself directly in the path of a sunbeam solely because she knew it lit up her gray hair like a halo and gave her a heavenly impression. She turned as they walked through the door, and horror suffused her face. "Oh, Journey."

She felt Frank stiffen behind her and reached back to take his hand. *Trust me.* "Grandmother." She braced for the accusations or demands for explanation. There was no way Esther wouldn't blame her for what happened on that boat. It didn't matter what the truth was—she'd lost a son today and she'd react accordingly.

Esther clasped her hands in front of her. She wore a pale yellow dress that somehow made her look stronger while playing up her age all the same. "I am so terribly sorry. If I'd been more careful with dismissing Elliott..." She pressed her lips together in the same move Journey did more often than she cared to think about. "But I wasn't. The harm my son did rests on my shoulders."

Several long seconds passed as Journey tried to make reality and expectation mesh into something recognizable. It didn't work.

She knew better than to argue that her grandmother was well aware what Elliott was capable of when she'd set him on his children like a rabid dog. It was his sole purpose for being in Houston, and this kind grandmother act didn't change how ruthlessly Esther had worked to bring them to their knees. "Is there anything else, Grandmother?" Her voice came out steady despite the exhaustion weighing her down. All she wanted was a shower and to collapse into her bed for the next twelve hours and give herself some time to process what the hell had happened.

Something like respect flickered through Esther's blue eyes. "I'll be staying in town for a while." She smiled and it was almost—almost—warm. "I'd like to see you—all of you. And I'll be stopping in to visit with Eliza regularly."

She wasn't exactly asking for permission, but then she didn't really need to. She owned properties locally, and the Bancrofts had several smaller businesses in Houston. The timing was nothing less than suspect—she no doubt planned to ensure her wayward grandchildren agreed to her terms, and held up their end of the bargain.

We'll see about that.

Game on, Esther.

After her grandmother left, some of the tension bled out of the room. Anderson rubbed a hand over his face. "I'm glad you're okay, Jo."

"Did you..." She hesitated, but the question had to be asked. "Did you have something to do with Elliott's boat going down?"

Her brother looked her straight in the face and lied. "Of course not." His mouth twisted. "You weren't supposed to be aboard." His blue gaze flicked to Frank. "Neither of you were."

God, Anderson. She kept her thoughts to herself. They made it out alive and she didn't think for a second that her brother would have endangered her on purpose. *Journey* pulled the trigger that ended their father's life.

She didn't exactly have a pedestal to stand on when it came to patricide.

He cleared his throat, the subject effectively closed. "It's going to take some work to reverse the damage Elliott did in the short time he was here."

Journey perched on the arm of a chair and tried to pretend it wasn't because her legs were about to give out. "We put out the biggest fires first and then deal with the rest. The next order of business needs to be updating the budget." The list of things needing to be addressed seemed to grow by the second.

Frank's hand closed on her shoulder. "Not today. Not even this weekend. You need to rest and recover."

She started to argue, but Anderson was already nodding. "Take a three-day weekend, Jo." He pushed to his feet and crossed to pull her into a hard hug. It whooshed the air from her lungs, but she hugged him back just as fiercely. Anderson stepped back. "I'm glad you're okay."

"I'm going to be." And for the first time in a really long time, she believed it. There was no easy fix, no Band-Aid big enough, no magic spell to banish the pain of her past. But…maybe that wasn't the end of the world. She'd faced down her own personal demon.

Journey survived.

He didn't.

After this, she was damn near bulletproof.

"Get out of here." He smiled, though the expression faded as he looked over her shoulder at Frank. "Thank you. I haven't always been gracious when it comes to you, but I was wrong."

And then there was nothing left to say.

Journey and Frank left, which was just as well. The strength abandoned her legs, and she weaved on her feet as they took the elevator down. She caught him looking at her with brows drawn. "I'm fine."

"I didn't say anything."

"You didn't have to. You're getting all frowny at me, which means you're considering scooping me up and hauling me back to your lair." She made a face. "Okay, I'm punch-drunk. We really do need to go home."

"I have a car waiting out front."

Of course he did. He must be as exhausted as she was, and he'd still stood at her back and let her handle shit that probably could have waited until they recovered. She was glad to have gotten everything out of the way now, to put a period at the end of the nightmarish sentence that was Elliott's time in Houston.

He's really gone.

Forever.

She wavered, and Frank was there, slipping his arm around her waist and keeping her on her feet. "I've got you, Duchess."

"I know."

It seemed like they made it back to her apartment between one blink and the next. She managed to hold it together long enough to shower with Frank—neither of them having the energy to do more than wash each other's backs—and then she let him wrap her in one of her silly pink fluffy towels and carry her to bed. If there was an energy meter for the day, hers was at zero.

But when they lay under the covers, her cheek pressed against Frank's broad chest, she couldn't quite still her racing thoughts. "He's gone."

"Yes." Frank pressed his hand to the small of her back, bringing her more firmly against his side. "It's okay to feel conflicted about that."

"I'm not." It was the truth. Elliott might have been her father, but he was the monster under her bed, the boogeyman in her closet, the footsteps stalking her through a dark and deserted alley. She felt nothing but relief when she thought about his being dead. She turned her face into his chest and inhaled. "I don't know how this is going to play out. We're both workaholics who have people depending on us. How does a relationship even develop in those conditions?"

"One day at a time." He pulled the covers up higher around their shoulders. "Close your eyes, Duchess. Give that impressive brain of yours a rest for a little while. I'll keep you safe."

She obeyed, but she wasn't quite through. "I'll keep you safe, too, you know. I'll never abandon you, no matter how tough the stakes." *Not like your parents.* She didn't say the last. She didn't have to.

Frank pulled her tighter to him. "I know you will." He smoothed a hand down her spine and back up again. "I've never had a white knight before. You look good in armor, Duchess."

"You're a terrible damsel in distress, though." She

gave a tired laugh. "Let's both be knights to someone else next time, okay?"

"Deal." He pressed a kiss to her temple. The last thing she heard was her audiobook clicking on, the soothing tones of the narrator sucking her under and into an exhausted sleep.

CHAPTER TWENTY-FIVE

Three weeks went by before they managed to schedule that date. Journey spent most of the time closeted in with Anderson and the heads of the various departments of Kingdom Corp. It took all of her not-inconsiderable negotiating skills to get everyone to agree to their respective budgets, but things were looking positive going into next quarter.

And she hadn't even needed to fire anyone to make it happen.

Every single night for those three weeks, when she staggered home to bed, she found Frank in her apartment. He was always camped out on her couch with a computer and files, and a phone that seemed permanently attached to his face, but he was there. Every single night, they fell asleep in each other's arms. Despite the professional stress and her worry about Eliza's road to recovery and concern over what Esther was planning next, Journey had never been more at peace.

She leaned forward to look out the windshield of Frank's car as he took a familiar turn. "The airport? I thought this was a date."

"It *is* a date." His route took them to the private hangars, but not the area she recognized. The planes were smaller here, ranging from looking like they weren't flight ready to something that could have been yanked out of a sci-fi movie. He pulled up near one that lay somewhere in the middle, the open propellers making her heart pound a little. Journey didn't make a habit of flying in planes the size of a tuna can, and she wasn't sure she wanted to start now.

This was Frank, though, so she was willing to give him the benefit of the doubt.

Following his lead, Journey climbed out of the car and smoothed down her deep red dress. She'd chosen one with a wicked short hemline and a plunging neckline that barely covered the essentials, thinking this date was going in an entirely different direction. Frank crossed around the front of the car and took her hand. He led her up the narrow stairs and into the plane. "Sit here."

"Frank, you really don't need to exact revenge for my saving your ass. I know you have your pilot's license, but now you're just showing off."

The door closed and then Frank was in the seat next to her. He handed her a headset. "I promised you an extraordinary date, and I fully intend to deliver. Trust me, Duchess."

"I do." It was the truth. After what they'd gone through together, a little death-defying flight barely ranked notice. She carefully put on the headset and settled back into her seat. Not wanting to distract him while he got them moving, she saved her question until they'd accomplished a surprisingly smooth takeoff. "Tell me the truth—you're just looking for some plane head, aren't you?" She shot him a look. "Or is it air head? Flight head? Is there even a term for getting your dick sucked while you're flying a plane?"

He laughed, the sound rolling through her like the best kind of buzz. "The weather's a little tricky today, so that might not be wise."

Tricky? She leaned to look out the window and instantly sat back, her heart in her throat. They were flying over the Gulf. "You ever have to do a water landing in this thing?"

"No. Because I'm an excellent pilot." He reached over and squeezed her hand and then went back to flying. "How was your day?"

She took a careful breath and tried to pretend they were sitting at her kitchen island instead of God-alone-knew-how-many feet above the water. "Good. We've managed to get the budget squared away, which was the headache of the century. Esther called today, though. She wanted to inform us that the merger with Cardinal Energy will be postponed until Eliza is recovered—but not a second afterward. It gives us time to figure out a way out of the deal, at least in theory, but the language is tricky, and Cardinal Energy is being difficult. It's going to take some serious muscle to get out of it." It wasn't the merger she disagreed with—it was the price they demanded. Eliza marrying Asher Bishop. After everything Journey's sister had been through, that merger would continue over her dead fucking body. Thankfully, both her brothers were in agreement, and Anderson was the one actually handling negotiations. If anyone could see them through things, it was him.

"What does Eliza want?"

That was the question. Journey had seen her sister
every other day since she was transferred to Lydia's old
place, but the spark that made Eliza *Eliza* was showing
no signs of reappearing. It hadn't worried Journey in the
hospital, but it did now. "I don't know how to get her
back on her feet." She shook her head. "Hey, I've been
meaning to ask you—since we're banging like bunnies
and I'm totally your girlfriend, are you going to sell me
that damn building?"

He glanced at her, his lips quirking up. "I'm prepared
to be convinced."

"Ooooh, in that case—I can make an excellent argument." Her ears popped and she frowned. "Are we about
to fall out of the sky?"

"Faith, Duchess." He guided them down to a tiny
little island just off the coast. It barely had room for
the runway Frank used to bring them to ground, but she
caught sight of a house through the trees. He pulled the
plane to a stop and worked some magic to kill the engine
and get the door open. "Come on." He claimed her hand
the second they hit the ground, and tugged her along a
well-manicured path toward the house.

Journey stared. It was a little bungalow that was no less
fancy for its relative size. Spanish tile spread out around
one side, showcasing an outdoor patio area around a
gorgeous abstract fountain. Frank bypassed the house and
took another path that led them to the beach. He stopped
just short of the sand. "I know the water doesn't exactly
hold happy memories for you...but I thought it was time
to start making new ones."

The scene before her looked like something out of a
romance novel. Two lounge chairs sat on either side of a

low table laid out with all her favorite foods, an oversized umbrella keeping the worst of the sun off them. "Wow." She couldn't keep a stupid grin off her face. "Just... wow, Frank. I love it."

"I love *you*." He pulled her into his arms and laced his fingers through her hair. "Did you pick that dress just to torture me? How the fuck did you think I'd get through a meal without ripping it off you?"

She laughed against his mouth. "That's kind of the idea." Journey ducked out of his arms and pulled the dress over her head. She walked naked to the lounge chair and draped it over the back. A quick glance over her shoulder told her that Frank hadn't moved from his spot. "You said you want to give me some better memories."

"Yeah." The word was so low, it was a growl.

Every muscle in her body clenched at the promise written all over his face. "I've never had sex in the ocean."

"You don't have to tell me twice." He stalked to her and scooped her into his arms. He waded into the water and shifted her so she could wrap her legs around his waist. The expression on his face—love, desire, tenderness— made her so happy, it hurt. "We have a lot of years ahead of us, Duchess, and I plan to fill them with the happiest of memories." Frank kissed her. "Starting now."

Opposites attract in the first book of a red-hot new series from *New York Times* bestselling author Katee Robert.

Keep reading for an excerpt of

The Last King.

CHAPTER ONE

Beckett King was a monumental pain in the ass.

The man was a force of nature, and he never did what Samara expected, which made it impossible to counter his moves.

Probably shouldn't have slept with him, then.

Shut up.

There was no point in stalling further. Samara had a job to do, and the longer she took to do it, the later her night would run. She smoothed down her pencil skirt, bolstered her defenses, and marched through his office door before she could talk herself out of it.

Beckett himself sat on a small couch rather than behind the shiny desk, his head in his hands. His dark hair was longer than she'd seen it last, and he wore a faded gray T-shirt and jeans, looking completely out of place in the sleek, pristine office. His broad shoulders rose and fell in what must have been a deep sigh.

If Samara didn't dislike him so much, she might almost feel sorry for him.

She shifted, her heel clicking against the marble floor,

and Beckett raised his head. He caught sight of her and stood, his expression guarded, his mouth tight.

"Are you here on behalf of my aunt?" he asked. "She really hates my father so much she sends someone else for the reading of his will?"

Samara considered half a dozen responses and discarded all of them. Tonight, at least, she could keep control of her tongue. "I'm sorry about your father."

He snorted. "It was no secret there wasn't a whole lot of love lost between us." And yet the exhausted lines of his face showed that no matter what he said, he cared that his father was dead. It was there in the permanent frown pulling down the edges of his lips, and in the barely banked fury of his chocolate brown eyes.

He sighed again. "If Lydia doesn't want to be here herself, fine. We might as well get this started." He stalked to his desk and pushed a button. "Walter, Lydia's..." He glanced up at her with smoldering eyes. "...*representative* is here."

A few seconds later, a thin man opened the door she'd just walked through and shuffled his way to the desk. He wore an ill-fitting suit and looked about thirty seconds from passing out right where he stood. His pale blue gaze landed on her, his eyes too large in his narrow face. "Ms. Mallick. I'd say it's a pleasure, but the circumstances are hardly that."

"Mr. Trissel. It's nice to see you again." Empty, meaningless words. So much of her job required her to spill white lies and smooth ruffled feathers, and Samara was usually damn good at figuring out what a person needed and leveraging it to get what *she* wanted.

Or what her boss, Lydia King, wanted.

That skill had abandoned her the second she walked through the doors of Morningstar Enterprise. Her movements lost their normal grace, and words she had no business saying crowded her throat. Beckett always made her feel like an amateur, and they'd been going head-to-head for years, his aunt's company against his father's. But right now, he looked like the walking wounded and she didn't know how to process it. Samara wasn't a nurturer. Even if she was, she wouldn't comfort *him*.

Beckett doesn't matter. The will does.

The reminder kept her steady as Walter separated two folders from the stack and looked at each of them in turn. He passed one folder to Beckett. "It's a lot of legalese, but the bottom line is that Mr. King left you nearly everything. Morningstar and all his shares are yours, which puts you firmly in the role as majority shareholder. As of the moment you sign this, you are acting CEO."

No surprise showed on his face. Why would it? For all his tumultuous relationship with his father, Beckett was the only King suitable to take over once Nathaniel was gone. Of course he'd been named CEO.

Beckett leafed through the file but didn't appear to read any of it. "You said almost everything."

"Yes, well..." The lawyer fidgeted. "There was a change in the most recent version of the will."

He went still. "What change?"

The lawyer passed Samara the second file. "Nathaniel King has left the residence of Thistledown Villa to Lydia King and her children."

"The fuck he did!" Beckett slammed his hands down on the desk, making it clang hollowly. "There's been a mistake. No way in hell my father left the family home to her."

"I'm sorry, Mr. King, but there's been no mistake. As I mentioned earlier, the paperwork is all in order. Your father was in his right mind when he signed this will, and I stood as his witness. While you're welcome to contest it in court, I have to advise you that it's a losing battle."

Samara read through the paperwork quickly. She'd been told to expect the family home to be willed to Lydia, but she still wanted to make sure everything was in order. As Walter had said, there was a lot of legalese, but it was exactly what he said. *Good.* It meant she could get the hell out of there. "Thank you for your time." She turned on her heel and headed for the door.

She barely made it into the hallway before a large hand closed over her upper arm, halting her forward progress. "Let me go, Beckett."

"Samara, just hold on a damn second." He released her but didn't step back. "That house should have been mine and you know it. My father leaving it to Lydia makes no sense. She hasn't set foot in the place in thirty years."

"It's none of my business what your father did or didn't leave to Lydia. I'm not a King." She forced herself to move away despite the insane urge to touch him. It was second nature to inject her tone with calm and confidence. "Nothing you can say is going to change what that will said. I know it's your childhood home, but your father obviously had a reason for leaving it to his sister. Maybe he was finally trying to fix the hurt *his* father caused by passing her over for CEO and cutting her out of the family. It's not like you were close enough for him to confide in you if he *had* decided to fix things with Lydia."

Hurt flickered through Beckett's dark eyes, and Samara

battled a pang of guilt in response. The King family's messed-up past wasn't Beckett's fault any more than it was hers, but that didn't mean she had to throw it in his face.

His jaw set, hurt replaced by fury. "Stop trying to handle me. I'm not some client you're trying to talk into an oil lease."

She took him in, from the top of his hair that looked like he'd been raking his fingers through it for roughly twelve hours straight, over the T-shirt fitted tightly across his broad shoulders and muscled chest, down to the faded jeans that hugged his thighs lovingly, ending on the scuffed boots. "If you were a client, I would already have a contract in hand. You're easy pickings right now, Beckett." *That's it. Remember who you are to each other: enemies.*

He reached out and twisted a lock of her hair around his finger, pulling her a little closer despite her best intentions. "Don't try that snooty attitude with me. It doesn't work."

"You're just full of orders tonight, aren't you?"

"You like it." His thumb brushed her cheek, sending a zing down her spine that curled her damn toes in her expensive red heels. "You like a lot of things I do when you're not thinking so hard."

She had to get the hell out of there right then and there, or she'd do something unforgivable like kiss Beckett King. *Never should have let him get this close. I know what happens when we're within touching distance.* It had only been once, but once was more than enough to imprint itself on her memories. No amount of tequila could blur out how intoxicating it was to have his hands on her body, or the way he'd growled every filthy thing he'd wanted to do to her before following through on it. Things would be a lot easier if she'd just blacked out the entire night and moved on with her life.

He lowered his head and she blurted out the first thing she could think of to make him back off. "Beckett, your father just *died*."

"I'm aware of that."

Nathaniel King was dead.

That reality was almost impossible to wrap her head around. For all her thirty-two years, Nathaniel had loomed large over Houston. The King family was an institution that had been around for generations, all the way back to the founding of Houston itself, and Nathaniel was its favored son. It was that favoritism that caused his father to pass over Lydia for the CEO position. The unfairness of that call had driven her to cash out her shares and start her own company—Kingdom Corp—in direct competition with her family. Thirty years later, it didn't matter what Samara had told Beckett, because that rift was nowhere near closing. Time might heal some wounds, but it only cemented Lydia's ill will for the family that had cut her off when she wouldn't play by their rules.

And now there was nothing left of that side of the family but Beckett.

He released Samara and took a step back, and then another. "Just go. Run back to your handler." He let her get three steps before he said, "But make no mistake—this isn't over."

She wasn't sure if he meant contesting the will or *them*, and she didn't stick around to ask. Samara kept her head held high and the file clutched tightly in her grip as she took the elevator down to the main floor, walked out the doors, and strode two blocks down the humid Houston streets to Kingdom Corp headquarters. The only person lingering at this time in the evening was the security guard near the front door, and he barely looked up as she strode through the doors.

Another quick elevator ride, and she stepped out at the executive floor. Like the rest of the building, it was mostly deserted. Kingdom Corp employees worked long hours, but no one worked harder than Lydia King. She was there before the first person showed up, and she didn't leave until long after they'd gone home. *She* was the reason the company had made unprecedented leaps in the last two decades. Samara admired the hell out of that fact.

"I have it." She shut the door behind her and moved to set the papers on the desk.

"I appreciate you going. It's a difficult time." Lydia leaned forward and glanced over the paperwork. She didn't *look* like she was grieving, for all that her brother had died in a terrible car accident two days ago. Her long golden hair was twisted up into a more sophisticated version of Samara's updo and, despite a long day in the office, her white and gold color-blocked dress didn't have a single wrinkle on it.

Samara glanced at the clock and resigned herself to another long night. "Is there anything I can do?"

Lydia smiled, her berry lipstick still in perfect condition. "How did my nephew look?"

"He's in rough shape." It wasn't just the fact that he'd obviously dropped everything in Beijing and come directly home upon hearing the news of his father's death. Everyone in Houston knew that the King men could barely be in the same building for more than a few days without clashing spectacularly, but that didn't change the fact that Nathaniel was Beckett's father, his last remaining parent, and now he was dead. "I was under the impression that they didn't have much of a relationship."

Lydia shrugged. "Family is complicated, my dear. Especially fathers."

Years of building her defenses ensured that she didn't flinch at the dig. "What's the next move?"

But Lydia wasn't through. She ran her hands over the papers almost reverently. "Was he upset when he found out about the villa?"

She pictured the look in Beckett's dark eyes, something akin to panic. "Yes. He didn't understand why Nathaniel would leave it to you."

"He grew up there. We all did." Lydia's smile took on a softer edge. "Nathaniel and I were born there. So was Beckett. My children would have been if not for how things fell out."

It was just a building, albeit a beautiful one. Samara didn't understand the reverence in Lydia's tone, or the pain Beckett obviously felt to lose it. Who cared about an old mansion on the outskirts of Houston—especially after the King family had essentially cut Lydia off when she wouldn't dance to their tune?

Doesn't matter if I get it. It's important to Lydia, which means I have to plan on dealing with that damn house in the future.

She realized the silence had stretched on a little too long and tried for a smile. "That's nice."

"Oh, Samara." Lydia laughed. "Don't pretend I'm not boring you to death with my nostalgia. At least Nathaniel managed to do one thing right before he did us all the favor of dying."

There she is. This was the Lydia that Samara knew, not the sentimental woman she'd just been talking to. "Nathaniel was handling the upcoming bid personally. With him gone, it will leave Beckett scrambling to catch up." Her fingers tingled, and she clenched her fists. *Excitement. Not guilt. I'm beyond guilt when it comes to men who have had everything handed to them from birth. Losing this contract won't sink Beckett's company, but it* will *damage it.*

"Yes, well, don't get cocky. This is important, Samara."

"I won't drop the ball."

Lydia looked at her for a long, uncomfortable moment. Staring into those hazel eyes was like glimpsing a lion stalking through the tall grass. Samara was reasonably sure the danger wasn't directed at *her*, but her heart still kicked in her chest. Finally, Lydia nodded. "I know you won't let me down. Why don't you get some rest? You need to hit the ground running tomorrow."

Samara paused. "I hope you'll be able to get some rest soon, too." When Lydia just shook her head and chuckled, Samara gave up and left before she could do or say something else ill advised.

She hesitated on the corner. The smart move would be to go back to her little condo, have a glass of wine, and go over her proposal for the government contract yet again. She *knew* she had it locked down, but insidious doubt wormed through her at the thought of facing Beckett King. *I have the advantage this time.* It didn't matter. He had advantages she couldn't even see, ones that had been gifted to him just because he held the King last name.

Samara closed her eyes. She wanted to go *home*. She wanted to call a Lyft and travel across town to the little house her mother had lived in since she was born. She wanted to hug her *amma* until the fear of losing her only parent dissipated.

Get ahold of yourself.

Amma would already be asleep, her alarm set for some ungodly hour so she could get to work on time. If Samara showed up now, it would mean a long conversation while her mother tried to figure out what the problem was. No matter how nice that sounded, Samara was stronger than this. She couldn't lean on her *amma* just because seeing Beckett's grief left her feeling strange.

She was *not* weak. She refused to let a man she barely knew derail her path. Kingdom Corp needed that contract, and *Samara* needed to be the one to get it. It was a shame Beckett's father had died, but ultimately she couldn't let pity for him take root.

He was the enemy.

Samara couldn't afford to forget that.

ABOUT THE AUTHOR

KATEE ROBERT is a *New York Times* and *USA Today* bestselling author who learned to tell stories at her grandpa's knee. Her novel *The Marriage Contract* was a RITA finalist, and *RT Book Reviews* named it "a compulsively readable book with just the right amount of suspense and tension." When not writing sexy contemporary and romantic suspense, she spends her time playing imaginary games with her children, driving her husband batty with what-if questions, and planning for the inevitable zombie apocalypse.

Learn more:
www.kateerobert.com
Twitter @katee_robert
Facebook.com/AuthorKateeRobert

Looking for more romantic suspense?

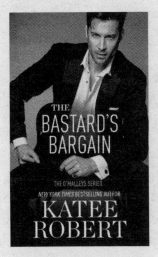

THE BASTARD'S BARGAIN
By Katee Robert

Dmitri Romanov knows Keira O'Malley only married him to keep peace between their families. Nevertheless, the desire that smolders between them is a dangerous addiction neither can resist. But with his enemies circling closer, Keira could just be his secret weapon—if she doesn't bring him to his knees first.

THE FEARLESS KING
By Katee Robert

When Journey King's long-lost father returns to make a play for the family company, Journey turns to the rugged and handsome Frank Evans for help, and finds much more than she was looking for.

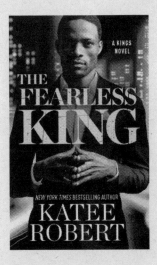

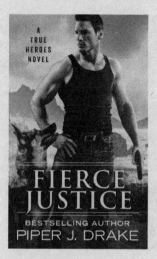

FIERCE JUSTICE
By Piper Drake

As a K9 handler on the Search and Protect team, Arin Siri needs to
be where the action is—and right now that's investigating a trafficking
operation in Hawaii. When an enemy from her past shows up bleeding,
she's torn between the desire to patch Jason up or to put more holes in
him. Then again, the hotshot mercenary could be the person she needs
to bust open her case.

Find more great reads on Instagram with
@ForeverRomanceBooks.

TWISTED TRUTHS
By Rebecca Zanetti

Noni Yuka is desperate. Her infant niece has been kidnapped, and the only person who can save her is the private detective who once broke her heart.

Follow @ForeverRomance and join the conversation using #ReadForever.

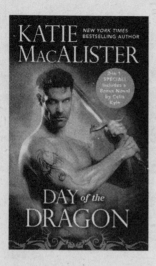

DAY OF THE DRAGON
By Katie MacAlister

Real scholars know that supernatural beings aren't real, but once Thaisa meets tall, dark, and mysterious Archer Andras of the Storm Dragons, all of her academic training goes out the window. Thaisa realizes that she really should worry about those things that go bump in the night.

TIGER'S CLAIM
By Celia Kyle

Cole Turner may act like a wealthy, gorgeous playboy, but he's also a tiger shifter determined to bring down the organization that's threatening his kind. Leopard shifter Stella Moore will do whatever it takes to destroy Unified Humanity, even if that means working with the undeniably annoying—and sexy—Cole.

Visit
Facebook.com/ForeverRomance

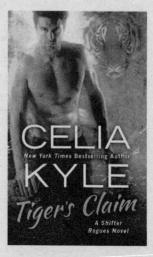